UNSPOKEN

SAM HAYES

ISIS

LARGE PRINT

Oxford

First published in Great Britain 2008
by
Headline Publishing Group
an Hachette Livre UK Company

Published in Large Print 2009 by ISIS Publishing Ltd.,
7 Centremead, Osney Mead, Oxford OX2 0ES
by arrangement with
Headline Publishing Group
an Hachette Livre UK Company

British Library Cataloguing in Publication Data
Hayes, Sam
    Unspoken. – Larg
    1. Mothers and d
    2. Family secrets
    3. Lawyers – Ficti
    4. Murder – Ficti
    5. Suspense fictio
    6. Large type boo
    I. Title
    823.9'2 [F]

ISBN 978–0–7531–8242–0 (hb)
ISBN 978–0–7531–8243–7 (pb)

Printed and bound in Great Britain by
T. J. International Ltd., Padstow, Cornwall

UNSPOKEN

For Joe, my brother, with love.

Acknowledgements

Huge thanks and respect must go to my agent and my editor, Anna and Sherise — two talented, insightful and hardworking women. Heartfelt thanks also to the wonderful Becky at Headline for getting me "out there". And, of course, I am eternally grateful to the entire team at Headline. Thanks, guys!

As ever, my love to Terry, Ben, Polly and Lucy. Couldn't do it without you! A special thank-you to Audrey for Wednesday tea; Gwen Richard at SARDA Wales for invaluable search and rescue advice; Vicki for insightful chats about the human mind; the White Watch crew — you know why; and Sandra — your magic goes on.

PROLOGUE

As a child, there are things you learn not to talk about; that the very utterance of certain words sends some people into a flat spin.

I was four when I first spoke of my father, having just started nursery. "Where's *my* daddy?" I asked my mother. It appeared that all the other little girls had a father, and until I discovered this fact, the absence of my own had meant nothing to me. It was simply never spoken of. As if he never existed.

That first day at nursery, we'd been asked to paint a picture of our family. I'd done one entirely of him; just my daddy standing tall and proud and gazing at me with handsome blue eyes, exactly the same shade as mine. He was smiling, his arms outstretched, as if he was beckoning to me to run into them, knock him back a few paces as I hurled myself against his body.

"Look, it's my daddy," I told my mother, waving the paint-wetted paper at her. We were walking home. She suddenly let go of my hand. I squinted up at her, the brightness behind her protecting me from focusing on her fierce scowl.

All my life, she only ever said one thing to me about my father and it was then, the sun flashing on our backs that September day, completely alone down the lane that led to the farm. "You do not have a father, Julia. Never, ever speak of him again." And she pressed her forefinger to her lips and whispered a firm *shhh*, silencing me eternally.

Now, grown up and with children of my own, I am left wondering, from that brisk walk home with my mother all those years ago, how you can speak of something you've never had. How do you know which words to use when they simply aren't there?

It's the very nature of language, the shape of the syllables, how they slide off the tongue and linger in the air, that makes each of us unique.

But it's when those words take on a life of their own that the real story begins to unfold. When the unspoken past collides with the present.

JULIA

I discovered her completely by accident. She was lying in the field, twisted on her side in the brittle iced grass. Her lips were violet and her eyes wide open, drilling holes in the winter sky.

She lay perfectly still, her pale skin sparkling from frost and her red nails spread like a broken string of beads.

"Grace!" I fell to my knees, fumbling in my pocket for my mobile phone. I tore my jacket off my back and made her into a parcel. Her bare legs protruded, askew of their natural position. "Grace, what happened to you?" I still wasn't sure that she was alive.

She turned her head and a tendon in her neck snapped against my wrist. Her mouth opened, revealing a salty crust on her lips.

"What *happened*, Grace?"

Last time I saw her she had dropped her English essay on my desk and left the classroom in a flurry of teenage urgency. It was the end of term and everyone was full of Christmas excitement. With everything going on in my life — with Mum, with Murray — I'd not even marked her work yet.

"Doc . . . tor," she rasped without breath to force out the word.

"I've called for an ambulance, Grace. Sit tight." I pulled her broken body closer and encased her in my arms, my legs, my hair. Milo bounded across the field and instinctively slumped on her legs, panting, his breath falling in bursts of steam on her knees. Warming the life back into Grace.

It was twenty minutes before the paramedics crowned the rise that splayed from the end of the footpath. Everyone walked their dog down Lightning Lane but not all got as far as the unnatural quarry bowl of amphitheatre-like proportions beyond. As a kid, I used to run down, my knees buckling, my hair a mess, our dog barking at my madness as we descended into the man-made hole. Murray always pretended to race me and always let me win.

"Can you hear me, sweetheart?"

Grace was levered from me by a paramedic. There were three of them, two men and a woman, while a couple of police officers left staccato prints on the white-green grass.

"I just found her like this," I said, fumbling for an explanation. Nothing seemed real. "I was walking my mother's dog." I wasn't shivering, even though Grace was shrouded in my coat; even though the breath fell from my mouth in icy clouds. I was already used to being numb. "I thought she was plastic." A mannequin, dumped. A useless shop dummy, fly-tipped.

"What's your name, love?" the female paramedic asked.

"Grace. Grace Covatta. Her father's Italian," I said when Grace didn't reply.

"Grace, can you hear me, sweetheart?" While the woman coaxed her to talk, the other paramedic wrapped her in foil blankets and opened a small case containing portable monitors. She was hooked up to a mini oxygen canister and a machine beeped, registering her barely alive. "Has she told you what happened?"

I shook my head. "I was walking my mother's dog. He started to chase a rabbit and I turned to call him off and that's when . . ." That's when my eyes had blurred, squinting through the morning mist, disbelieving. "That's when I saw Grace. Will you take a look at her feet? They're hurt."

"She'll be looked after in hospital. She's not bleeding now." The paramedic turned to Grace and spoke to her as if she were deaf. I should know. People do it to Flora all the time, as if she's stupid. "We're going to put you on a stretcher, Grace. We're taking you to hospital." His mouth was big and wide, a goldfish trying to communicate.

Grace said nothing. She stared. Her tongue, swollen and dry, tried to lick her lips as if she was about to speak. She didn't. "Oh God," I cried and turned away, yanking on Milo's collar. It was something familiar, purposeful, reminding me of the reason I was out in the fields early on a freezing December morning.

The crew moved fast while the police cordoned off the area and called for backup. Grace was loaded on to a fold-up stretcher and I followed beside as they carried her down the footpath. She said nothing, just jolted in time with the steps of the paramedics, her tongue caught between the roof of her mouth and her dry lips.

"Grace, your English essay was fabulous. I gave you an A." I touched her foil shoulder, hoping I might register a link of normality. I'd got the class to write a two-thousand-word essay on their interpretation of evil. It was a broad-spectrum assignment, a shot at inspiring my lazier students. I hadn't marked them yet but I already wanted Grace to have an A.

"Do you have any idea what might have happened to her?" I asked as we headed back to the village. "Is there any evidence of . . .?" I couldn't say it. I panted, half running to keep up, pulling hard on Milo's lead so that every breath rasped in his throat. I wanted him close.

"The doctors will examine her. Are you a relation?"

"I'm her English teacher."

Lightning Lane eventually dissolved into the road at the edge of the village in an estuary of mud and frozen leaves. It's always been called that, since way back when I was a child and beyond.

Mum said it was because for three winters on the trot an oak, a beech and a chestnut were taken down by storms.

Mum said.

Mum also once said that bad things come in threes. Neat triangles of trouble. In all that mess, I was reminded of her, of Murray, of me. Our own triangle of pain.

An ambulance and a police car barricaded the lane, their blue lights ticking through the murk. The sight had drawn a crowd of curious onlookers and I knew that the ripple of news would already be reaching neighbouring villages, towns, journalists, front pages. Within hours the local presses would be rolling, Grace's name at the top.

We marched up to the vehicles like a team of Arctic explorers and just the very faces that I would have expected to be there came hustling forward for news. They reminded me why we had moved from the small village with its tittle-tattle and messaging system faster than email. Had Grace not been on the stretcher, I would have walked on, thankful not to be a part of it any more. Eight miles wasn't much, but living in Ely provided enough anonymity.

I ushered the onlookers back — I was a storm wall against the tide, protecting Grace from their invasion — but because of this, I didn't see the medics get her into the ambulance. I didn't wish her well or bon voyage or let her know I hoped to see her at school soon. Just what *are* you supposed to say when someone's like Grace?

Within seconds, the vehicle was pulling off down the lane with a single blast of its siren to clear the gathering. Extra police had arrived. As I slumped on to the frozen grass, they asked me to make a statement. I told them what had happened and they wrote it all down, including the single word Grace had spoken.

That was Friday and I'm still here, staying at Mum's farm, coping on her behalf. It's what you do, isn't it? Walk the Labrador, discover the victim of a brutal attack, come home and read the paper. A nightmare threaded through normality.

"Mum," I say gently. I clasp her hand in mine; bring it to my lips. "Grace is still in hospital." Four days she's been there. She can't walk or talk. She has head injuries and the tendons in her feet were damaged. They don't know how long it will be before she recovers. No one likes to hazard a guess about Grace.

Mum stares and I wonder if there was a slight turn of her head, a glimmer of interest. She doesn't know Grace but I've told her that she's one of my pupils. Over the last week I've told Mum lots of things — mostly light-hearted babble and stuff about her grandchildren and the two teens she fosters. For now, because of what's happened, I've temporarily taken over their care.

I thought perhaps the shock of finding Grace down Lightning Lane would elicit a reaction, but there's simply nothing in her. Mum is empty. Her eyes are drained and her lips thin and unwilling. Only when I pass her a cup of tea or slide a plate of food in front of her does she move. I'm sure I hear her bones creak while she's eating, as if they are whispering behind her back.

"They say poor Grace will be in a wheelchair for ages and have months of physiotherapy. They're very worried about her head injuries." I sigh and wonder if that is a mini sigh in Mum's chest too; an echo of mine; a tiny heave of sadness beneath her brittle breastbone. "I'm going to visit her soon." I plant another kiss on the top of her head.

I put the children's sandwiches on the table just as my two come bowling into the kitchen. Alex curls his mouth around the soft bread before he is even seated. I trail my fingers through Flora's hair and tuck her chair under the table. The teenagers make a slower appearance for their food.

Orange juice? My hands form the words for Flora. She nods and smiles, cheese poking from her mouth. I prepare more plates of sandwiches for the foster children and they slip out of the kitchen with their lunch. They've kept out of the way these last few days, wisely avoiding all the fuss that revolves around Mum.

"Thank you," the girl says as an afterthought. She gives me a nervous glance, a half-smile. Her brother is silent. I am concerned about him. He disappears for hours at a time, often coming home filthy.

I clatter glasses on to the table and stop, looking around the kitchen. Nothing much has changed in this house over the years. The window still rattles from the wind, and if the rain comes from the north, a bowl is still needed to catch the water on the window ledge. Old pine cupboards and dressers line the room, insulating the walls with a vast stash of family crockery, glassware, chipped dinner sets, children's paintings, lace tablecloths, drawers full of string, glue, tape, broken pens and ancient bills. The flagstones are perhaps a shade darker than I remember, the walls more yellowed, but the whole place smells the same: of wood smoke, cooking and love.

"Why don't you wrap up warm and take Flora down to the rope swing after lunch?" I say to Alex, but then I stop, halfway to the sink. "Actually, it's probably too cold. Why not watch a movie?" Someone did that to Grace. Someone bent and cut her body and left her naked in the field. I embrace each of my children. They will not be playing outside while we are staying at Grandma's house.

"No, we want to play in the fields. It's not cold." Alex doesn't whine but rather states his case. Did he learn that from his dad? Like his father, he knows it won't do any good. When things are final, they are final. I shoot him a look.

"Mum," I say gently. "Cheese for you, too?"

I know she won't answer but I feel I have to ask. I'm finding it hard to remember her voice, even though it's only been a week since she fell silent. No one knows why.

I put the sandwich on a tray and rest it on her knee. "If you sit any closer to that fire, you'll turn into toast." I realise I'm talking to her in a voice fit for a kindergarten class. "Anyway, Alex, your dad's taking you out later." I say it like it's good reason for them not to play outside. "He's coming at five."

Alex grins and immediately turns into a little Murray, his face broad and alert, his eyes filled with more anticipation than the situation warrants. He is a memento of the husband I thought I knew. Flora pulls at my arm and signs, What? Her finger is an annoyed scribble in the air, her eyebrows tucked together.

Dad, I tell her. He's coming to fetch you at five. Flora abandons her sandwich and runs to nestle on her grandma's lap, competing with the tray for space. It seems she doesn't want to go.

I sigh and snap on rubber gloves to tackle the dishes. Mum doesn't have a dishwasher. Neither does she have a washing machine, a tumble dryer, a television or even an electric kettle. When we visit Grandma's house, we put on an extra sweater and the children bring their portable DVD player.

"Where's Dad taking us?" Alex asks, chomping on the last of his sandwich. He drains his milk.

"I hope to God not anywhere on that boat. Not in the dark." I plunge my hands into the soapy water and imagine Flora slipping off the side of the narrow boat, her mouth unable to do anything but drink the River Cam. "He'll probably take you bowling or to that nice pizza place." I comfort myself with the thought of them having an evening in the city. Surely nothing can go wrong there.

"Or to his friend's house," Alex adds.

"His friend?" I know I said it too quickly. I hope Alex didn't notice. Male or female? I find myself wondering. Our lives are already diverging.

Alex shrugs and I don't press him because there is suddenly the sound of breaking china. Flora has knocked Mum's plate on to the floor.

Don't worry, I tell her with my wet yellow hands. She tries to hide the smile and pushes her face into Mum's shoulder, who vaguely curls an arm around Flora's waist. It is the most animated I have seen her in days.

★　★　★

Murray is an hour late. He stands in the doorway and I throw my car keys at him a lot harder than I intended. He clutches them to his chest, surprised, hurt, but then his expression tells me he understands completely. His car is at the garage for repairs and is likely to be there for a while longer. I'm praying that the use of my car will discourage him from taking the children on the boat and also from drinking. Surely I can trust him.

"Sorry. I was —"

"Kids!" I don't want to hear why he was late or, indeed, why he is only wearing a T-shirt when a frost has already set a glaze on the courtyard beyond. "Come in and shut the door. You'll freeze." Come and join my kindergarten class, I think, yet I still find myself wanting to wrap a blanket around him, to huddle under the curve of his shoulder. I sigh through the realisation that such moments are gone for good.

"How are you?" he asks. "How are you after finding —"

"Tea?" I interrupt, then wish I hadn't asked. It'll take the kettle an age to boil on the range and I don't want the children back late. It will also mean awkward conversation as we sip our scalding drinks, blowing ripples on the surface to prevent what needs to be said but never will be. It's too late now. "And I'm doing OK, thanks. There's no more news on Grace."

Murray nods thoughtfully. "Yeah, tea would be good." He goes to stand with his back to the fire. "Mary," he acknowledges. He doesn't know what to say to her. "How are you?"

Mum happens to be staring at Murray's knees now he is beside the fire. She doesn't reply, just a swallow and a blink. I ease between them and put the kettle on the hotplate.

"She's the same," I say. It's the wrong thing to do, talking for her, but David said to include her in conversation as if everything's normal. "David . . . I mean Dr Carlyle . . . comes to visit her regularly."

"Do doctors make house calls these days?" Murray rubs at the stubble on his chin.

"Are you growing a beard?" I shouldn't have mentioned David in front of Murray.

"How often does he come?" Murray presses on.

I concentrate on making the tea. "He came yesterday and he'll be back tomorrow." I spoon tea into the pot. No quick-fix teabags here at Cold Comfort Farm. "I think Mum likes his visits."

"And you?"

I stop, sigh and make my face into a picture of weariness. "I'm not sick, Murray. I don't need a doctor."

"Do you like his visits, I mean?" His voice is dry and determined.

My head hangs instinctively. "Murray, please . . ." But Alex hears that his dad has arrived and runs into the kitchen, begging him to take a turn on his Nintendo, interrupting me. "Why not wait until you're in the restaurant to show Dad your new game?" I say, thankful for the reprieve.

"We're going to a restaurant, are we? The four hours of time with my children has already been planned. That's nice."

"Well, you wasted one of them by being late," I mutter.

Swiftly Murray unhooks Alex's coat from the overburdened stand and tucks our boy inside. Then Flora spills into the room — delighted to see her father even though she hates the upset of being taken from me just for an hour — and she too is padded in coat.

I am struck by a slice of freezing air as they leave. "I'll have them back by ten," Murray commands in a voice I recognise from way back.

"*Nine!*" I call out, but the word gets caught in my throat. For the rest of the evening I sit in silence with my mother and wonder what happened to my family.

MURRAY

It was going to be better than that. I was going to kiss her when I arrived. I was going to say she looked good even though her eyelids were a little heavier today and she'd forgotten to brush her hair. I was going to wear my new trousers and have my car fixed and perhaps, if things had gone really well, I would have asked her to come with us. Flora signs that she needs a wee.

"Guard the table, mate," I say to Alex. He's already done the puzzles on the table mat.

"Sure, Dad."

It wasn't that she didn't want me there. I know Julia. God, I've known her practically since she was born. But because she never quite looked at me, never quite managed not to look at the teapot, the floor, Mary, her own fingernails, there is still hope. What Julia doesn't look at, she generally wants. So maybe she still wants me.

With that in mind, I'm grinning as Flora comes out of the ladies' loo. Did you wash your hands? I gesture, and instead of signing back she shows me tiny glistening fingers. We go back to the table.

The pizza's OK, although each bite is automatic. Alex struggles with the spice of his pepperoni sausage so I give him half of mine. I get him to tell me again what Santa brought last week and he likes scooting down the list of things I've never even heard of; likes telling me that Santa's not real and I shouldn't treat him like a kid. I'm asking again because in all honesty I can't recall what he said the first time he told me on the phone. I can't even remember a phone call.

Flora, I sign. Don't interrupt your brother. She's being impatient, begging for vanilla ice cream, and when it arrives — because I can never say no to her for long — it has the same colour and smell as her hair. It reminds me of when she was a baby; of when things were whole and sweet.

"What's wrong with that girl Mum found in the field?" Alex finishes his chocolate ice cream in record time.

"Grace Covatta?" I say. There's no point in hiding her name. It's been all over the newspapers. Witherly — where if someone bumps their head it's big news — is steeped in Grace Covatta. Within hours of Julia's discovery the press were camped along the muddy verges of the village, their satellites pointing skyward beaming out the shocking news. Even days later, the Three Horseshoes is still base to a couple of journalists still hungry for information as well as the home cooking. "She got hurt, buddy. But she's going to be fine."

"Who hurt her?"

"The police are trying to find out." I don't have the words to explain such a vicious attack to an eleven-year-old.

"But how will they find out?" Because of his Uncle Ed, Alex wants to be a policeman when he's grown up.

"Through forensic testing. By talking to her. Searching the area." I've had enough of this. I've seen what it's done to Julia and I'm not getting my son involved, however manly he's trying to be. "Come on," and I sign this for Flora. "Anyone fancy hot chocolate on the boat?"

I'm grateful that the muddy towpath is frozen solid tonight. Dirty shoes would flash a beacon of deceit to Julia, and really, deceiving her is the last thing I want to do. She would say I am an expert at it.

"Careful, now." Alex steps across the small gap of water on to the rear deck and Flora gasps when I scoop her around the middle and place her beside her brother. Keep back from the edge, I tell Flora for the thousandth time, and she thumbs the side of her head in disgust.

I know. At eight, she is wiser than me.

I settle the children with steaming mugs of hot chocolate, and before long the cabin is warm and cosy. Half an hour after I shovel in extra coal, the stove puts out more heat than we can stand. I slide the roof hatch open a little.

"How come Grandma Mary won't talk?" Alex asks. "Is she deaf like Flora now?" My son wears a premature moustache, and before I answer, it dawns on me that he will probably start shaving in years that I can count on one hand. "Mum says Grandma is a mute."

This is Julia's territory. I feel the ice creaking beneath my feet before I even answer. "Your grandma's been sick, as well." Why I put her alongside Grace Covatta isn't clear, but with the two incidents hammering against Julia's life, the problems have fuzzed around the edges.

Aren't you having hot chocolate, Daddy? Flora is thoughtful.

No, I tell her. And when she asks why I'm not thirsty after all that salty pizza, I realise that I am and pour myself a Scotch. For the next hour, we laugh and tell stories and bundle ourselves up in blankets on the roof of the boat, waiting for the moon to shine bright enough to reveal the face of a pike in the water below. All we see are our own shiny grins.

When Julia was twelve she nearly drowned. I can label every childhood nick and scar on her body and give dates and reasons, too. It was a summer so hot the lanes felt like melted treacle as we hammered our bikes along the tarmac at midday.

"Slow down," she cried. Even then her hair was thick and lustrous and fell behind her in plumes of red gold as she struggled to keep up with my frantic pedalling legs. At my age, I should have known better, but showing Julia that I was faster than anyone else was more important than waiting for her to catch up. It was Mick, five years my junior, who helped her cart her bike down the bank and over the stile to the pond at the bottom; hoisting her bike way higher than necessary just to show how strong he was. And I was meant to be in charge.

The three of us sat in a row on the jetty that stretched out into the man-made pond. It was Mick's rod but I'd brought along the bait. Julia lay back on the hot wooden planks while we argued over who should thread the worms. The sun stung our necks and made the fronts of Julia's skinny legs go red.

"Who wants to swim?" she said, sitting up suddenly. Perhaps she was sick of our bickering or the heat had got to her, but before we could even answer, she'd slid her halter top off and was standing in her bra and shorts at the end of the jetty.

"Don't dive, Ju," I said, remembering my promise to her mother. But I was worried about the worms. "There's a whole scrapyard down there." I still didn't look up. In fact, neither of us looked up until it was time to cast the line, by which time, Julia's dive was nothing more than a series of ripples fading away at the shore.

"Where is she?" I peered over the end of the jetty. "Julia!" I yelled. I shielded my eyes from the sun, expecting to see her eager face break the surface, gasping for air, grinning. "*Ju-li-a!*"

"I dunno," Mick said. "She'll be OK."

And if it hadn't been for the sunlight as sharp as a razor, I'd never have seen her waterlogged face bobbing a foot below the murk. She was floating on her back, nostrils flared, her lips fat and eyes wide open with a slim streak of blood winding its way from her temple.

"Shit," I heard Mick say behind me as I leapt off the jetty. As soon as my legs cut the surface, I reached out and grabbed her body, yelling for Mick to help me haul her in. I don't know how we did it — her back got grazed from the rotting wood scraping against it as we manhandled her — but somehow we hoisted her to safety. What I remember most about that day is the softness of her lips the first time I ever kissed Julia Marshall.

"You're late," she tells me sternly. I want to crack a smile to see if she crumbles, like we did as kids. But laughing won't appease Julia. The children filter inside and I am kept in the kitchen doorway, half in, half out of the house in which I spent three-quarters of my childhood hanging out.

"Only half an hour," I say, glancing at my watch. I'm not wearing one. It takes me a few moments of staring at my wrist to realise this and a few more to accept that I can't remember where I left it.

"*Two* hours!" she screams. "I've been worried sick."

Then she slams the door but can't because my foot is in the way. That's when I laugh, even though it hurts. Julia lets out something between a scream and a growl and her cheeks turn pink. She flings the door open again and gets up close to me. It is a distance at which she should either kiss me or slap me. Our noses are nearly touching and something stirs inside me, a warning, a pre-programmed instinct to back off quickly.

But I ignore it just to stay close to Julia for another second. I might not get the chance again.

"You've been drinking. You've been in charge of my children, in my car, and you've been bloody drinking." She breathes in deeply and recoils. "Christ, Murray. How could you?"

She bangs her fists on the wall.

"I mean, the kids . . . the car." Her face is softening a little now, as she thinks of our children. "God, Murray, you are the biggest dick I know."

She slumps on to the chair and cradles her head in her hands.

"It's not what you think. I drove *before* I had a drink."

She looks up. "Then where did you have a drink?"

"On the boat." I kick myself for letting it slip.

"When will you understand that I don't want my children on that hulk?"

"I made them hot chocolate and we looked for fish in the moonlight."

Julia sighs. "What if they'd fallen in and you didn't even realise because you were . . ." She can't bring herself to say the word.

"Drunk, Julia? Did you mean to say drunk?"

She nods. Not looking at me.

"And do you mean drown, like the time you fell into Beck's Pond and I pulled you out?" I say.

We are both back there, the sun burning holes in our skin and me sucking the brown water from her throat. Mick shouting beside me as I worked. Julia's chest sputtering back to life and the blue finally seeping into her eyes again. I hardly admitted to myself — the big brother of her best friend sent to keep watch — that my kiss of life was way longer than necessary.

"One Scotch, Julia. One or two is all I had. Out on my boat with my children, watching for fish. They had fun. They were bored with pizza and ice cream. I'm sorry. I didn't mean to upset you."

"One now. Two tomorrow. Three the next." She feels the weight of the kettle.

"It's not like that any more."

"Isn't it?" She turns from the stove and I don't recognise her. Her curves, her softness, her glow, have gone. She's lost weight and there's something brittle about her, as if she might shatter.

Then he walks into the kitchen, striding to Julia's side, breathing the air that I was just about to, saying the words that I should have spoken. Julia doesn't know where to look as my eyes zig-zag between them.

"Everything's going to be fine." His rich voice even convinces me. He's not noticed me yet, but I see his hand on Julia's shoulder. "Trust me." The smile is indelible.

Julia is startled. She looks at me, her eyes wide. She tucks a chunk of hair behind her ear. "David," she says nervously, and I know she just wants to get it over with. Julia would never flaunt this. I know she doesn't want to hurt me. "This is Murray, Alex and Flora's father."

David turns and eyes me for a second. "I'm very happy to meet you, Murray. Your children are a credit to you." How he traversed the room without me noticing, I don't know, but his hand is there for me to take, to shake, to formally let him know I'm OK with this. "I'm Dr David Carlyle," he adds. "I'm looking after Mary."

I pause, then say, stupidly, slowly, curiously, "Are you?" And as I take his hand — the smooth, warm skin pushing against me — I realise that this is it, the moment when Julia finally slips through my fingers.

"Your mother is sleeping now," he says, turning back to Julia. "The medication will help her rest."

"Thank you for coming out at such short notice," Julia says softly. She doesn't look at me any more. Instead, I see her roll her lips together, smooth out her sweater, stand a little taller. She is relieved that the moment she was dreading has been traversed without incident.

"I didn't think the NHS budget ran to house calls."

David pauses and considers my remark. His face relaxes into a spread of friendly lines. "Generally speaking, you're right. But Mary is a special patient. Julia was worried about her so I decided to come out. Really, it's not a problem." The doctor smiles, floodlighting the entire kitchen.

I can see quite clearly that Julia is dazzled.

JULIA

It was Christmas Day. We'd opened the stockings, eaten turkey, pulled the crackers and, as usual, we trundled over to Witherly to see Mum in the afternoon. She didn't like to leave the farm if she didn't have to. But this year Christmas was different, as if something vital had been chipped off all our lives.

"Will Dad get any turkey?" Alex asked as we pulled down the lane towards Northmire Farm.

"If he bothers to cook one," I replied. Murray's Christmas dinner wasn't something I had considered. I tried to strike the thought from my mind, but it wasn't easy.

"What about presents?" he continued, worsening the image of his father's lonesome festive season. As we pulled up to the farm, I cursed Mum for leaving days' worth of newspapers stuck in the gate. I yanked on the handbrake, jumped out of the car with the rain and wind lashing my face, and gathered up the wet papers.

I leapt back in. "Perhaps we could wrap something for him before he fetches you tomorrow." I wiped the rain off my cheeks and steered the car down the long drive.

Alex didn't seem enthusiastic. "But you and Dad always buy each other presents. And you get something for Flora and me to give you both."

It's different this year, I wanted to tell him. Your dad and I are separated now. Not in love. We don't give gifts. Instead, for Alex's sake, I agreed to buy something for them to give their father the minute the shops reopened. We would wrap it and write a card and Alex and Flora would present their father with it on Boxing Day. But then Alex had to go and suggest a bottle of whisky, "Because Dad likes that, doesn't he?" just as we pulled into the yard.

I unhooked my seatbelt and then unbuckled Flora.

We're here, her hands announced cheerily, and she bowled from the car to greet Milo in the yard. He was muddy and shaking and hardly had the energy to welcome us.

"Milo," I said. "What's wrong, boy?" Then I saw the animal muck spread across the usually spotless cobbles; the two loose goats scoffing whatever winter herbs and greenery they could find in Mum's pots. The washing line had come down at one end and several sheets dragged on the ground, while the chickens clucked at the goats' feet.

This wasn't the picture of rural perfection that Northmire usually boasted. Not Mum's farm. Not Mum's way.

I banged on the back door but didn't wait for a reply. I shovelled my key from my bag and we went straight in. The kitchen fire was out and that was strange in itself. From September to March, the grate glowed with orange coals. It heated the entire house.

"Mum?" I called. "We're here." My stomach cramped.

"Where's Gran gone?" Alex asked. None of us took off our coats.

"Mum!" I pushed open the door to the inner hallway and called through all the doors of the house. "Mum, it's us. Are you here?"

I half expected the two new foster kids to come charging through the house, excited that people had arrived for the day. I'd not met them at that point; knew nothing about this brother and sister recently delivered for Mum to shelter. But there was nothing except the sound of our own breathing and Milo's claws clicking on the flagstones.

"Kids, wait in the kitchen. Keep Milo with you for company. He looks like he could use some love." I signed as I spoke for Flora's benefit, my hands shaking, causing my little girl's face to crumple with worry.

I went upstairs first. She probably has 'flu, I remember thinking, or a stomach bug and has gone to bed. I tried to recall the last time we had spoken — always once a week — and with our Christmas Day visit approaching, our last conversation had been only four or five days ago. She'd seemed fine, cheerful about the festivities even, although she never once agreed to come and spend the day at our place. She was bound to Northmire Farm, mind and body. It was where she felt safe.

"Are you home, Mum?" I stopped shouting, trying to sound upbeat in case I discovered her perfectly fine, reading a book by the bedroom fire, tucked up with hot soup and a box of tissues. "Mum?"

I zig-zagged a path between all five bedrooms and then checked out the converted attic rooms above the barn, which were always kept for the foster kids.

"Oh, hi," I said as cheerily as I could when two pale faces stared at me from the gloom. "I'm Julia. Have you seen Mary?" Mum always insisted the kids call her by her first name.

They shrugged. A boy and a girl, somewhere in their teens. By all accounts, Mum had taken on a bit of a handful this time. "Have you even seen her today?" I noticed wrapping paper on the floor, as if they'd been given presents.

"Yeah," the girl said. "She's around somewhere. Hasn't said much, though. Not even happy Christmas."

"Well. Happy Christmas to you both. We can get to know each other later."

Back downstairs, I poked my head around the study door, the dining room, the snug and finally the drawing room, which honestly, I can't ever remember using since Grandad's funeral. Generations of Marshalls have lived in this house.

"*Mum*," I said, sighing with relief when I saw her small frame propped in the blue velvet chair. "I was worried. Are you OK?" She faced the unlit fireplace. The house was so cold I could see the fog of my breath. I stepped in front of her, crouched down and froze.

Was she dead?

"Mum!" I screamed. Her eyes flickered open. "What's wrong, Mum? Talk to me, for God's sake." I touched her arm, tugged her sleeve and brushed the back of my hand down her cheek. There was some warmth beneath the cool powder of her skin, but her eyes were staring vacantly ahead.

"Just tell me you're OK. Nod or something. Have you been hurt? Are you ill?"

"Grandma!" Alex said and skidded across the room, closely followed by a more cautious Flora. "Happy Christmas!"

I put up my hand to prevent them leaping on to their grandmother. Looking at her, she would have crumbled under their weight. "Alex, go and get a glass of water."

Flora ignored me and plopped on to Grandma's small lap. Happy Christmas, Gran, she signed. I got a Barbie horse and this dress is new. Flora smoothed out the satin folds of a plum-coloured dress she had fallen in love with back in November.

Alex returned with the water. "Thanks, love," I said while sizing up Mum's face. Her mouth was pursed and her fine eyebrows — always shaped into perfect thin arcs — pulled together in a cruel frown. Mum just didn't seem to be inside.

Grandma, Flora signed. Say Happy Christmas to me. She slid off her knee, suddenly fearful of her usually jolly grandmother. My mother remained blank, moving only by default as Flora escaped.

"What's Grandma doing?" Alex asked. He thumbed his Nintendo frantically, not looking up as he spoke.

"She's perhaps a bit tired," I suggested. "A bit too tired for Christmas.

"Come on, Mum," I said, taking her hand. She was freezing. "Let's go in the kitchen and stoke the range. We can have some tea and chat." I pulled gently on her hand and to my relief she stood up. Her knees were bent and her back formed the shape of the chair, but she was upright and showing some degree of comprehension and willingness.

"That's it," I crooned. "Let's go and get warm."

But still she didn't speak.

David is coming again today. I suggested tentatively, not meaning it, that he shouldn't put himself out. He wouldn't hear of it. Even though he only saw Mum last night, he wanted to check up on her. He said he'd like to see me again too. I can't help but feel flattered.

Alex runs to answer the door, thinking perhaps it's his father, but I beat him to it. Today, it is slightly warmer and the wind has dropped. Everything outside looks weary, fed up, spent. I am reminded of myself.

"Hi," I say and pull the door wide. Alex hovers behind me, ignoring David's friendly greeting — a ruffle of his hair. My son skulks away. David bends forward and leaves a kiss on my cheek.

"Hi," he says back without stifling his grin. He takes off his long overcoat. He's wearing jeans and a V-necked pullover that shows me his shoulders are broad yet slim. His stomach reveals no sign of overeating this Christmas.

"This looks new," I say, then feel embarrassed as I take the coat.

"A bargain in the sales," he replies, amused by my interest. "I admit, I'm not one for shopping, but I lent my old one to . . ." He stops, looks me up and down and says, completely forgetting the coat, "I'm worried about you, Julia. You've lost weight these last few days." The grin drops away and is replaced by a frown. I'm touched that he's noticed. He reaches out and lays his hands on my shoulders.

"I'm fine. Really." I can feel myself blushing and quickly change the subject. "Mum's stopped hyperventilating but her heart is still racing. Shouldn't the medication have settled it?"

His eyes narrow, concerned yet inquisitive, and for a second, I'm convinced he knows what I'm thinking. "Come on then, where's the patient?" He picks up his doctor's bag and walks ahead of me, assuming that Mum is still in bed. I follow him upstairs.

"Mary," he says fondly, as if he has known her all his life. He stands at my mother's bedside. "How are you feeling today? Have the tablets helped?" He doesn't wait for a reply because he knows he isn't going to get one. He lifts her limp wrist off the bedspread — exactly the same place where he left it last night — and measures the tick of her pulse. I swallow, watching him deal with my mother. He is so kind and patient, I know she is in safe hands.

"Normal?" I ask when he's finished.

"Pretty much." He removes a stethoscope from his bag and listens to her chest through her nightdress.

"And?"

"Fine," David replies. Then he takes Mum's temperature, and again it's normal.

"But she's not normal, is she?" I say. Seeing my mother lying ghost-like in bed and not being able to do a thing to help her is agony. "I'm sorry," I add to cover the shake that takes hold of my hands. "I haven't been sleeping well." Haven't been sleeping *at all*, I should have said. Because of Mum. Because of Grace. Because of Murray.

"Come." David puts his hand on my elbow and guides me out on to the landing, clicking the bedroom door shut behind us. Suddenly I feel warm, secure, childlike, as I know Flora does when Murray scoops her up in his arms. At the window, we look out across the fields, across the meadow of mud and stubby grass picked to the root by the few goats and sheep Mum keeps. I'm doing my best to keep everything going.

"Something must have happened to your mother to cause this." David flicks his glance away briefly, swallows and thinks. "Do you have any idea what that might be?" He stares at me as if I should know; as if I can tell him exactly the reason my mother is not speaking.

I shrug. "No, I don't," I answer honestly. "There's nothing in Mum's life that could have made her like this." I'm standing in the sunlight that's spilling through the window and he's staring at me as if it's the first time he's ever seen me. I smile and my cheeks feel hot.

"I promise that I'll do my best for her now, Julia." His words are slow and reassuring.

"Mum's life has always been . . . well, great. Like that." And I point at the farmyard below and the kitchen garden beyond. Even in winter, it still looks idyllic with the pretty fields spread around us. "See? Perfect. Maybe she's upset because the washing line came down and the goats got her towels." I try to laugh but it doesn't come out right.

David breathes in and sighs seriously. "She's going to need a few tests, Julia. It's time for brain scans, psychological screening, a full blood work-up. Telling your mother this is one thing, but I suspect getting her to comply will be quite another." He's already got an uncannily accurate measure of her. "She clearly needs help and I want to give it to her. The best way I can."

I wish I'd had such a concerned doctor when I was pregnant with Alex and Flora. Briefly, I recall the dismissive young man who completely missed the signs of pre-eclampsia. "Well, if she disagrees, it's a good thing," I say, blocking out the disturbing memory. "It will mean she spoke." My face crumples with anguish. "Oh David, she's barely eating and won't do anything on her own. I've had to wash her and take her to the toilet for over a week." What could have made her like this?

David glances down. The carpet is threadbare and I recall running barefoot over its dated pattern as a child. "Without the test results, I wouldn't like to say. Maybe she's suffered a trauma . . ."

"An accident?"

"There are other kinds of trauma," he says. "And it doesn't have to be purely physical." He pauses and thinks. "Maybe a problem will show on the brain scan."

We walk back downstairs — David's hand sitting naturally in the small of my back. By the time we reach the hall, I feel calm again.

"I've looked over your mother's medical history and it appears perfectly normal. In the last decade, she's only seen Dr Dale, my predecessor, a couple of times for minor things. I started practising at the medical centre in November and apart from her visit to me for her finger, she's been as healthy as a horse."

"Her finger?" We're in the kitchen again, the heart of the old farmhouse, and David plants himself in the ancient sofa beside the fire. I like seeing him there but then I remember all the times Murray has folded himself into that sofa.

"It was nothing serious. She had an infection around the cuticle. To be on the safe side, I prescribed antibiotics."

I think back. Mum never mentioned an infected finger. When we last spoke, we talked about Christmas arrangements. She told me what she'd bought for Alex and Flora and I told her off because I'd wanted the surprise too. I'd promised to make the mince pies and bring them over and, finally, she'd had a quick word with each of her grandchildren. Everything had been normal.

"She never mentioned a bad finger to me."

"I've been keeping an eye on it these last few days. It seems fine now. She must have taken enough of the antibiotics to clear it up."

"Could that have caused her not to speak?"

David smiles at my ignorance but then quickly stops when he sees how worried I am. "No, Julia. I'm afraid it's something a lot more serious than that."

Somehow I end up on the old sofa next to David. We sit for an hour, talking and drinking tea, and gradually find out that we have a lot in common. When our shoulders brush together, he suggests that we have dinner. He says he would like to get to know me. When I nod, when I agree, I realise I have gone my first hour without thinking about Murray.

MARY

Living alone is my favourite pastime. When I say alone, I don't quite mean alone. To start with, the house has enough ghosts to populate an entire village. The memories within these walls keep my eyes wet with tears and my face wrinkled with laughter lines. So really, despite my attempts at solitude, I have failed miserably. I am dragged through life by snatches of happiness and admit that my knuckles are permanently white. I am a skilled tightrope-walker — holding on fiercely to a wire so taut that a breath would snap it. I have promised myself that I will never fall off. Not again.

There are the animals of course, in varying numbers — mainly chickens and goats now, and Milo, my Labrador. He's the man of my house and in charge around here. I once had a rare breed of sheep but it eventually died, and the half-dozen ducks waddle between the marsh in the east paddock and the village pond. There have been cats, rabbits, a Shetland pony years ago when Julia was young, and dogs galore.

Then there are the kids. Hordes of them over the years. Expect the unexpected, they said. That was twenty-five years ago when I started. A day or two training and off you go. It was a kind of medicine, although I didn't realise that initially. As Julia was growing up, I wanted more, needed more to keep me focused, busy, purposeful. Slipped in alongside Julia and me in our content, safe, controlled existence were other people's unwanted children. Bad children. Disturbed children. Runaway children. Frightened children. Abused children. None of them very happy children. Respite foster care, that's what I provided, and still do. Some days I could do with a respite myself. Some days I add up all the kids in my head and realise that the total of their sum is me. They have been the answer to all my pain.

So, like I said, not quite alone.

Brenna and Gradin — it's as if their parents dipped into the Scrabble bag and made whatever names they could — have come to stay for a couple of months. Their father has been abusing them since they could walk and their mother burned down their house three days ago. She did what she did to save her children — an eradication attempt. Take away life as they knew it and blow it all apart. I will pick up the pieces of their fragmented lives and do my best for the children. In this way, I am doing the best for myself.

Sometimes it's hard to believe this is the east of England. Brenna and Gradin come from the serene epitome of traditional English life — Cambridge, a city steeped in education and culture, opportunity and hope. They are surrounded by glorious countryside, bracing walks, the Fenlands, interesting rivers, and we aren't far from the coast. Yet their father saw fit to shatter their childhoods — smash up their lives from an early age for his own gratification. It is the least I can do, therefore, to provide them with a little stability, comfort and love. For me, it is a way of life; for them, it's the key to their future. Between us, I reckon we stand a chance.

I've seen kids like Brenna and Gradin a thousand times before. Each time I fix one up, and gently nudge them back out into the unknown, a little part of me is healed. What worries me, though, is that there aren't enough screwed-up kids in the entire world to make me better.

When Brenna and Gradin arrived, I knew we were in for trouble.

I've just found out that thirty pounds has gone missing from the tin on the dresser. Our treats fund.

"Where's Brenna?" I ask Gradin, sucking on my finger. It's been throbbing a while now. I can see he wants to say the right thing but he is completely unable to tell the truth. Instead, he shrugs. I can smell his unwashed body.

"Did you shower this morning?" I squint at my finger.

He shrugs again.

"Did you take the money?"

"No."

"Did Brenna?"

"No."

"That was for the weekend. You could have seen a film and had a meal out. Pizza, perhaps." He's already told me it's his favourite food.

Gradin sneers and whistles. I thought he was going to confess but he doesn't. That would have been too soon. "Baby," he croons and turns to his sister as she comes into the kitchen. He grins at her, and even though at sixteen he is two years her senior, it could be the other way round. "Baby, she says we took her money." Gradin's voice is rounded and childlike; his consonants without edge and his vowels wrapped in a blanket.

"Course we didn't. We've not taken it." Brenna, on the other hand, is as bright as a button and slips her arms on to her brother's shoulders. "You probably spent it already." Her eyes whip a keen defence at me. I am almost knocked off balance.

"I think not." I stay perfectly calm, watching them, studying every muscle twitch, every blink and breath, the way Brenna's fingers lie flat on Gradin's shoulders before she needles her nails between his muscle fibres. Lying is an art form.

"Ow!" he squeals. "What you do that for?"

Brenna shrugs and I make a mental note of that, too. "It were probably that coal delivery man who nicked it. When he came in to use the loo."

She's holding her own, I think. Staying cool and her actions are congruent with her words. Gradin, on the other hand, is squirming in his chair as if he's about to be accused of all the world's crimes. "That's probably it," I say and turn to prepare their lunch.

"I never nicked it!" Gradin suddenly yells and explodes at the kitchen table, upturning it and sending cheese and bread and knives and glasses on to the floor.

I jump back to avoid the knife from stabbing my foot but I don't shout at Gradin. He's had enough of that in his life.

Believing him is important. It doesn't do to live a life stacked on lies. "If you say you didn't take the money, then I believe you, Gradin. Will you help me clear up?"

And just like that I have them calibrated — their baseline reaction to accusation when they know they haven't done anything wrong. There wasn't any money in the tin in the first place.

By late afternoon, my finger is so sore that I can't do anything with it. After Gradin's emotional outburst, I really don't want to leave the youngsters alone while I visit the GP, but I have no choice. I have an infection, and as much as I dislike doctors, I now need to see one. It all started last week with a splinter from the chicken house. I thought it would go away if I ignored it, but it hasn't.

Witherly is a twenty-minute bus ride from Ely. They're not for me any more, towns and cities — too much happening, too much going on, too many people getting on with their lives, with what they always planned to do. I might be clever walking a tightrope, but it's never taken me anywhere.

The bus will drop me directly at the surgery on the city's periphery. This I can manage. But keeping within the boundaries of my farm is what I strive for, and infected fingers are the kind of nuisance that throw me off course, make me wobble on my rope. For a moment, I understand completely why Gradin upturned the table.

As the bus plunders the patchwork of desolate fields, I recall the last time I saw my GP — Dr Dale, a fairly pleasant man in his sixties. It was a chest infection, years ago, and Julia insisted I make an appointment when I lost my voice. She was right to make me go, of course, and Dr Dale was right to fill me with antibiotics, but I can't help wondering what would have happened if I'd overruled Julia. Would I have found my voice again?

As the bus rolls to a stop, I remind myself that this is only a quick visit to the surgery and nothing to worry about.

I stand alone on the pavement, perfectly still in the plume of diesel fumes as the bus rumbles away. I am doing the right thing.

At the surgery front desk, I receive a scowl from the receptionist when I reveal that I've made a short-notice appointment for such a trivial complaint. *But it's agony*, I want to say, *and filled with pus*, but she only has eyes for the two dozen patients racked up and waiting to be seen before surgery ends at lunchtime.

"Take a seat," she says, sighing, banging the computer keys.

I do as I'm told and take my book from my bag. I don't like being idle, and time spent sitting in a waiting room needs to be filled.

It's twenty minutes before the overhead display beeps and flashes my name to proceed to the blue room. My finger is on fire. Each consulting room door is colour-coded. I head for the correct sign, remembering that we are out of milk. I decide to walk to the shop around the corner before catching the bus home. As my hand reaches for the door handle, I think of Brenna and Gradin. I hope they're being sensible. All these perfectly normal, everyday thoughts on the way down the long white corridor and it strikes me that perhaps the coloured doors match the type of illness. I go straight in without knocking.

I see not the bent frame of Dr Dale hunched over a stack of files, but another man tapping away at a computer. He doesn't look up.

"Take a seat and I'll be with you in a moment."

"Thanks," I say in a whisper. Is it Dr Dale's absence that has thrown me, or is it something else?

When he finally does give me his attention, when he slowly looks up and our eyes meet a thousand times over, the pain in my finger is nothing compared to the pain that reaches through my chest. Around me is a thick band of strapping pulled so tight that I can't breathe, can't speak. I want to scream but I can't even open my mouth.

He is staring at me. Thirty years condense into a second. "How can I help you, Mrs . . ." He hesitates for a moment, perhaps not sure if Mrs is correct. He swallows and allows a tiny frown, although I'm shaking too much to notice for certain. He glances at the computer screen, checks my name, and then, composing himself, stares right at me with his steely eyes on full beam. ". . . Miss Marshall?" And there it is.

The smile, the nose, the ears, the neck, the shoulders, the back, the legs, the hands, the everything.

After the split-second decision, he doesn't miss a beat. His eyes slide into eager slices as if he has been waiting for this moment all his life. I half expect him to pat me on the back, shake my hand, peck my cheek.

I breathe — the only thing left for me to do. It takes all my courage, all my pride, all my strength not to run out of the surgery. I attempt a reply, calmly, as if I don't know, as if I have no idea who he is, just so we can get this over with. Then I can go away, climb back up on to my tightrope and begin all over again. I want to tell him that my finger is sore — *my finger is sore* — but no words come out. Instead, I hold out my hand.

"Let me take a look."

Do not shake, I beg of my body, but it does and he has to hold my wrist steady.

"Your finger is infected. How did it happen?" He is so near. I can feel the heat from his body. Is that his jaw tightening as he touches me?

My mouth opens but there's still silence. I want to tell him that a splinter from the chicken house snagged under my nail but the words catch in my throat. Not only is my finger filled with pus, but now my head is too and it's crazed with fuzzy images of the chickens and the incessant rain and Gradin tipping over the table and the lake and . . .

The doctor smiles. His crooked tooth has been fixed. "Don't worry, it's just a minor infection. Not allergic to anything, are you?" He laughs — perhaps nervously —

and scans my notes. He wants to make me better. Honestly, I don't think he knows what to say.

I shake my head.

Seconds later, a prescription is printed and he hands it to me.

"Three a day for a week." He smiles again. He pauses, then opens his mouth to say something but shies away from it, clipping his head as if he can avoid everything that easily. "Bathe your finger in hot salty water and keep it elevated whenever you can." His voice becomes shaky, tense, his words tied up and strangled. He leans forward on his elbows. His face is close. "And no self-lancing," he instructs before grinning again, suddenly returning to easy-doctor mode. He reclines in his chair and clicks the computer screen on to his next patient.

He is as slick as that. As if he doesn't know, as if he doesn't recognise me, as if he's never seen me before in his life. He is done with me.

As I leave, floating out of the consulting room, I see his name stuck on the door: Dr David Carlyle.

MURRAY

"Dinner? You're having dinner with your mother's doctor?" I weigh this up. Perhaps it's not as bad as it sounds.

"We'll be discussing Mum. Other stuff. It's not what you're thinking. Really." Julia is standing, shivering, holding our children's hands, not really wanting to pass them over, but she knows if she wants this dinner badly enough, she's going to have to.

I can't help the grin, a shake of my head. "Suddenly my boat's not so bad, then?" I like it that she needs me; I like it that there must be a remnant of trust. I don't like it that she's going out with another man.

"Just keep them inside. I won't be late."

Julia is wearing a grey duffle coat and a pale pink mohair hat. I know that she has gloves to match but she isn't wearing them. Her cheeks are pink, too; pools of excitement on her tired face.

"What if we want to go out?" I say snappily, and then wish I hadn't.

"Then don't."

"But . . ."

"Murray, for God's sake. Just keep the children warm and happy for three hours while I have dinner. Is this such a big deal?"

Of course it is, Julia. This is a huge deal. We've known each other all our lives; we have two children together; we're still married. I know what happens when I kiss the dimple at the base of your back; I've seen you give birth, twice; I've saved your life; you've washed my face when I've thrown up. Now you're having dinner with a doctor. This is a fucking big deal. But I don't say it.

"You're right. It's no big deal. Going anywhere nice?"

Julia sighs with relief. She even smiles. "David recommended the Three Feathers in Burwell. Apparently their steaks are to die for." She bends down and kisses first Alex and then Flora. She signs that she is to stay inside the boat. Whatever Daddy says.

I do good steaks, I think. I could cook you steak. "Shall I keep them overnight? They'll be asleep when you get back. It seems cruel to wake them."

"I'll fetch them tonight. They can sleep in tomorrow. School's not back until Monday."

There is no use arguing with Julia. Not now we're like this. It was once true that if I didn't like the colour she wanted to paint the bedroom or wasn't keen on the shirt she'd bought for me, I'd say so. Say it strongly, if I had to. Sometimes she would buckle over these wonderful, trivial, but most important issues. Sometimes she wouldn't budge. Either way, we were still together.

"What if I'm asleep?"

Passed out, more like. We're both thinking it.

"Then I'll knock loudly. Or I'll rock the boat."

"There's a programme on," I lie. "I'll be awake."

Julia slips her fingers from the children's hands — I can see she is reluctant to leave them — and kisses them once again. "Thanks, Murray," she says and walks off down the towpath to the bridge at the junction where Burwell Lode meets the River Cam. Her car, I am assuming, will be parked nearby and she will scoot off to Burwell to meet Dr Nice.

"Hey, kids," I say loudly, "fancy playing blindfold games on the roof of *Alcatraz*? With knives?"

Julia's steps lose their purposeful beat for just a moment and then she resumes her pace until she is out of sight.

"What's *Alcatraz*?" Alex asks.

"My boat, dummy." I help him aboard.

"Duh. Yeah, but what *is* it?" At eleven, I can't expect him to know.

"A prison," I reply, and realise that's exactly what it is.

I am five and a half years older than Julia. Not such a big deal; not when you're our age. But as kids, I was angry that we were lifetimes apart.

I first fell in love with Julia when she was less than a week old. With her skin as delicate as the wing of a butterfly and her eyes barely able to focus, I kissed her tiny hand when no one was looking. Her fingers coiled around my bottom lip, and when I pulled away, her nail snagged my skin. As she sat propped precariously on my small lap, Julia had an impact on me for the first time.

It wasn't that I hadn't experienced babies and their ways. Six months earlier, I had acquired a baby sister of my own. It took me a few weeks to realise that the wrinkled, squawking creature that took up all of my mother's time wasn't a temporary glitch in our otherwise settled family life. No, Nadine was here to stay, and however hard I tried, I couldn't get used to her. I preferred Julia.

But then if it wasn't for Nadine's arrival, I wouldn't ever have known Julia. Babies brought people together, and even though my mother was slightly older than Mary Marshall, the two of them became firm friends. They had babies in common. They had time to spare; time to meet, share, play and compare, and over the years the Marshall household became my second home.

We didn't stay long, that first visit. There were lots of people there besides us. And I remember thinking, why is the vicar here, consoling, passing between groups of visitors as if someone has died? Surely having a baby is a happy occasion? Beneath the smiles and coos delivered to baby Julia, there was a layer of sadness that even a five-year-old could detect.

Mary Marshall got lots of presents that day, mostly for Julia. Knitted hats, rag books, crocheted blankets, towelling baby suits and tiny vests. My mother gave her a stuffed rabbit and some cream in a pot. Both were home-made. But Mary Marshall sat coldly in a chair beside the fire — the chair that, as kids, we were always told not to sit in — and she hardly even acknowledged her baby.

The next time I fell in love with Julia was at Christmas. I'm not sure which one, but she was walking, just, so she would have been one, maybe two. Me, I was a big fat seven. I taught Julia the meaning of giving that season when I urged her to hand over all her sweets and let me play with her new toys. She protested at first, howling in her uncomfortable nappy, but then she watched in awe as I set out her painted blocks. I placed them in a crooked wall, letter side out, so they spelled our names. Julia and Murray locked together. She howled when they fell over. Why, every time that baby cried, did someone scoop her up and feed her or change her and take her away from me?

I remember that Mary Marshall didn't go out much, if ever. Kids pick up on these things, file away meaningless slices of adult information until decades later, when they piece them back together. Mary had an illness, they said. A fear of open spaces, unfamiliar places, other people, strangers. People would come and sit with her in those early days, cajoling and laughing around her. Trying to bring her back to life, I overheard my mother say. But I understood perfectly why Mary didn't want to go out: she had Julia.

At my young age, I didn't realise that being an unmarried mother wasn't something you broadcast; that taking care of a fatherless baby carried particular stigma. Not even in 1977, when the entire country was dressed in red, white and blue and the summer was filled with street parties and fetes, egg-and-spoon races and fancy-dress discos. Great Britain was celebrating; the people were happy. Then, amid the streamers and good spirit, the patriotism and first-day covers, someone said that Mary Marshall should have been ashamed of herself.

When Julia started at St Augustus Primary School, I was almost ready to move on to the local comprehensive. One year, that's all I had, to teach her the ways of the playground. I remember her standing there, in the whitest of white socks pulled up on legs that took nearly two decades to gain any shape. She looked like an angel, a sad one. Her hair fell across her face and tears welled in her eyes. She was alone and she wanted her mother.

I started off across the playground. I didn't care what my friends thought of me hanging out with a first-year girl. I wanted to protect her, scoop her up and take her back home where I knew she would be safe.

In the previous five years, Mary Marshall had somehow gathered herself together and become the perfect mother for her daughter. It was a long journey but a necessary one. Julia needed her mother as much as her mother needed Julia. They reared lambs together, sowed lettuce seeds with freezing fingers in January; they made ginger beer in the summer and served it up with ice and a sprig of mint when I visited. Mary and Julia's café, they pretended. Julia rode a pony, a stocky Shetland called Alfie, and she laughed when I tried to ride him. My legs nearly touched the ground. More than a dozen summers, over a dozen winters, and packets and packets of memories. Mary

Marshall — no wonder — had fallen right in love with Julia too.

A ball smacked her in the side of the head. I watched as Julia fought back the tears on her first day at school. Her chin quivered, her lips puckered and her eyes watered. I froze, halfway across the playground, so near and yet far enough away to be of no use at all. From that moment, I made a promise. I would never let anyone ever hurt Julia Marshall.

Yep, the kids are fine. The portable TV crackles a grainy picture at them and Flora isn't even bothered that there aren't any subtitles. They are watching a crime show; an investigation into an old murder case where they are exhuming bodies all over the place. I asked if they would prefer a cartoon.

I stand up and knock over my drink.

"Sshh, Dad," Alex whines when I swear. "This is a good bit."

Flora has a little doll who's buried under the cushions. She makes a fuss of digging about for it and then mothering it and cuddling it when she finds it. She pops it back in and does it all over again. It makes me wonder if she is copying what's on the television. I flick the channel and ignore Alex when he yells out in protest.

"Anybody for another drink?" I ask, forgetting to sign at Flora. I pour another whisky. "Cheers, then, me old mate," I say when no one replies, and flop back on to the beanbag.

There's only room for that and one small sofa inside *Alcatraz*. Built in 1972, she boasts a certain vintage appeal — mainly through the mustard curtains and the faux-wood interior. But her engine runs sweet and her body's just about holding out. *Alcatraz* is now my home.

"Are you all right, kids?" I check again. If I can smell it on my own breath, Julia will. Not that I care, at this time of night, after this much whisky. I should care, I know that much, but the quantity inside me makes it impossible. Alex grudgingly confirms that they are fine and changes the channel back. I can see they are OK. They are six feet away. They are watching dead bodies on television and their father is drinking whisky. We are all OK.

But is Julia OK? I wonder, suddenly remembering where she is when I've spent all evening trying to forget. Is she leaning across a table, her face inches away from Dr Nice? Is he flashing a brilliant smile at her that outshines all of my smiles added together? Does Julia ask him about his career, what car he drives, where he takes his holidays? Does she notice that he's a good deal older than her — and richer, able to provide everything that I couldn't?

I stand up and pace across the beam of the boat, rocking it in the still water. "Definitely very much the wrong side of forty," I say, the realisation of my comparative youth some comfort. Then I laugh. "Even pushing fifty. What's she doing going out with an older man?" What, I wonder, as I drain the bottle into my tumbler, is wrong with me?

JULIA

Grace Covatta looks like an angel. I stare at her and fleetingly imagine Flora, all grown up, lying in her place. I shudder and close my eyes for a second to erase the image. It's difficult to trace the thin line between the white hospital sheets and the edge of Grace's frail body. She didn't used to look like this in my classroom — she was always a happy, outspoken, gutsy girl with lots of answers.

She doesn't know I'm here. She's been given her own room on the trauma ward and I'm staring at her through the observation window. A policeman guards the entrance to her room. When I arrived, a couple of journalists were trying to get in to see her. They were sent away. This is Grace Covatta's new world. I wonder where her mother is, knowing that if it were Flora tucked thinly between those sheets, I would have already climbed in beside her. Nothing would make me leave.

I show the guard the pass that Ed, my brother-in-law, gave me. He's a detective in the CID. The police have finished questioning me, for now, and until an arrest is made, it's unlikely they will want anything more. The guard glances at it and stares back at me. "I'm her English teacher," I say in case he mistakes me for her mother. "The one who found her," I add in a whisper, almost shamefully, as if without my discovery, none of this would have happened. The guard nods and lets me through.

"Grace," I say gently. She's awake. Staring at the ceiling. Her chest rises and falls beneath the sheets. "It's Mrs Marshall. From school." Grace blinks. "How are you feeling?" It's a ridiculous question when half of her face is swollen and mashed with bruises. The parts of her body that I can see — her neck, her hands and forearms — are similarly decorated. None of this showed up in the frost. When she was lying in the ditch, she appeared shrunken, pale, corpse-like to combat the cold.

"We're all thinking of you, sweetheart." She doesn't reply. The ward sister told me that she still can't speak. She points at the jug to ask for water and makes gestures when she wants to be turned. The words are still stuck behind her enlarged tongue. She hasn't been able to tell anyone exactly what happened. "I would have come to see you sooner but my mother's not been well."

I want Grace to know that I care. I want to tell her that Ed will catch whoever did this and get him put away for a long time. "But I'm here now," I add in a lighter tone. "Milo sends his love and lots of licks."

Grace turns her head to me. She blinks three times and opens her mouth. Her tongue falls out, swollen and patterned with black stitches. I close my eyes and shiver through a single breath.

"Oh, Grace," I say, and drop my head on to the bed. "They'll get the evil bastard, don't you worry." Yet I wonder how likely this really is. Ed told me the forensics team is hard at work but so far there has been little conclusive evidence. Grace has been thoroughly examined and swabbed for DNA but the results aren't back from the lab. I wonder how much Ed would tell me even if he knew.

I take her hand, surprised at how warm it feels. Grace Covarta, my grade A student, is still alive. She stares at the glass of water on the table over her bed. "You want a drink?" She nods and I put the straw between her lips. She holds it in place with two fingers that are strangely normal.

"How are your feet?" I ask when she has finished sucking.

Grace's hand quivers on the bed. She is trying to tell me something, trying to be brave. Sister said the surgeons spent four hours reconnecting the tendons of her left foot and setting the tiny bones on her right so that after months of physiotherapy, she may be able to walk without much of a limp.

"I hope they heal soon," I say and then I'm stuck for words. "Oh, and everyone in JM1A did this for you." I delve in my shoulder bag and pull out the card that the kids in her year have all signed. One of Grace's friends organised it and got her mother to drive her around collecting signatures. Heartfelt wishes and lines of pity and hope are scribbled into a large card with an elephant on the front. *Don't Forget to Get Well Soon* it says in inch-high blue lettering.

Grace will never forget.

Just for one night I want to escape Grace's beaten body, my mother's silence and the fact that Murray still hasn't signed the divorce papers. I haven't been on a date for twelve years. I've been married to Murray ever since I can remember so there's been no need. But now that we're separated, nearly divorced, there is a need. I admit that it takes my breath away, the thought of someone wanting to be with me, to find out about me, open doors for me and perhaps hold my hand. Of course, I've had dates before. Murray was my first but we broke up, got back together, broke up, got back together, countless times.

Until now. Where the break-up is punctuated with a final full stop.

In between the Murray interludes, there was Mick Hopkins, a mild-mannered lad who used to follow me around with a traffic light lolly stuck between his teeth; Damien McRory, brain of Britain, who only liked me because of my grandfather's immense collection of books; James Eaton, who was the best looking — I've since heard he's gay; and finally, the one I thought would be mine for all time, Pete Duvall, sports champion, good all-rounder, who managed to kiss me with tongues a whole six months before Murray. Even now, my heart flips at the thought of Pete Duvall.

But in the end, it was Murray, my forever Murray — me aged seventeen, him aged twenty-two, and we declared undying love for eternity. Seriously, we did. We believed it was written in the stars — our very own constellation up in the heavens mapping and planning our future. Sometimes I think it's fallen out of the sky.

I have two hours before my date and I'm panicking about what to wear. I feel guilty even thinking such thoughts, what with poor Mum and Grace the way they are. I tear through my wardrobe, flinging long-forgotten clothes on to the floor before collapsing, exasperated, on to my bed. It's not at all like me to become agitated over something as simple as choosing an outfit for a date. And as I lie with my face buried in the pillow, I realise that just for now it feels good not being like me.

After my visit to Grace yesterday, Flora and Alex went to Nadine, their adored aunt's house. That was when I dashed back home to our place in Ely to grab some clothes for my evening with David. Plus it was a chance to check up on things and fetch the mail. Brenna and Gradin were content exploring the farm and promised not to leave the property. I've been staying at Mum's house way longer than the planned Christmas Day afternoon.

My small house was cold, slightly damp-smelling, and in the short time the kids and I had been away, my perception of where home was had altered. Walking through the fusty-smelling rooms — the small sitting room, the tiny dining room where Alex and Murray used to twang on their guitars and play Clapton CDs so loud the neighbours complained — I struggled to remember the happy times.

"Things move on," I said to myself. "Change is OK," I dragged my finger across the top of an antique sideboard. It was nothing special — just a nineteen forties piece — but when Murray gave it to me, I melted with happiness. He used to notice the tiniest things, how I'd spotted it at the antique shop, how I'd mentioned it on the phone once, briefly, to Nadine. Murray was like that. Was.

Back at the farm, after a desperate dash to the shops, armed with new clothes and the kids tagging along, bribed with sweets and toys, I find that Nadine has left me a message. She can't baby-sit again tonight because she has to work at short notice. Nadine is a nurse and I have to understand.

I hang my head as the answerphone beeps at the end of the message. "Murray," I whisper desolately and close my eyes for a beat as I serve spaghetti on toast to my children.

It shouldn't be like that. It shouldn't be that when I think of my husband — *the children's father* — taking care of them for an evening, my heart is filled with worry. He loves them, of course; that's never been in question. I see the way he watches them as they're lacing up their shoes when he's come to pick them up, the broken, deeper breaths he takes as Flora runs up to him and hugs his waist or when Alex takes a manly swipe at his shoulder. Murray loves them all right. It's just that he's grown to love the bottle more.

"What's this?" It's a trick question. Alex speaks through a disgusted look but really he is thanking his lucky stars he's not got a plate of broccoli in front of him.

"Pan-fried monkfish served with a salsa of vine tomatoes, chilli and coriander." I dry my hands on a tea cloth. "Eat it up then." I give him a wry smile. I never usually serve up spaghetti on toast. But tonight is different. I'm in a rush and the lack of vegetables on their plates is a small price for a few hours of . . . of letting go.

"You know I don't like chillies." Alex grins, forking in the orange hoops.

I laugh, and pretend to take away my son's plate. Flora struggles to cut up her toast. I curl my arms around her and help her saw the soggy bread. I kiss the top of her head and believe, when I think of the evening ahead, that I'm seventeen and starting all over again. I then realise that's exactly what I need to do if I'm to move on from this mess. I owe it to the children to find some stability. Someone strong, someone reliable, someone who really loves me.

Before I leave, I clean my teeth twice. Just in case.

The first time I smelled alcohol on Murray's breath was when I was eight. I didn't know what it was. It was sweet and grown-up and reminded me of summers at the pond when he was put in charge.

I had no idea why he lolled in the grass with his mates, why his eyelids drooped, why he laughed at the silliest things, why he allowed Nadine and me to do as we wished while he swigged the diluted liquor from a Coke bottle. It made him fun. It made all the days fun.

Then, when I was twelve and Murray was old enough to know better, he brought me my own mix of rum and blackcurrant.

"It tastes like Ribena," he said. "Drink it and see how you feel. If you don't like it, no harm done." I stared at him. I wanted to please him and prove to him that I wasn't a kid. Murray had been in my life since I was born — almost like a brother to me. The thing is, I knew you weren't allowed to fall in love with your brother. I knocked back the drink and grinned at Murray. He laughed at my purple lips.

Whether it was the rum or a virus, I don't know, but I spent the next three days being sick. I've never touched alcohol since.

"Wine?" David offers.

"No thanks," I say, my hand trembling as it shields the glass. "I don't drink." I pour water instead and David doesn't insist or make me feel guilty. "Besides, I'm driving." Of course I'm driving, I think. I didn't need to say it. If I wasn't driving, it would mean David would be driving me somewhere. And what does that bring to mind?

"Oh God," I whisper because of what I was thinking, not meaning it to be audible.

"Pardon?" He smiles warmly, dissolving my angst. Everything about David Carlyle is calm and together and held in place by an aura that bursts with confidence yet is quietly compassionate. The nature of a GP, I assume.

"Oh, nothing. I was just thinking about the children." I'm lying, of course, although this in itself makes me think of them and wonder if they are playing on the towpath while Murray drinks himself into a stupor.

"Are they with their . . . father tonight?" He hesitates and frowns over the word *father*.

"Yes." I nod and gulp my water so I don't have to say anything else. Mixing Murray into our conversation so soon has thrown me. Thoughtfully offering me a reprieve, David insists on fetching me something more interesting to drink from the bar. He brings back two menus and a pineapple juice.

"Have you been here before?" He glances around, seemingly satisfied with the choice of venue. It's busy, warm, cheerful and filled with the smell of home cooking. Just the kind of place I can really get to know David. Now I'm alone with him, I'm starting to sense there really could be something special between us.

"Never," I admit, and for a moment I see Murray sitting beside the fire instead of David, his features highlighted by the flames, his neck arced over the menu, his finger running down the meals.

"Their steak melts in the mouth. But the whole menu's good here. You can't go wrong."

"Do you own shares in the place?" I joke.

Now we are out of Northmire, now he's not visiting Mum, I don't know what to say to him. My conversation feels awkward. I am a soon-to-be divorcee on a date with a man who I have met only half a dozen times. I try not to notice his razored hairline as it dips beneath the collar of his shirt or the way his eyes narrow when he smiles. His hair is speckled with grey and sits in a slightly tousled, longer style on the top. He clearly takes care of himself and his clothes are stylish. I wonder if he notices how many women in the room have glanced at him since we've been here.

"No, I don't." He laughs. "I just like eating out and discovering new places." He sips his wine, barely letting any into his mouth. Murray would be on his third glass by now; thinking about ordering another bottle. "Besides, it gives me somewhere to bring beautiful ladies." He passes me a menu.

I press my toes into the soles of my boots, the only things I am wearing that aren't new. I can't help but smile.

"Ladies," I tease. "How many are there?"

"Aha." He laughs and gentle lines flicker around his eyes. "Hundreds," he jokes. "Seriously, though, I'm not seeing anyone. No one special." He looks at me intently. "To be honest, when I've finished work there's little time for socialising. I expect I'll meet lots of lovely women in the area soon enough." He sips more wine. "Hey, I already have." He gestures at me and I'm not sure if I can swallow any more compliments for the time being. He's trying to tell me that he's available, that he's interested, that he wants to take things further.

"I'm going to have the crab cakes. Have you decided?" I change the subject.

"The fillet steak, of course. And it must be rare." His eyes twinkle at the thought.

Suddenly, all I can think of is Grace Covatta lying in the field, covered in blood. There is a moment's silence, broken only by the crackling log on the fire. I must look miserable because he's staring at me quizzically, wondering what's wrong. "I'm sorry if I seem maudlin from time to time," I explain before he has the chance to ask. "It's been a strange couple of weeks."

"I understand completely," he says, resting a hand on mine. But because it's not Murray's hand, because it's an unfamiliar hand, I freeze — feeling guilty for liking it — and my whole body tenses.

David squeezes my fingers and goes to place our order at the bar. I watch him standing there — at least six feet tall, maybe more — telling the young waitress how he likes his steak, ordering more drinks. I also notice the way his body language suggests to me that he could be flirting, making her giggle, knowing exactly how to get his steak the way he likes it. It's harmless, I tell myself, and stare at the flames as he returns to the table.

"All sorted," he says, placing a new drink in front of me. I want to ask if he knows the young girl but that would be rude. He's a doctor; he's bound to know people of all ages in the community.

We chat nonstop. About where we've travelled, what our favourite books and films are, what sport we like — a kind of skirting around each other's lives in a mix of genuine laughter and warmth but so far at a safe distance. Our meals soon arrive. We eat, glancing up at each other with food balanced on our forks — me trying not to spill anything and David tucking into his rare steak. Conversation flows as if we have decades of catching-up to do.

"So am I your first?" he asks. The crab falls off my fork and splats into the salsa. "Meal out since you and Murray separated," he says, underlining what I should have known. He didn't say *date*, I notice; no implication of any strings attached. I feel slightly empty.

"Yes." It sounds as if I'm confessing to having no experience at a job interview. "Murray and I have . . . well, we were together for a long time. Meeting other people isn't so easy when you've . . ." Do I admit Murray was my first and my only lover? "When you've only had . . ." I can't do it. "Murray and I were childhood sweethearts." David seems intrigued by this bit of news. "You can understand that it's hard for me to . . ." I'm trying to let him know I see this evening as a date — the first of many, I hope. But I just can't say it outright, in case he doesn't feel the same.

"Of course I understand." His eyes say it all. They are full of compassion. "So, I imagine that Murray would know you better than anyone else." He rests his knife and fork down.

"I guess," I reply, drenched in my husband once again. A deep breath, half a glass of pineapple juice, a visit to the ladies' — it all helps me not think about Murray. I have to concentrate on why I am out with David, and really, it shouldn't be so hard.

"He's gorgeous," I say to myself in the mirror above the washbasin. I wipe off the remainder of my lipstick. I don't want it to smudge. "So stop being so bloody stupid."

One glance at him across the room rights my feelings as I return to our table. I get on with my meal — him offering me a mouthful of the legendary steak *on his fork*; me tentatively asking if he'd like to try a crab cake. We laugh when it falls on to the table. All the while I can't help wondering how the evening is going to end.

An hour or so later, David helps me into my coat and we leave the warm pub for the windswept street. The cold air is welcome after the crowded bar. Anything to blow away the moment when we part, don't part, kiss, don't kiss. "Look, do you fancy a ten-minute walk?" He's drawing it out. He starts walking anyway, as if it's a given.

"Sure," I say too quickly and he hooks his arm through mine when I catch up.

The streets of Burwell are quiet. It's a pretty place, with everything you'd expect in a Cambridgeshire village; a place where nothing out of the ordinary ever happens. Except maybe tonight.

"You've changed your name already," David says.

I recall the fuss that Murray kicked up when I chose to keep my maiden name after we married.

"I've always been Julia Marshall," I reply. With hindsight, it was the right thing to do. I don't have to worry about changing names now the divorce is underway.

"When did you and Murray actually separate?" David looks down at me.

"Last July," I say. "Saturday the fifteenth at three twenty p.m."

"That precise, huh?" He tugs on my arm. A belated gesture of sympathy.

"It was the exact time the locksmith finished changing the locks. Murray wasn't even around. He was at . . ." I stop. Not yet. Don't colour David's picture of me with the stain of Murray's drinking. "Well, he just wasn't there, that was all. It was for the best." I remember Murray at the bar, the look on his face when I approached him. By then, he didn't even know who I was, let alone that he was supposed to have picked Alex up from the ice rink.

"Have you ever been married?" I ask. David's been carefully protective of his past. He's more interested in finding out about me, my childhood, than revealing his own story.

"No," he says with a laugh. "I've always managed to put it off, wriggle out. There have been women . . . a woman." He swallows and his pace slows; drags almost. "But the time has never come." He stops walking. "It obviously wasn't meant to be." I can tell he doesn't want to talk about it. We are beside a bus stop. He turns me to face him. "I think we have a lot in common." A breath, a pause, and then he leaps. "I'd like to see you again." Then, "I want to know all about you."

"That would be nice," I say far too quickly, without even considering what it all means. I grip his forearms, giddy with pleasure, because they are the nearest things — strong, supportive, just where I need them — and suddenly his hands are holding me in return. In a flash, I am seventeen again, when Murray and I finally got together properly. He was strong. He was there. He was everything I'd ever wanted.

"I'm not quite thirty," I say absurdly, perhaps thinking of all the roadblocks that we will encounter. I am completely unable to remove the grin from my face. He wants to see me again. Surely he knows there's an age difference. It's ridiculous but the only thing I could think of to say.

"Lucky you," he says, laughing. There is no shock.

"But it's OK. I like older men," I say, grinning back. And it's true. As of now, I do, because when he walks me back to my car, he kisses me. Just a dusting of skin, his lips missing mine by a fraction. I feel the heat in them anyway, his warm breath on my cheek, the passion I know he's holding back. He stays there for a beat too long, causing my heart to kick up in my throat all the way back to the children.

MARY

After my visit to the surgery, after all the words I wanted to scream got wedged in my gullet, the woman that I'd become over the decades quickly unravelled and fell apart. The result was silence. I couldn't speak a single syllable. It was self-preservation of the highest level. There was no one immediately available to talk to anyway, and by the time I got home, a few hours later, the vile bung that was trapped in my throat was as stubborn as a blocked drain. And it stank as much.

Everything I ever feared had come right back at me; a full circle of horror. And this time, I had more to lose.

Initially, I don't think Brenna and Gradin even noticed my silence. Of course, they knew that something was wrong but their already troubled minds made it impossible for them to grasp what needed to be done. They were barely able to function normally themselves. My condition certainly made them unsettled, but ultimately, they were simply content to be out of their abusive home. They still took guesses at what I'd got them for Christmas, shrugging when I didn't reply; they still squabbled and left the bathroom in a mess and ate up all the food in the house. During the first day or so, I managed to cook for them, just enough to make toasted sandwiches, a casserole, hot chocolate, and I washed their clothes. I got through the day hour by hour.

Until the telephone rang.

"Mary . . . it's . . ." There was a sigh. A hesitation. "It's David . . ." I hung up immediately.

I stood for ten minutes, staring blankly at the wall ahead. My hand was pressing down on the receiver, pinning it to the base as if that would prevent it ringing again. It didn't. He called twice more that evening.

"It's for you, Mary." Brenna answered and held out the phone to me. She frowned when I didn't take it; when I didn't stir from my chair. Even across the room I could hear him. *Hello, hello?* Each word ripped out another organ from my body. Piece by piece, David Carlyle was tearing me apart.

Stunned that he'd made contact, that he'd dared to enter my home — even if it was just his voice — I fell on to my bed and wept silently.

By Christmas Eve I was even worse. It wasn't just that I couldn't speak — although the words inside my head still flowed at a thousand a minute trying to unravel the mess, formulate a plan — but by now, my body had lost its tone, too. A fuse had blown in my brain, short-circuiting pretty much everything about me. I transformed from an active, stubborn, determined woman into an incapable, terrified shell.

"There's nothing to do," Brenna moaned, and the pair of them lurked through Christmas Eve, grumbling that they wanted a television, some sweets, something nice to drink. It wasn't like Christmas at all. I dipped into my purse and fished out twenty pounds. They knew where the village shop was. It would still just be open.

"What about you, Mary?" My catatonic state had even prompted concern in Gradin. Before this, I'd been very concerned about his destructive behaviour. Now all I could think about was mine.

Christmas morning, they didn't care whether I spoke or not. They'd already sniffed out the gifts I had hidden away and gorged on the chocolates, played the games and even read the books I'd bought for them. They were teens acting out a missed childhood and I was supposed to be helping them. It was all I could manage to breathe in and out.

In the afternoon, Julia arrived. She found me in the blue velvet buttonback chair that was only ever sat in when something was wrong. She didn't know my heart was bleeding.

Today she's back to take me to the hospital. "Are you still willing to have the tests, Mum?" Julia sighs — all the weight of her worry pouring out. She is doing her best under the circumstances. I can't even bring myself to look at her. I'm scared she would see the truth in my eyes. I twitch my finger. She knows what I mean. "Good. It's cold out. Let's get you into this."

She holds my coat in a welcoming spread in the hope I will slither into it. When I don't, she fumbles one arm into the sleeve, then the other, then hauls me upright by the hands. She truly believes she's helping me; that her kind actions will make me better. What she doesn't know is that there is no getting better.

"Let's get you into the car then, eh?" Suddenly, everything is *let us*, as if that familiar, uniting use of words will make everything all right.

Oh, *Julia*. They say that what you don't know can't hurt you.

The hospital is busy and noisy. Doctors and nurses are rushing around and patients are shuffling along the polished floors. I look back at the entrance — a cluster of dressing-gowned women are smoking outside. One of them catches my eye and turns away. Her dressing gown is as bright as the tumour on her leg. Already I am regretting agreeing to this. I don't need any tests. They won't find anything.

We wait in the neurology department for my appointment. Julia talks to me but I don't hear her. My ears only pick up fragments of sound — shattered remnants of other people's lives. She mentions cuts and guilt and suddenly, even without hearing her words, I know exactly what she is talking about. She says she will perhaps visit Grace while we are in the hospital. I think of Julia discovering the girl and wonder how much more my daughter can take.

"Mrs Marshall?" I leave it to Julia to reply. I hope she tells them I never married; that I'm *Miss*.

"It's my mother," she says, gesturing to me. "Come on, Mum. Our turn." She pulls me upright and I go dizzy.

It's hard to believe that I'm shuffling like an old woman when two weeks ago I was chasing the chickens around the yard and repairing the goats' pen. My previous foster child had returned to her family and I was looking forward to getting on with my next challenge — Brenna and Gradin. I was convinced I could help them; certain I could make a difference. Instead, it's my life that's pulled inside-out. Julia leads me into Mr Radcliffe's office.

I don't like doctors. My skin prickles.

"Well, Mrs Marshall. Dr Carlyle has referred you to me as an urgent case. I've known him personally for a long time and we chatted at length about you. He's extremely keen for you to be assessed as soon as possible. I'm going to ask you a few questions and most likely refer you for some tests. How does that sound?"

He is speaking to me like I am a child. His desk is laminated, not real wood, and there is a snag of cotton on the edge where someone has caught their clothing. The carpet is a medium blue, worn near the door but otherwise serviceable. "Mrs Marshall, do you understand?" I wish he'd call me Miss. The spider plant on the corner of the desk has trailed miniature plants right down to the floor. A slice of winter sunlight cuts across the room and dust motes hover, swirling and lost.

"Mum," Julia says, although she knows I won't speak. "Shall I answer for you?"

I would like to nod, to glance at her, to smile even or twitch my finger, but I can't do it. There is simply nothing there. Julia's boots have a rim of pale mud around the sole and the heel is a little worn. Brown leather, crinkled at the ankle, with a zipper up the side.

Warm boots. Julia's boots. I recall fighting with her to wear sensible shoes as a child.

"I'll answer for her, Mr Radcliffe. Will that do?"

"Under the circumstances, it will have to. Dr Carlyle explained to me about your mother's mutism. He said . . ." Radcliffe trails off, leaving me wondering exactly what was said about me. "Look, selective mutes can be surprising. They'll talk to some people and not others."

Does he think I *selected* this?

"Are you suggesting that Mum is choosing not to speak? That she could if she wanted to?" Julia sounds angry.

"If she is a selective mute, then yes, to a certain extent she can choose who she speaks to. But I'm more concerned with the neurological side of things — her brain, to be precise — in case she doesn't have a choice."

"You mean like a tumour?" Julia is always direct.

"That's one possibility. We need to look at everything. When did Mrs Marshall stop speaking exactly?"

Julia pauses and I know she's looking at me. I can feel the burn of her stare on my face; the plea in her eyes for me to become normal again — the pair of us, mother and daughter, invincible against the world. "That's hard to tell. We chatted on the phone a few days before Christmas, and then when I visited her on Christmas Day, she was . . . like this. So it must have happened any time in between, I suppose. Dr Carlyle said . . ." When she says his name, her voice turns to double cream.

"Dr Carlyle didn't seem to think she should go to hospital straight away. I think he was hoping that with rest and close monitoring, she would recover. As if she'd just had a big shock."

"And has she spoken a single word since, or even made any kind of vocal noise? A grunt or squeal perhaps."

I don't grunt or squeal, I yell in my head so it aches. My farm animals grunt and squeal.

"She whimpered when I lifted her out of the chair on Christmas Day. I think I hurt her arms. But nothing else. Not a sound."

Julia glances at me, praying I'm suddenly going to join in their repartee. They are talking about me as if I'm not here, which certainly makes my feeling of not being real all the more tangible.

"And what about your mother's movements? Does her physical ability seem impaired in any way? Does she limp? Is there any sign of paralysis?"

Julia pauses and thinks for a moment. In my head I interrupt, try to whisper the truth, but she can't hear me. Frustrated, I turn to Radcliffe and silently mouth the answer he requires. Like Julia, I doubt he will believe me.

To begin with, Doctor, my mobility was perfectly normal. After several hours had passed, I somehow got myself home from Dr Carlyle's surgery. It wasn't until it all . . . sank in . . . until I understood what was now going on . . . that my joints gradually stiffened and my tendons creaked as they slid across my bones. Once released, the poison that I'd worked hard to contain for thirty years spread quickly through my body. It reached every part of me. Several days later, my eyes became gritty and dry, my heart barely beat in my chest and my skin started to peel. Walking crushed every joint in my body and eating felt as if I was swallowing thorns. Tell me, Mr Radcliffe, what is wrong with me?

"It's so weird. Mum's always been full of energy. She's fantastic for her age. She eats healthily and keeps fit on the farm. So to see her like this, it's impossible to say she hasn't been affected physically. Of course she has. Whether she's capable of moving more, well, I don't know. My guess is no, she is not choosing to be taken to the toilet and bathed by me. If she could do it, she would. Whatever it is has hit her entire body."

My entire soul.

"Mr Radcliffe said the MRI scan is booked for Monday, Mum. That's good news, isn't it?" Julia is driving me home. "We just have to stop by Nadine's house to pick up Alex and Flora." She's being how I used to be with her — patient, understanding, driven to the ends of the earth with exasperation.

I think about the MRI scan. The doctor explained that I will be slid into a tube, where the machine will image my entire body, map my brain, my internal organs and trace the path of my blood vessels to make sure they are not bleeding inside my head. I will be slammed by noise as the machine goes about its business, probing a magnetic field into parts of me that no one has ever seen. Mr Radcliffe will study the results and report back what's wrong. What they don't yet know is that the scan, the precision picture of my entire being, will not show up a thing.

Outside Nadine's house, Flora and Alex climb into Julia's car. They smell of Coke and sticky sweets. Normally I would remind Julia to tell her sister-in-law not to fill my grandchildren with junk. She would eye me in a way that told me not to interfere, and then explain why Ed and Nadine enjoy spoiling their niece and nephew. Later, we would laugh about it and I would apologise.

But things are far from normal, and as we drive back to Northmire, Alex bombards his mother with news of Ed's new case. The boy is clearly obsessed by his uncle's job and talks nonstop about how he has to make sure no more women are hurt.

"Uncle Ed is in charge of the case, Mum. He says I can go down to the station and interview the officers for a school report." I can't see him sitting behind me but instinctively I know that he is beaming, already planning the questions. Alex is set on joining the police force when he is old enough. He looks up to Ed almost as much as to his father. Then I'm thinking about Murray and wishing he was here for Julia; to hold her and support her through the inevitable, because I can't. I see an abyss so deep that when she is at the bottom, no one will hear her call.

"Alex, you shouldn't ask your uncle so many questions." Julia's voice is shaky, like her driving.

"Oh, Mum," he moans. "Uncle Ed says I can. He's going to find the man who killed Grace."

"Grace is not dead," Julia retorts. She sighs and pulls the car straight after hitting a pothole on my drive. "She's very poorly, though, and I sincerely hope that Uncle Ed catches whoever did this to her."

"I want Uncle Ed to catch him otherwise it might happen to you or Grandma or Flora."

"Enough, Alex!" Julia explodes, as if being in the neurology department has stripped all her nerves raw. "Inside, kids, while I help Grandma." She paces her movements with short, sharp breaths, each one taking her to the next minute.

As Julia helps me out of my seatbelt and leads me inside, I think about what Alex said. How can I tell him it's already too late?

MURRAY

There was no point in the world trying to hide my mistake. We could have died, I admit. With not a speck of air left in the cabin from the hungry furnace-like stove, Alex and Flora had heaved open the heavy wooden hatch of *Alcatraz* and stepped out on to the rear deck to gasp lungfuls of icy night air. Their bodies hungrily drew in the oxygen and I was saved only because they left the hatch open.

"How *could* you, Murray? They could have suffocated. You're irresponsible and selfish and useless and . . ." Julia screamed at me from the deck, her barrage dissolving into the freezing night. She didn't set foot inside the cabin, which smelled like a distillery and blew out hot, dry air from the over-coked stove that I had lit to keep my children warm. That was all. I'd not wanted them to go back to Julia and complain that Daddy had let them shiver. But I'd drunk Scotch and fallen asleep on the floor with my neck bent crooked and the empty bottle between my knees.

It was eleven fifteen when Julia, reeking of Dr Nice, finally stormed back down the towpath, dragging our bemused children with her. They were *sure*, I heard them tell her, that they had seen three giant pike lurking in the light of the moon. When I looked up — Julia's cross words still ringing through the night — I saw that the moon was obscured by cloud. Had the children imagined the pike, just as I'd imagined I could take care of them?

I've made it into work today. Odd, considering my head feels like a demolition ball has crashed through it, and also odd because I'm about to lose my job. Any sane person wouldn't have bothered showing up under the circumstances — pride or shame or simply the hangover keeping them away. Me, however, I'm desperate, and turning things around is what I have to do. If I can keep my job, there's a chance that I can keep my family.

"French!" Sheila Hanley — boss and all-round demon — is in my office snapping orders. "Do these. Today." A pile of files lands on my desk, the thud of them sending shockwaves through my body. I wince. "And get yourself some coffee. You look like shit." A fiendish smile slices up her face and she ruffles my hair. "You know how much I love you."

"Good morning to you too, Sheila. You look . . . as beautiful as ever."

She shakes her head, and I realise flattery will get me nowhere. Her lacquered hair doesn't budge. The neck of her crisp cotton blouse is open a little too low for a woman of forty-five, and her waist is unfeasibly trim. Her heels are high and her lips are red — always bright red. Somehow Sheila Hanley, senior partner of Redman, Hanley and Bright, carries off the look.

"There's a road traffic accident, a matrimonial case and a debt recovery for you." She pats the files as if they are her children. "Nothing too hard for you today, eh, darling?"

It's what I was expecting. The bottom of the pile. Then, just when I think it couldn't get any worse, the last face in the world I want to see pokes into the cupboard that is my office. Suddenly, I am a sideshow. "Hey, Frenchie, it's been a while. They let you out of rehab, I see."

I breathe in and quickly count to ten. "Dick," I reply, dragging out the syllable although that's not strictly his name. I don't bother looking up. I open one of the files and pretend to read while concentrating on sipping my coffee without my hand shaking. I flip through the papers.

"Where did you park the boat, then? In the multistorey?" Dick squeezes into my office and stands beside Sheila. They loom over my desk. This is one cruel hangover.

The shakes come and I put the cup down just in time. I take off my reading glasses but it doesn't help. My vision is still blurred "Richard." I nod my head. "Very clever. As usual." Sheila is waiting for me to crack.

"Then how did you get to work? Didn't I hear that you lost your licence?" Dick presses on.

"No, you didn't." Not quite. "As it happens, I came on the bus. My car is in the garage being fixed. How did you get to work? In a spaceship?"

"In my new Porsche, actually. I could give you a ride home later, if you like. As long as you don't throw up in it." He smiles broadly.

"I can't guarantee that, Dick. The bus will be fine."

"Suit yourself." And Dick Porsche strides off to the partner's office that would have been mine — the one with the extra-large desk and the view over the city — if I hadn't decided to become an alcoholic instead.

"So," Sheila says, closing my door. "What's going on in Murray-land?" I know when Sheila is serious, and this is one of those times. Her eyelids semi-close — an almost feral expression — and her arms fold around her body. She perches on the edge of my desk. In the five years that I've been working for Redman, Hanley and Bright, I've never quite managed to figure her out. Mostly she's indomitable lawyer, courtroom queen, but occasionally she's quiet and reserved — usually before an explosive outburst — and sometimes I've witnessed her almost maternal with the young female staff. Sheila's most reliable quality is that she's unpredictable. If I didn't respect her so much, I'd hate her.

"Really, you don't want to know." Coffee spills on my desk, and without even thinking about it, Sheila has a tissue soaking it up.

"That bad?"

"And I guess you're about to make it worse, right?"

It's no secret there was a partners' meeting last night. The three-monthly get-togethers are largely an excuse to run up a big bill at the Square, a favourite venue for the Cambridge legal set. But apart from ordering expensive wine and eating enough langoustines to fill an entire ocean, they do talk shop. They discuss figures and cases and staff and assets. And liabilities. Like me.

"I should be," she says, lobbing the wet tissue in the bin. "But," she stands and props her hands on her hips, "I got you a reprieve." She raises her hands to stop me interrupting. "Just don't bloody ask me why I grovelled and begged on your behalf, Murray French. Don't ever bloody ask me why."

I won't, I think, and keep my face solemn. Sheila doesn't like emotional outbursts and would hate it if I hugged her, which is what I feel like doing.

"But if you ever, ever . . ." She pauses and takes a breath seemingly too large for her chest. "If you ever let me down and make me look a fool again, then —"

"Oh for God's sake, Sheila, I won't let you down, right?"

"Why don't I believe you?"

"Let me think," I say. "Is it because I've missed five court appearances in the same number of months, or lost more cases than I've even taken on?" Each of us is suppressing a grin. I can't help it. I get up and give her a hug. "Thanks," I whisper in her ear. "I'm the dick, not Dick Porsche."

"Oh no, take it from me. He's one as well." Sheila exits my office, leaving nothing behind but the scent of expensive perfume.

I turn to the files on my desk. I open the first one. I read the brief. Just as the sigh of gratitude settles inside me, just as I reach out to touch the glimmer of hope that maybe I can claw my way back into all this, I read in the file that the driver I will be representing mowed down a girl Flora's age. He was three times over the legal limit.

When I was thirteen, when alcohol started to really mean something to me, I would have done anything to be one of the gang, to hang with the cool kids. That's when I started the Secret Drinking Club.

The thing is, I was too stupid to realise that there was nothing much wrong with my life in the first place. True, I was surfing on hormones, dodging schoolwork, desperately waiting for Julia to grow up so that she could be mine. The Secret Drinking Club helped pass the time but only served to make things worse. After that, I really was a freak, an oddity, the boy who the normal kids avoided.

We met several times a week in various places — sometimes a bus shelter, sometimes a hedgerow by the river, sometimes a farmer's barn — it depended on the season. Each member would be obliged to bring at least a cupful of any alcohol they could lay their hands on. Two failures to turn up with the goods and they were out. Of course, as club leader I received a share of the offerings, and in return, well, I didn't give anything in return except the privilege of belonging to such an elite club and a rip-roaring good evening with the chance to forget our schoolkid worries.

The club lasted exactly four months, two weeks and three days. I know this precisely because having to hit my parents' drinks cabinet on a regular basis after the club folded took its toll. I'd run out of willing kids in the village to supply me with booze. Some decided it was a bad idea all by themselves, or their parents hauled them home by their scruffs. I was either a very skilled liar or my parents were blind. By this time, I was completely dependent, and having to reduce my intake to what my parents wouldn't notice resulted in anxiety, the shakes, depression, not to mention headaches and insomnia. I was bad-tempered, foul-mouthed and a total pain in the butt.

Now, I wish for those easy symptoms. Now, I wish I'd never gone to that party in the first place.

It was only because I'd wanted to impress a girl. Not Julia — she was still only a kid, and there was a long while to wait before our ages didn't seem like a million light years apart. It was another girl — she was in my class and I can't even remember her name. But it was her fault, anyway, that I took that first drink laced with the promise of being more confident, more attractive, more of a man, with my skinny arms and legs and constellations of spots. The alcohol worked. We snogged. We danced. We went out briefly. She ditched me but I didn't ditch the booze. Either way, girl or no girl, it was always there for me. And so started the club.

As I hear Dick Porsche talking on the phone loudly in his office, I resolve never to drink again. Again. What have I lost because of alcohol? My wife, my children, my home, my dignity, my money, and, oh yes, if I don't get a grip, my job too.

When I rummage around in my old desk drawer for a biro, my hand rests upon the slim body of a half-bottle of Scotch. I pull it out from beneath the papers and other junk — my vague attempt at concealing the evidence — and realise that this is what I will have to do for the drunk driver who killed the little girl. Conceal the evidence. By midday, having stared at the empty bottle for several hours, I'm not sure I can do it.

JULIA

There is no other option. I have to take time off work. Call it annual leave, I told them on the phone, whatever you like. I just can't come into school for a few days. I explained it was because of Mum, and of course that's true, but with the weight of everything else, the thought of teaching a classroom of rowdy teenagers fills me with dread.

"They'll have to get a supply teacher to cover my classes," I say to Mum as I brush her hair. "And as for Brenna and Gradin . . ." I'm hoping she'll respond. Beg me not to give up her latest challenge. "I guess they'll have to be re-homed now." I pause, the brush halfway down Mum's hair. In the mirror, her face is blank, completely untouched by the prospect of giving up on two needy kids. "And that's sad. A real shame," I finish.

But calling social services and turning them over to the authorities is not something I truly want to do. I'm still hoping that Mum will wake up one morning and throw some breakfast on the stove, round up the goats, snap out the sheets on the washing line, chattering away as if nothing has happened. I would forgive her. I would never ask what happened. We could just pick up where we left off.

I know there's no point telling her any of this.

"So, I'll make the call then, shall I? About Brenna and Gradin?" One last attempt elicits nothing. It will be hard to see them go because there's something reassuring about Gradin's slippery grasp of reality and his sister's determination to keep them locked together. Given the choice, they would beg me not to turn them in. Despite all the upheaval at Northmire, they seem quite at home here, although living on the street would have been preferable to what they endured at home. Before they arrived, Mum had told me all about their history.

I stop brushing again and realise that I'm forgetting what my own mother's voice sounds like.

"They'll end up back with their father in a hostel or be bundled off to another foster carer." I'm talking to myself rather than Mum. Change piled upon change piled upon the stress of somewhere new would not be good for Brenna and Gradin. I decide to keep them at Northmire while I am here to care for them. The authorities don't even know that Mum's sick, and I reckon I can persuade David not to let on.

That's when the smile comes, flashing across my lips as wispy as Mum's greying hair. "I saw your doctor last week." I hadn't bothered her with my news on the day of her first hospital consultation, but now that he wants to see me again, at his place for supper, I'm happy to tell the goats if they'll listen.

Unexpectedly, Mum breathes in and parts her lips.

"Yes, go on," I urge.

She coughs, and then her eyes are as vague as ever, staring beyond my shoulder. Her body slumps again, as if it took every ounce of fight left in her to even cough. I bow my head. What, then, will it take for her to speak?

"Mrs Mary Marshall?"

"Yes," I reply for her.

"Date of birth?"

"Twelfth of February nineteen forty-nine."

"Address?"

"Northmire Farm, Back Lane, Witherly."

"Can you confirm her GP?"

"Dr Carlyle," I say slowly, allowing his name time on my tongue. "David."

Then Mum is taken from me by a nurse. She is led down the corridor to a changing cubicle and I wonder how she will ever get into one of those hospital gowns all by herself. She glances back at me just before the curtain is snapped closed. I should be in there, helping her.

"Julia, I'm so glad I caught you." David is suddenly behind me, making me turn, making my lungs fill with air, making my cheeks flush. I smile even though I'm worrying about Mum. I haven't got any mascara on.

"What are you doing here?" It sounds confrontational. I stand on tiptoe and plant a kiss on his cheek. I didn't mean to do that, not under the circumstances, but for a second it makes me feel good. He seems to like it.

"I'm a doctor, Julia. And this is a hospital." He is grinning, winning me over, making me shed my concerns for Mum. "I have a private clinic here on Mondays."

"Oh," I say, still surprised, still pink, still glancing back down the corridor to where she is.

"I run a teen pregnancy clinic. It's a particular area of interest for me."

"Oh?" I'm not giving him my full attention, because my mother is going inside a noisy tube and she hates small spaces and I don't know which way to turn. To David, or to run after Mum.

"It's a confidential service. We offer the girls advice, choices, a safe place."

"Mum's gone in for her scan." I'm hardly listening to him.

"Julia. There is nothing you can do now except wait." His hand is on my back, patiently reassuring me. "She'll be fine. Let's get a hot drink, sit, and talk. I won't leave your side until she's out and safe. How does that sound?" The scent of him overpowers me and buckles me into agreeing. He leads me away from the MRI reception and down a series of corridors to the staff canteen. He buys me coffee.

"Tell me the worst, then," I say. "The most awful, wretched scan results you can think of. Then when we get the real results, maybe they won't seem so bad."

David remains calm and not even a little fazed by my gloom. "Your mother is a puzzle, I admit." He looks away. "What I do know is that I want to help her. I desperately want her to talk again. There's so much —"

"*David*," I say. "Tell me the worst."

He just stares, then sighs. "Brain tumour. Damage to the primary auditory cortex, perhaps due to a head injury. A stroke, again resulting in lesions and tissue injury to the speech centres in the brain. Brain aneurysm, which may not kill her now but if it bleeds —"

"Please, stop." I raise my hands. I don't believe him. I don't want to have Mum boxed and buried before she's even out of the scan. "OK, so what's the best scan result we could hope for?"

"That her brain looks perfectly normal, of course. It's what we all hope for, Julia." David reaches across the sticky table and takes my hand. "I'm looking forward to spending more time with you."

It will be a relief, I admit, not to think about Mum for an evening. "So, can you cook?" I ask, grinning. "I'm expecting a feast when I come round, you know, and stimulating company as —"

"As much as an old man can manage, huh?" David's face is solemn, seeking confirmation of what I have already told him. Then the smile spreads. I wonder why he says *old man* when he is clearly not.

"Older man," I correct. If I am honest, I would say that it excites me. "It's attractive," I admit, blushing because it's only been one date and a butterfly of a kiss. Barely there, really.

"Come on," he says tenderly. "Let's see if they've finished with Mary yet. She'll probably be a bit disorientated." We walk back down the corridors.

Then I have a thought. "Perhaps I should visit Grace Covatta while I'm here?" I suggest, hoping he might come with me. "You have heard about the case, I take it?"

"I'd have to be deaf and blind not to have heard about it," he says, and then, "Sorry. That was insensitive. The Covatta case is terrible." He bows his head respectfully.

"How do they solve a case like that?" I ask. Ed has sometimes spoken about his work, about forensic science. It amazes me how so much can be gleaned from specks and samples invisible to the eye. "Grace still can't talk and they've got nothing much else to go on. The police have scoured the area where I found her and come up with very little so far." I make a mental note to call Ed, who is technically still my brother-in-law.

"Look, see? She's fine," David says, pointing away from me.

Mum is standing halfway down a long white corridor, looking first one way and then the other. She doesn't know which way to turn. "David," I say, halting him with a hand on his arm. "How did Mum act when she came to your surgery? Was there anything to suggest that something was bothering her, something more than an infected finger?" It's a question I've been meaning to ask him.

He pauses and thinks. "Not at all. Of course, if I'd noticed anything unusual I would have probed. She was very quiet, a little nervous perhaps, but many people don't like seeing doctors. The visit only lasted a couple of minutes. In fact, it was as if she couldn't wait to leave."

"That's Mum all right," I say, remembering how hard it had been to get her to see a doctor when she had a chest infection. I fetch her from the corridor and tow her back towards David. She glides like she's floating a couple of inches above the floor. "Dr Carlyle came to see how you got on. That was kind of him, wasn't it?"

Suddenly Mum's arm — its bony thinness contained in my grip — tenses into a strap of muscle. Her eyes widen. She is reacting, responding. The way she stiffens her neck, her shoulders, and the way her pace gains purpose, I almost think she might speak.

Hello, Doctor. Thank you for being here. Thank you for taking care of me.

Then Mum, even though she is dressed in the open-backed hospital gown, strides as purposefully as any healthy person down the corridor and into the bowels of the hospital. It takes me half an hour to find her.

And there she is, standing, staring through the window that separates Grace Covatta from the rest of the world. Mum's fingers trace a smeary line on the glass before she allows her arms to fall by her sides.

Grace slowly turns her head and her empty eyes connect with Mum's just as I lead her away. "No time for visiting now," I tell her, realising that Grace and my mother are both locked in the same silent world, at opposite ends of their lives. I sigh and wonder what they are trying to say to each other.

After I strap Mum safely inside my car, I have a breathless word with David. He is having a private chat with the neurologist, Mr Radcliffe, about my mother.

"The outcome must be conclusive," David says quietly but firmly. I *think* that's what he says, but his back is turned so I can't be sure. "Mary Marshall is —"

"David," I interrupt, "I'm going now. I found Mum in the trauma ward." He turns suddenly, smiling at me, melting my heart like Murray once did. "What were you just saying about Mum? Do you have the results yet?" Mr Radcliffe and David stare at me blankly, as if they don't know how to tell me bad news.

"There are dozens of images for the radiologist to report on. It will be a day or two before we have any idea of what's going on inside Mary's brain." David puts a hand on my arm. "This isn't my speciality field, but Andy and I go way back, so no doubt he'll give me the heads up when there's news, won't you, Andy?" David raises his eyebrows at Mr Radcliffe and for a second there is a moment of silent tension between the men. "I trust the results will be what we are all hoping for."

"We'll see," Mr Radcliffe says.

"You will call me if there's any news, won't you, David?"

"You have my word," he replies, and leans down to kiss me on the cheek. It turns my bleak day into one filled with sunshine, and as I'm walking away, I hear the voices of the two doctors knitted together again in deep diagnosis.

MARY

I've heard that when you die, you travel down a long tunnel with such a bright light at the other end you can hardly stand to look. For me the tunnel is dark, noisy and the second most terrifying place I have ever been in my life. There are no guardian angels or harps or trumpets, just the banging and whirring of this great metal machine, the guts of which I am stuck inside. Getting into it was like being fed through a drinking straw.

They gave me headphones with music and said that the test would take a little over half an hour, so to pass the time, I count in time to the beat. I only get to forty-three before my mind wanders away from the numbers and vague notes, perhaps dragged off course by the massive amount of magnetism that is passing through my body. A film reel of my life flashes before my screwed-up eyes. They say that happens, when you die.

I was pretty back then. So pretty, with a figure to match, and oh, didn't I know it. I was going places, or so I thought. Looking at me back then, knowing who I am now, you'd think I was a different person.

Take the hair, for a start. It was halfway down my back and screamed out at least as much as the rest of my body. It was the way I wore it, half covering my face and spilling over my shoulders in a semi-coy, semi-provocative manner. Then there were the clothes — not so much concealing my body as showing it off — the purple, yellow and brown mini-dress with a plunge neckline, and knee-length boots. I was a stunner, for sure, and mostly cheerful even though my dreams had veered somewhat off course. At eighteen, I'd been desperate to go to university, become a zoologist, a marine biologist, a doctor, a lawyer, a scientist or a professor of modern languages.

I was smart, too smart perhaps, and even though my excellent school results reflected my determination, I never made it into university. I applied to Cambridge — it was on my doorstep. They rejected me at the first round, crossed me off their list. I tried to tell them what they were losing, that there must have been a mistake, that I was better than Rupert and Tarquin and Jeremy and whoever else had been offered places from public school. They slammed the door in my face.

In the mid sixties, the quota of female places offered at such a prestigious institution didn't stretch as far as a farm girl who had bothered to do her homework. A country bumpkin made good. Perhaps they were worried I would turn up in my wellies or smell of cow muck. Or end up getting pregnant.

There I was, armed with grade A results in mathematics, physics, biology and English, and absolutely no prospects. I could speak three modern languages, had read classic literature from an early age, was taught Greek and Latin by my grandfather, and I was an accomplished dancer. After Cambridge, I applied to a dozen more universities. None of them accepted me.

My father suggested a secretarial course. My mother hinted she could use the extra help around the house, and because I could drive a tractor, I was invaluable at harvest time. Besides, she said, a nice boy with his own farm would soon come along and whisk me off my feet.

Resigned to temporarily giving up on university, I moved into the city. Living where we did — Northmire Farm was stuck between waterways, blankets of green, gold and brown fields, and absolutely nowhere — meant an hour-long round bus trip to Cambridge every day. But it was where I needed to be if I was to get a job, the only option left to me if I wasn't to become someone's wife within a year. I would work and save and study and reapply. They couldn't ignore me for ever.

The bus service to the city was unreliable and would have eaten up most of my wage, once I was lucky enough to find a job. Besides, I didn't want to live at home. Life at Northmire was not what I aspired to. Everyone else was having fun in the city — it was the sixties — and I wanted a piece of it too.

I resume my counting . . . fifty-five, fifty-six, fifty-seven . . . and the technician's voice suddenly comes to me through the headphones inside the machine. "Just relax, Mrs Marshall. There'll be more noise but we'll soon be finished. Keep very still, now."

Miss Marshall, I mouth silently.

It was freedom and adulthood and fun mixed with regret and anger and jealousy that I wasn't one of the students strutting around the city with a pile of books clutched to my chest. Some days I would do just that to make everyone think I was one of the lucky ones, that I was studying medicine or science at Cambridge. I visited the trendiest cafés, bent over my books while chewing on a sandwich, blending with all the other students who had gone there to study and socialise. I frequently trekked to the city library to harvest the most challenging reads I could find — both fiction and non-fiction. I discovered a love of psychology and read everything I could get my hands on. I meshed with the other students flawlessly and considered, once or twice, slipping into a lecture, just to see if I was noticed.

At eighteen, I was congruent and didn't stand out at all as I loitered around Newnham College, my mouth watering as I followed a group of girls to the dining hall. It wasn't the food I was after. It was their company, the prestige, the knowledge that whetted my appetite. Oh yes, I was hungry. Starving to be educated. But I stopped at the door, let them carry on without me, and as the years rolled by, I became too old to be credible. As my late teens finally flowed into my twenties, as the sixties turned into the seventies, I was no longer a viable student. People didn't think my clutch of books or the fake glasses I wore were symbols of student life; rather they took me to be a schoolteacher or someone's secretary, or really saw me for what I was. What I'd always been since leaving school. A café waitress.

Suddenly there is noise, as loud as roadworks, and it's not so much through my ears that I hear it — even though I am wearing headphones — but through my body that I feel it. The machine is delving deep into my tissues, trying to find out what's wrong with me. They explained, in language they would use for a child, that the magnets take pictures of my body so they can see if I am poorly; to see if there is a problem with my brain. Because I am silent, they assume I am stupid.

What they don't understand is that I have read about a hundred science textbooks and already know that the nuclei of the hydrogen atoms in my body are being pulled into alignment with the scanner's magnetic field. Radio waves then kick my poor nuclei out of kilter, and when those waves are stopped, the nuclei effectively pop back into position, releasing their own signals as they do so. It is these signals that are captured and analysed and translated into images of my brain.

If only they'd ask, I would tell them they are looking in quite the wrong place. I'd tell them, if only I could speak.

By the early seventies, I was renting a tiny bedsit. I lived alone, and even though I sometimes craved the company, sharing accommodation with a group of other girls didn't appeal to me. I was a private, serious person most of the time, intent on achieving academic success any way I could — although that didn't mean I wasn't enjoying the social life in Cambridge. I'd soon built up a circle of friends and there was always a party to go to.

Café Delicio was a favourite with King's and Corpus Christi students. It wasn't my first job. I'd already lost several of those by daydreaming and reading and writing notes on a thousand subjects I planned to study. But Café Delicio was by far the best place I'd worked since leaving home and so I made sure I didn't get sacked. Apart from the regular college students, we took in a large lunchtime trade from businessmen and university staff. It was my delight to serve these people, to eavesdrop on their conversations.

"Can I take your order, sir, and by the way, I think you'll find that it was in the central part of Plato's version of Socrates' *Apology* that the condemned man antagonised the court. Really, he didn't stand a chance." They chose spaghetti and meatballs and I served them extra-large portions.

"Don't you have a home to go to?" Abe, the café owner, asked me a week after I began work.

"Yes, but I prefer it here," I replied while folding tea towels. My shift had ended twenty minutes earlier. I smiled at Abe, convincing him that I wasn't unusual or weird or going to scare off his customers if I hung around. I just liked being with them. They were educated. They were who I wanted to be, and I thought if I stuck around long enough, then some of their lives might rub off on me. I would be a scholar by proxy.

"Make yourself at home, then," Abe told me, and paid me overtime as well as a generous share of the tips.

Within three months, I had qualified as his longest-surviving employee. Mostly he'd hired no-hopers or students who couldn't hack the demands of a busy café, so when I came to Café Delicio, stayed for more than a few weeks, rearranged the interior and — having coaxed Chef to be more adventurous and pasted up new menus — I was suddenly in Abe's good books.

Before long, he gave me the title of café manageress. It meant I got to wear a badge with my name on. It meant that the customers, after glancing at my chest, would call me Mary.

It meant that when he came in and eyed me up, when we flirted over scrambled egg and rashers of bacon, when he demanded a recount of his change and a cloth to wipe his spilled tea, there was a vague hope that he would remember who I was.

Mary Marshall, the girl with the long blond hair at Café Delicio.

I certainly remembered him from one visit to the next. With his fresh face and white teeth that were always on show, one of them crooked so that sometimes his lip snagged on it. It gave him a quirky appeal; almost roguish in a beautiful way. He had skin that gleamed and light brown hair that fell about his face in a long, slightly tousled style.

Occasionally he came alone, but mostly he herded a posse of fellow students to take up half of Café Delicio with their book bags, their huge egos and their mountains of knowledge. I served and adored every one of them.

Especially him.

After his first visit, he squeezed a fifty-pence tip into the knot of tea towel that I wrung between my palms.

"Your tea was good," he said in a voice that rivalled any movie star. There was something about the way his eyes narrowed, drank all of me in in a second. I was dumbstruck.

"Thanks," I finally managed. "Would you like some more?" The pot shook in my hand.

He nodded and I poured. When his group of friends left, he stayed. Sipping from his white china cup, glancing casually around the café, he watched me work. I felt the heat of his eyes on my back, saw him tracking me in the big gilt-framed mirror. He sat there for nearly two hours, all the while drinking tea and pushing more coins into my hand with every refill. I busied about with other customers but never ignored him. I brought him food when I thought he was hungry and wiped his table so he could lay out his books when he wanted to study.

"*Gray's Anatomy?*"

"First-year medical student," he replied, looking up from his work. His half-smile lit up my life. His outstretched hand made me belong; pulled me into another world. His world. "I'm David," he said. "It's a pleasure to meet you and your teapot."

It was 1976, and even before it began, I knew it was going to be a long, hot summer.

"Mrs Marshall, we're all done now. We're going to take you out of the machine. Just relax. You've done very well." The invisible person still speaks to me as if I am a child.

I'm very dizzy after the scan, and the nurse who was looking after me has gone on a break. No one notices as I stumble unaided into the toilets.

When I come out, there is no one around to help me. They have taken what they wanted from me and now I am forgotten; an empty husk with the life sucked out of her by a giant magnet. If only it were that easy.

I am standing in a corridor and there, up ahead, is Julia. A splash of colour in the white tunnel but with a deep, dark shadow by her side. I turn one way and then the other, searching for a way out. There isn't one, but then, after all this time, I'm used to feeling like that.

"Dr Carlyle came to see how you got on. That was kind of him, wasn't it?" Julia takes me by the arm and pulls me where I don't want to go.

Suddenly I am a young woman again, and before I have time to think how that feels, I march off down the corridor like I should have done thirty years ago.

JULIA

Nadine and Ed Hallet's house is neat and tidy and lies on the edge of Cambridge. They like it like this. They like the perfect crescent of their street and the way the birch trees are spaced evenly along the pavement. They like the milk float and the corner shop and the newspaper delivery boy. Nadine once said their neighbourhood reminded her of a perfect heartbeat on a patient's trace; the perfect life. The life that she and Ed had set out to achieve. They've got it all, too, except there's a hole the size of a planet in their lives.

Alex and Flora go some way to filling the gap, and that is why I am determined that my break from Murray will not separate my kids from their adoring uncle and aunt. It would crumple Ed and Nadine if contact wasn't regularly maintained — although perhaps not so much when Flora draws a pencil line around the fresh white paintwork of their semi-detached so that she doesn't lose her way.

"Oh, Flora!" Nadine scolds, when she sees the wobbly line going all the way from the telephone table in the hallway into the dining room, through the kitchen and back to the hallway. A map of intent, a dose of good sense, Flora is a survivor and would never set forth on an adventure without leaving a trail to find her way home.

"What's she done?" I say, emerging from Nadine's living room to find her rubbing a wet cloth on the paintwork.

"Look at this!"

"Oh dear," I say, amazed at how incredibly straight Flora got the line.

"Silly girl," Nadine pouts, hiding a smile, as Flora trails past with a Lego creation.

"Nadine," I say, placing a hand on her shoulder. "Do it this way." And I show her the ballet of hand gestures she will need to use if she is to tell my daughter off.

"I'm sorry. It doesn't matter." Nadine stands up. Is it that she suddenly realises my daughter's deafness is more important, more tragic than the pencil line on her wall?

"The final results came yesterday. I'm just a bit tetchy."

I fold her body against mine. It is conclusive. Nadine and Ed will never be able to have children.

Nadine was my first friend. As Murray's little sister, she took a fair few knocks and grew up chasing footballs, riding bikes and playing tricks on Murray. Five years younger than her brother, we took delight in letting down Murray's bicycle tyres, hiding his house key so he got into trouble and putting jelly in his pyjamas. It was all very happy; all very childish — a collage of delicious memories of hanging out with the big boys.

So what I'm saying is that Nadine grew up tough and spunky. She was raised with a coat of varnish, and honestly, with all the tests and trials she's suffered recently, it was a good job.

"I don't know what to say," I tell her. "I'm so sorry." She turns her nose up at the tea I made her. "Not enough sugar?" I ask.

"Too much," she says, and watches intently as Flora pulls apart her Lego model. Alex harvests all the pieces for himself. A frantic signing battle then ensues, but Alex turns his head so he can't see what she's saying.

"How's Mary?" Nadine asks.

"Not so good. I'm taking her for the MRI scan results tomorrow. A friend from the village is keeping her company at the moment." I sigh. "I can't rely on other people to help with my problems for ever, though." I wonder if life will ever return to normal. "It's a relief that Brenna and Gradin are going to school now. It would be hard to cope otherwise."

I look at my watch. I'd only called in briefly to see Nadine after I'd picked up Alex and Flora from school. The bus would be dropping the teenagers back at Northmire shortly. Besides, I know Nadine's going to mention Murray soon. She'll bring him up in conversation any way she can and squeeze glue on to the pair of us. She does it every time I see her.

"Julia, you look done in." Nadine tilts her head and pulls a sympathetic face. She's right. On the floor, Alex tentatively offers some Lego to Flora. He doesn't want to give it up but knows he has to.

"With what happened to your student and Mary being ill," Nadine continues, "you need a break. And looking after two teenage tearaways is hardly what the doctor ordered, either."

"It's not that easy, is it? Nadine, you know if you want to talk about the test results, I'm a good listener."

"Don't change the subject," she chides.

"*Me* change the subject?" I stay calm. "You're the one —"

"How's my big bro?" Even though she says it with a grin forming, I know her question digs deep. I am giving up on her brother — probably going to have to fight him in court over the kids, the house, money — and Nadine wants answers. We love each other as much as any two friends could. We have known each other for ever, but she can't help feeling the loss.

"Did I tell you about David?" Instantly I regret mentioning him. But she's my friend. She knows I've been through so much with Murray — she sees people like him every day, with addictions making up the bulk of her work — so surely she understands a little of what I've been through? I look at the kids again. Beacons of light. They keep me strong.

"David," she ponders. "I don't think so."

I have mentioned his name in passing twice already. I know she is humouring me even though her tone is weary. She curls her socked feet on to the pale sofa and, after only a moment's thought, plucks a chocolate from a box sitting on the table beside her. She hands the box to me and I take a strawberry cream. "He's a doctor and we've been out for dinner. I'm going over to his house on Thursday. He's going to cook." I am talking with my mouth full, trying not to make any of it sound too serious. I couldn't stand it if Nadine and I fell out over this.

"Have you slept with him?" Nadine sucks her chocolate slowly, eyeing me through fronds of loose hair. Whatever I say will get straight back to Murray.

"Nadine!" I feign shock and get a flash of pain as the pink strawberry filling settles on a tooth. "He's very nice," I say. "But no, we haven't slept together. I think one pub dinner is a little premature to be suggesting such things. He's Mum's GP, actually."

"Ah." Nadine curls her head in an arc of understanding. I don't know if this revelation makes things better or worse.

"He's older than me." I want her to know that I've thought about this.

"How much older?"

"A little bit, but he looks good for it."

"*Julia*," she warns.

I've said enough. I know Nadine will tell Murray everything when he finds out I've been visiting.

"Look, we just really hit it off." I trust Nadine to drip-feed what she sees fit. "I called the out-of-hours surgery number on Christmas Day when I found Mum poorly. David was there nearly every day afterwards checking up on her over the holiday period. It grew from there. He's been good to me, Nadine. A really decent person." I wish I'd not said that. It implies that Murray never was.

"That's the medical profession for you," she jokes rather too sourly. "We're all such darn fine folk." She stretches, and her pale arms poke from her baggy sweater. It's her day off and she looks like she needs it.

I can't leave allowing her to think this is a fad, that I'm fickle and have intentionally broken her brother's heart.

"Do you think it's possible to feel such a deep emotional connection with someone that you wonder if you've known them all your life?"

"Bloody hell, Jules. Talk about rebound." Nadine takes another chocolate. "Christ, he's that amazing and you haven't slept with him?" She's smiling now but not without a glint of loyalty. What can I expect? They are brother and sister.

There is a sudden chill as the front door opens and closes. Ed is home. Nadine already told me that he has been working twenty-four hours straight out of the last thirty. She greets her husband as he comes into the room, reaching her arms around his neck. I see a flash of Murray in her profile — the long neck, the square jaw, the slightly crooked angle of her nose as she kisses her husband. I busy myself with packing away the Lego.

We have to go, I tell Flora.

Even though I have known Ed for years and years, seeing him makes me think of Grace. I'm considering visiting her family, sending flowers, anything to help ease the shock of finding her. I almost feel party to the crime in some way. So far I've convinced myself they wouldn't want to see me, that I represent every parent's fear.

107

"Hello, Ed," I say quietly when Nadine slides off him. Envy sears my heart. I recall Murray and me greeting each other in a similar way. Another day over; stories to tell; a familiar set of arms to fold into. "You look done in." It's true. Exhaustion is pasted all over him and the lower half of his face is overcast with stubble.

"I am," he admits, grimacing as Nadine digs her fingers into his shoulder muscles. He has sauce on his shirt.

"Come on, Alex. Help Flora pack up the toys."

My son scuffs the coloured blocks across the carpet towards the bucket. He'd rather listen to what Ed has to say about his work, although I fear it won't be suitable for an eleven-year-old.

"Are you going to catch whoever hurt that girl?" Alex can't resist asking what I daren't. Leading the Grace Covatta investigation makes Uncle Ed, in Alex's eyes, the coolest man in history. "Did you arrest anyone yet?"

Ed drops on to the sofa. Nadine pours him a Scotch and I glare at her. Then I glare at the drink, and finally I glare at Ed.

"We're working on it, mate." He swirls the whisky around in the glass "Forensics are gathering evidence and piecing it all together. The weather conditions at the time didn't help."

"You mean the snow and wind we had?" Alex snaps Lego apart and tosses it into the bucket, never once taking his wide eyes off his uncle. "Shall I go out into the field and see what I can find?"

Ed leans forward and grabs his nephew by the arm, hauling him on to the sofa beside him. A kind of rugby tackle crossed with a tickle fight ensues, and at the end of it, Ed looks a whole lot better.

"Tell you what, mate," he says, glowing from either whisky or laughing. "I'll make a date and get you down to the station one day after school. You can hang out with some of the team. What do you say?"

"Yes, please. That would be cool."

"Alex, why don't you go and track down Flora's coat and those books she left lying around," I say. He does as he's asked without grumbling. "He's a good lad," I say to Ed. "I don't want my family mixed up in all this."

"Look, I'll be honest with you, Julia. You're involved in this whether you like it or not. You found her. You're her teacher." Ed stands. Again I feel guilty, as if without me none of this would have happened. "It's wreaked havoc in the whole community. The pressure for us to make an arrest is enormous." He paces the living room, as if the answer is written on the wallpaper. "The public are calling the station, desperate for news, worried their own kids are at risk." He stops and stares out of the window. "*I* am concerned they are at risk."

When he turns, Ed is a silhouette. Even without taking into consideration the broadcasting vans settled outside the police headquarters, the newspaper headlines or the local television news bulletins, I can see the strain written all over his face. At the very least, he needs to offer the public reassurance that strong leads are being followed. The plain fact is, he can't.

109

"Has Grace said anything yet? Can she give a description?"

He sighs. "She's still suffering major trauma from the incident. She received several very severe blows to the head." He glances at the door. There's no sign of Alex.

"Was she . . ." I can't bring myself to say it.

"I'm still waiting for results. Early indications from the doctors are that there was no sexual trauma. We'll know more when she's able to speak. Plus, the doctors are very concerned about her head injuries. They won't let us at her."

I hardly dare ask. "Who do you think did this?" I'm shaking. I think back to my hospital visit, upset that I couldn't do more for her.

Ed looks away, telling me he's revealed too much already. "Let me do my job, Julia. When there's any news, you'll hear about it."

"I hope you make a breakthrough soon," I say. "For her parents' sake, as much as hers."

Flora climbs on to my lap at just the right moment. Nadine sees my hands shaking as I cradle my daughter.

"Julia, are you OK?" She squats beside me. For now, our differences about Murray fade away.

I nod. "No," I laugh. I bury my face in Flora's hair and Alex comes back carrying the things I sent him for.

"Julia, if you need help coping with this, I can arrange something." Nadine speaks earnestly, softly. She means someone to talk to, counselling. "With everything else going on in your life, you're going to need all the support you can get."

Unintentionally she makes me feel like a failure, incomplete, as if everything I'm involved with falls apart.

"I'm not bothered about support for me," I say, wondering how Grace's family will ever function again. "I just want Ed to find out who did this."

"Is this about Grace, Mum?" Alex is all ears. I hold up a hand to silence him.

"I just hope he doesn't strike again." Ed stops when I glare at him. "Look, I haven't slept in twenty-four hours and I'm back at the station this evening. When there's news, I'll let you know." He removes his jacket. He is plainclothes in the CID. His stomach pushes against the buttons of his shirt. "You get home and look after Mary. She needs you. And lock the doors." Ed kisses my cheek and goes upstairs. He wasn't joking about security.

"Nadine," I say, hefting Flora on to my hip. She is too big to carry but I do anyway. "Look after yourself, won't you." We link eyes, each understanding the preciousness of life.

"Go and date the lovely Dr David until you're full and satisfied. Stuff your face with him," Nadine orders, although I know it hurts her to say this. Perhaps she's hoping that I'll rebound so fast off David, I'll end up right back in her brother's arms. Maybe I'm hoping that too.

"I will," I promise as we leave, and as I watch her wave us off, I see her mouth, "Be careful."

MURRAY

Alcatraz is sinking. The bilge pump isn't working and the rot in the hull is worse than I thought. It only takes a hole the size of a nail for the water to enter my home. Half an hour each morning is needed to return it to the river, but today the pump spluttered and died.

It all sets me up for wanting a drink, but I ball my fists and pull on my overcoat. Instead of drinking, I tramp down to the boatyard to find out about getting *Alcatraz* fixed. Shame, I think, that the same can't be done with my life.

"Leave the keys with me," the yard owner says, agreeing to take a look at the damage before dusk. "I'll get the pump going at the very least." He shakes his head, already familiar with my boat. "Not so sure about the rest of it, though."

Satisfied that I won't be spending the night underwater, I decide to drop in on Julia. It's a spur-of-the-moment decision, partly to see the children, but I also want to find out how Mary is doing. Mostly, if I'm honest, it's because I want to see Julia, to see how she is coping with everything, to stock up on another dose of my wife — even if it means spying on her through the window while I lurk outside in the dark. Besides, I want her to know that I still have a job; that I can still just call myself a lawyer. It's not only smart doctors driving Range Rovers who are deserving of her respect.

I tramp across the fields in the frosty half-light, near to where Grace Covatta was found, and when I reach Northmire, to my disappointment I find that Julia's car is gone.

Milo stands in the courtyard, lazily snapping at a chicken as it parades around his legs. He half-heartedly wags his tail as I stand outside the back door.

I go inside, using the spare key that I know is pushed under a pot of herbs. The kitchen is as I would expect. A stack of dishes sitting beside the deep sink, the remains of a fire, and the cats jigsawed together on the armchair so that it's impossible to tell them apart.

"Julia," I call, even though I know she's not here. There is a certain ritual, a comfort even, in saying her name. Honey, I'm home.

In my head, she replies. She calls back to me with years of memories — mental snapshots of picnics, birthdays, sleepless nights with babies, first days at school, grazed knees, dirty laundry, fireside nights with a bottle of wine . . . It's all there, on hold, in boxes, waiting to be unpacked.

"Mary," I shout. It would be good to hear a mistaken reply, to be the one who got her talking again. Julia would thank me for that. But it seems, after looking around the house, that Mary is gone too.

It's then that I know I'm being watched. Two pairs of eyes glint from behind the doorway that leads to the accommodation Mary reserves for her foster children.

"Hello," I say with a smile. "What are you up to?" Some of the kids Mary harbours are timid and unwilling to speak. Not these two. When they realise they've been spotted, they march right into the room, one dragging the other by the sleeve.

"What are you doing in our house?" The girl strides forward. Mary has obviously been doing a fine job if the girl already considers Northmire *our house*. She looks about seventeen, but beneath all the make-up and bravado I can see that she is a lot younger. There's a twinkle in her eye, and her curled mouth, her skinny neck and her defiant expression suggest she's up for trouble when it's around. I can tell she's had a tough life.

"Looking for my wife, actually." The word rests on my tongue as if I only have a certain number of times left to say it. Technically, Julia and I are still married.

"If you mean Julia, then they've gone off in the car," she continues, daring to come right up to me. She drags the boy by the arm. He is older and much bigger than the girl but I can see straightaway that his thoughts are way behind hers.

"Who is he, Baby?" he finally asks. His words are as deliberate as the slow blinks forming in his eyes. His cheek twitches involuntarily. He smells sour and his clothes are stained.

"Who are you, then?" the girl demands. "You can't just come barging in."

114

"Like I said, I'm looking for my wife, Julia. She's the one taking care of you while Mary is sick —"

"Yes, we know who Julia is." The girl rolls her eyes. "I could call the police, you know." Her posture is defensive and she uses the boy as part shield and part weapon, holding him out at arm's length while verbally challenging me. This, I suspect, is how they've behaved all their lives.

"My name is Murray," I tell them. I push the cats off the chair and sit in their warm patch. "What are your names, then?" I know already, of course, from Julia, although we haven't met formally.

Waiting for them to respond, I pick up yesterday's local newspaper from the floor and briefly consider that the foster kids could be the cause of Mary's mutism. They would be a hard pair to manage, I can see that much, but with Mary's experience, it's unlikely that she couldn't cope. Over the years she's had a lot worse than this. And that's exactly what worries me about her current state. She is as strong as iron. Why has she crumpled?

"I'm Gradin and this is Baby," the boy says.

"My name's Brenna," the girl says and then slaps Gradin's head. "Don't call me that, right?"

I smile and casually turn the pages of the newspaper, glancing at the columns, pretending to take no notice of the bickering pair. Then one story grabs my attention and I am only vaguely aware of the kids squabbling over food in the refrigerator.

Vicious Attack Leaves Teen in Coma.

115

I scan the short article. A small picture of Grace Covatta in her school uniform sits squarely beneath the words.

Injured local schoolgirl Grace Covatta remains in a critical condition after the brutal attack twelve days ago, which left her hospital-bound and unable to talk or walk. Neurologists treating the teen have medically induced a coma — a controversial treatment according to some experts — in order for her brain to recover from its injuries.

"Pressure and swelling in the skull can sometimes cause further damage if the brain isn't rested and allowed time to heal. It was essential that we take action. The patient's life was potentially at risk," said a hospital spokesman. He refused to comment further on her injuries.

Detective Inspector Ed Hallet made a short statement. "I have a team of experts working round the clock. I feel confident an arrest will soon be made."

Grace Covatta is a pupil at Denby High School studying English, history and music A levels. Mrs Julia Marshall, a teacher at the school, discovered the victim early on 29 December.

I stare at the ceiling and imagine what Grace's parents must be going through. I can't. There would have been forms to sign — forms allowing the doctors to put their daughter into a sleep from which she may never wake. I think of the hundreds of nights I have watched Alex and Flora sleeping peacefully in their beds. These days, I am not there for them.

As darkness spreads across the countryside, I am suddenly filled with a worry for my family. An attacker is still stalking the area.

"When is Julia back?" I demand of Brenna. "Where have they all gone?" I am out of the chair and standing close to her. She recoils even though I haven't been drinking yet.

"I dunno. To the hospital or to see a doctor or something. That man was with them." Brenna has a mouthful of cheese and isn't particularly fazed by my outburst.

"What man?" I back off, not wanting to scare her. But I already know who she means. I know that David is with Julia and my children, and for some reason, while it should at least make me feel better about them being safe, it doesn't. They should be with me.

When things changed between us, Julia was seventeen. I went to meet her at the station, watching as her train grumbled to a halt. It was pouring down; a musty and humid rain, lightly fragranced by the wet earth. She jumped on to the platform with her coat slung over her arm. Her face was fresh and eager, seeking me out. Beads of water collected on her neck and wound beneath her collar. She carried an overnight bag and she couldn't help the grin when she saw me waiting.

"Hi," she said sweetly, coyly. She ran up to me and dumped the bag at my feet. She was squinting through the rain, allowing me to kiss her on the check as she wriggled into her coat. It was a pretty peach colour, like her skin, and never before had I wanted to wrap someone up so much with my love; to promise to take care of them for ever.

"Let's go," I said nervously, slinging Julia's bag over my shoulder. These feelings were new for each of us, even though our silent passion had been there ever since we could remember in one way or another. It was only a chance telephone call that had us admitting it, our words tumbling down the line, bumping into each other. It was the end of the way I had always known Julia but the beginning of the way I wanted her.

In fact, that phone call was more about what *wasn't* said; the hidden meaning in our conversation that taught us it was acceptable to feel like this; that loving, truly loving, the person you've grown up with, been a big brother to for seventeen years, was OK. Julia suddenly slid into a fresh compartment in my mind — girlfriend, lover, future wife. After all, it wasn't like we were blood relations. It was allowed.

By the end of the call, we knew we had to see each other. Desperate didn't describe how we felt. So there we were, walking along the platform at King's Cross station, wondering what would happen next — a silent continuation of our telephone admission, only this time it wasn't just our words that were tangling.

Already, my arm was slung around Julia's waist, as indeed it had been in the past. But this time was different; this time we both knew it meant going back to the tiny flat I shared with three friends, setting Julia's bag in my room, turning down the sheets of my bed, shyly undressing each other, making love without a word, without a sound, without anything except a release of everything that had built up between us over the years, while praying that my flatmates wouldn't hear. Our feelings, however explosive, would have to remain silent.

Afterwards, we went to see a movie and ate ice cream. We held hands, only it was different now. Gone were the days of walking her back from the school bus or leading her back to Northmire with a cut knee. When we held hands now, our fingers interlocked to match the synchronised beat of our hearts. It was real. It was serious. We were both grown up, or at least thought we were.

Julia returned to Witherly that Sunday night. A small kiss on her lips — held perfectly still until the stationmaster blew the whistle — sealed our love until next time. I waved her off, back to her mother and her grandparents, who were expecting to hear all about Julia's exciting trip to the city.

She didn't tell them that there were no sights; that the only thing she saw was the inside of my bedroom or the sweat dripping down my back or a movie theatre packed with couples soaking up a French love story. Julia went back to her studies, but from that moment on we knew we would always be together.

When she got pregnant the next summer, we married before Alex was much more than a gentle arc on her smooth belly. When he was born, we weren't much more than children ourselves.

★ ★ ★

I set about preparing Brenna and Gradin a meal — or rather, insist that they make the food under my strict supervision. It keeps them out of trouble and helps pass the time until Julia returns from the hospital or wherever it is she's gone with the kids and Dr Nice. It's that or hit the bottle.

When headlights flash a wide beam through the window and my heart unclenches a fraction, Gradin sinks his hands into a bowl of pastry. I made him scrub his fingernails, which were stuffed with a strange mix of rust-coloured paste, and now he is kneading the flour and fat in readiness to drape over the steak and kidney combination that Brenna is frying up on the range.

"Something smells good." But it is not Julia's voice that accompanies the measure of cold air when the door is opened. David Carlyle is breathing in our cooking as if he has returned home for his evening meal. Across the kitchen, we lock stares, and only when Julia pushes through the taut link do I look away.

She is exhausted, pale, fragile. Beautiful.

"Nice work," I say to Gradin as he hammers the pastry with the wooden pin. I'm waiting for Julia's voice to channel through the tension; questioning what on earth I am doing. "But try it like this." I show him how to press and roll, back and forth, but when I leave him to try again, he takes to bashing through the lump of pastry as if it's a rat running across the table. When I tell him to stop, he doesn't. He just carries on pounding and pounding until the table wobbles and Julia intervenes with a firm demand for him to stop.

"Murray, what's going on?" She looks at me as if I am answerable for Gradin's outburst. The boy is obviously troubled. Mary shuffles past him and takes her seat beside the range. Julia shakes her head wearily. Then, "Why are you here?" Her tone is accusing, impatient, frazzled.

"I came to see . . ." I pause, trying not to sound hurt. "I came to visit the kids. Perhaps take them out for a walk."

Julia glances out of the window. She shakes her head and her eyebrows peel into thin, incredulous curves. "It's dark, Murray. And Flora has the sniffles."

I glance at my little girl to see that she has already curled up on her grandmother's lap; each of them silent and content in their own way. I hate explaining my presence in front of Dr Nice. "When I got here, these two were alone and bored and in need of company. We've been cooking."

I go up to Julia and lower my voice, not wanting Carlyle to hear our discussion. Julia glances around the messy kitchen, probably searching for a secret glass of wine. "But I'll go now that you're back." I sign a private few words to Flora and indulge Alex by having a quick go on his Nintendo. I drop him back six levels.

"Oh thanks, Dad," he moans and snatches it from me.

"How's Mary?" I ask, shrugging on my coat. "Any news?" Looking at her, Mary seems to have less of a grasp on life than ever.

David steps in when Julia folds into a wooden chair. She drops her head into her hands.

"Julia has had some disturbing news about her mother," he announces. He stands behind my wife and places his hands on her shoulders as if it's her that's ill. "Mary's MRI scan showed that she has vascular dementia." He keeps it short, technically inaccessible to the non-medical so that I have to ask what he means. "The principal findings were lacunar infarcts. This means that Mary has had a series of strokes deep inside her brain. There were also abnormal findings in the cerebral white matter, where axons — the wires, if you like, that connect one nerve to the next — travel." He bends to kiss Julia's head. "This would explain Mary's mutism and sudden inability to cope."

"Dementia?" I say slowly. He's packaged this very neatly. A tidy diagnosis explaining everything away. "Surely not, Julia? She's too young for dementia." I look at my mother-in-law. "She wasn't showing any other symptoms before the loss of speech, was she, Jules?" I sit down opposite Julia, my coat half on. Between us, we know Mary best in the world. God, she practically brought me up. "Can it just come from nowhere?" I'm not sure who I am asking.

"If I'm honest, there have been signs." Julia's head is heavy, her eyes ringed. "I guess I just didn't want to admit it."

I understand what she means. Mary has always been there, the immovable wedge that held the Marshall family together. Julia is realising she must step up to the mark. I am not sure that she can face it.

"What does all this mean?" I grudgingly ask David.

He sighs heavily. "I want to admit Mary to hospital."

Julia suddenly looks up. This is news to her, too. "Hospital?" She is on her feet, standing beside Mary like an impenetrable barrier.

"It's a necessary precaution to allow further testing. Mary can't continue to live in this state. She must be professionally assessed in a suitable institution. She needs a treatment plan." David hesitates for less than a second. Julia misses the swallow that sinks down Dr Nice's throat. "It's impractical and exhausting for her to travel back and forth to the hospital in Cambridge for all the tests she will need over the following weeks." He pauses again. "Besides, someone like Mary needs . . ." Each word is measured and spaced, painfully laden with a hasty diagnosis. What does he mean, *someone like Mary?*

I am about to disagree, but Julia speaks, already resigned to her mother's fate. "Well, where else can she go apart from Cambridge?" I know she is considering logistics, the children, her work, trying to make life as normal as possible even though it has never been so askew. She is also hoping that David will ease her burden; whisk her mother away, make her better, and send her home again.

David settles his hands on her shoulders. I fight the urge to push them off. "There's a place that will be ideal for your mother. It specialises in . . ." Another break as Dr Nice thinks of the most appropriate words. He doesn't want to upset Julia, I can see that. "It specialises in this kind of illness. Best of all, it's not far from here and set out in the countryside. She'll be well looked after by the medical team there. It's more like a home away from home than a hospital."

"A home?" Julia is quick to catch on. She slips from beneath David's palms. "An old people's home, you mean?" Her frown has doubled in size and crumples her entire forehead.

"Not at all." David smiles in just the right place. "It's a hospital for patients with conditions similar to Mary's. Sadly, brain diseases can strike at any age and this place is filled with all sorts of patients, from the young to the old. And the therapies . . ." He's thinking again, measuring every word against the tiniest of muscle twitches on Julia's face. "The therapies on offer are second to none. Your mother will receive first-class care."

Julia is torn, I can see, and it dawns on her about the same time as I realise it. "It's a private hospital, isn't it?" The hopelessness in her voice is obvious. Mary doesn't have private medical insurance and there's no way, on a teacher's salary, that Julia can afford it.

"Yes, it is, Julia, and I know what you're going to say —"

Julia interrupts with an unintelligible noise but stops with her mouth open. Her protest hangs there. She realises that Mary will have to take her place in the queue for an NHS bed. We are thinking the same.

"It's already taken care of," David says. And then, as if I'm not there, he imprints a kiss on Julia's stunned lips. Afterwards, she touches a finger to the spot, as if he's just told her a thousand things I'll never be able to say.

★   ★   ★

Back on *Alcatraz*, the bilge is working, after a fashion. The man at the boatyard handed me back my keys and suggested that I have her lifted from the water for a major hull overhaul. He also suggested I get a large bucket in case the pump packs up again.

I light the stove and fill the kettle. It's as I'm fishing about in the engine chamber searching for a spanner that I stumble across the emergency bottle of Scotch, hidden deep in the heart of the boat.

I take several slugs direct from the bottle, sitting on the rear deck and squinting out across the still river. No amount of whisky is going to erase the look that settled in Julia's eyes when Dr Nice took control. That's something I have to take care of myself.

JULIA

Just for this evening, I am going to forget the sick feeling that pervades me from the minute I wake up to the moment I pass into brief sleep. Perhaps selfishly, I have left my problems behind, and for a few hours I will pretend that I am Julia Marshall, desirable woman without a care in the world; Julia Marshall, out to explore new possibilities. Julia Marshall — an exciting prospect.

My hand hangs heavily on the knocker and slides down the wood with the weight of my life.

The door opens and David is standing there.

Never before has anything, anyone, so timely happened to me. Never before have I needed someone as much as I need David now, however briefly we've known each other. It's his confidence, his experience, his wisdom, and I'm pretty sure, his concern for me that tightens the thread of hope inside. I won't let go; not for anyone.

David is clutching a tea towel and wearing an apron. He looks good enough to eat.

I can't help the landslide of laughter. "Oh my God, I promise not to tell *anyone*." Truth is, I like it. I like the ridiculousness of it; the normality of it and everything else it suggests. I also like the freshly chopped herbs that I can smell layered upon searing meat, and the log fire in the lounge as David shows me round his house. To begin with, neither of us mentions Mum.

"Your home is beautiful," I say when we're in the kitchen. It's obviously very old but has been renovated to a high standard. I hadn't envisaged David in such a place. It's a family home — albeit without the family — but that sets me thinking, only for the briefest of guilty moments, about how it would feel to have Flora and Alex tumbling through the many rooms. Their laughter and footsteps would echo through the tiled halls and beamed corridors. Their toys would leave a childhood trail between the large rooms. Thinking all of this makes me feel even more apprehensive, yet excited that something, possibly something good, could be happening in my life. It's a bittersweet turn that I have to make. It already feels as if I've known David for ever.

"I saw you as more of an apartment-in-the-city kind of guy." I lean on the worktop, watching him. David smiles and passes over a glass of mineral water. "Have you heard anything about Mum? Any news?"

"Be patient, Julia. She's only been there a few hours." He smiles again, and the way it makes me feel, he may as well have taken me in his arms and pressed me close. It's a brief moment but one that spans decades. We have a link, something in common on a deep level. I wouldn't fall for just anyone.

"You're right. I'm being silly. I'm just worried about her, that's all." I tuck a loose strand of hair behind my ear. David notices. It makes my stomach tingle.

"I understand," he tells me, and I can see quite clearly that he does.

"I can't be too late home," I say out of the blue, which suggests that I was thinking I might be. The children are at Nadine's for the night, and with Mum admitted safely to The Lawns, the evening ahead looms like a heavy moon. I glance at the floor and immediately feel fourteen years old. "It's because of Brenna and Gradin," I add quickly. "I can't leave them overnight." It was just me thinking out loud, but now I have pretty much declared that I was contemplating staying the night. "I did already tell you this, didn't I?" My voice is fragile, shattered in fact.

David laughs and I like that. The broad smile on his face tells me that he thinks I am both funny and attractive as I dig my hole. "They'll have to be re-homed soon," I continue, hoping he doesn't see my mind skipping way ahead to the future. Our future.

I heave myself out of the hole. "The Lawns seemed perfect for Mum. Whatever strings you pulled to get her in there, I can't thank you enough." I harvest an olive from the bowl sitting on the work surface. "I thought I even saw an improvement in her before we left. She seemed at ease, as if it's where she should have been years ago. As if she was grateful. And I swear I saw her sign at Flora."

"Julia . . . don't get carried away." David's medical training warns him off promising a full recovery. "Your mother is a long way from being cured." With this sobering thought, he turns his back on me. He's becoming personally involved, allowing the weight of whatever is wrong with Mum to sit squarely between us. He briefly turns back to me, and when he faces me again, there is a glaze in his eyes.

"It's highly unlikely that she signed with Flora. For now, anyway." Suddenly he is being professional, speaking as if I am just any patient's daughter. "The scan . . . it showed recent infarctions. Recovery, if ever, may be long and slow." He's not telling me everything. "I personally know the head of the team that will be caring for Mary, and he's promised me the best care for her. I've discussed the case in great detail."

"I'm very grateful," I whisper. "You seem to know a lot of people."

"Well, that's not unusual in the medical profession. You have friends in teaching, I presume?" For a second, I detect a defence; that perhaps in the past he has been accused of pulling strings, bending favours and twisting arms to get what he wants. In this instance, I have no objection. He's going to great lengths for Mum, for me. It would be rude to question his motive.

"Let's eat," he says and leads me to the table.

It's not until we are relaxing on the biggest sofa I have ever seen — David enjoying the last of a bottle of Bordeaux and me content with a coffee — that I have to pretend it's Murray sitting beside me. Until a couple of weeks ago, the very thought of anyone wrapping their arm behind my back or edging closer so that the inevitable brush of lips happened as naturally as breathing, would have scared the life out of me. But here it is, imminent, natural, beautiful, although for now I am sitting stiffly at one end of the sofa, while David watches me intently from the other. Does he see the panic in my eyes, or the hidden excitement?

"That was a wonderful meal. Thank you." My vision of him cuts in and out of focus. I am so new to this, it terrifies me. One minute it's David's face staring back at me — talking about things I don't hear — and the next it transforms into Murray.

There he is, reclined on the sofa as easily as if we were in our own living room. Just Murray. And that's how it's been as far back as I can remember. Only Murray. Together, properly, for the last twelve years, and friends for ever, there's never been room for anyone else; never any need. Part of me, only a tiny part now, begs him not to leave, while the rest of me yells at him to get out of my life, to make way for someone I can count on, someone who doesn't let me down time after time.

"Julia?" David notices the tears collecting in my eyes and leans forward.

"I'm OK." I laugh through it. A sniff and a smile.

It's clear that letting David into my life is going to be harder than I anticipated. What happens when I feel the unfamiliar touch of another hand on my shoulder, my back, my arm, my breast? Will my heart pound with excitement, or will I crumple and fold and never be able to do anything else — be *with* anyone else — ever again? When I consider what the children would think,

130

that's when Murray appears again, frowning, begging, pleading with me to give him another shot.

With every last ounce of resolve and energy, I promise myself that falling for David is the right thing to do; that he is the perfect person to replace something that is so long gone, so painfully missing, that for years I never even questioned why it was absent.

"Did I do something to upset you?" David leans closer still and kisses my forehead fondly. I feel the slight tremor in his hand as he twists me round to face him. Is he nervous too? I wonder. He breathes in my scent, as if he's downloading my entire life in one gulp.

Oh, Murray, I beg in my head, *what happened to us?*

But before Murray can answer, I close my eyes, hoping any second now that David's mouth will be on mine, lingering over my skin, keen to rip open the join of my lips. I'm guessing that his hands are aching to spread over my body like spilled treacle, but when nothing happens and I open my eyes, I see that he has sat back again. Even from a distance, I see the flicker of his pupils, his lashes, his desire. But he didn't lay a finger on me.

"You didn't upset me," I tell him, coughing my way out of embarrassment.

"That's good. There's so much I want to know about you."

I shift closer to him on the sofa and breathe in deeply, hoping the heave of my chest will urge him to push his fingers into my hair, my skin, and cup my face, rather than delve into my soul. David delivers a further brief kiss; a tiny torment placed carefully on the top of my head. "And plenty of time," he adds.

"Wow," I say, when he stands up and walks to the drinks cabinet. Did he feel it too? David doesn't say a word. He pours himself a glass of brandy from a decanter and stares at me as if I pose the biggest question in the universe.

Mary, I think he says, each syllable as wide as the horizon. I swear he mouths my mother's name.

But before I get a chance to ask him what he means, someone is hammering on his front door. As David strides to open it, a large male figure looms at the front window.

That's when my heart stops beating.

"Ed?" I call out, tearing into the hallway. Something's happened to Alex and Flora. "The kids," I cry breathlessly. "Has Nadine sent you? Are they OK?"

Ed ignores me. He pushes past with another man while two uniformed officers flank the porch. "Ed, what's going on?" All the blood drains from my head. Not the kids. Dear God, please not my children.

"Dr David Carlyle?" Ed asks flatly, flashing his CID badge.

"Yes," David says calmly. "Would you mind telling me what —" He stands tall, dwarfing Ed and his men. He doesn't get the chance to finish his question.

"I am arresting you on suspicion of the assault of Grace Covatta on the night of Thursday the twenty-eighth of December two thousand and six. You do not have to say anything, but it may harm your defence if you fail to mention when questioned something which you later rely on in court. Anything you do say will be given in evidence." Ed flashes the arrest warrant and then signals to the constables, who immediately surround David. "Do you understand, Dr Carlyle?"

David's eyes go wide and black, and for a second he looks at me. In that instant, I see a thousand truths, although nothing I understand. Everything is underlined by dark fear.

"David?" I say weakly. "Ed?" I'm dizzy and lost. Nothing is real. David is being arrested for the attack on Grace Covatta. It's impossible. I put out my hand to David, to offer some comfort, but he is handcuffed before I reach him. I can see that he wants to say something, but he doesn't get the chance.

"David, what do you want me to do?" I'm there for him, by his side, shaking yet still managing to pluck his coat off the stand and wrap it round his shoulders.

He is escorted out into the night. "I'll sort this out," I call after him, but he doesn't turn to acknowledge my help, doesn't say a word. He just allows himself to be led out to the lane where a constable shields his head as he lowers himself into the unmarked car. "I'll get you a solicitor," I cry weakly. The scent of him still lingers in the hall.

Assault? I stand alone in the hallway with the door gaping open to the blackness of the country lane. My heart thumps so heavily, I can feel each beat in my throat. I watch as the police vehicle becomes nothing more than two dots of red light through the trees. The sudden chill makes me shut the door. I lean back on it, sealing me alone in David's house.

"He would never hurt anyone," I whisper, shocked and shivering. "Let alone Grace." My words are fireflies, ricocheting off the thick stone walls; setting light to everything. I remember when I found her — her broken body an unreadable map of what had happened in the hours before. It is impossible to hold David and Grace in the same thought.

I stand alone for a few minutes, barely able to keep upright from shock. Numbed, and not knowing where else to turn, I lock up David's house and head to the only person I know can help.

I tear down the towpath, each dangerous footfall a step nearer to assistance. My need goes against every grain of reason and sense.

The light from the boat windows casts ripples of silver across the murk of the water and guides me to Murray's domain. There is laughter coming from deep inside *Alcatraz* and I hesitate before knocking on the hatch. It hasn't occurred to me that Murray might be entertaining. I go ahead and knock. Either way, I need his help. Either way, I don't have time to hesitate.

The painted hatch opens in bursts of effort and expletives. Murray's head pokes up and he squints into the night, not instantly realising it's me standing on the towpath.

"Julia?" he says, puzzled at my presence. "Where are the children?"

134

"They're fine. They're with Nadine." I'm breathless, panting, and while I would like to fall down and sob out everything in Murray's familiar arms, I know I can't. "Could I have a word? It's serious."

A pause. A frown. "Of course, of course. Come aboard."

I've never been inside *Alcatraz*. It smells of alcohol and Indian food and looks like it's not been touched since the seventies. Sprawled on a beanbag is a bearded man I don't recognise. I barely notice the relief that it's not a woman enjoying Murray's company. The man looks at me through drunken eyes.

"It's David," I say, finally catching my breath and not caring if this other man hears everything. By the looks of him, he won't remember anything tomorrow anyway. "He's been . . ." To actually say it gives it reality, and that I can't stand. "Oh Murray, he's been arrested." My mouth is dry, barely able to form words. "Arrested by Ed, of all people."

Murray doesn't initially understand the gravity of what I've just said. He sways a little, or it could just be my arrival on the boat throwing him off balance, and squints at me as if I'm not really there. His world drags with the Scotch flowing in his blood. He finally seems to understand. "Really? That's bad. What for?" A heavy frown crosses his face, but I still notice the tiny smile beneath.

"It's ridiculous," I say. It tumbles out, sounding as crazy as any word ever *did*. "Assault."

Everything is silent. *Alcatraz* continues to rock, making me feel even more nauseous. The man in the

135

beanbag struggles to stand, declaring his departure. At least he has the decency to sense the seriousness of my visit. He leaves the boat with a stumble and a brief goodbye to Murray.

"Assault?" Murray is busying himself, straightening up the place. He rearranges the cushions on the ancient sofa, pats a spot for me to sit, lights the gas stove and boils the kettle, glances briefly into the shard of mirror that hangs crooked from the bulkhead. He squints and ruffles his hair. "David's been arrested for *assault*?"

"Oh for God's sake, Murray, yes!" I slump into the sofa. "I was at his house and Ed came with three other officers and arrested him. Ed didn't say a word to me. It was like he didn't even know me." I cover my face. "David's a doctor. He wouldn't hurt anyone, let alone a young girl."

I get up again and pace the length of the boat, wondering how anyone can live in such a confined space. It makes me think of David holed up in a police cell. "I have to call him." I jab the buttons on my phone, but the call is directed to his voicemail.

"Who?" Murray asks. He's not stupid, and the full seriousness finally breaks through the drink. I nod in confirmation when he mouths *Grace?* "Ed's a damned good detective, Julia. I think on this one you have to —"

"But David didn't do it! One minute we were . . ." How can I tell Murray that we were about to share a kiss? "One minute we were eating dinner, and then David was being arrested and hauled away. I don't know what to do."

136

"Firstly, you need to go back to the children and get them tucked up in their own beds." Murray hands me a cup of tea, and I can tell from his tone that he is disapproving of me leaving the kids yet again.

"They'll already be tucked up. It's Nadine's night off and she was happy to take them overnight. There's no point disturbing them at this hour."

Murray reluctantly agrees and squats on the floor in front of me. "I guess what I'm trying to say, Jules, is that the man you've fallen for has been arrested for a very serious crime. He's a suspect in a very high-profile case. It's shocking, it's ghastly and wretched for you. I can hardly believe it myself. But you have to let Ed and his team do their job. I'll be honest, I've never liked the man —"

"Oh for heaven's sake, Murray. This is hardly the time to air your macho jealousy." I sip the tea but burn my mouth. "Unless David's found guilty, there's no way I'm giving up on him."

"So why did you come to me, then?" Murray asks gently. He always backs off when I'm upset, and he hasn't lost that flicker of kindness.

"Because . . ." I bury my face in my hands. "I . . ." I look up again, my cheeks flushed, my hair spilling from its clip, and my eyes filling with what I don't want to admit are tears. "I don't know," I whisper honestly. I shrug. "I came to you because I always have done, and old habits —"

"Die hard?" We're both thinking about the drink. "I can't help him, Jules, if that's what you're here for."

"I'm not," I add quickly, and it's the truth. I'm still reeling from admitting I *needed* Murray on an emotional level. I haven't yet considered the obvious — that David will require legal help, and fast. "But he will need a solicitor. A damn good one. And a barrister if it all goes to court." My thoughts tumble over each other. So much to arrange. David will be relying on me.

I watch, not daring to breathe, as Murray soaks up my admission. Did he think I was here to beg for help? He stares at me, his hair a mess — it's grown long over the last few weeks — and his clothes not much better.

"Julia . . ." But he doesn't say what I think he's going to say — that if I do ask him for help, he expects something in return. "Julia, I . . . You're right. David needs the best legal representation you can find. It's not me."

"For heaven's sake, I don't want you as his lawyer. But he will be in a police cell right now, and for all I know he'll have the duty solicitor dumped on his case. I must go down there. We must go down there. I need some support, Murray. Please. Just for tonight."

"Julia, David is a grown man with enough resources of his own to procure a decent solicitor. Whether he chooses his own or makes use of the duty solicitor is hardly any business of mine. I really don't think me coming with —"

"*Please*, Murray." The deepness of my voice silences him. I hate myself for this — that I'm not strong enough to go through this alone — and I hate it that he's fighting the effects of the drink. But here I am

138

desperate for his help, desperate for him to be sober. "Please." I close my eyes.

After a moment, I hear his exhalation. "Get me a gallon of black coffee, find me a clean shirt from somewhere and I'll come with you down to the police station. Nothing else."

I open my eyes and mouth a silent thank-you.

"And Julia." Murray pulls his dirty shirt off over his head. "I'm doing this for you, not David."

I know that what he really means is he is doing it for *us*.

MARY

I told him that we had to get a few things straight. I didn't want sex. Not that I wasn't attracted to him — far from it. He was handsome and intelligent and I knew that he was crazy for me too. And the problem wasn't that I was twenty-seven and he was only eighteen — although David had never questioned my age outright. No, the big problem was that people like him held the key to my future. He had contacts at the university and I didn't want to jeopardise them by having a relationship with him. Getting on a course via the back door was fast becoming my only option, so I couldn't afford to let things turn sour between us.

"I get the feeling you want to leave," he said. The landslide of his grin did untold things to me, but I had made a promise to myself: I would not sleep with him. I cherished David's friendship and his world far too much to mess up. I was living the life I'd always wanted, but one step removed. It was vital that we remain firm friends.

The party had only just got going. The music was good, the house was filled with intelligent people —

albeit drunk ones — and the walls were alight with disco ball sparkles. I'd had a hard day at the café.

"You mean *you* want to leave." I grinned back at him and sipped my drink. It was all hidden messages with us, a secret language of the body and mind. Me, I wanted the luxury of his brain, adding him to my collection of super-friends. David, well, he just wanted to get me into bed. He considered me a challenge. An older woman. All of this, the sum of what we had, in my mind, was nearly-sex. A mind mess of innuendoes and games, each of us trying to sidestep the other's next move — David so he could get what he wanted, and me so he couldn't. I admit, it was fun. It kept us going.

"It's quieter upstairs," he mouthed above the music. We swayed against the wall to Abba's "Fernando", Wings, and the Rolling Stones, and not once did I lead him on. Not once did I respond to his further temptations that we should explore the house, find an empty bedroom and make out.

"That's what kids do," I said, winking, with a look that showed my age. I was referring to the idea of seeking out a vacant room for gratuitous sex, and it didn't occur to me until later, until he dropped me home without a word, that I'd upset him.

There's talk of hospital. Their voices wither like autumn leaves, the news of my future fluttering around me. The results of my MRI scan are not good. They say I have a kind of dementia. All the experts agree that I will be better off in hospital. Perhaps they're right, but I worry for Julia. I worry so much that I can't even tell her. It's too late.

I watch her pack a bag for me. She wishes I would show some inclination for a pink nightdress or a blue one, ever hopeful that I will leap up and cry, *Not that old thing, for heaven's sake,* like I once would have done. But she can pack what she likes. It no longer matters.

When she has finished laying out slippers and underwear and several skirts and sweaters that haven't seen the light of day in decades — doesn't she know I always wear trousers? — she sinks bottles of shampoo and perfume into the mound of clothes. Then, in a fit of desperation, she tosses in the mobile phone she bought me last birthday. I have never used it.

"Just in case," she says, zipping up the bag.

As Julia is making my bed, smoothing the sheets and blankets flat as if I might never slide beneath them again, her foot catches on a forgotten pile of clothes stuffed under the bed. "More washing," she says, grimacing, and pulls out the bundle of dirty garments. "God, Mum, what did you do, go rambling in these? They're filthy." She holds up my trousers and an old sweater, bound around my muddy work boots, before untangling them and tossing them into the washing basket.

I don't say a word. She knows I would normally defend myself, argue about mucking out the goat pen or hefting bales of straw in the rain.

Later, before we leave, I retrieve the filthy clothes and boots, wrap them in a plastic bag and stuff them in my hospital suitcase. No one should leave their dirty laundry lying around.

It seems appropriate that David drives us to the hospital. There's something final about it. To him, I'm nothing more than baggage, and after all this time he's finally remembered where he left me. There's something full-circle about it that, back then, I'd never have anticipated. I sit in his great big car, going along for the ride, trying so hard to remember what it felt like to love him.

The Lawns Private Hospital is at the end of a long drive, lined on either side by chestnut trees. I spy a couple of patients winding across the vast lawn like flotsam. A nurse chases after them, and it's then that I realise exactly what is happening. I catch a glimpse of David's eyes — just his eyes — in the rearview mirror. Never before have I wanted to scream out so much. Never before have I been quite so unable.

"Here we are," Julia says, because no one else does. "It looks more like a hotel than a hospital, Mum." There is forced lightness in her voice. "They'll have you better in no time." She is speaking to me as if I am a child again.

Alex and Flora tumble out of the car first and I follow slowly, levered from the back of David's vast vehicle by several pairs of hands. Going along with them, letting myself be swept along for the ride, is easy. The alternative is too painful.

The process for booking me in to the hospital is similar to that of a hotel, except here, in a private office, two nurses rifle through my possessions as if they are bargain-hunters at a jumble sale. They make a list of my meagre belongings. They confiscate the nail scissors and tweezers that Julia packed, and open and sniff my shampoo and other liquid toiletries in my washbag as if we are at an airport.

"Right," says the first nurse. "Let's get you settled into your room."

Instead of a metal bed in a crowded ward, I get a private space with my own bathroom and a large window overlooking the chestnut-treed drive. I can smell lavender. There is a television. A dressing table.

After a few minutes of arranging clothes, chatter and excitement, Julia, David and Alex are led away by the nurse. I am left sitting on my bed. They have forgotten Flora. She climbs on to my lap.

I want to stay here with you, she signs. Her perky little face stares up at me. Her nose is a button pressed into the pale palette of her skin. Her lips pout, as if she's trying to say something. It's then that I realise Flora hasn't grasped that I'm not speaking. One silence is pretty much the same as another in her world.

I wish you could stay too, I sign back. It nearly kills me.

Then, suddenly remembered by Julia, Flora is plucked from my lap and taken away.

David didn't come back into the café the next day. Understandable, really, seeing as he was gearing up for first-year exams. That's what I told myself, anyway. I imagined him in the library with his fellow students, hunched over piles of books, memorising anatomy, microbiology and a multitude of pathogens. But I couldn't help thinking that perhaps he was stewing over my careless comment.

Meantime, I polished the tables until they shone, waiting to catch a glimpse of David behind me in case he surprised me by calling in for tea and cake.

He didn't. In the end, a week after the party, I made a point of seeking him out. I called his college, left countless messages, but they were never returned. I visited his boarding house, lurked outside and asked his friends where he was. They were vague and avoided me. David, it seemed, was more upset with me than I had imagined.

Then, after a lengthy trek around university rooms and poking into places that I really shouldn't have been — it was a thrill to venture deeper into the institution that had stolen my heart — I finally found David in a medical sciences laboratory. I crept inside, out of place yet feeling strangely at home.

For company, David had enlisted the help of a cadaver, and before he realised I was there, I eavesdropped his one-sided conversation with the body. As I neared, I saw that it was in four pieces. Four quarters of a person.

"David," I said cautiously. The longer I spied on him, the more dangerous the game I played. "I found you." I was wearing a floral summer skirt. It swooshed when I walked and my top was a knitted halter. I knew I looked good. As ever, when I ventured inside the university campus, I carried a clutch of books. They were my identity badge.

"How did you get in?" David scowled at me and then returned to his work. Ever so carefully, knowing I was watching, he peeled back the layers of skin, muscle and bone to reveal a shrivelled heart. There was no blood.

"I walked right in through the door," I explained, grinning. "I wanted to see you. I've missed you." I had to look away from the body but couldn't escape the smell of formaldehyde mixed with . . . something else; something vile. "You've not been to the café for ages."

"I've been busy," he replied. He stood back from the cadaver and I noticed the tiny gems of sweat on his forehead. He looked me up and down, his eyes peeling back my living layers as his hands had just done to the corpse. I was close to retching. "It's fascinating, don't you think?" He beckoned me nearer and so I stepped up to the challenge. A farm girl I might be, but if I'd made it into medical school then I'd be elbow deep in death too.

"Amazing," I said, trying not to breathe. The cadaver didn't look very old. It was a woman and her skin clung drily to the chest wall. "What are you studying?"

"The vascular system," David replied. "See, this is the coronary artery." The pale vessel had been snipped in two and peeled away from its host organ. "Clean as a bell," he said and poked a metal instrument inside. "No heart disease here."

"How did she die?" I asked. The striations of muscle binding her features to her skull were delicate. I think she would have been pretty.

146

David shrugged. "Who knows?" He prodded the organs. "Perhaps it was a broken heart." Then he gave me his sexy grin, pulled off his white coat, and clattered the dirty instruments into a metal tray. He beckoned me to follow him out of the lab. We walked in perfect step down the tiled staircase.

"What about . . ." I gestured back to the cadaver.

"She'll get put away," he replied, leaving me wondering how he could cast aside death so easily; just walk away from a body.

We stepped out into the sunlight, each of us squinting, each trying to focus on the other. "Now," David said seriously. He pinned me against the wall, his arms barricading me to the left and right, his thighs pressed against mine. He still smelled of the cadaver. "What would you like to do?"

I suddenly felt happy. Finally I'd got David back. Anything was possible. We could have seen a film, taken a walk on Jesus Green, browsed the bookshops together, hired a punt and trailed our fingers in the river as we glided nowhere in particular. I thought very carefully before I answered, blinded by the sun behind David. His hair was long and unkempt and cast a silhouetted aura around his face as I decided our fate for the afternoon.

"How about you show me your college room?" I suggested. To sneak into the boarding house would be a certain thrill. Even now, so many years after academic rejection, I was keen to infiltrate the premises. There might be a chance contact, a new opportunity . . . I wasn't ready to give up.

"Fine," David said and released me. So that was what we did.

I watch them drive away, rustling the leaves of the chestnut trees as they go. My world is now not only silent, but empty too. Julia and the children are gone. It is ironic, I think, that David should be taking them away. Loving him is such a distant memory. I can almost convince myself it never happened.

Periodically, a nurse comes to check on me. I haven't moved since Julia left. I have had my blood pressure taken, my pulse measured and the dilation of my pupils checked with a bright light. She carries a clipboard and jots down her findings.

"Well then, Mrs Marshall. What would you like for your dinner tonight? You can choose from fish pie and broccoli or vegetable lasagne."

She thrusts a menu at me but I don't look at it. Food has been slivers of cheese and crumbs of bread eased between my lips by my desperate daughter. That they want to stuff me with pie shows how little they know of me, my illness.

"Fish pie, then," the nurse suggests, and when I don't object, she scuttles off.

Sitting perfectly straight on the bed, I wonder what will become of my goats, my chickens, Brenna and Gradin. Me. A single tear leaves my eye when I consider what will become of Julia.

MURRAY

I arrive at the police station exactly ten seconds before
Sheila Hartley struts through the automatic doors. Her
face betrays annoyance at being there. She is wearing
an evening dress and scarlet lipstick.

"Sheila." I greet her as if this is all perfectly normal.
My slow body is unable to cope with action, my mind
unable to make decisions. "What are you doing here?"
She can't be on duty, not Sheila. She always delegates.

She looks me up and down, and even though Julia
helped me into a clean shirt, it's creased and below it
I'm still wearing dirty jeans and ancient trainers. "Oh,
Murray," she sneers, avoiding my question. I try to
detect humour mixed in with her words but I can't.
"Been arrested?" She strides up to the custody officer's
desk, ignoring me, as if I am just another nuisance in
her life. "Why?" she demands, slamming her hands on
to the counter. The desk sergeant recoils. "Was I called
away from the hottest date of my life when I'm not even
on duty? Mel bloody Gibson is waiting for me at his
hotel. His five-star hotel. With champagne. In the
penthouse suite." She draws a sharp breath. "Na-ked."
Sheila takes a packet of Marlboro from her bag and

lights one. She only smiles when the smoke from her first drag, blown deliberately over the sergeant, makes him cough.

"Really?" I ask.

Sheila glares at me for a second, remembering that I'm there, before turning back to the sergeant. "Well?" she screams.

"You're on the list, ma'am, and no one else was answering or available. Someone's been brought in . . ." The sergeant coughs again. "A big case, I believe. He wanted the duty solicitor and . . ." The sergeant shows Sheila a laminated list of the poor suckers who've drawn the short straw at Redman, Hartley and Bright. Thankfully I'm not on it. Not likely to be, either. Only reliable solicitors, ones with lives that haven't fallen apart, are able to step up to the mark.

"What about Schilder's firm? He can get his bloody ass down here." Sheila turns to walk away, satisfied she's taken care of the matter.

"Ma'am, it's your firm's turn. I can't call anyone else."

Sheila stops and pivots on her stilettos very slowly. She stamps out her half-finished cigarette on the grubby tiled floor before immediately lighting another one. She grins, holding the filter between her teeth, and walks towards me.

"No problem." She smiles at the desk sergeant as if they have only ever exchanged poetry for conversation. "No problem at all," she says, looking me up and down again while nodding her head, rolling her lips together. Sheila takes me firmly by the upper arm — her talon-like scarlet nails digging into my flesh — and leads me over to the waiting area. "I like you, Murray. I always have done." She pauses for effect; stares into my eyes, knowing that she is blurred to me. "But we all know that you've been letting the side down recently." She grins again and I nod, because it's the only thing I can think of to do. Half of me can see where this is going and half of me doesn't even want to look. If I was sober, it would be easy. "Thing is, I *really* don't want to let down my date."

"Of course not."

"And the other thing is, you really need to score some serious points if I'm to convince the other partners that you're worth hanging on to. You need your job, don't you, Murray?"

Of course I need my bloody job. "But I thought you said I was —"

"Sshh," Sheila says, placing a finger over my lips. It smells of smoke. "Just take the case, Murray. Get the guy some bail. Get him through his interview. Get him a suit and a tie if he's up in court in the morning, and for God's sake, Murray, get yourself a bloody wash and a shave before dawn breaks." She steps back and says sweetly, "OK?" As far as she is concerned, the problem is solved. She can go back to the penthouse suite.

"Oh no," I say, my eyes widening, my heart thumping. Through the glass doors I see Julia running along the pavement. She has been to park the car. "You really don't understand, Sheila. I *can't* take this case. I'll do anything for you, *anything*, but don't make me do this." I gesture to where the cells are located, but already I know it's hopeless. Sheila's made up her mind.

151

Julia pushes through the doors and comes up to me, panting, freezing, smelling of the night. "What's happened?" she asks. "Is there any news?"

"Plenty," Sheila says, butting in and tapping the side of her nose. She stares directly at the back of Julia's head. "What were you doing here anyway, Murray?" But she doesn't even wait for my answer. "See you . . . back . . . in . . . the . . . office, then," she sings deliberately, coded to say that if I want to keep my job I'm going to have to do exactly as she says.

"What was all that about? Why was Sheila here?" Julia has never particularly liked or understood my boss. She stares after the older woman as she strides down the street, leaving another cigarette butt in her wake. "Murray? Are you OK?" Julia is breathless; beautiful. She is puzzled as she draws up to me. "Have you found out about David yet?"

I snap back to some kind of reality. "No, not yet." Suddenly, I feel very sober.

"Why was Sheila here? She looked really angry."

"Here you go," the grizzled sergeant says, handing me a load of paperwork. "I couldn't help overhearing the good news." He briefly looks at Julia as if he's not seen anything so beautiful in the station for a long time. "I'd smarten yourself up a bit if I were you, mate. You'll be hitting the breakfast news in about five hours."

I assimilate this observation before Julia can reply, which, of course, she will. My drunken world slows everything to poured treacle. The sergeant is right. The assault on Grace Covatta has caused a flurry of interest from journalists both locally and nationwide. Television crews and newspaper reporters have already latched on to Grace's story as one to watch. Public sympathy is running high, especially as there's always the chance this could be the work of a serial attacker.

"What does he mean?" Julia asks. "What does he mean, you'll be on the news?"

"Julia." I plant my hands on her shoulders but she shrugs them off. I worry that my breath still smells of whisky. "Julia, Sheila was here because she was called in as the duty solicitor. Our firm is part of the Criminal Litigation Accreditation Scheme." That was hard to say.

"And?"

"And it means that, because Sheila had a date with Mel Gibson . . ." I stop for a second and then it all comes out wrong. "Julia, I've been assigned as David's duty solicitor. Just for tonight until . . . just because . . . I didn't want to . . . Sheila said . . . She made me and . . ."

Julia has already walked away with her face buried in her hands. "No way," she whispers, peeking between her fingers.

"It's OK," I say, knowing it isn't. "Just a formality. It was a case of wrong place, wrong time. Sheila was on a date and didn't want to take the case, so she forced —"

"It's not right. It's not ethical. You're hardly going to give it your best shot, are you?" Julia rarely gets hysterical, but she is doing a fine job of it now. She paces back and forth across the width of the waiting area. "Murray, you have to call someone else."

I shrug and turn to the desk sergeant for support. I know he's been listening to every word. My face implores him.

"He's right, love. Ms Hanley threatened this chap here with losing his job. I've seen some things in my time, but —"

"Will you be able to help him?" Her words cut through everything; shatter as they drop on the tiles. Julia is cold and the skin on her face has hardened to alabaster.

"I don't know yet. I have to read the file. But Julia . . ." and I go up to her; allow myself within an inch of an embrace. "I will treat him as I would any other client. You have to believe me on that." Our eyes lock for a second, just long enough for her to see a glimmer of honesty in me. "I won't let you down."

"Thank you," she replies, and hugs her coat around her body. The shivers don't stop. "Thank you, Murray."

Her desperate tone, poorly concealed beneath a measured voice, makes me believe she's known the man for twenty years; that he's been a long-standing friend of the family; that he is her brother, an uncle, a long-lost relative, or worse . . . her lover.

"Do you want to help?" I ask, trying to lighten things up. Julia nods solemnly. "Then fetch me a suit," I say. "The grey one in the cupboard at the front of the boat." Her face slumps when she realises she won't get to see David.

I fish in my pocket for the keys, turning away from the custody desk. I pull in close to Julia and speak into her ear, taking the opportunity to let her hair brush against my lips. "Old Groucho here is right. Once the press find out there's been an arrest in relation to the Covatta case, it'll be headline news. Bring me a toothbrush, aftershave. The whole damn bathroom."

And it's at that moment, as Julia nods and sets off to begin her mission, that I realise two things. One, I am more deeply in love with my wife than I have ever been, and two, if David is charged, I have very limited experience of this type of case. Earlier in the week I was dealing with a client who had thirteen unpaid parking fines. However hard I try, it's going to look like I messed up on purpose.

David's back is broad and square and facing me when I enter the interview room. His arms splay out to the sides, his cuffs are unbuttoned, and his shirt stretches in a fine cut across his shoulders. "Dr Carlyle?" I don't know why I'm asking. It's clearly not going to be anyone else. Rather I'm giving him the chance to recognise my voice, to kick up a fuss at my presence and send me away before we are locked in together. It would be a relief if he did. The bang of the door destroys any chance of that.

"Guess what?" A pause for effect. "I'm your solicitor." Slowly, he turns. "Murray French," I add. "At your service." I suppress the bow, the smile of triumph when I see the flash of shock widen his eyes and raise his brow. I've still got a decent amount of whisky inside me.

"I asked for a solicitor, not a clown." He ignores my extended hand and speaks like a careful machine, already one hundred per cent on guard and very different to the man I met at Northmire. His expression is rock solid now and betrays no concern at his predicament. I wonder if this is how he treats his patients in the surgery.

"No extra charge for the entertainment." I resist the urge to punch him and dump my battered leather bag on the table. Julia gave it to me aeons ago, when I first qualified. "Assault, Dr Carlyle. Grievous bodily harm, aggravated battery. Call it what you like. Call it murder if the girl dies." I remember the newspaper article. Grace's current lifeless state. "That's the unsavoury little cocktail you're about to be questioned on and possibly charged with. I suggest if you want to be out of here in time for breakfast, then we get down to discussing things."

Carlyle draws a breath that seems to suck the walls closer to him. "In that case, there's nothing to discuss."

"Oh, I think there is."

I drop down into the chair at the small table and take out a pad and pen. The first glimmer of a headache stretches between my temples. I write down the time and date, badly, because my hand is shaking. I reek of Scotch. "From the beginning, Dr Carlyle. The very beginning, up to and including this evening when you were with my wife." That's all I want to hear, what they were doing as the police hammered on his door. Were they kissing, or hadn't they quite got that far? Had he touched her by then, on the back, shoulder, face or somewhere more intimate? Worse, perhaps the police interrupted them already in the bedroom. Julia is hardly likely to tell me of how they hastily struggled into clothes when Ed and his men arrived.

"So do you want me or not, Dr Carlyle? There's no one else available to fight your corner tonight. You'll be questioned, possibly charged, and then it'll be off to the magistrates' court in the morning." I lay down my pen. The gauntlet.

He pauses thoughtfully and stares somewhere beyond me, and for a moment I see not contempt or jealousy but a whip of vulnerability. In a flash, I know that the doctor needs me, really needs me. The thread of hope spun between Julia and me is stretched to virtual invisibility but not yet broken. I fight the urge for another drink, just a small one, to wash it all away.

"Doctor." A deep breath. "There is a detective in this building waiting to interview you about a very serious crime. He wants to put you in prison." He might as well hear it straight. But David's eyes close, as if picturing another place, another time. His skin glistens with a thousand tiny sweat beads. "Dr Carlyle, did you attack Grace Covatta on the twenty-eighth of December?"

His eyes flash open, making me visibly jump. They are as dark and unfathomable as anything I have ever seen.

Before he answers, I step in. "You realise that if you are charged with this crime and you confide to me that you actually are guilty of . . ." I swallow, not wanting to think of Grace's injuries yet again. ". . . of these current allegations, but you choose to plead *not* guilty, then I can no longer be your solicitor." Hope above all hope that this happens. Now. Tonight. To get me out of here.

"But I am not going to tell you that I'm guilty, am I?" David smiles, perfectly in control again, as if he's only got a parking fine.

157

"The evidence against you is extremely serious." I know. I've read the file. Carlyle isn't going anywhere tonight except back to a cell. I wipe my hands over my face and catch the length of my hair in my fingers. I'm reading the headlines already: *Suspect Represented by Alcoholic Dropout.*

"I'm telling you that I didn't assault or hurt or injure anyone, Mr French. When the police discover that any evidence they have against me is purely circumstantial, they'll release me. It's as simple as that." Carlyle is completely unfazed by the seriousness of the allegations against him. I have no idea if he's telling the truth or not.

"The police recovered a waxed jacket in the field close to where Grace Covatta was found." I think of Julia, how bravely she coped after finding the girl. "The jacket had one of your bank statements in the pocket. As we speak, forensics will be officially confirming it's your coat. It'll be riddled with DNA, hair, bodily fluids." I wait for a reaction. There's nothing. I feel sick.

Just get through this, Murray. Get through this for Julia.

I continue. "Based on Grace's parents' statements about their daughter's movements, DI Hallet has CCTV footage revealing that you and Grace were together in your car on the afternoon before she was attacked."

"That's easily —"

"Plus there's a statement from a café owner stating that you were with Grace Covatta, apparently arguing, a week before her attack." I'm skimming through the details. "And you . . . you were seen kissing her. You

158

clearly know her well, Doctor." His face is deadpan. "In Julia's statement to the police, she says that the first and only word Grace spoke when she found her was 'doctor'." It's ironic but I like it that Julia's statement has helped bring in Carlyle.

"She asked you to help me, didn't she?" He says this with a vapour-thin smile, as if something magical has dawned on him. When I don't respond immediately, he says, "Julia made you." He is ignoring everything I have just told him.

I shake my head. "Actually, no . . ."

"So are you going to, then?"

"What?"

"Help me."

"Of course —"

"Let me offer you a bit of advice, Mr French." His turn to interrupt me. "There's this joke I know about solicitors. I think we could both do with a bit of a laugh, don't you?" He stands up and there's no way I can compete with the size of him. He looms across the table, hands outspread, face warped by anger, guilt, denial. He pauses for maximum effect. "How do you get a lawyer out of a tree?"

I shrug. "I haven't a clue." I know I've heard this before. I've just set myself up. It's not jokes we need, it's a miracle. "I don't know. How do you get a lawyer out of a tree?"

"Cut the rope, Mr French. You cut the rope."

JULIA

Ninety minutes a week visiting rights and he gives them all to me, just like that. An entire week crammed into an hour and a half.

"This is absolutely shocking. Terrible," I say earnestly, whispering so no one overhears us. But however I say it, it still sounds as if he has been caught by a speed camera or had a parking ticket slapped on his windscreen; as if he'll be out by teatime. "Ridiculous!" I laugh, showing him I believe he's innocent. Besides, it would be an insult to my judgement if he were anything else. I know, I just know, that we have a future together. There's no way David attacked anyone. I won't let it be true.

"I went to visit Grace Covatta again," I tell him. I can see by the look on his face, the way his eyes suddenly bleed their colour, that he doesn't like me bringing up her name. "She's been put into a coma to let her brain heal. She's just a husk; as if the life's been sucked from her. It's frustrating for the police, let alone you. I want her to be able to tell them that it wasn't you who hurt her." I stop. David is miles away. Doesn't he want to hear about Grace?

"I understand," David replies flatly. It could mean anything.

I swear he's lost weight since I last saw him. Looking at his gaunt face and the yellow-grey circles around his eyes, I doubt if he's sleeping. "It's so sad. She has a police guard on her ward and a couple of reporters were hanging around the corridors. Ed let me in." He looks annoyed. Ed is the enemy, after all. "I wanted to find things out for you, David. To get information. Until Grace is able to speak again you're stuck here." I flick my hand wide and a guard glances over. "It could delay the court case."

"It's more important that Grace recovers. The trial can wait." He's resigned to his fate. I admire him for that, even if being separated is already driving me crazy. His face is a carving of new lines and I see the worry stretched between his eyes in a knotted frown. "I'm sorry you've been dragged into this."

"I was in it neck deep already," I remind him, half laughing. "That's the irony of it all."

"A real family affair then," he says.

"What about *your* family? Can I call anyone for you?" David hangs his head, frowns, making me wish I'd not asked. "How are they treating you in here? Do you eat well? Do you have your own room?" I must look terrible myself with everything that's been going on.

A surprise smile cracks his face and his eyes light up. "They're called cells, Julia. And no, I have to share." For a moment, he's the David I know — charming, confident, assured. "But I've stayed in better hotels.

Wouldn't give this one any stars, and the food's not up to much. As for the other guests, well, they're incredibly noisy and inconsiderate. I have to share my room with a convicted paedophile." He pauses for maximum effect but quickly stops the charade when my shocked expression gives away my concern. "This is a category A prison, Julia," he says. "Bad people."

"But you're not a bad person, David. You shouldn't be in here. I believe you're innocent. Really, I do." I take his hand across the table. Prisoners in custody have more lenient visiting rights than the convicted inmates. I am grateful for that at least.

"Maybe it's the best place for me, Julia." David locks his hands around mine, like I've seen Murray do to Flora a thousand times. Then, "I'm sorry." He bows his head.

"Don't give up hope," I say. It's only as he closes his eyes and turns away from me that the first flicker of doubt seeps from under his skin and into mine.

After David was arrested and hauled off, there was nothing for me to do except wait. Murray promised he would handle things down at the police station and tried to console me before he went into the interview room. He reckoned that after a few hours of questioning they probably wouldn't have enough evidence to even press charges. I took his suit and the other things he'd requested in to the police station.

"Go home and sleep, Julia. You need to be rested for the kids' sake." Murray tried to sound upbeat, as if he actually wanted to be David's lawyer. I tried to believe he would do his utmost, but the whole situation was ludicrous. In the morning, I'd phone around the best law firms I could find.

"Surely if Sheila had given you the chance to explain the circumstances, she wouldn't have forced the case on you." I waited for him to agree, my eyebrows raised.

Murray brought his hand towards my face, as if to stroke my cheek, but then his arm dropped away along with his explanation.

"Trust me," were his last words — fragile as moths' wings — before he was led off to the prisoners' section.

I once did, I thought, before calling out a weak "Thanks."

I didn't sleep. Early the next morning, Murray called me.

"Julia." A pause, perhaps him not knowing how to say it. "David has been charged."

"Really?" Even though I knew this was bad, I was still hoping the news might herald the end of all this mess. "With what?"

A sigh. "Grace's assault. Aggravated GBH. Kidnap. Attempted murder."

"But I thought you said they didn't have enough evidence to charge him." It was true. I remembered him saying it.

"He's going to appear before the magistrates' court this morning."

Then I asked loads of questions but Murray was evasive. He didn't want to worry me.

"I'm sorry," he breathed down the line. "I'll still do everything I can. These are indictable offences, Julia."

He waited for my gasp before continuing. "It's a long way from over."

"Will he have to appear at the crown court?" I asked. I'd regained control of my voice and imagined Murray nodding his head even before he confirmed my worst fears. He said a brief goodbye.

David appeared before the magistrates' court. Bail was refused and he was immediately remanded in custody. He would be sent for trial by jury as we feared. There was no chance to do anything — wash my hair, eat, make phone calls, bring him clothes. He was transported to Whitegate Prison in an unmarked van. As quickly as he had entered it, David was taken from my life.

A vengeful crowd gathered outside the courthouse when the press learnt of his arrest. I fled the courtroom with my jacket over my head, stumbling on the stone steps as I left. I was a teacher — the teacher of the girl who had been attacked — yet I was also involved with the man accused of the crime. Grace had already won the country's hearts. If they found out who I was, the media would have a field day with me, and no doubt so would the head teacher at my school. Journalists and TV crews were everywhere, while parents nationwide wanted to know that their kids were safe. Me, I just wanted David back.

"Don't think I didn't pull out all the stops, Julia." Murray looked wrecked. The official slot allocated for his hangover had been filled with David's police interview, charging and court appearance. He hadn't slept all night. "But it's not over yet. I'll lodge an appeal. I'll take advice from the senior partners. I'll do whatever it takes to win this."

Later, I fetched the children from school, and soon after that Murray came round to the farm.

"I'm not leaving. Not going anywhere." He said this as soon as I opened the door. "If you're right about David, if he really is innocent, it means there's still a madman loose around here. And if you don't let me inside the house, I'll just go and camp in the barn." Then came the boot in the door, wedged in my heart for good measure. "Will you sleep well, knowing that I'm freezing and uncomfortable outside?" There was his smile, eclipsing the rest of his face, outshadowing his tiredness. It took me back a thousand years — or at least it seemed that long ago.

So I made up the spare room reluctantly and Alex skipped cheerfully round the house chanting that Mummy loves Daddy again. We did a funny dance ourselves when it came to using the bathroom, preparing food, saying good night. We do-si-doed between memories and the necessity to eat; we waltzed through our impending divorce and sidestepped around how it would affect the children. Murray and I had been separated since the summer and now here we were, however temporary, living together again. The oddest thing about it was that after a short time, it didn't feel odd at all.

"I'm moving back to Ely soon," I told Murray on Sunday evening. It was a hard decision. That morning I'd been to visit Mum — the first time since she'd been admitted. I was exhausted, and relieved that she was getting the care she needed. "The kids need some normality. They've been palmed off on Nadine and friends too much recently and Alex's teacher said that he's been disruptive in class. That's not like him."

We sighed in unison.

"What will you do about Brenna and Gradin?" They're not his concern but I like it that he cares. I'd had to call on several other friends to look after the teenagers. It wasn't ideal.

"Call social services, I guess. They'll get re-homed." I realised I'd made them sound like stray kittens. "And then there's Mum's animals to consider." I was finding reasons to stay put, even though the kids' routine was important. "I just want things to be ordinary again." And although neither of us said it, we both knew that that was impossible.

I busied about tidying the kitchen, stacking crockery and clattering cutlery into the sagging drawer. I had to hang on to every shred of normal life — for Mum, for Alex and Flora, for David — even though I had let go of every tattered piece of mine.

That was earlier. Now we're standing awkwardly in the shadow of our collective memories, each waiting for the other to leave the room, wondering who will flick off the light, check the door is locked, settle the embers of the fire so sparks won't jump out of the grate. It's as these night-time rituals take place just before midnight that I make a grab for Murray's hand. It scares the life out of him.

"What?" He's just turned out the kitchen light. His hand is tense in mine, a ball of uncertainty, and he's unsure whether to pull away or hold me back. "Julia, what is it?" He knows it must be serious.

"Nothing," I say. I feel silly.

"You can't grab my hand and then say nothing." The straps of tension in his fingers loosen and he spreads them wide. He weaves them with mine.

"Do you remember when Alex broke his elbow?" This is crazy. We're standing in the doorway, the one that leads out to all the other rooms, with Murray hunched under the low lintel and me backed against the frame. His fingers ensnare mine.

"It was dreadful. Worst day of my life." A moment passes as we each relive that dreadful time. "*Nearly* the worst day of my life." Now he's thinking about when I broke the news; recalling the sour taste, the bitter words, the slam of the door.

I want a divorce, Murray.

"Well," I say, hesitating. "Do you remember how we thought it would never heal? How we were convinced Alex would be broken for ever?"

"He was perfect until that day." Murray's shoulders drop forward an inch or two as if he's carrying the pain of the accident all over again.

"He still is," I confirm, and Murray nods. One thing we'll always agree on is how amazing our children are. "But do you remember how it happened?"

"The baby-walker," he states.

"What about that chain reaction of events? You calling me from the office and the phone ringing over and over when I was busy with the kids. Then the doorbell, Flora spitting up her food, you calling again, my headache, the power cut from the storm, me slicing my finger on a knife when I was talking to you, the phone pressed between my shoulder and ear. And I didn't even know the baby-walker was upstairs. You must have left it there."

"Oh, I see. This is a blame-Murray-for-Alex's-accident night, is it?" A cold breeze slices between us.

"What?" I pull my hand away but it won't come. It's locked in Murray's grip. "Of course not. You weren't even there."

"We went over this years ago, Julia. It was me who forgot to bring the damn baby-walker downstairs that morning." Sweat erupts on Murray's palm.

"Hey," I say gently. Once, I would have followed it with a kiss, a stroke, something tender. "Don't get upset."

"He was in agony." Murray leans back on the door. With his free hand, he covers his face. "If only —"

"If only I'd shut the stair gate, then Alex wouldn't have gone mountaineering up the stairs all by himself, somehow climbed into the baby-walker and hurtled back down the stairs again. You clearly weren't at fault, Murray. I didn't *have* to answer the telephone or see who was at the door." I stick up my left index finger and angle it in the light from the hall. "See? That's the scar from when the knife slipped through the tomato and into my hand. A reminder of that awful day."

Murray blows out. Not so much a sigh as a hurricane. "You want the truth about that day?" He screws up his eyes and grips my hand tighter. "I was drunk, Julia. Too drunk to drive home from the office.

168

That's why I kept trying to reach you. That's why we were on the phone when Alex climbed up the stairs."

I shiver even though the embers are still warming the room. I'm trying to understand this. "What? But . . . you said that your car had broken down. That it had been towed away. You'd been working so hard that you'd not had time to sort it."

"Well, I lied. I'd spent the day in the pub. I was drunk and I couldn't drive home. That's why I called you. And I kept on calling you because I was too stupid to know when to stop."

I had been about to remind Murray how good we were together; how every time something didn't go our way we roped in the resources and dealt with it. Alex's injury was an example — a brief clip of how we'd got through it, moved on, grown stronger. Perhaps all we'd learnt was that we're not invincible.

"You were *drunk*," I whisper, as if it's never happened before. It's then that I realise Murray is doing exactly the same thing now — calling for me, because he doesn't know when to stop. Despite everything, he will never give up.

Slowly I unwrap his fingers from mine and leave him to switch off the light.

Mum was staring out of the window when we arrived. She was wearing a hospital gown that clearly wasn't hers.

"Mum, I packed clothes in your bag." I crouched beside her. I thought it important that she didn't lose her identity. "Why are you wearing this?" She didn't turn at the sound of my voice; just stared as bulbs of rain hit the window. The sky had darkened since we left the car. "Alex, stay here with Grandma and Flora while I go and find someone."

I trekked down the corridor to the nurses' desk. "My mother," I began, slightly breathless from annoyance. "Mary Marshall. She's in a hospital gown. Is there any reason for this?" I'd heard of patients becoming institutionalised and unable to adapt to life at home again.

Two nurses greeted me with the efficiency and courtesy of a five-star hotel. One pulled up my mother's notes on the computer. Then they glanced at each other, hesitating before answering. "She's had some tests today, so that's probably why she's wearing the gown. Perhaps you'd like to take her to her room and change her back again? She'd enjoy that." A white smile accompanied the suggestion. I didn't believe her for a minute.

"Thank you," I said quietly, and walked away. "What tests?" I stopped and turned back.

The nurse shrugged. "It doesn't say exactly, but you'll be notified when we have results." She turned to answer the telephone while her associate chased after a stray patient. They were being cagey and I didn't like it. It was my mother they were talking about.

I returned to the day room to discover that Alex wasn't with Mum. A quick glance round the room and I saw him helping an old man with a jigsaw puzzle. They were forcing a piece into a hole that was clearly too small. Flora was sitting on her Grandma's knee, chuckling away like she'd just had the tickling of her life. Then she fell serious and signed something I couldn't make out. I paused behind them, in case Mum signed back, but Flora's expression had already given away my presence in the doorway and any conversation, imagined or otherwise, was lost.

Did Grandma talk to you? I signed frantically as Flora slipped off Mum's bony legs.

Flora looked up at her grandma before answering. No, she signed at me, her fingers hesitating. When will she get better? I want Grandma back.

Soon, I hope, darling. Soon.

It was as we were shuffling up the stairs — seemingly one forward and two backward — that I realised The Lawns was a very special kind of hospital.

"Excuse me." I stopped a young man trotting past us down the stairs. He looked like he knew his way around the place. "This might seem a very strange question, but," I gripped Mum's arm, "can you tell me what kind of hospital this is?" It sounded crazy but I had to hear it for myself. I trusted David, didn't I?

The young man's pupils enlarged into big black buttons and he slid against the banister rail. He licked his lips furiously and started rubbing his shoulder. "They're trying to kill me," he whispered. His eyes darted everywhere. "All of them trying to kill me." Then he ran down the remaining stairs, chanting as he went.

With my head bowed, I ushered Mum up to her room. David knew what he was doing and I had no right to question his decision. If I had any doubts, I quickly decided that for the time being they were best not mentioned. I couldn't take any more complications; perhaps I couldn't take the truth.

"I expect Murray will be here first thing in the morning." It's no consolation to either of us. My time with David is nearly up and I don't want to waste a minute of it.

"Let me check my diary to see if I'm available." He's laughing now, holding on to my hand, and we might as well be sitting at my house, his house, or the pub where we shared a meal. Nothing that he has said during this visit makes me think David is a violent criminal. I trust the legal system. I trust David. Most of all, for now at least, I have to put my trust in Murray.

"I'll get him to bring you some clean clothes. At least you don't have to wear prison overalls."

"One of the perks of being a remand prisoner. See, it's not all bad in here."

He's trying to make the best of this. I study him, wondering why I am falling for a man who, in truth, I hardly know. Am I on the rebound? Perhaps, but it's undeniable that there's something deep between us; a connection spanning the universe yet invisible to the naked eye. David makes me feel like a different person — someone I never thought I could be. I can see quite clearly that he was meant to be a part of my life.

172

"Was it awful?" I ask. "Being in court." What I really want to know is how well Murray did. Did he do a good job? Was it his fault that bail was refused?

"It was as I expected." His face remains layered with calm and ease. "Murray did his job well," he continues. He obviously knows what I'm thinking, confirming that we are in tune with each other. "A barrister will take over once the case is prepared." Then there is a silence because there aren't words to describe the interminable wait in custody that David will have to endure before this actually happens.

"What if Murray just puts in the appeal for bail. Then I'll find a . . ." I trail off. ". . . a more experienced lawyer to put the case together." I didn't think I'd feel so disloyal. "This really isn't his speciality."

"Julia, Julia," he says. "Slow down. Let things take their course. And besides, what's wrong with keeping it in the family? Everyone else seems to be involved."

"You know that Murray and I are getting a divorce, David. That makes it very difficult for him to . . ." The look on David's face tells me to stop. That discussing lawyers and barristers and the state of my marriage is simply more than he can tolerate after the last three days. "I'm sorry. I'm being selfish."

I change the subject. I can't have our last few minutes together ruined. "I think that Ed . . . that the police are clutching at straws." I want to give him hope but we're back to family again. In our small community, it's easy for lives to cross. "As for the evidence, it all seems rather circumstantial." Murray explained why David had been arrested but I could tell he was worried about upsetting me. "It's probably all a terrible misunderstanding." I lean across the table. "And Murray says they don't have any positive DNA results yet. That's a good thing. Their whole case rests on that coat. He says there's a chance the case could be chucked out before you even have time to zip up your prison boilersuit."

The buzzer sounds and the guard calls out that we have two minutes left. Two minutes out of what could be a life sentence.

"Goodbye, David." I stand up. Visitors are being ushered from the room; being searched on the way out. "If you're still here, I'll come back next week." He doesn't move but I lean down and kiss him. My lips land on his cheek when he tilts away from me. I stay quite still for a moment, breathing in, ashamed that I'm searching for the scent of guilt.

"Julia," he calls. "Look after yourself." I nod and walk away, catching a whiff of something on the air.

Gradin cries like a child when I tell him, and Brenna twists her hair in such a tight knot that the skin on her scalp starts to pull away from her head.

"You'll be placed with a nice family. Everything will be fine, you'll see." If ever a voice is insincere, this is it. "Think of it as a holiday before you find something more permanent." I am preparing their supper. Not quite the last.

"Don't want a holiday," Gradin wails. "I want to stay here with you and Mary."

Brenna slaps her brother round the head. "Don't be such a baby." She wiggles her fingers to dislodge the nest of hair that has come out of her head. "If you send us back, we'll just run away. We're not damaged goods, you know. We have feelings too."

I stare at them. Brenna is right. Gradin is so emotionally unstable that he's hardly able to form a sentence. I can't imagine what his future holds. My son is the product of a happy, stable, solid home, while Gradin is . . .

I squeeze the brakes on my thoughts. Happy, stable and solid? I laugh, making Brenna frown. So what will become of Alex and Flora when Murray and I finally break apart? What, indeed, is it doing to them now?

"I know, I know. OK?" I don't mean to snap. Brenna is bitter and full of pain and shouldn't bear the brunt of mine. The onion I'm chopping skids on to the floor. "But you must understand that Mary is very sick and can't look after you. It's time for me and my kids to go back to Ely so that I can return to my job." Return to normal, I think, whatever that is.

Brenna sneers, looking me up and down. She's trying different techniques until I respond. Quite skilled, but it leads me to wonder what drove her to it. Whose hands shaped a little girl into such a bitter, messed-up thing? "I know your type," she snaps. "You kicked your husband out and now you're doing it to us." She spits on the floor and yanks Gradin out of the room with her. Her timing is perfect because Murray is suddenly standing in the doorway, overhearing all this.

"Whoa, what was all that about?" Murray's face spreads with surprise pretending he doesn't know what's been going on.

"Oh, the usual," I say flippantly. "Teen tantrums. Hormones. Me kicking them out. Being homeless. Having abusive criminals for parents. That kind of thing." My eyes are streaming tears now. Murray hands me a tissue.

"You told them they have to leave?" Murray takes the knife from my hand. "Let me do it. You always did howl." He has a vested interest in the teenagers staying at Northmire. He thinks there's a chance he will be able to stay on for protection.

I fill a big pan with water and set it on the stove. "What option do I have, Murray? I need to go back home, for the kids' sake, and I certainly need to go back to work." I am about to say *because I am a single parent now* but realise I would be setting myself up for a harsh comment. "Can you chop the onion smaller? Flora won't eat it otherwise."

Suddenly we are back in our old home, chipping around each other with a daily update of our lives during snatched moments while the kids argue over some game, the kitchen smelling of laundry and spaghetti sauce. Evidently Murray realises this too. "Just like old times, eh?" He grins and I have to look away as another salty tear leaves my eye.

I clatter knives and forks on to the old table that's been in Northmire's kitchen for ever. "I really have to go back to Ely the day after tomorrow. I'm exhausted, driving all over the place. I can't please everyone and now I have to visit Mum regularly at The Lawns it makes more sense. There's Flora's ballet class to think about and Alex's swimming club and the hospital's up that way and —"

"Steady, there. Steady." Murray lays down the knife. "We may not live together any more but the kids are still partly my responsibility. You know I'll help share the load."

Well why didn't you convince me of that a year ago? I scream in my head and Alex walks into the kitchen, preventing it from bubbling out. "Hungry?" I ask, and then quietly to Murray, touching on the subject I hardly dare mention, "Just get David out of that place, that's all I ask of you, Murray."

A look passes between us — me because I need David freed, and him because he's still hanging on. Still believing there's some hope for us. "For Mum's sake at least. So he can continue caring for her." It softens the blow, sharing the need for David with Mum. "Anyway, last time we played Mummies and Daddies we weren't very good at it, if you remember." I instantly regret being so harsh when he was only offering to help. I slam down the table mats to compensate. Even Murray doesn't deserve that.

"So, you want me to be his solicitor now?" He gives me an incredulous glare and his forehead crinkles. I can't stand to look at him because he reminds me of everything familiar; everything how it should be. But all I need to do, to mask the guilt for smashing it up, is overlay the scene with a crate of beer, a few empty bottles of Scotch, evenings spent alone and a row each night at midnight.

I recall my conversation in prison with David. He didn't seem to have a plan; appeared oddly content with Murray's services. "No, Murray. I don't *want* you to help David at all. The idea sucks." I fill a jug with water. There isn't anything else to drink. Murray eyes it warily, realising the implication. He glances at his watch, wondering, no doubt, if the nearest shop is still open. "I think the sooner David finds a —"

"What, a proper lawyer?"

"No. I was going to say a *different* lawyer. A different one, Murray."

He looks at his watch again.

"It's shut, by the way."

"What is?"

"The village shop. Booze is about half an hour away unless you want to pay over the odds at the pub or are desperate enough to knock on someone's door and beg." Murray doesn't answer, which I take to be a good sign. "Look, David needs help. Won't a decent judge see how ridiculous this is? He has patients that need him." Like Mum. Like me.

"I'll submit an appeal," Murray says keenly. It makes me wonder why he isn't throwing his arms up in despair and leaving the whole mess to someone else. Surely he can't want this case either. There's clearly more at stake than Brownie points from me. Why doesn't he just walk away?

I screw up my eyes in silent protest. It's all too complicated. Only when I open them again, only when the pan of potatoes bubbles over on to the hotplate and I start breathing again, do I realise that we've been holding hands all this time.

MURRAY

Holding hands with your wife is perfectly normal. It is not a good reason for irregular heartbeats and sweating palms. God knows, we did all that when we were teenagers. But the dinner ensures that our connection is only fleeting because Julia flies across the kitchen to rescue the potatoes.

"Bloody hell, what a mess." She tips the contents through the colander and I watch, quite unable to move as she pounds them with a masher. "Well, wipe the stove then." She glares at me.

I pick up a cloth. I have to go easy on her, ignore her snappiness. Julia has a lifetime of worries dished up on her plate. But when I remind myself that she doesn't love me any more, that she is falling for another man — possibly a *criminal* — my blood runs cold and sympathy is stretched to its limit. "All sorted," I say calmly, wishing it was.

With the panic over, the six of us eat in silence and Gradin shovels his food like he hasn't eaten for a week. The boy intrigues me. I'm certain that buried beneath his exterior is a capable young man. It's doubtful that side of his character will ever see the light of day. For a

180

second, I am reminded of myself; the real Murray that never gets a look-in these days.

So it's a deafening silence this mealtime, with only Flora talking, chatting away with her hands, oblivious to the tension. No one is paying her any attention and everyone except me misses what she says about her trip to the hospital yesterday.

Grandma says she's sorry.

"Grandma says what?" I say, incredulous, signing at the same time. My fingers tangle in knots.

"Oh, very funny, Murray." Julia lays down her cutlery and shakes her head. "Grandma says nothing. That's the whole darn problem, in case you hadn't noticed."

In Julia's eyes, everything I do is wrong. If I did manage to secure bail for Carlyle, then no doubt it would have come too late or have too many conditions attached to it. I've considered begging Sheila to take me off the case.

But maybe, just maybe, I can make this work in my favour. Ever since Alex came along, Julia always had a thing about security. She was desperate for me to have a decent career. Once, she even talked about having another baby. I liked the idea. It warmed me from the inside out.

"You'll never learn, will you?" she said just before I fell off the bar stool. I remember Alex was there; had to witness it. "Another baby?" she said. "With you? I'd not do that to another child." And she walked off. Her reasons were good. I don't blame her.

"I'll prepare the appeal in the morning," I say quietly, efficiently; just what she wants to hear.

Stepping out of court with Dr Nice on my arm, blinking at the reporters' flash bulbs, recounting how he couldn't have got off such a heinous charge without my expert help . . . Well, Julia can't help but respect me again. Perhaps even love me. Maybe, at a push, want me back. My brain is screaming for a drink. "I'll get David bailed for you, Julia." I stand up and blindly spoon more food on to everyone's plates.

Only later do I remember what Flora said about Mary.

I was always scared of Mary Marshall. Even more fearful of her than Mrs Wraith at school. As a kid, I believed that Julia's mother was the keeper of terrible secrets and vessel of all things dark. It was something about the way her eyes were focused on another time, another place, while her body went about perfectly normal tasks. When she stared at me, I wondered if her secrets would spill out all over me.

Mary Marshall's legs were straight and strong and her jaw jutted forward. Her pale eyes beaded into suspicious jewels whenever I followed her daughter into the house.

"Not got a home to go to, Murray?" she would ask, and because she said it so many times, I ended up believing that she was right. Perhaps I didn't have a home to go to.

It suited my parents just fine that Northmire Farm was open house. Summer or winter, Julia had a circus of kids dotted about the property — climbing up the hay bales in the barn or following the stream at the bottom of the east paddock with our jeans pushed up to our knees.

Mary didn't seem to mind the other kids' presence, but she singled me out. Looking back, it was probably because I was a good deal older than Julia and appeared out of place stuck amongst her younger peers. "Not got any friends of your own age, Murray?" Looking back again, it was clear that Mary was trying to avert disaster. Our age difference, she once told me when I was slurping greedily from the kitchen tap, would only end in tears. It always did, she said.

So I decided to ease off on my friendship with Julia. Mary was right. Her daughter should be allowed friends her own age without being tailed by me.

Pete Duvall, sports champion and all-round smooth operator, was the one I most wanted to punch. I found Julia sitting on the village green bench waiting for him, tears held back behind a surprised smile when she saw me walking my dog. Truth is, I never walked the dog along that road but I'd heard that was where Pete was meeting Julia before taking her to the city — the cinema, the burger bar, the games arcade.

"Julia," I said, acting all amazed. I stood in front of her, shielding her from the setting sun. "What are you doing —"

"He's stood me up, before you ask." The sniff was barely detectable.

I already knew that. I'd walked the perimeter of the common a dozen times, waiting for Duvall to show his smarmy face. He lived in the big new house in the village.

"He's such a loser. Mind if I sit down?" She was too young to be out alone.

"Yes."

I did anyway. "Do you love him?" My dog nuzzled around Julia's ankles.

She sighed. "Not now, I don't. Not unless he's got a really good excuse. Like he's dead or something." Then we both laughed and that's when the tears started, hot and fast, and they got all over my T-shirt.

I walked her home, cursing my parents for not having waited a few years to conceive me, and that's when she told me something amazing. Julia Marshall, standing on her tiptoes in the muddy track leading down to Northmire Farm, whispered in my ear. "I only went out with him to make you jealous." Then she ran on up to the house without looking back, her skinny legs bending as if they might snap.

"Not jealous. Not me!" I called out after her, and on the top step of her house, she turned and blew me a kiss before darting inside. I walked home, desperate to know how she did it. Julia Marshall was playing me like a puppet.

It is the same upside-down thrill that always stops me in my tracks when I tuck my daughter into bed. But tonight, I ask Flora to repeat what her grandma told her.

Nothing, she signs stubbornly. Grandma's not speaking.

I sigh. Yes, I know, Flora. But when we were eating dinner you said that Grandma said sorry. What is she sorry for? Has she done something wrong?

Flora tunnels her way down the bedclothes and peeks her head out of the other end. She giggles too loudly, unable to control the volume of her warped voice, and ducks under again when I lunge for her. I grab her small body, padded up by quilt, and tickle between her ribs until she surrenders with her little finger thrust at me. I stop when she protests.

We stare at each other for a moment, and I see a replica of a young Julia staring back at me. I want to be a child again myself. I would tell her everything about our lives to come; make her promise never to leave me; beg her, this time: let's get it right.

"Time for lights out." Julia is suddenly behind me, breaking our connection. Come on, Little Miss Cheeky, it's bedtime, she signs, and snuggles Flora under the covers.

Night, Flora, I gesture, and leave the bedroom door open a little, just how she likes it.

"Get some sleep yourself, Murray," Julia tells me coolly on the landing. "You need to be fresh for tomorrow. I don't care how you do it, but David can't spend another night in that place." The secure future she craves is slipping away. "I need him out of there."

I nod, catching a glimpse of myself in the gilt mirror at the top of the stairs. I don't blame her for any of this.

"Good night, Julia." And I go to my room, still insanely jealous after all these years.

"So," Sheila asks. "All happy families again then, is it?"

I've just finished explaining that I'm currently living at Northmire, to help Julia while she's at the farm, but

185

she glazed over when I got to the bit about Mary not speaking. Sheila sees clients, she sees cases, she sees meetings and profits and reputations. She doesn't see my problems.

I don't bother explaining further. "No, it's not happy families, Sheila. More like bloody snap."

"Well, how about you play Cluedo instead and get down to the police station to figure out who the key witnesses are in the Carlyle case. Isn't it exciting for you, Murray? A proper, juicy client and a chance to prove what you're made of." She pauses and a hurt look sweeps over her face when I don't reply. I ignore her sarcastic tone. "You are grateful, aren't you?" She perches on the edge of my desk and knocks a pen on to the floor. It was a present from Julia. "Get this one under your belt successfully and I'll have Gerry take a look at you."

I lean back in my chair and it creaks, making the same noise as the one in my head. "Take a look at me?" I ask incredulously. "Sheila, I'm very grateful that you're trying to help save my ass here, but what you don't understand about this case is —"

"I always knew you were a fighter, Monsieur French. Why do you think I took you on all those years ago, fresh-faced and eager?"

Quickly, I think back. Was I fresh-faced and eager? I don't remember. With each day that passes, another ten get bumped off the list of memories thanks to the booze. If I'm honest, it's hard to remember much these days. Alcohol is a powerful detergent. "Sheila, do you know who David Carlyle is?"

"Yes. Yes, of course I do," she says, sliding off the desk and smoothing out her skirt. Her heel catches on the pen and skittles it under my desk. I retrieve it but feel sick. "He's your client, stupid. A rather dashing doctor caught up in the Covatta girl assault. Total cock-up, if you ask me. Pressure on the CID has forced a premature arrest. Anyone vaguely in the wrong place at the wrong time was bound to get it. Still, good for us, eh?"

"But Sheila, it's not that simple." I might as well pack up my desk now.

"Well make it simple, Murray darling." She leans forward, presumably to offer her secrets on successful practice. Her perfume is making me nauseous. "Look, Murray. Gerry is shuffling again. Things are going on here that you don't need to concern yourself with, but I took a punt on you when you first came to work here and I don't want you to mess up. It will reflect badly on me." She strides about, her pencil skirt limiting the space she can cover with each pace. "Your boozing is no secret. If it were left up to the other partners, you'd be long gone." She makes a slicing gesture across her neck. "I've bought you a reprieve, so damn well use it. Get your ass down to the prison, get your appeal lodged, get your case together and get into court. It's where you belong, Murray, not dealing with parking fines that our newest intern could manage blindfolded."

"Finished the lecture?" I'm calm. I'm not shouting. I'm not shaking or banging my fists about. I'm even smiling. "I don't want the case." There. I said it.

187

Sheila remains silent while she lights a cigarette. She opens the window. "Don't want it?" Her words hang incredulously on the smoke as it curls out into the street. "So you don't want your job either, then? Is that what you're saying?"

"Of course I want my job . . ." I shrug and think. Then it occurs to me. Maybe I don't. There's a photograph of Julia on my desk. I took it on the day she chose her wedding dress. I pick it up and trace my finger over her hair. Julia's eyes are starbursts and her cheeks swollen to pink crests. Her mouth is a perfect O and I recall that she was holding a copy of *Bride* magazine out of shot. We were so excited about getting married. We'd not long found out she was pregnant and I couldn't keep my eyes off her.

"She always looked like that," I comment. "Right through her pregnancy, she glowed and spread . . . I don't know . . . sunshine. Does that make sense?"

"What are you talking about sunshine for, Murray? Are you completely off your head? Are you drunk?" Sheila stares at me.

"It was a beautiful dress." I smile, surprised by the sudden clarity of the memory. "Cream with tiny blue flowers around the neck. It rained and the hem got muddy. Julia was going to have it cleaned but I told her not to. It was our wedding-day mud, I told her."

"You have, haven't you? You've bloody been at the bottle already." Sheila thrusts her face near mine and breathes in. All she'll smell is coffee.

Oh Murray, don't blow it. You need that job. You know we can't live on my teacher's pay alone. Julia

188

speaks to me from within the shiny paper. I touch her face.

"I won't blow it," I tell her. Sheila sighs and heads for the door.

"I should think not," she says, believing I've seen sense. "Like I said, Gerry is conducting a staff review soon. I'm far from mentioning the partnership word, Murray, but if you want a job, if you want to keep that pretty little wife of yours happy, then I suggest you get to work."

I place Julia carefully back on the desk, wishing I could make her happy. "Odd," I say as a warm feeling settles in my mind. I shake my head and gather the papers that I'll need for the day ahead. When I glance back at Julia, the feeling is still there — a glimmer of something I remember from way back; the one I thought the booze had destroyed. It's only when I bring the photograph up to my lips that I clearly remember it's called love.

HM Prison Whitegate is a maximum security institution for male category A and B offenders. The rush of pleasure I get when I see Carlyle incarcerated is better than any bottle of Scotch.

"Dr Carlyle," I say grimly. He is sitting with a guard in the small interview room, a slight hunch to his shoulders. Surprisingly, he doesn't look as broken down as he should. The guard leaves and waits outside the closed door, occasionally glancing through the small square of glass. It is our privilege to have complete privacy.

I've only been inside a couple of prisons before. The rigorous security procedure has put me in a bad mood and I'm shaking from the coffee I drank in the car. Or it could be because since I've been at Northmire, I've not had a drink.

"So. How's things?" I sit at the small table and lay my hands out in front of me. Carlyle stares at me, either resigned or amused by my presence. "And before you ask again, yes, I'm doing this for Julia. There are plenty of good criminal defence lawyers out there. I'm not one of them. But . . ." I breathe in deeply, sigh it out. ". . . I will get you out of here." I flinch at the sound of what I just promised. There's no way I'm letting Julia down.

"Then that makes two of us."

I raise my eyebrows, unclear what he means.

"Two of us doing things for Julia," he finishes, and I wonder which part of aggravated grievous bodily harm is for my wife. "Oh, and I didn't hurt the girl," he adds casually.

"Let's start with where you were when the incident took place." How will I get through this meeting, let alone a court appearance? I continue. "Grace Covatta was found early on the twenty-ninth of December. I don't have an estimated time of assault. The forensics report hasn't come back. Perhaps lucky for you that Grace is in a coma?" I say it as a question, in case there's a glimmer of agreement, a glimmer of guilt. "It's early days yet for medical or coroner's reports. No one's implied sex attack yet, but who knows what they'll discover, eh?"

Carlyle sits still and calm, unfazed, almost bored.

"Either way, the girl was messed up bad."

"So I believe," he says. "It's tragic." There is coldness in his voice, as if it's all a great inconvenience.

"Firstly, I need to know where you were on the night it happened."

David sighs. "I was at the surgery until six p.m. I drove home. I made myself a meal." He gestures briefly, flicking the memory away casually.

"Just like that. You remember just like that?"

"You said it was a Thursday. That's what I usually do on Thursdays."

"But can you prove that you did it on that one?"

"No."

"And what about your relationship with Grace? It's clear from the evidence that you know her."

"Yes, I know the girl."

"Just how well do you know her, Doctor?"

David's words are vapour thin, sending a shiver through me. He swallows. "People were talking." He bows his head. "I knew it had to stop."

"What had to stop, David?" I hold my breath, already knowing what he's going to say. How will I tell Julia that the new love of her life was having a fling with a teenager?

"I knew it wasn't right. All the appointments, secret meetings, phone calls." He sighs.

I go cold from the admission. "So you were having relations with a young girl." I hold it together. "Did anyone else see you with her the afternoon she was hurt? Apart from the CCTV cameras."

David is vague, somewhere else entirely. "Yes, a few people, I would imagine. Her mother saw me with her. She came with Grace to my surgery for an appointment the morning before she was hurt."

"What happened while they were in your surgery?"

David wipes his hands across his face. "Grace argued with her mother in my consulting room. Her mother stormed out and left her daughter alone with me."

"What was the row about?"

David searches the ceiling for an answer. "Grace was pregnant. Her mother wanted her to have an abortion, but Grace didn't want to. I spent a long time comforting her. She was incredibly distraught."

"Christ," I say, considering the implications. I have to ask. "Who is the father?"

David pauses before answering. "I can't say." He stares blankly ahead, wringing his hands together in a knot of deceit.

I don't say anything else; can't say anything else. My lips have frozen together. I have to take a break. To get some air. To think. To work out why everything is folding in on me. I need a drink.

I stand up, gather my belongings and leave the room. The guard immediately slides into my place.

"How did it go?" The bilge pump is noisy so I don't hear her the first time. I leap on to the towpath.

"She's sinking," I say matter-of-factly.

"Murray! I said how did your meeting with David go? Did you make an appeal for bail?" Julia's cheeks are glazed pink and her breath spurts out in shots of hope.

She is wearing her pink mittens, clapping them against each other as if that will hurry me up.

"Even God couldn't get him out of there at the moment. Coming aboard?" I'm moving the few things I had at Northmire back on to *Alcatraz*. There's no point staying at the farm any longer, not when Julia's returning to Ely.

"No. Flora has a ballet lesson."

There's a thread of sadness to her voice and I'd like to think it's because she doesn't have time to come inside. But of course it's because there's no progress with David's case and her mother's in hospital and one of her students has been battered into silence.

"I understand," I say, not even beginning to. "Send the kids my love."

"I will." Julia turns to walk back to her car at the junction. "Did David say anything? How is he?"

"We made a good start," I reply vaguely. I could end it all for her, with one sentence — *Grace Covatta is pregnant with David's baby* — but I haven't even digested the news myself yet. "I need to see the coroner's report and the police are waiting for DNA samples to come back from the lab. Don't worry," I tell her, meaning the opposite. "The evidence is largely circumstantial. I'm shocked he was even charged." I smile, offering a little warmth for her shaking body. "And he's bearing up well. He's eating and sleeping. He sends . . . he says hi," I add.

Julia nods appreciatively, her lips tight. "Will you be in for dinner?" she asks, and I wonder why. Then I realise she still thinks I'm staying at the farm.

"No." I smile, enjoying the flash of irony. "I've gone and left you."

Julia finally walks on, shaking her head, trying to figure out how you can leave someone who was never there in the first place.

MARY

I remember the sun on my back as we walked, his warm hand settled there too — fingers spreading like molten lust between my shoulder blades. He commented on my back, saying it was the prettiest he'd ever seen. That I had good muscle tone, and he even named them all, his finger tracing their striated path. Even these days, with my back hunched and my skin sallow, I can still feel his touch as he delved between my bones.

David's university room was not how I imagined. Firstly, it was furnished with antiques and was actually more of a suite than a room. Already a cut above the average student. He had a living area, a bedroom and his own bathroom. It was all decorated in deep rich colours and two entire walls were lined with books, many of them antique.

"Courtesy of my parents and their contacts." He grinned when he saw my mouth hanging open. "That's just how they are. By furnishing me like this, by dumping funds into my bank account each month, they believe themselves to be . . ." He paused. Another stroke of my back. ". . . parents. Rhomboideus minor.

Arising from the seventh cervical and first thoracic vertebrae inserting into the spine of the scapula. And you are *very* tense."

I sensed he had issues with his family but didn't pursue it. It was a neat explanation for his flash outbursts of anger. I understood perfectly. "Shall we have tea?" I suggested. He was right. I was tense. I perused his books, trailing a finger over their spines, as David had just done to me. "You still smell of death." I turned and grinned at him but his smile dropped away.

"I'll make you tea," he said, approaching me, leaving a tiny imprint of his lips on my bare neck. It's still there all these years later.

We sat in the bay window of his room sipping on a Chinese blend, watching student life from the first floor. For that hour, I felt special, part of the elite group I had obsessed about for years. "I'd got it all figured out," I told him, but David didn't seem particularly interested.

"Hmm?"

"My career. Veterinary science. Astronomy. Philosophy. Classics. History of Art. God, I didn't really care." I laughed away the pain that spiked through my heart and counted myself lucky that I was at least taking tea with an intelligent, cultured and privileged young medical student at Corpus Christi. Second best; all that was left for me. "But still, I like my job."

"You're a waitress," he said flatly, and pulled out a packet of Embassy. He lit one.

"Maybe I'll open my own café some day." Smoke rolled through the sunlight and tumbled over me. It was the same air that had just left David's lungs. I sucked it up in case there was something of him to be had.

"Why do you like me?" he asked. Through squinting eyes, through a confident demeanour that a young man of his age had no right to possess, he appraised me. I knew he wanted me.

"Well," I said, trying to keep things light. I was way out of my depth. I dabbed tiny drops of sweat from my top lip. It was hot in his room, a hot day everywhere. "You have nice eyes." That was true. Crazy dark irises swam behind a mop of hair that had been hand-picked to match. "And you're intelligent. I like intelligent men." Yes, it was flirting. Yes, I crossed my legs one way and then the other, and yes, the fabric of my pretty skirt fell from my knees. "I have great admiration for intelligence. I find it —"

"Sexy?" He was grinning again, switching flawlessly from indomitable to childlike. That's what I liked about David. Traversing the depths of his psyche had become an impossible yet enchanting puzzle. "I like older women," he confessed. I smelled his smoke again. "It's all about experience, isn't it?"

I remembered my vow and crossed my legs away from him. I respected David and I wanted him to feel the same way about me. I was an older woman and I wasn't about to take advantage of the situation. I knew better. That was not what our relationship was about. For me, it was way deeper than that. I wanted to learn from him; absorb by osmosis the life I should have had.

"Is twenty-seven old, then?" Suddenly, I felt like his big sister.

"Terribly," he confessed, and leaned forward so that his shirt stretched across his shoulders and his sleeves hoisted up his elbows. He dropped the cigarette into an ashtray and it continued to burn until it went out at the filter. I watched the smoke wind up to the ceiling. "That's why I like you." And suddenly he was on his knees in front of me, trying to press his lips on to mine and fumbling with the tie of my top.

I dropped my cup to the floor — china smashing around my ankles. I pushed him away. "David, no!" My voice was smothered by his lips.

It all happened so quickly. Fear told me to fight him off, yet it was fear of our friendship ending that made me want him to continue. His hand was on my breast, the hot cup of his palm sending a wave of lust to my brain.

"I'm so sorry." As quickly as it had begun, it was over. David was back in his chair, his cheeks flushed, his eyes smoking like the dog-end dying in the ashtray. For a second, I felt eighteen again myself.

It doesn't really matter where I sit. Here, at home, in the past. It's all the same to me. The nurse has brought me to a clean white room where, even though it's dismal and raining outside, everything makes me believe I'm on the verge of heaven. I sit and stare at a wall, just catching a whiff of all the smoke from the past that's somehow seeped into the present.

198

It was only the shower curtain that smouldered. And apart from the smell and the black on the tiles, you'd never know that there had been flames or fuss at all. But because the window only opens an inch, the stench will take days to clear. It was the clothes that I'd wanted to burn, not the hospital.

Julia is visiting. I couldn't look her in the eye when she arrived because of where she's heading with her life. It's hard to watch your daughter fall over the edge of a precipice; hard not to be able to tell her. But I hear her voice, shrill and seeking, cheerful yet veined with sadness, and here I sit, unable to answer. She mutters something about clothes and the hospital gown, and suddenly little Flora is climbing on to me, rocking what's left of my world. Julia walks off.

Hello, Grandma. I don't like it here. Flora shakes her head and her curls bounce against my cheek. Her hair smells of vanilla and I wish I was her. Everyone understands her reason for silence. When will you come home? Milo is missing you. She wriggles and positions herself better, wrapping and unwrapping the string of my gown around her fingers; effectively silencing herself.

Don't you want your animals any more, Grandma? Did you lose your way home? Mummy says that your brain is sick and you might die. I heard her talking to Daddy. Flora's hands whittle the air into wisps of words and I understand her perfectly. Saliva pools in my mouth.

When Flora was born, no one knew that she was deaf. Alex, instinctively acting as big brother, spoke for her as they grew up, so even before the doctors broke the news, it never seemed that Flora was without a voice, without comprehension. If she wanted something, she'd somehow communicate it to Alex through expression, crude signing or perhaps just a sibling sixth sense. Despite her disability, Flora never seemed different, never an outcast, never blamed or judged for living in her silent world.

Alex stands across the room. He looks so like his father — his body lean and pliable with the awkwardness of youth that never quite left Murray. His blue eyes poke from beneath messy brown hair that refuses to lie flat. He bends to compensate for his gangly limbs and precocious height. Bored, Alex walks off, despite his mother's instructions.

It's just Flora and me now, stuck in our mute worlds. My grand-daughter rests her head on my chest and her quick child breaths fall into line with mine. She raises her hands in front of my face.

Isn't there anything in your ears either, Grandma? Is everything hollow too?

She searches my face, desperate to communicate any way she can. She is allowing me into her mind through those pretty blue eyes, offering a helping hand like Alex did for her. Flora is safe, silent, a locked cabinet for my thoughts.

Yes, it's all hollow, I tell her with fingers that bend from the first knots of arthritis. There's nothing left.

Flora nods and rests her head on me again, as if my communicating with her had simply picked up from our last chat. Are you sad, Grandma?

No, I sign quite clearly. Just very, very sorry.

Before Julia leaves the hospital, she takes me back to my room, but we are intercepted by a nurse because they have moved me to another, less salubrious wing of the building. My new room doesn't have a view of the chestnut trees, rather a tiny window about eight feet off the floor. There is no private bathroom, the floor is covered in linoleum and the bed is a metal-framed cot. A tiny smile catches the corner of my mouth but, thankfully, nobody sees. This room suits me perfectly.

"Why is my mother in here? Her last room was much nicer than this." Julia's voice is caught on the sharp point between tears and yelling.

"I'm sorry, Mrs Marshall, but we don't have unlimited facilities. Your mother set fire to the last room, and until we have cleaned and redecorated, she will have to stay in here."

I sit on the bed, the middle of it sagging under my weight, and absorb the heat from Julia's eyes as she stares at me. Suddenly she is on her knees in front of me, nothing coming out of her mouth except a thousand unanswerable questions.

JULIA

It's Brenna who eventually persuades me to stay on at the farm. When she wants to, she can turn on the charm, and for a mixed-up teenager she doesn't do a bad job.

"Oh please, Mrs M. We like it here." Simple words strung around her imploring face and they get to me. Then she hoists a surprised Flora up on to her hip, although the weight of my daughter soon sends her sliding down Brenna's side again. But the girls keep hold of each other and Flora is touched by the teen's attention. It's clear that my daughter craves something that I've not been providing.

Want to play with me? Flora signs, but Brenna just stares dumbly at her.

"Wow," she says. "That's amazing when you look at it." Brenna stoops down to Flora's height and says, "It's crazy cool! Teach me something, Flora." I translate what Brenna says and she stares intently at Flora's hands as they shape words in reply.

"She says she'd like you to play dolls with her. She wants you to help dress them. Now she's asking if you like dolls."

"I *love* dolls," Brenna says overenthusiastically, clearly lying. This is an easy scam compared to the rest of her life; easy to worm her way into my heart via Flora. It doesn't do for me to think about the abuse and suffering she's put up with. That would make me treat her differently, and what Brenna needs now is to be dealt with like any normal teenager — praise, love, an occasional reprimand dished out fairly and consistently. Whatever her past holds, she's doing a marvellous job of speaking with Flora without knowing a single word of sign language. Maybe I can encourage her to apply the same aptitude to her schoolwork.

Three times the head teacher has called because Brenna didn't turn up at school. Each time I conjured a hurried excuse why Mum couldn't get to the phone — busy with the goats; just popped out to fetch something for tea; in the bath. If the head suspected that Mum wasn't home looking after the kids, she'd have to notify social services. Brenna and Gradin would be whipped away before I could put the phone down, and I'm not entirely sure that's what I want.

Stupidly, as I watch Brenna mess about with Flora, making her giggle, I realise that I have grown fond of the pair. Against my better judgement, I decide not to turn them in. When I think of all Mum's hard work and dedication, the years of love and effort that she has unconditionally donated to her foster kids, I can't waste it all by giving up so easily.

I tip the last of the coal from the scuttle on to the range and sigh as I remember Mum doing this a thousand times a year throughout my childhood. I wonder where her devotion to me, the farm and her foster children, came from. It was a place inside her mind that she never allowed me to visit. Of course, she was always a loving mother to me. Strict at times, yes. Evasive and stubborn when I questioned her about my father, certainly. From an early age, I learnt that probing the subject raised a taut anger that no good little girl wanted to provoke. The result was a seamless erosion of any desire to delve into the past. "Never look back," was Mum's motto.

"OK, OK. You win," I say, even though I know it's only a matter of time before we are found out. "But you're going to have to pull your weight around here. Make it worth my while."

"Oh, we will, Mrs Marshall. We will." Brenna licks her finger and sticks it in the sugar bowl.

"That means going to school and staying there," I add. "And don't do that. It's disgusting."

She gives me a wry smile as she studies her frosted finger. "Come on, Flora. Let's go and find those dolls." Amazingly, Flora seems to understand, and the two girls trot out of the kitchen. I hear their footsteps tread the creaky stairs and my heart dares to warm by a degree. For just a moment, I feel like my mother.

It's only later that evening, as I am creeping around the house checking the doors and windows are secure before I go to bed, that I wish I had called social services after all.

The old oak floorboards give away my presence. The youngsters' accommodation is above the hay barn but accessed through the farmhouse up its own winding staircase. The area is cross-hatched with beams and a mix of old painted furniture that I remember from my childhood. Just the smell and sight of it evokes dusty memories, of Murray, and of long, carefree days.

Mum has put feather-filled mattresses on the brass bed frames, and with the old sofa, several rugs, and posters on the whitewashed walls, it makes a comfortable teen retreat. There have never been any complaints. In fact, the kids love the independence that the loft provides.

The first thing I smell is the alcohol. The sweet vapours tingle my nose before I even reach the door at the top of the stairs. I'm calibrated to sniff out even the most secretive of drinkers. The loft-room door is open a few inches.

I stop suddenly, my heart an axe inside my chest.

The kiss — from a boy aged sixteen who wears teddy bear toggles on his coat — lands clumsily on Brenna's mouth. I stumble from shock and the floorboards creak beneath me. Gradin slowly looks up, whereas Brenna is on her feet quick as a hunted doe.

I burst into their room. "No, no, you mustn't kiss your sister like that, Gradin," I say as if I have caught him stealing biscuits. "It's not what we do." My voice is shaking.

"It's OK, missus, because Brenna likes it. She says that makes it all right." Gradin is on his feet, stomping towards me, intimidating me. The boy is at least six feet tall. From the corner of my eye, I see Brenna shaking and bowing her head.

"Brenna is your *sister*," I tell him. My eyes flick to her. She is shovelling her way through her school bag, searching for something. "And we don't kiss our sisters or our brothers or mothers or fathers. Not like that, anyway. It's nature." I'm flailing in the dark, not having a clue how to handle this. I can't bear to think what would have happened if I'd not interrupted.

Gradin smiles. He believes he hasn't done anything wrong. He takes my arms and grips them tightly, one in each hand. I don't move. "It's just a kiss," he tells me. "It's nice." His eyes bulge, and it makes me wonder, frozen in his grip, what else he is capable of. I smile weakly, hoping it might make him let go.

I turn slowly, not wanting to startle him. Brenna has lit a cigarette. She is sitting cross-legged on a pile of cushions, squinting at me through black eyeliner and smoke, elbows propped on her knees. Quite different to the girl who enchanted Flora earlier, she doesn't say a word.

"No, no, it's *not* nice, Gradin . . ." His grip on me grows until I can feel the bruises pushed into my skin, until his eyes look fit to explode, until I stop talking, until he makes me promise that I never saw him.

If it wasn't for Murray, who had been passing, seen lights on at the farm and come to investigate, I don't know how far Gradin would have gone.

"I think you're blowing this out of proportion, Ju." Murray is incredulous. He hardly believes me. We are in the kitchen, hovering around the fireside chairs, no one daring to sit.

"The boy was kissing his sister. His hands were about to grope her by the looks of it. He was *kissing* her, Murray. Full on the lips. More than just a 'good night, sis' kind of kiss."

"What about Brenna? Did she protest?"

"She didn't look very happy about it. She was sullen and wouldn't speak. And she was *smoking* up there."

Murray laughs. "God, Julia. Don't you remember what we were like?" He paces away and then paces back.

"What *you* were like," I add quickly. "You were the one who rebelled at every chance."

Murray sighs and makes a decision. "In that case, if you really think it's serious, I don't want them in the same house as Alex and Flora. Gradin needs help, and you're not qualified to give it." From his expression, I can tell that he's not sure whether to go or stay.

"Look, Julia, your mother's in a psychiatric hospital. A girl you teach has been brutally attacked and the man you are clearly falling in love with has been charged with GBH. And that's not to mention the mess that is us." He paces around some more to lend weight to the "us" part. "Get rid of Brenna and Gradin, Julia. They're bad blood. You don't need them."

"Is it that obvious?" I say quietly.

"Is what obvious?" Murray asks. He stomps to the back door.

"That I'm falling in love with David," I whisper. And even though it makes things worse, even though I'm temporarily grounded with guilt from the expression of sudden and deep loss on Murray's face, I clap my hand

207

over my mouth. He looks as if he's just found out about our divorce all over again. "However much of a mess we're in, Murray, you'll always be . . ." I stop. I'm just making it worse. I didn't mean to admit my feelings to myself, let alone Murray. "I didn't mean . . ."

"It's OK," he says when it's obviously not. "I'm glad you can still be honest with me." I swear there's a tear beading in his left eye. "Do you remember when we were kids and we said that if we ever had a secret, it wouldn't be a proper one until we shared it with each other?"

Of course I remember.

"Well now I know, now you've told me how you feel, it's an official secret," he says, smiling, crushing me with kindness. For a moment, I glimpse a Murray of the past; a Murray who always tried to make things OK, even if they weren't; even if he didn't succeed.

"Do you want me to stay?" he asks.

I hesitate, part of me desperate to say yes, the rest of me already pushing him out of the door. "No. You go. I'll be fine," I say, my voice still barely more than a whisper. "I'll sleep on the camp bed in the kids' room if you like so that I can make sure lovesick Gradin doesn't come sleepwalking." I stare at Murray, holding the unexpected snapshot of the man I used to know, as carefully as I would hold a butterfly wing.

"Perhaps I'll hear more news in the morning about the appeal. If I do, you'll be the first to know."

"Thank you, Murray." I plant a kiss on his cheek before he finally steps out into the night.

★ ★ ★

Ed isn't being funny with me exactly, but he steps around me, doesn't look at me directly.

"I'm going back to work tomorrow," I tell Nadine, hardly believing it myself. Most things I plan these days don't seem to happen.

"How's Mary doing?" She slides a sandwich in front of me. "You've lost weight," she comments. "Hey, maybe I should get myself a bit more stress, and then perhaps . . ." but she stops, realising how insensitive it would be to continue.

"Help yourself to some of my stress, by all means." It's the only retort I can think of. I'd hate it if we fell out too. "Thanks, this is good." I bite into the tuna sandwich and the sweetcorn pops between my teeth. "And before you say anything, I know I look a mess." I drag my fingers through my hair. "It's a wonder David even looked twice . . ."

My turn to trail off as Ed raises his head at the mention of the man he has just put behind bars. He has a crust poking from his mouth and he's glancing through the pages of a newspaper so fast he can't possibly be reading anything. He's working round the clock at the moment — because of the Covatta case, but perhaps also as a reaction to the news that he and Nadine can't naturally conceive.

He's about to say something, then thinks better of it. If I hadn't known him for so long, I'd be intimidated by his rough veneer, the tough cop image he strives to maintain. But behind all that there's a gentle, sensitive man.

"Mum's doing OK, the same really," I say, changing the subject. "But I'm worried about her treatment plan now that . . ." Another glance at Ed tells me he is listening. "Anyway, I'm going in to visit her again later. I have to make sure that she's getting all the tests she needs. I need to know who's taken over her care."

"It's a shame she wasn't admitted to one of the wards at my hospital. I could kick ass." Nadine is dressed in her white tunic top and matching trousers. It's a coping uniform; a getting-on-with-things outfit. "What's the name of the place she's at?"

"The Lawns. It's a private hospital and . . ." My words dissolve again. I don't want to tell them that David is taking care of the fees, although I feel the need to explain.

"The Lawns?" She whistles through her teeth. "It's expensive. A friend of mine, Chrissie Weaver, works there." Nadine is thoughtful for a second. "Julia, The Lawns is a . . . Well, Chrissie is a psychologist. Your mother has been put into a psychiatric hospital."

"I know," I say in quick defence. Ed is still listening, more intently now. He scans the paper, one ear open. "Apparently the problem in Mum's brain is giving her symptoms similar to dementia. She can get top-class psychiatric care at The Lawns as well as the medical treatment. David was liaising with her consultant over further tests at another hospital, but now . . . he can't." I glare at Ed when he looks up. Whatever he thinks about David, his arrest has interfered with Mum's treatment.

210

Ed's had enough. He slams the paper on the table. "Julia, your mother's doctor has been charged with a *very* serious offence. Your involvement with the man only complicates issues."

I'm sure he wants to hug me as he's done countless times in the past. As a compromise, he replaces the hug with softer words. "Look, you're still my sister-in-law, just, and you know that I love you. But for your own good, you're going to have to trust me on this one. Keep well clear of David Carlyle." Ed grabs his keys, stamps a kiss on Nadine's head, and leaves the house.

"I'm so sorry," I say when I hear the front door close. I break down in tears. Then, between sobs, I say sorry a thousand times more and let my face drop on to Nadine's shoulder, smearing a trail of mascara on her white uniform. I look up and apologise again, and we both laugh, me through bursts of snot and misery and her because she has the spark of an idea.

"Look, Julia, I'll call Chrissie later. I'll get her to find out what's going on with Mary. I'm really not sure it's in her best interest to be treated at The Lawns. Leave it with me and I'll see what I can dig up."

"Thanks, Nadine. I owe you." I blow my nose.

"No. You owe it to yourself to survive this." She clears our plates away. "How's Murray?" she asks, and I tense again because talking about Murray with his sister is always strained.

"Murray is fine," I say, lying, wondering when it was that I lost sight of that.

★ ★ ★

When I drive into Witherly after fetching Alex and Flora, Brenna and Gradin are stepping off the school bus in the centre of the village. Brenna has tied her hair back and is wearing the correct uniform, while Gradin has his book bag slung over his back. The rock narrowly hurtles past his temple and I flinch instinctively on his behalf. He seems unaware the missile even came close to him.

"Oi!" Brenna yells, turning like a wildcat to the pack behind her. "Fucking leave him alone." Only then does Gradin look up from watching the trudge of his footsteps on the verge.

I pull up alongside them and wind down the window. "Hop in," I order. "Slide over, Alex." Gradin tumbles in beside my son and Brenna sits next to me in the front. I can smell the cold country air on their bodies. Their breaths are hot and grateful.

The lane narrows as we approach Northmire and the Clio drives heavily, bouncing over the potholes. "Good day?" I ask. Brenna shrugs. "Gradin, is everything OK at school?" I glance in the rearview mirror.

"He's being bullied," Brenna says for him. "The kids call him names, kick him, steal his stuff, nick his lunch money." She pulls a face — a frown combined with a plea: *do something*.

How can I tell them that what Murray said made sense? I doubt very much that they'll understand why I called social services earlier; why I left a message with the woman responsible for their placements, their well-being, asking her to call me to discuss their future.

Flora begins to jiggle in the back seat. "Hang on, darling," I say out loud, and in the mirror I see the flick of Alex's hands as he translates for me.

We swing into the cobbled yard, which looks shabby and uncared for now that Mum isn't around to tend to it. I haven't had the time or inclination to take care of jobs like that myself. I pull up the handbrake and my mouth drops as Murray steps out of the back door. It makes me angry that he still feels he can come and go as he pleases.

He strides up to the car. "I remember where Mary keeps the spare key," he excuses, noticing my frown.

"I don't need you to baby-sit me, Murray. Things are fine here." I am unnecessarily snappy with him but can't help it. I lock the car and all the kids file into the farmhouse. I have no idea what to feed them for tea. Grocery shopping is something I haven't had time for.

Murray takes me by the arms and I wince. They're still sore from where Gradin grabbed me. "Listen, it's early days but there may be some news."

I stop. "Oh?"

"The Crown Prosecution Service is demanding a review of the police evidence. It seems they're not entirely convinced there's a strong enough case."

"Come in," I say, trying to stay calm. I shoo Alex and Flora into the sitting room, feeling guilty because it will be chilly in there and all they have for company is a portable DVD player with a choice of exactly one film. Flora has made up her own signed version of *101 Dalmatians*.

Murray sits by the embers, pokes at them for me and adds some kindling. "To put it in simple terms, the CPS have to consider two main points when bringing a case like this to court. Firstly, they have to ask if there is enough reliable evidence to get a conviction. The case will be dropped if evidence is insufficient or not of a good quality."

"However serious the case is?"

Murray nods. "Yes. The Crown Prosecutor also considers if it is in the public's interest for the case to be tried in court. Unfortunately, if the evidence is stacked against Carlyle, then of course the answer to this will be yes. But with evidence that isn't as strong as we first believed, there may be a chance, a tiny one, of the whole thing falling apart. Bail, at the very least."

The breath is knocked from me when I consider that some part of my life may be normalised again. "How can they just arrest him one minute and then suddenly decide that he's innocent after all?"

"It's not quite as simple as that, Julia." I can tell by Murray's expression that he doesn't want to have to explain it to me. "The CPS has to decide if the recent information is reliable enough —"

"Do they have witnesses?"

Murray looks away; shuts his eyes and gathers up our little girl in his arms when she comes back into the kitchen, bored with the movie. "Not as such, Julia." He glances down at Flora and makes a face, as if we shouldn't say anything with her present.

"She can't hear you, Murray. For Christ's sake, just tell me who. What do the police know?"

He pauses and lifts his eyebrows before he speaks, bracing me for a shock. "The police believe that David was ... involved with Grace Covatta. They have witness statements, CCTV of them in his car together and ..." He's trying to be gentle.

"So?" I say immediately, defensively, not daring to ask what comes after the "and". *Grace was in David's car?* I feel sick. I consider the implications but nothing makes sense. "Why didn't you tell me this before?" My voice is a whisper but then deepens to an indignant tone. "So what if Grace was in David's car? I've driven her home once before. It doesn't mean I assaulted her."

"Look, most of the evidence is just as flimsy. Don't fret. Remember what I said about the CPS. If they can't stick this one together with solid facts, then in the bin it goes."

"Are you sure you've told me everything you know?"

"Really, that's it. Really, it is." He hoists Flora up high and makes her squeal as he pretends to drop her. Suddenly Murray stops messing about. "Julia, it's a serious charge with serious implications. Don't expect to hear things that you're going to like."

He's right, although I don't want to admit it. I'm stuck in a time warp, still back at David's house, waiting for the moment when he returns so we can pick up where we left off. I want to rewind to the point just before Ed and his officers arrived.

"The washing-up," I say slowly, as if it is the solution to all my problems.

"What are you talking about? What washing-up?" Murray isn't looking at me. He is swaying one way then

215

the other as Flora tries to outwit him at tag around the kitchen table.

Enough! I sign and she pouts. I'm trying to talk to your father.

No! she gestures back, pushing her luck. I raise my eyebrows at her and widen my eyes in warning.

"The washing-up is still sitting in the kitchen at David's house. I'm going to go and do it." For some reason the thought of dirty dishes and pans going mouldy in David's home is more than I can stand. I don't want him to come home to a mess, to feel that everything's been neglected. Murray sees the tremor in my arms.

"Julia, you're out of your mind. What are you thinking of?" He doesn't understand. "You want to do the washing-up?" Then he pauses, frowns and lifts Flora to one side. "The house will be sealed off to gather evidence. What are you going to do, break in?"

"No, dummy," I say, reaching for my bag. "I'm going to use the front door keys."

And, after a second's thought, Murray takes the keys I've plucked from my bag and slams the door as he leaves.

MURRAY

After all this time, the house still smells of their cosy dinner. Maybe it's my imagination, but there's a sweet fermented blend of lamb and rosemary hanging in the stale air with the dizzy scent of lust mixed in. A semi-evaporated glass of red wine sits forgotten on the worktop.

All the curtains are closed, and even though it's dark outside, there's no way I'm putting the lights on. My torch is risky enough. If I'm caught here, they'll take me off the case. Hang the lawyer who simply couldn't help himself. Briefly, I think of Sheila and what she would say if she knew I was here, stalking through my client's house.

I have to find out if Dr Nice is hiding something. Getting him out of prison is one thing, and may well keep me my job and prove to Julia that I'm not a loser. But if he walks free, there is of course a chance that he did attack Grace. I have to assume the worst. I don't want him anywhere near my wife and kids.

I'm surprised that there isn't a police guard on duty, but then again, if Ed has already scoured the place, and forensics have taken what they wanted, then the cost of manning such a remote property is unlikely. It makes my job easier.

I decide to get straight to the heart of the matter. The bedroom. I need to know how far it went.

I kick open a random door off the landing, hoping it's his. But I am wrong. It looks like a guest bedroom, sparsely yet comfortably furnished with few personal belongings. I pick another door and open it. Behind it, I half expect to see Julia and David entwined on the bed.

My heart thumps as my hand touches the door with a tissue sheathing my fingers. I push it open and step inside, flashing my torch around to get a quick look, a sense of the size, the contents. Apart from the torchlight, the whole house is dark.

My breathing quickens. It's a small room used as an office. I see an antique desk, a filing cabinet, and piles of files and papers everywhere. I beam the torch over the four walls and notice that the wall above the desk is dotted with dozens of drawing pins, Blu Tack and peeled paint where tape has been ripped off. "Photographs?" I ask myself quietly, and I wonder if the police seized whatever was up there as evidence. "Or perhaps Carlyle got there first," I ponder.

Being careful not to touch anything, I twist my head to read some labels on the stacks of files. Bank statements, insurance, credit cards, mortgage . . . the regular household files of a man who keeps his affairs in order. By torchlight, I see that there is a darker square in the dust on the desk and a couple of loose cables feeding up from behind. I can't help the smile. The police have seized Carlyle's computer.

Using the tissue, I try to pull open a filing cabinet drawer but it's locked. I have a quick scan around with the torch for a key but I don't see one. It's then that I notice the corner of shiny paper poking out from beneath the base of the cabinet.

Heaving my shoulder against the metal drawers, I tilt it enough to pull the paper out. I forget to hold it with the tissue, and now that my prints are firmly marked, whatever it is will have to come with me when I leave.

It's a photograph with tiny holes punctured in each corner — one from the wall, perhaps? I turn it over and shine the torch right at it. Julia is standing beside a car — *my old car* — getting something from the boot, her gaze set to the distance and the wind lifting up her hair.

"I *remember* this," I whisper incredulously. My heart is really thumping now. "We went for a picnic but it was ruined by the bad weather. Alex was only seven or eight." And sure enough, there's my son in the background, carrying a red toy car. A quick calculation confirms that this picture is at least four years old. Why, I ask myself while turning it over and over, does David Carlyle have it?

The sudden voices downstairs make me forget the implications of the picture — what it actually means that a photo of my wife and son is in David's study. I stuff it in my shirt pocket.

"Hell," I whisper. I edge up to the window and see a police car parked in the lane. As the smell of Indian spices and garlic wafts up on to the landing, I realise that the police guards had taken a chance and slipped out for a curry. Just my luck, then, to have come calling when the coast was temporarily clear.

"Hallet won't even know," a young voice says to the tune of rustling packaging. "Don't see the bloody point of us sitting here all night when nothing's going to happen."

"You're right about that. This place is so remote, I doubt even the bloke who lived here managed to find his way home every night."

"Probably exactly why he did live here. It was safe to lure young girls back. Wants his balls chopping off."

There is a pause, laughter, and the crack of a can. Then they are chattering again, forks clattering, mouths full.

"I overheard the boss. Reckon he knows for sure that this bastard did it. Says he has a sixth sense about it. Don't say anything, but Hallet's worried all right. Worried there isn't a strong enough case. If you ask me, they did the right thing hauling him in. He could've been planning another attack. It could have been my Sally next."

"Mmm," the other one agrees. "Or my sister." But I don't wait around to hear any more. They'll be up to use the bathroom before long. There's no way I can go down those creaky stairs without being heard, so I tread as carefully as I can down the landing to a room I'm praying is on the end wall of the house. I remember a lean-to, a kind of conservatory, and it's at the opposite end of the house to the cops. There's a chance I can slip out on to its roof, shimmy down a drainpipe, or jump for my life. Either way, I can see myself limping back across the fields with a broken ankle to the gateway where I left the car.

Carefully, slowly, I open the door at the end of the passage, shutting it behind me before I turn on the torch. With a little bit of light, I can see quite clearly that I'm in Carlyle's bedroom. My eyes widen and focus on the bed; the thing that drove me here in the first place. It's huge, perfectly made up with an undisturbed quilt. I stare at it, just to make sure. Holding my breath, I silently open the window.

JULIA

"So? David's allowed to have a picture of me." Murray is holding a photo in front of my face, clasping it triumphantly.

"This picture was taken about four years ago when we went on a picnic. Do you remember that day?"

"Yes, I think so." I take the photograph, stare at it. I was heavier then; rosy and plush. "Alex broke that toy car on the way home and howled." I smile at the memory. I like it that David has a photograph of me. He kept it in his study.

"So how do you think David Carlyle happened to have this photograph in his possession? Not to mention what else might have been plastered all over his study walls. The Blu Tack was there. Tape and pins too. Evidence of the evidence." Murray is breathless, like a kid unwrapping presents at Christmas.

"What *might have been* on the walls? That's all you think about, isn't it, Murray? What might have bloody been." The razored comment is only a cover for the anxiety that is starting to build in my stomach.

"Julia. Think. Why would David have this?" He flicks the picture with his finger. "It's a Polaroid photograph. An instant snapshot."

"And?" I say, dizzy with delusion. "Perhaps he found it." It's suddenly obvious. "He'll have seen it on the dresser with all Mum's other knick-knacks and taken it as a souvenir." I like it that David wanted a piece of me.

"Julia, concentrate. We've never owned a Polaroid camera. It wasn't me who took this picture. Your mother didn't come on the picnic. It was just the four of us on that day trip, and none of us took this."

"Well I don't know then," I whisper. "Is it really me?" I peer up close, hoping it's someone else.

"It's you," Murray whispers back. "And it makes me wonder what the other pictures on his study wall were. Were they of you? The kids?" He pauses; allows me a breath. "Or perhaps Grace."

"Murray!" I exclaim with a last shred of hope. "Are you seriously suggesting that David had a hit list and I was on it?" I laugh. I really laugh. "The only list of people David has is his patient list. You're crazy. Crazy and jealous." My mouth's gone dry. "Totally mad."

I'm not sure if I'm really spinning in circles or it just feels like it. Murray is everywhere at once, swirling round me. "Anyway, Ed would have told me by now if they'd found photos of me stuck all over David's wall. That would just be plain creepy." The thought alone stops me spinning and gives me the strength to kick Murray out. "Just go. Please. Isn't there something you can do to get David out?"

"It's late, Julia. There are procedures to follow and there's nothing I can do tonight."

And like a ghost dissolving through a wall, Murray leaves. Just the whisper of his suspicion still hanging in the air.

My phone wakes me even though it's not particularly late. My neck is stiff and I realise that I've dozed off beside the fire. "Nadine?" Her number is displayed. For a second, I don't remember if she's looking after Alex and Flora, but then I recall tucking them into bed earlier.

"Hey," she says. "Are you OK?" I don't answer. I sit upright and muss the tangles from my hair. "I just wanted to tell you that I spoke to my friend Chrissie, the psychologist." A silence, and I think it's poor reception, but my phone still shows five bars. "We need to talk, Jules. Murray too. Can you meet me in the morning?"

"I have work," I say quietly, wondering if this is a Murray-fuelled dream. He has sown the seed of suspicion and it makes me wonder if my whole life is make-believe. "Sure," I reply when I register the gravity of her voice. "Can you come over to Ely during morning break time? We can have coffee."

"No, Julia." My name beds on her tongue before she lets it go. "We need to meet at the police headquarters."

In all the years I've known my mother, I'm sure that she has never lied to me. She is a staunch believer in the truth, and apart from instilling this moral in me throughout my childhood, she also set new foundations of integrity in her foster children.

This was one of the reasons why she was sent the most difficult kids from the local authority. They trusted her to get on with her work. It's no surprise then, just as I'm leaving for school, that a social worker comes calling at Northmire. I'd all but forgotten the message I left at their offices.

"I'm Larry Crest from the foster care department. I'm new and doing the rounds getting to know all our foster parents. Mary Marshall, I presume?" He's young, eager, and wants to make an impression. He pushes the tiniest glasses I have ever seen back on to an equally tiny nose. It takes less than an intake of breath to lie.

"Yes," I say, smiling and extending my hand. "But I was just going out." I don't know why I am doing this.

"Oh, I'm sorry." He almost bows. My mother has made quite a name for herself. "It won't take long."

"No," I reply tersely. I stare at my watch, trying to hide my face. He obviously doesn't know how old Mum is. "Brenna and Gradin have already left for the school bus." I unlock my car. An image flashes through my mind. Gradin locking on to his sister in a gateway — love at first, then anger. The girl never makes it to school. Then Grace is in my thoughts, naked, bloody.

"It isn't them I've come to see, actually. I'm responding to a phone message that was left at our department. It seemed rather important. Perhaps a private meeting is in order?"

Flora and Alex rush out of the house and fight to be first to the car. Damn. He stares straight at them, frowns, but says nothing.

225

When I look at my two children, I can't help superimposing the dismal lives of Brenna and Gradin over the top. What hope do they have? What chance of ever having a life one tenth as stable as Alex and Flora's exists for them? "None," I say, answering my own thoughts. They are misguided kids. They need me, Brenna because she needs a mother figure in her life and Gradin because, despite his age, he is still a child.

"Sorry?"

"I mean none. No reason for you to come. Everything's fine now." Larry looks puzzled. I draw him close. "Look, there was some trouble between them. Sibling stuff. I was going to ask for more background information, but it's all sorted now. Better than ever, in fact." What am I saying? The way Larry's face is easing and a relieved smile is forming, he'll be back in his car, crossing me off his list of concerns.

But I couldn't help it. I couldn't help pretending to be Mum, just to see what she would say if she were speaking. I push my doubts about Gradin's behaviour from my mind and remind myself again that he's only a kid, not capable of much at all.

"Hurry up, Mum," Alex yells from within the car. He hates being late for school.

"Look, I have to go. But Larry," I touch his arm, smile warmly, swallow down all the thousands of reasons why I shouldn't be doing this. "I really appreciate your concern. If I ever need anything, I'll come straight to you. Trust me, Brenna and Gradin couldn't be doing better."

"Well, that's great. Goodbye then, Mrs Marshall." And Larry gets into his car. I wait until he has disappeared from sight before shutting myself in my own car. "Oh God," I say, head welded to the restraint. "What have I done?"

"What, Mum?"

I turn and clasp Alex's hand. He is old enough to never miss a trick. "Sometimes adults have to tell white lies. I didn't want to lie to that man but it just came out." I grimace, realising I sound like a kid myself.

"You did the right thing. You saved Brenna and Gradin from being taken away." He squeezes my hand, being brave, when I know that what he wants more than anything is to go home. As long as Brenna and Gradin are my responsibility, we're staying at Northmire. "Will Dr Carlyle have to tell white lies so they don't lock him up in prison for ever?"

I glare at my son, let go of his hand and start the engine. I'm left wondering what it is that an eleven-year-old sees and I don't.

MARY

Today I am going to tell Julia everything. Everything.

I test my mouth. Flexing my jaw, I accidentally bite my tongue — a sign perhaps that I should keep quiet.

I need to practise. I take a deep breath when a nurse walks past. I stick out my hand like she's a taxi. She turns with an impatient sigh and frown. "Yes, Mary?" They all know my name. They say it a thousand times a day. Then her eyes widen and incredulity sweeps over her. "*Yes*, Mary." Amazing, she's thinking. The one that never speaks has, in some small way, communicated. She's crouching beside me, hopeful, feeling lucky to be the one who finally gets me to talk.

It's like this, nurse, I begin. *If you've got a while, I'd like you to listen to a story.* I wait for her reaction, but she simply tightens her frown, puzzled now, as if I'm wasting her time. She doesn't seem to hear me. *Please, will you help me? Will you help me tell my daughter everything?* It's not like me to beg.

The nurse says nothing. She just blinks at me, and everything that I want to spill out, everything I've ever wanted to confess to Julia crams my head so full that I swear it's oozing as tears from my eyes.

228

"Never mind, love." And before she walks away, she hands me a tissue.

Perhaps it was pride that drove David into the café the very next day. I'd not expected to see him for several weeks. But there he was, bright and breezy because he knew that's what I wanted more than anything — to keep our friendship alive. Anyway, he was the one who'd overstepped the mark.

"Mary," he said, and kissed me in front of Abe. A slice of his respect stamped on my cheek. I touched it. "Coffee and poached eggs, please. And two pieces of toast." He was chipper, happy, and didn't mention our last heated encounter.

I stood motionless for a moment. Abe watched the exchange from behind the counter. The swallow caught halfway down my throat and then the relief came. David still liked me. He still wanted us to be friends. The way he'd forced himself on me in his room had slipped into the past and I saw the fog between us clearing as he sat at his usual table. He unpacked his books. I didn't admit it, but a little part of me was terrified of him.

"Fine," I said about the order, but he didn't hear. David was already brain-deep in revision. I was surprised then — and nervous with guilt, excitement, delight and fear in equal measure — when later he invited me along as his guest to a wedding party.

"It's a big event," he said. "A society wedding." He didn't look up from his books, but I knew he wasn't reading them. He didn't even turn the page as I stood behind him, wondering what it all meant, why he was inviting me, a waitress.

A friend of the family, he'd said. A top Harley Street consultant's daughter, son of a landowner, country house, wealthy guests, publicity . . . it all got mixed up just at the thought of going somewhere with David, at his side, on his arm, as his guest.

I calculated the risk, the implications of attending such an event with David. If we played it right, if we trod carefully, if we kept a glass screen between us, nothing need go wrong. David was my friend. A good friend. I was a café waitress. I served him tea and we chatted. We were mates, chums, acquaintances. That was what it was, wasn't it, because if I'd got it wrong from the start, if I'd misread his intentions, then I didn't think we'd survive another misunderstanding.

The risk assessment complete, I didn't hesitate. "I can't wait," I said, and immediately wished I hadn't.

"I want you to meet some people there," he said. And then he told me that those people were his parents.

David and I suddenly became us. I either had to put a stop to this completely, or succumb to what he wanted. "Your mum and dad?"

He turned right round to face me and tried not to smile. He lifted my hands out of my apron pocket and sandwiched them between his. I was self-conscious because they were rough from the washing-up. "My mother and father are my parents, yes." It was a smile that should have been delivered by an older man, not someone nine years my junior in his first year at medical school. When he was like that — full of confidence, charisma, passion, humour — that was the David I found hardest to resist.

"Silly me," and I spun on my heel hoping it would force him to release my hands, but he held on so tight that my shoulder muscles pulled.

"I want to show you off," he continued, "so make sure you wear something nice." Only then did he let go. I scuttled off to the kitchen feeling like Cinderella.

"He's just a boy. Just a boy," I muttered a thousand times as I waited for the order to be cooked. I wrung out a tea towel so that the rope of it burned my palms. "Yet I'm playing with a man." Nothing could have stopped the rush in my stomach as I delivered David's breakfast. "I'll look stunning," I promised calmly, defying my true feelings. "You won't recognise me."

All good weddings take place on sunny days. In truth, summer hadn't let up for weeks, and someone had been watering this particular lawn, going against the drought regulations. There was a marquee, a string quartet sending delicate notes fluttering between the guests like confetti, flowers jostling in the pre-storm breeze that came most afternoons now, and little girls in crumpled silk dresses which would have started the day perfect.

The marriage ceremony had only been open to close family and friends. The village church was too small to seat all the guests, and afterwards, the chosen few walked down the leaf-lined sunny lane back to the manor. David, of course, had attended the service and sent a car to fetch me to take me to the reception. I would be returning with him in the morning, after a night in a nearby hotel.

The words wouldn't come out — *never* came out — about separate rooms, about slipping between the sheets together, about me wanting him more than anything despite knowing it was wrong, or about waking up alone. In the end, the decision never needed to be made.

"It's a beautiful house," I said, staring up at the weathered stone. I was getting that feeling. The same one I got when I first moved to Cambridge. I knew it would pass. I just needed some more wine. I threaded my arm through the crook of David's elbow and knew we looked ridiculous. Older woman — sister, even — vying for a go with the young doctor. I didn't care what anyone thought.

"The Boseley-Greene family has owned this estate for aeons. All of this crowd come from similar backgrounds. They're all loaded." I imagined he was including his own family in this. He rarely spoke of his parents, and since I'd arrived, I'd been looking out for them. I wouldn't rush him. We had all evening. I wasn't even sure I wanted to meet them.

"Rich, then?" I said, laughing. We ambled through the guests.

David laughed too. "You don't know. You just don't know." He gave me that older man smile again. I was growing to like it.

Suddenly, David brought us to a halt. "Sarah, Nigel, Vicki, Pete, Tanya . . ." The recital was endless. "I'd like you to meet Mary."

232

And there I was in the centre of a group. They were all young like David, all beautiful, all self-assured, all not like me. I didn't think they were Cambridge students. I didn't recognise them from David's posse at the café, if they were. A dozen pairs of eyes watched me, expectantly. They knew instantly I wasn't one of them.

"Hello, Mary," Sarah had scorched red hair and a gown I swear I'd seen on the front of *Vogue*.

"Hi." I was determined not to feel inferior. I looked good, stunning even. I'd saved my tips and spent them on a cream dress and a hat. The neckline dipped low and a purple corsage matched my shoes. David hadn't taken his eyes off me since I'd stepped from the car. "I'm Mary Marshall," I added in case they cared.

"Are you a friend of the bride or groom?"

I wasn't sure. "Bride, I think. Is that correct, David?" But when I looked round, David was gone. A void where he once was, and when I looked again to double-check, another man had stepped into his place.

"I'm Jonathon," he whispered to me. His hair shone like faded copper coins, an unusual touch of red that glinted in the late afternoon sun. "David's best friend from school."

I could tell instantly that he was the brother of Sarah, the young woman with the fiery hair. Piece by piece, I was patchworking a life around David. He had always been so evasive when it came to discussing his past.

It was dizzying, and I was almost as taken by Jonathon as I was by David. I loved the fun of it all — the people, the music, the designer clothes and expensive cars, the backdrop of the manor house. Besides, Jonathon was nice to me while David was gone. He confirmed that he was Sarah's brother. He held out his hand and I took it. "I'm charmed," he said. Like David, he was young. Like David, he was fascinating, and I felt utterly beautiful in his company.

"I see you've met the enemy." David was back, passing me champagne, blinking in the sunlight. "Good to see you, Jonno." The two of them exchanged a brief handshake, a pat on the back.

They both wore tailored grey suits, and I soon learnt that their parents used to take holidays together. Jonathon's father, like David's, was a surgeon. We chatted, and once or twice, when the conversation turned to me, to my life, to my meagre existence, to my tiny flat, my dead-end job at the café, my failed entry into university, that's when I skilfully sidestepped and threaded their words back to their privileged existence. I winked at David. I was enjoying being part of this threesome.

"Have you met Elizabeth yet?" Jonathon asked, but I didn't hear him initially. The passing guests milling in and out of the blowsy marquee were too attractive to ignore. All those prominent, educated people at my fingertips. "Mary?"

"Sorry?" The champagne was fizzing my thoughts.

"Elizabeth Carlyle. I asked if you'd met her?"

"No, Jon, she hasn't." David answered for me. "She has that treat yet to come." Both men laughed. "Mother is around somewhere but seems to be avoiding everyone. Last time I saw her, she was sobbing into a pillow."

"Oh, that's terrible," I said. "Shouldn't we find her?" Another piece for the patchwork. A clue about David's mother.

David laughed. "If you haven't met her, you won't understand that she *likes* to sob." He gave a devious grin. David's mother was an enigma, just like her son. It wasn't until I saw her that I understood completely.

Matron walks past but then stops; a second thought. "If you've got something to say, Mrs Marshall, you can say it to me." She believes it's that easy. I want to demand that she fetch Julia, bring her to my side so that I can tell her everything, warn her, plead with her to get away before it's too late. But how do I do that when the right words don't even exist?

"Perhaps your daughter will visit today, and that pretty little granddaughter of yours. What's her name now?"

Flora, I tell her silently. I can only hope that yet another generation doesn't become infected. Seeing him with Julia, with the children, it's a glimpse of what might have been. All I can do is silently watch, holding my breath, praying that my daughter treads a different path. How can I risk losing everything I've ever loved? She'd hate me after all these years.

Matron is right. Some time later, Julia and Flora arrive. "You don't look any better, Mum. You're very pale. Are they feeding you enough? Have they done any more tests yet? What medication are you on?" My daughter reaches out to touch me but then thinks better of it. Her questions float between us, brushing our faces like cobwebs. "Anyway, Flora made this for you."

Flora creeps up to me — not the perky little girl who used to chase chickens and gather fallen apples in her skirt, but rather a tamed, forlorn creature who has obviously been told that her grandma is very ill.

I made you a card with things at your farm, she signs. Her little hands pass over a piece of brown cardboard box squashed in half. She places it on my lap. It's smeared with white glue that's still wet in places. Wispy feathers, spongy moss, twigs and tiny stones cling on. Flora pushes a twig back into its bed of glue when it falls off.

It's to make you better, Grandma, she signs.

And by one ounce out of a million tons, it does.

Julia spends most of her visit fussing with the nurses. She's agitated, that's for sure, and doesn't seem in the least bit interested in talking to me. She flits between the day room, where I'm sitting with Flora as she colours, and the nurses' station. Down the corridor I hear her voice spinning demands at the staff. I know from experience that they will smile politely and tell her they'll mention it to the doctor when he does his rounds.

"You don't quite understand what I'm saying, do you?" Julia has followed the matron back into the day room. "There are conflicting reports and I don't know what to believe."

"Mrs Marshall." Matron looks up from her clipboard. She is trying to tick off and account for all her patients. Someone does this every hour. Now she has been interrupted, she hangs the board by her side. "It's a matter for the doctor," she explains predictably. "Your mother is stable. I will certainly mention your concerns to the consultant on Monday."

I hear something from Julia — a protest that she can't visit on Monday, something about mixed-up reports, something about prison. Then her voice washes away down the corridor as she tries another nurse. Flora looks up at me from the floor. She is sitting in a patch of temporary sunlight. An angel sent.

Flora, I sign, and if hands could whisper, this would be it. Come and sit on my knee.

Flora frowns and glances around for her mother. What have they told her?

Come on, I won't bite. Perhaps my words aren't clear for her. My fingers form limited outlines as I don't want to draw attention to myself. Come here so Grandma can tell you a secret.

At this, Flora hops up, abandoning her felt pens like she is about to learn all the mysteries of the universe. It's as easy as that to win a child's attention. I could coax her into my car with the promise of puppies and candy. I could drag her into my mind by pledging a glimpse of my past and a flash of her future.

What is it, Grandma? Are you getting better yet?

The truth is, I tell her carefully, that I am not ill at all.

★ ★ ★

Elizabeth Carlyle was see-through thin. She made a brief but memorable appearance just after the food was served, just as the meringue and gateau plates were being cleared away. Shortly before this, David had disappeared from my side once again, and I later discovered that he was inside the big house with his mother, discussing things, he told me, as he downed yet another glass of champagne at the table. We'd both had too much.

"Here she comes," he said, as if he was announcing royalty. The other guests seemed to instinctively know when to turn their heads. "Bloody decent of her to make an appearance at last." David had removed his jacket and his cuffs hung wide open around his wrists. He loosened his tie. "She's getting more attention than the bride." The bitterness was palpable.

"Introduce me," I said, leaning over to David, but only because I'd had the champagne. Elizabeth Carlyle looked terrifying. She cruised the cream carpet that led to the dance floor with the elegance of a black swan gliding on a still lake. "She's beautiful," I whispered truthfully. David was sprawled in his chair, playing with the cutlery he hadn't used.

He clattered the knife on to the table. "No. No, she's not," he said brusquely, resignedly, angrily. He stood up.

David strode over to his mother and roughly intercepted her on the dance floor. The string quartet started to play. I watched the battle taking place between mother and son. Elizabeth danced reluctantly, wanting to escape, although still desiring to steal the show. From the unnatural tightness in David's steps to the ice in his mother's eyes, it told me there had been sour words between them earlier; perhaps all of David's life.

David gripped Elizabeth as they tracked a path across the floor. His fingers laced between her ribs as if he would never let her go. But a minute later, he did. Elizabeth Carlyle swept from the dance floor as soon as her son's arms fell to his sides.

"What's going on?" I asked Jonathon. He had come to sit in David's vacant chair.

"They hate each other." Jonathon poured me more champagne and left me wondering. "So what's a nice girl like you doing with David anyway?" By now, a cluster of his friends had drawn around — Sarah, his sister, included. They all wanted to hear my answer.

"Yes, tell us how you met?" Sarah asked. Her cheeks were touched with red, to match her hair, and the same colour showed up in her eyes as she waited for my reply.

I laughed nervously. I didn't know how much David had already told them. "We met in Cambridge," I began. They would probably assume I was a mature student or worked on the university campus.

"Hey, Mary," the young man opposite said. I'd forgotten his name. "Any chance of . . .?" He grinned and held up his empty champagne glass.

"Oh." My reaction was instant. I didn't stop to think. The bottle was next to me, and I stood up, grateful for the reprieve. I circled the table and refilled his glass.

"While you're there, Mary," his partner said, "can I have a top-up too, please?" But the bottle ran out halfway through her measure. They all looked at me expectantly. "I'll go and get another one," I said, still not realising, not even as a round of laughter trailed me to the bar. When I returned and filled all seven glasses at our table, there were more requests.

"I see some people have cheese and biscuits."

"And coffee."

"Yes, can we have coffee, Mary?"

"I appear to have lost my napkin, Mary. Could you fetch me another?"

The comments came with increasing accuracy, and it was only after I returned from the buffet with platters of cheese and extra napkins that I began to understand what was going on.

Finally, ending the cruel banter, it was Jonathon who stood up and barked, "Enough!" The group instantly ceased their play, although none of them appeared particularly sheepish. "Come with me, Mary," he said and led me away. I was furious but too intimidated to show it. Still dazzled by their wealth, their status, their proximity, I allowed myself to be saved by Jonathon. I didn't know where we were going or why, but I was thankful to be out of the marquee and plunged into the fresh evening air.

"Thanks," I said when we were well away from the reception party. I bowed my head in shame. "I wonder what happened to David." I'd cast a glance around the dance floor before leaving.

240

Jonathon smiled and placed a hand on my shoulder. "They're a cocksure lot but they had no right to treat you like that. I apologise on their behalf." He didn't mention David.

"Accepted," I said weakly. I swept a glance around the terrace in case David was leaning against the wall, smoking within the boughs of wisteria. I couldn't see him. "Before you ask, it's true. I am a waitress."

"David already told me how you met."

Suddenly, I couldn't have felt more separated from their world. David had seen fit to tell Jonathon where I worked, as if prior warning was needed to get over the shock of him associating with a mere waitress. I tried to cling on to the last shreds of self-respect. "I like the work. I meet all sorts of people." I was lying, of course. The work was mostly tedious and hard. After each shift, my feet ached, my mind stagnated and the pay was terrible. "Our customers are interesting, educated and come in from the university."

"Interesting like David," Jonathon added, slipping his arm through mine. We walked down to the lake — a spreading expanse of shimmering indigo — and all the while I was searching for him, David, in case he was near. The early moon broke from behind the willow fronds, killing the trail of orange still left in the sky from the setting sun.

"Yes, like David," I confirmed. "We've become good friends. *Just* friends," I added with a smile. It was an opportunity to let Jonathon know how I felt, as if my feelings would be better understood by David the more I spread them around.

"Mary." Jonathon stopped and turned, moving me to face him squarely. "David is besotted with you. He's in love with you." I felt Jonathon's breath on my cheek. It was as light as the breeze floating across the water. The words drifted away like litter and I wanted them back; I wanted to hear them a thousand times more even though I knew it was the beginning of the end. I stood with my mouth open.

Exactly what I had been desperate to avoid was happening. Once David succumbed to his feelings, it would follow that our friendship would crumble. I couldn't allow things to transfer to a different level, however tempting, however much I wanted to. I reminded myself daily that I was much older than David and that I needed him for other reasons. We were worlds apart and it was never going to work between us.

"He told you this?" I asked.

But before Jonathon could reply, I saw the silhouette of David's figure striding down to the lake's edge. My heart fluttered. So it didn't look as if we were parcelled up in secrets, Jonathon had the good sense to continue with our walk. He loosely wound a guiding arm around my back, leading me on. In a moment, we were perched on the edge of the small wooden landing deck at the shore.

"I've brought sustenance." David strangled bottles of champagne in his fists. Glasses and another bottle were bracketed under his other arm. He was breathless, exhilarated and grinned as he stepped on to the deck. His hair fell over his face and he didn't have a hand free

242

to brush it away. "God knows I need it after Mother." He didn't seem upset that I was alone with Jonathon.

A rowing boat was tethered to the landing by a rope. It bobbed in the water as David settled himself next to us. "You didn't introduce me to her," I said, thankful I had escaped the trauma. I relieved David of the bottles. Surely we'd had enough to drink already.

"Fuck, you don't need to meet her, Mary. She's cold. The original Ice Queen." David sat on the bleached wood and clawed back a bottle from me. He picked off the foil and unwound the wire. No one spoke as the cork erupted into the night.

I set out the glasses and David stared at me as he poured. His deep eyes gave away none of his thoughts. The champagne fizzed up to the rim and David topped up the levels when it sank down again. He didn't spill a drop. "To friends and lovers," he said, raising his glass. He continued to stare at me, leaving me in no doubt that what Jonathon had told me was true. The bubbles in my glass rose to the surface, popping, as if they never existed.

Music and laughter, sent to us from the party on the increasing breeze, broke the silence. I raised my glass. "To friends," I said, hoping to diffuse the weight of David's toast.

We sipped, smiling through the champagne, all apparently agreeing that we were drinking to friendship. I can't recall who suggested it; whose voice it was that changed the rest of my life.

"Let's take the boat out."

★ ★ ★

Flora, I say. Do you understand?

We've been signing away as if there's nothing wrong. In between asking about school, Milo and the farm, I explain things to her that I've not been able to tell anyone. Flora's silence makes it easy. She sits there, big-eyed, watching as my old hands offer a selection of child-friendly truths.

We connect — her young eyes dazzling mine. She nods. She understands.

With arthritic yet graceful hands I say: Don't tell anyone, Flora. It's a secret. Do you promise not to tell?

Flora pulls a face that convinces me my secret is easy to keep safe. Without another thought, she continues chatting about fun things again; things that are familiar in her world.

As long as someone knows, I think; just as long as I'm not the only one. I pull Flora close for a hug. This time her hair smells of marzipan.

I stare out of the window. There is a small lake at the end of the hospital grounds. I see a sparkle jump off the water before a cloud skims in front of the sun. There is a boat bobbing about. A single person on board.

You told me you don't like lakes, Grandma. Why are you staring at it?

I reply with my arms slung around her waist and my nose pressed into her curls. Because sometimes, my darling, it just goes that you can't help being attracted to the things that terrify you the most.

244

JULIA

At school, as I walk through the corridors to my classroom, the staff look at me with equal measures of pity and suspicion. The substitute teacher is sitting at my desk and treats me as if I'm an impostor. Apparently I didn't give enough notice for my return to work.

"Ah," he says with a telling lift of his chin. "Mrs Marshall. You're back."

"So no one told you that I was coming in today?" The sub shakes his head and there follows a silent battle for my desk. I put my handbag on the corner and hang my coat on the hook behind the door. He stays put.

"Hey, Mrs M. How's things?" A couple of kids greet me as if I've never been away, while several are apprehensive about talking to me. They associate me with Grace; don't want the same to happen to them.

"So," I say, leaning on my desk. "Looks like you've kept things in pretty good order." In fact, everything looks *out* of order because there's not much on my desk at all. There are a few assignments neatly stacked, but they appear to be marked already. I don't remember leaving my classroom like this, but then again, I don't remember things being in a mess. Not compared to how things are now.

"You have a class of willing and able students."

I think of Grace in hospital. Her spirit is still in this classroom; her bright, alert face always keen to offer up answers.

"Let's go and see the head," I say. The sub rises solemnly, as if we are about to appear in front of a judge. "Get on and read Act Two of the play," he tells the class. "There's a test later." I make a mental note not to have one.

Patricia, the head teacher, seems as surprised to see me at school as everyone else. "Good God, woman. Are you back?" She's always been like that. That's why she's the principal, I suppose.

"I did telephone. I know things have been a bit up and down recently, and for that I apologise. It's been —"

"No apologies. Everyone here is still in shock. You must be too." She speaks in bullet points.

"I am, and —"

"Mr Hargraves. Thank you for your assistance. I believe Year Seven is down a teacher today. Wretched virus. Would you be so kind?" He doesn't get a chance to protest.

We leave the head's office feeling like naughty schoolkids and depart where the corridor forks. "Thanks for holding the fort," I say, wondering how I will cope alone.

Back in the classroom, I take a deep breath. And then the register, skipping quickly past the gap that comes between Cochrane and Davies.

No one mentions Grace until period three. Her empty desk glows neon, somehow taking up far more space than the other, occupied desks. I can't stop looking at it; imagining her muddy, naked body sitting there; thinking of it now, lifeless in a coma. I deliver the essays back to my pupils.

"What did Grace get for her essay?" Josh leers at me. He's always been the one to push things too far.

"Other students' grades are confidential, Josh."

"What did she look like when you found her? Was there much blood?"

"Josh Ellis, this is not appropriate behaviour. If you don't settle down and get on with the tasks on the whiteboard, then I'll have no option but to send you to the deputy head."

"Or beat me up."

I should have turfed him out there and then along with the other pupils whose sniggers rippled through the class. But Grace wouldn't want that. She was tolerant and thoughtful, and I'd always seen her differently to the other kids. She was more mature, more able to relate to adults, perhaps therefore attractive to David. I swat the thought from my head.

The bell rings. "Remember, complete the English question sheet by Monday, because we'll need it for classwork next week. And if you have any completed homework set by Mr Hargraves then let me have it now." It's hard to compete against the scraping chairs and chatter as the class evacuates for mid-morning break, but suddenly there are twenty or so pieces of work slapped on to my desk as students leave.

The last to depart is Amy, a shy girl who is flipping through the leaves of a binder. "I did do it, honestly." Her fair cheeks flush crimson as I approach.

"The dog didn't get it then?" I smile.

She laughs without looking up. "Perhaps." Then, after rummaging in her pack, "Ah, here it is. Sorry it's creased."

"Thanks, Amy." She turns to leave, still not looking at me. "Amy," I say, halting her. "You're friends with Grace, aren't you?"

She nods. Hangs her head as if not talking about Grace will make it all go away.

"Was there anything unusual going on in her life before she was . . . before this happened? Was she upset about anything?" I see the girl swallow; too big a lump for someone who has no food in her mouth.

"Not really."

"Was she happy? Did she tell you any secrets? It's important, Amy."

She stares up at me through wisps of long hair. "I already told the police everything I know. Which is nothing." Her voice is fractured.

"OK, Amy. It's OK." The hand on her shoulder does it.

"She made me promise, all right, so just leave me alone." Amy charges out of the classroom, knocking over a chair on her way.

"Find me after school," I call after her, but with all the trouble banging about in her head, I doubt she hears me.

"Nadine, I can't possibly come to police headquarters with you. If I miss any more work, I'll get the sack." We are standing in the street outside Denby High School, having dodged the single remaining reporter who holds vigil at the gate. Now he knows I'm the one who made the discovery, he's not going to let up. He fires a couple of questions at me as we pass but I ignore him. It makes me wonder if he knows about my relationship with David. That would get the presses rolling. Teacher and doctor involved in schoolgirl attack.

Nadine is unimpressed. She has driven from Cambridge before her shift. "Can't you just tell me whatever it is here?" I continue, jamming a chunk of loose hair back inside my clip.

"I'm sorry, Julia. I understand." She stares hard at the journalist and turns her back on him, shielding me from the camera that's slung around his neck. Nadine's face stiffens and my heart kicks up a gear.

"What, Nadine? What is it?"

She takes my arm and we walk away from school, getting caught up in the tide of pupils heading down to the row of shops for sweets and crisps and cans of drink. For a second, I imagine everything feels normal.

"Chrissie Weaver called me. She looked into your mother's file at The Lawns." Nadine talks slowly, pacing the news in time with our slow steps. "It all seems a bit . . . unusual. Especially concerning her admission." Nadine's grip on my arm tightens. "For a start, there's no written report of any kind about the MRI scan that Mary had. Those results were what warranted her hospital stay in the first place."

"Well that's easy to explain." Nadine is way off the mark here. "It's bound to be a mix-up between NHS and private systems. The scan was done by the NHS and The Lawns is a private hospital." I consider other possibilities. "Or perhaps one of the doctors was reviewing the results and forgot to put them back in the file."

"I'm afraid not, Julia. Chrissie's checked out all these possibilities and she's talked to the nurses too. There's simply no reference anywhere to her MRI scan or the results." Nadine slows our pace virtually to a halt. It gives me time to think.

"That's just not possible. David should know about this. He'd be furious." Then I have a sick feeling as I remember where David is. My mother will not be on his list of priorities any more. "David's paying good money for that place. I must tell him." I'm thinking out loud, wondering what will happen to Mum if the account doesn't get paid.

"Thanks for bringing up the second issue." Nadine stops and turns through ninety degrees to face me. A turbulent stream of schoolkids flows around us. "Chrissie also checked with the accounts centre at the hospital and couldn't find out who's paying the bill. Naturally they're not allowed to release specific details, but they confirmed it wasn't David's name on the account. Chrissie said they implied a business or a trust."

"Nadine, I don't understand what you're saying to me. None of this really warrants a special trip to see me, let alone a crusade to police headquarters. Missing medical reports and mysterious hospital bills are hardly going to interest Ed and his team, even if the information does happen to come from his wife."

"Oh, Julia." Nadine takes hold of my hands and suddenly the swill of kids subsides and we are all alone, standing beneath an avenue of trees that looks like it's been charcoaled on to the bleak winter townscape. "There's more —"

"Stop! Right now." I've had enough. I snap my hands from Nadine's mercy grip. "Why is everyone out to nail David before he's even stood trial? Murray says that the CPS is teetering about his case anyway . . ."

My hand comes up slowly to my face, my fingers spreading to cover my mouth. But it's too late. I've just told the wife of the detective who's charged David that the CPS don't like the look of the evidence. "Nadine, I can't see you again. Not until this is all over." And the hardest thing to do as I turn and run isn't abandoning my sister-in-law but not finding out what else she was going to say.

I've seen Murray with other women before. He fanned through a variety of girlfriends before we got together, some suitable, some downright ridiculous. So when I see them tucked inside *Alcatraz*, laughing, impressing, overstating every move in an obvious mating ritual, it's tempting to pass judgement like I once would have done, when I was just a kid and waiting to grow up for Murray.

I don't mind interrupting their little get-together. She's about my age, a whole lot less stressed than me, and isn't wearing any make-up but still looks great. She holds a glass of red wine as if it's Murray's hand steadying her as the boat yaws from my arrival. The first thing he says is quite responsible.

"Where are the children?" This shows me that he's not had very much to drink yet.

My reply, however, doesn't sound much like it will win any parenting awards. "I left them with Brenna. She's quite capable." I added that to at least show I'd considered the arrangement. "I won't stay long." My mind races back. Alex had mentioned "Dad's friend". This must be her. If I'm honest, I don't like it.

"You're right. You won't stay long. In fact, not another minute. I want you to go right back and look after our children. Leaving them in Brenna's care is madness, Julia. The girl is a liability to herself, let alone our kids." By now, Murray has me backed up against the stove to make this as much of a private moment as possible. His friend tries not to watch our exchange but I can see she's sneaking a look. I don't breathe, which makes my reply barely there.

"Did you hear anything from the CPS?"

"Tomorrow, Julia. That will be tomorrow at the earliest."

Part of me relaxes and part of me wants to claw at Murray, to beg him to find out now, even though it's nine o'clock in the evening and everywhere will be closed. Don't drink any more, I beg him in my head. Be alert for David's case. I slip from entrapment and smell diesel and alcohol. It's Murray's personal cologne.

After I leave, I don't mean to stand on the towpath for so long, but when Murray shunts the hatch closed, the glowing rectangle of window in the side of *Alcatraz* gives me a glimpse into his life after me. It shows that his life is moving on — behaving in a way he hasn't done in years; teaching another woman about himself. Posturing, grinning, astonishing, leaving out the bad bits, bigging up the parts I probably ignored.

Not knowing I'm still on the towpath, Murray snaps closed the ghastly orange curtains. As I turn and walk away, sadness forces a sigh from my chest. I admit, it suits my needs for David to be innocent. Am I simply believing what I want to believe? Like I did with Murray for so many years, am I turning David into someone he's not? Walking down the towpath, I am left with an image of Murray and his lady friend burned on the inside of my eyes. As I blink, it morphs into David until my eyes are flashing open and shut so fast that they all become one.

Murray once had a girlfriend called Cynthia. She was taller than him and her knees and elbows, bursting with growth, were knotted like the joints of a young tree. Cynthia knew all the latest fashions, had hundreds of records, wore her hair big, flicked and backcombed. She was pretty much the coolest girl in school.

While Murray was dating her, I dissolved into the flat landscape of Witherly. I became a child again, especially when Cynthia was around. Them aged seventeen and me just turned a paltry twelve, I didn't stand a chance against Cynthia's long painted nails and shimmering court shoes.

I watched and waited, virtually held my breath for the entire eight weeks they dated, in case one day Murray should be back with his mates, back on the sports field, back hanging out with his younger sister's friend.

Then it happened. Cynthia was expelled from school and no one ever heard from her again. It was as if she vanished clean off the face of the earth. The only trail she left behind was a two-column-inch report in the local paper with a sullen mug shot balanced above. *Juvenile Thief Found Guilty*.

It took a while, but gradually Murray filtered back into his circle of friends, ripped around the villages on his bike, and teased Nadine and me when he baby-sat in the holidays.

"Cynthia wouldn't do anything like that," he insisted. "Someone got it wrong. She never nicked anything in her life." Murray was certain, wanted the entire world to know how certain he was, that the girl he loved was as clean as could be.

We all thought he was sticking up for her because he didn't want to look stupid for going out with her. He couldn't bear it that the love of his life had nicked all her trendy clothes, her chunky jewellery, her make-up and twelve-inch records. It made their true love fake as well. Defending Cynthia even after her court case was Murray's futile attempt at self-preservation. No one liked to look silly.

Truth was, he plain didn't see it. Love, devotion, need — the sheer size of his affection — simply got in the way of the truth.

The car is wedged on to the verge where river and road meet. I get in and turn the key. My mind is still on the towpath, stirring thoughts of Cynthia, wine, David and Murray. I drive home but don't recall any of the short journey.

When I step inside the house and everything is calm — Brenna and Flora are playing a lopsided game of snap — the notion that I have got it all so completely wrong, that my belief in David's innocence is foolish and blind, makes me feel ill. It doesn't take much for me to crack.

"You think keeping Flora up this late is responsible behaviour?" I glare at Brenna. The girl's cheeks colour and her eyes widen.

"I'm sorry, I didn't —"

"No, you damn well didn't, did you?" Whatever I'm saying, it's harsher than I intended. The laziest kid in my class wouldn't get this treatment. "She's eight years old, Brenna. For heaven's sake, she needs to go to bed and you're playing cards with her. You and your brother are a liability." She doesn't deserve my attack.

Flora slams her hand down on the pile of cards and makes a barking noise. Grinning, alert as a rabbit, she waits for Brenna's response. But Brenna simply stands up, the crescents of tears held back only by the tilt of her head. She runs out of the room.

"Damn," I say. And as Flora scowls at me for ruining the nice time she was having with Brenna, it's all the proof I need to know that my judgement has gone awry for sure.

MURRAY

Nadine is close to tears. "She won't answer her phone and doesn't return my messages. She told me she won't see me until this is all over. Whether we like it or not, Julia's lost her heart to a criminal."

I am stunned at what she's just told me. Chrissie has done more than her fair share of digging into Mary's case, making me wonder how much Nadine pushed her. Her dislike of the man, even though she has never met him, is almost equal to mine.

"None of what Chrissie found out goes any way to convincing me that this mess will ever be over. Not cleanly, anyway. One wily reporter will soon sniff out that Julia is involved with Carlyle." Nadine wipes her nose, trying to look as if she's not really upset. "Let's face it, Murray, Julia was the one who found Grace, and she also happens to be a teacher at the victim's school. It doesn't look good. Not good at all."

I'm trying to understand what she's implying, not to mention what Chrissie found out about Mary.

"You think that Julia will become a suspect by association?" I sigh. I'm hot; we're sitting too close to the log fire. I feel sick.

"It's a possibility. Your ex-wife might be forced to give evidence in return for relocation and a new identity. What's that going to do to your kids?"

"Not quite ex," I say, and for a second that hurts me more than everything Nadine is telling me. "Just how reliable is your friend Chrissie?" And I am slammed with a barrage of Chrissie's qualifications and dedication to psychiatric research, not to mention the societies and professional bodies she belongs to and just how deep the level of information that she has access to runs. "So she's reliable?" My pint does nothing for my churning stomach.

"Solid."

I run through what all this means. "And she was absolutely sure that Mary's admission had nothing to do with the MRI scan results?"

"Positive."

"And the treatment Carlyle requested for Mary isn't suitable for the problems he claimed Mary had anyway?"

"Yep."

I stare at my sister. She wouldn't lie to me. All the years I've known her tumble through my mind. She's always been there for me, hauling me home from the pub, giving me a place to stay, mopping up my spilt life. She's also married to the detective who arrested Carlyle. I happen to be the defendant's lawyer. The conflict rears up and slaps me in the face.

"Look, I might as well be honest." I know I'll regret this. "The CPS is currently reviewing the case and there's a rumour that the charges may be dropped altogether. Although I can't see Ed ever giving up on it."

"But . . .?"

"It's complicated. In simple terms, if they don't think Ed's got enough on Carlyle to secure a conviction, then they'll let it drop and he walks."

"Yes, that's what Julia told me about the lack of evidence. That's when she got angry with herself and refused to speak to me." Nadine drops a half-eaten bag of crisps on to the small round table. "Why on earth did you take this case, Murray? What in God's name did you think you were doing?"

It doesn't take me long to answer. "Loving Julia," I reply simply, when in truth none of it is simple at all. I resist the urge to down my pint in one go. "We had this game, Julia and I, when we were kids. Do you remember?" I don't think I played it with Nadine. "It was pretty stupid really, but it made her giggle and I liked that. I liked seeing Julia happy."

Nadine shakes her head. "What, Murray?"

"She would tell me to do things or say things to strangers, and if I didn't comply, I had to do a forfeit." We both step back in time, each remembering a slightly different view of a similar past. "Once she told me to half frighten an old man to death when he walked round the corner."

"And did you?"

"Of course," I say, sipping, remembering. "I nearly gave him a heart attack. He marched me right home to Mum but I didn't care. I did anything for Julia."

"*Do* anything for Julia," Nadine corrects, and we both know she's right.

"So," I say as we step out into the sunlight. It's cold but bright. "Where does that leave us?" Chrissie's findings don't make sense. Why would Carlyle lie about scan results and prescribe the wrong treatment for Mary?

"Us?" She knows she is in this too.

"Are you going to tell Ed?" I shiver and button up my coat. There are things I can't tell her about Carlyle however much I want to. I remind myself I have to win this case for Julia. For us.

"Of course I am." Nadine fishes in her bag for her keys. "Why would I want Carlyle to walk?"

"Why would *I*?" None of this is fair. "Either way, I get to fall on my sword. If Carlyle gets off, then he steps into the sunset with Julia. If he doesn't, then I'm bust anyway because I'll be the loser she suspects I always have been."

At that, Nadine looks sad. "You're no loser, Murray. But you've got to follow your instincts. Is Carlyle guilty of attacking that girl? If he is and he gets off, what about your wife and children then?"

"Oh God, Nadine. I love her. I want her back. I love her so desperately that I'm even defending her criminal lover." No sister should see her brother break down, so I cover my face with big gloved hands. It goes some way to hiding my pain. The few tears I manage soak into my palms.

"Then go get her," Nadine says before leaving. The look on her face tells me that she can't stand to watch me fall apart. She scuttles off to her car and I watch her drive away, feeling more alone than I've ever been in my life.

I receive the news that the CPS have bailed Carlyle at exactly the same moment I hear Dick Porsche pop the cork from a bottle of champagne. I can't decide if this is an omen. Another promotion for Dick, no doubt, and it draws quite a crowd in reception.

"Thanks for your call," I say and hang up, dazed by the news.

I step out of my poky office and join the happy throng at reception. "Don't mind if I do," I say to Dick as he passes out the flutes of champagne. "What's the occasion?" Drinking this stuff doesn't seem wrong, especially if there is good cause.

Sheila sidles up to me before Dick can reply. "Any news on the bad doctor?" she asks. "We can really work the publicity on this one, Murray. Don't screw up."

"I got bail," I say in a fake American accent, trying to hide the smile. Truth is, it wasn't *me* who got the bail; rather that the CPS has chucked out the case anyway. But Sheila doesn't need to know that yet. I tip up the champagne flute. It's just what I need and the only time I've ever been grateful to Dick.

"Who's a clever boy then?" she says, playfully swiping her finger under my chin. "Conditions?"

"The usual," I reply. "He's not to leave Cambridgeshire and has to report to the nick every three days." I don't tell Sheila about the third condition. She seems satisfied and wanders off to chat with Gerry. The pair glance at me occasionally, no doubt discussing my future.

"We've just got engaged," Dick says from a few feet away. He's grinning inanely, snuggled up to Olivia, the girl who answers the phone. I give up trying to lip-read what Sheila's saying and walk over to the happy couple.

"So that's why the bubbly's out, huh?" I stand over him, suddenly feeling powerful because Carlyle got bail. When I've cleared his name, this whole wretched business will be over. I'll still have a job, and a chance of getting Julia back. "Well congratulations, Dick." I say "Dick" very slowly. I stare at the tie he's wearing. It's horrible. "And to you too, Olivia." She squirms on the leather sofa.

Dick may well have a better job than me, an office with city views and a car that's more like a penthouse apartment than a vehicle. And now he has a pretty young thing with a fake tan, straightened hair and the whitest nails ever, suckered to his side. I don't care. Things are looking up.

"I bet your dick's bigger than mine too, isn't it . . ." A dramatic pause. ". . . Dick?"

The room falls silent — three senior partners glaring my way and everyone with their glasses halted halfway to their open mouths. It didn't come out right.

Shrugging, I knock back the champagne, which turns out to be cava, and fight the bubbles brewing in my nose — perhaps from the drink, perhaps from a dizzy sense that things are coming to a head. I leave the building. The thought of Carlyle walking free, right back to Julia, has done nothing for my mood.

★ ★ ★

I pay a visit to Whitegate Prison before returning to my sinking boat, before I allow myself to disintegrate completely. There are matters to take care of, and as his representative, I have a duty to brief Carlyle on developments.

"Looks like you're out of here," I tell him flatly, once I'm through security and we are seated in the interview room.

Carlyle's face relaxes, slowly absorbing the implications. "That's good," he says in a measured way. No thanks for me, no pat on the back. He doesn't know that I didn't really do much.

"The CPS isn't convinced by the police evidence." In my mind, I see Ed beating his fist against the wall, red-faced, yelling at his officers. "Of course, the inquiry will continue and the charges against you could be reinstated at any time should more . . . convincing evidence come to light. So don't go booking any holidays."

"I have complete faith in the justice system," Carlyle states blankly, as if he knows something I don't.

"So do I," I say, meaning quite the opposite. "For now, we need to build a case around what we know. Be prepared for the worst." It doesn't occur to me until much later that I'm acting exactly like his lawyer.

Alcatraz has several inches of water in her hull. I have a bucket that's effectively the size of an eggcup because there's a split just above the base. I start to bail out; hip flask in one hand, green water in the other. I'm chucking it all around — Carlyle's involvement with Grace, my feelings for Julia, the kids, Mary's health,

Chrissie's findings. None of it makes sense, least of all that my home will soon be on the river bed.

Someone's come aboard.

"Hello?" The boat tips from one side to the other, mini waves slapping at her arthritic hull. I straighten up and stick my head out of the engine hatch. "Julia." Instantly, I see she's been crying. "Where are the kids?" She gestures to the towpath and I see them giggling and sword-fighting with twigs. I haul myself up out of the hull and call them on board. "Not like I've got hot chocolate and biscuits or anything." I grin past Julia, putting her sadness on hold while I round up the children.

Alex leaps aboard and Julia gasps when she thinks he's going to plummet over the other side of the deck. Flora looks at me and grins when I sign to her about the treats.

"Alex, can you take Flora into the cabin and find the cookies?" They disappear down the hatch steps. "Julia, what's happened?"

"Nothing, nothing at all," she says, far too quickly for me to believe her. "Just that my life's crashed over the edge of a precipice."

"Funny, that," I reply. "Mine recently did the same." And we both laugh for a moment but only long enough to remember one millionth of the good times we've had together. Something stops me mentioning Carlyle's imminent release just in case now is the time she's come to say she wants me back.

Julia sighs. "The kids were missing you and I said they could visit before we went home for supper. Brenna and Gradin will be back soon and I don't like to leave them alone." She sighs out the remainder of her breath and smiles bravely.

"Anything else happened between them? Did you call the council about finding them a new foster home?" I want her to know I'm here for her. "And when are you moving back home? How's work? And how, of course, is Mary?"

Julia holds up her hands in a stop sign. With a pretty grin through mascara streaks, she answers my questions in order. I study the softness of her — her fragile cheeks, her once-shiny hair, her shapely body hidden beneath a thick layer of coat and poloneck sweater. Her voice. Her need.

"Come," I say. "It's warm inside." We both duck through the hatch — her first, then me with my hands a breath away from her back, guiding her from behind.

I fill the kettle and hand a pack of cards to Alex. "Solitaire, mate. Hours of endless fun." I keep Flora amused by tipping out a pot of coloured pens and rustling up a notepad from my briefcase. She adores drawing and sets to work immediately.

"Trouble?" I ask, to get things started.

"Nadine came to see me on my first day back at school." Julia slips off her shoes and flops into the beanbag. I like this. I feign ignorance about having already spoken to Nadine.

"Oh really?"

"She was only trying to help but we had a bit of a falling-out. It all started when she told me that there were no MRI scan results on Mum's file at The Lawns." Julia pauses for me to digest this, assuming I don't know. "She was implying something more sinister than clerical error, as if Mum had been put there by David against her will or . . . well, I don't know."

I pass Julia a mug of tea. Her face relaxes gratefully and she continues. "Then Nadine told me that whoever was paying the bill wasn't David. I mean, who else would be paying it? She was intent on causing upset, hoping I would think the worst of David." She studies my reaction closely. "Then Nadine was going to tell me something else but I couldn't stand to hear. I told her I couldn't see her again, not with Ed working on the case. Not until David is released and everything is back to normal."

We both flinch when she says normal.

I close my eyes for a beat. "You're right, you know. Nadine was only trying to help."

"Did you put her up to it?"

"No!"

"Sure?"

"Heavens, Julia. I'm David's solicitor. It's in my interest to get him off." I imagine Sheila firing me. Scarlet lips sending me packing; my career in tatters.

"And I've been thinking about that too." Her voice is curious, winding like the tail of a lost kite.

"Oh?"

"It's not really in your interest at all, is it, if David is freed? I thought you were going to hand the case over to someone else as soon as you could."

I sigh. "I want you to be happy, Julia. I never wanted the case, but . . ." How can I tell her the truth, that as long as Sheila's on my back, I *can't* shake the case?

"No, Murray. You don't want the case. You just want *me.*"

A sigh does for my reply. It could be taken either way, although we both know what I'm thinking.

"Anyway, that's not the worst news," she says. "Falling out with Nadine is nothing in comparison with what else I've discovered." She flushes and pretends it's because of the hot tea.

"I've been talking to one of Grace Covatta's friends at school. Her name's Amy. She's in my English class."

She sighs for about the hundredth time since she stepped aboard. I swear I see her eyes watering. A hug would do no good now. She'd accuse me of taking advantage, of levering my way back in through her sadness. She continues.

"It would appear that Grace Covatta had quite a crush on David. It had got to the point that she was becoming a real nuisance to him. And she wasn't the only teenage girl to feel that way, apparently. They all swooned over their new doctor."

Now this *is* news, although it fits perfectly with David's revelation about his relationship with the girl. But why is the story on its head? Why is she making Grace the bad girl when Carlyle is clearly the predator?

Suddenly, lack of sugar in my tea becomes insignificant. A shot of Scotch sloshed in would do nicely, but how can I do that without Julia noticing? "Carry on," I say, remembering the bottle in the cupboard. I could pretend to be looking for something else, more biscuits for the kids. "I'm listening." I take my tea to the cupboard and hold it in the cover of the open door while Julia continues.

"Well, can't you see? Poor David's been completely set up. To the police, it appears that he's been harassing Grace when it's the other way around. It's not going to look good." She pauses. "Is it?"

Oh Julia.

I slosh a generous measure of whisky into my tea.

"They're bound to think that poor David preys on young girls," she says. "It's hardly his fault he's the victim of a teenage crush."

"Unless he was the one who . . ." I bang my head as I stand up, lunging for the half-bottle of Scotch as it falls to the floor. It lands on my foot. "Ow!"

"Oh for God's sake, Murray. I'm telling you something important and you're sneaking booze." She smacks her hand into the beanbag, probably pretending it's me. Before we were separated, she would have gently taken the bottle and tipped its contents down the sink. Now, because all is lost between us, she doesn't stir.

"OK, so David's got a thing for young girls. Reason number ten why you having anything to do with him is a bloody bad idea." I sit down again, regretting snapping at Julia. My head hurts but my tea tastes a thousand times better now, helping me think. "Grace was clearly involved with David, Julia, regardless of who started it all off."

How can I tell her what David said about their secret meetings and phone calls? "The fact is, David was arrested and charged with Grace's assault." It's like jumping off a cliff. I lean forward. "Julia, I should also tell you that . . ." I stop. I can't do it. I can't tell Julia that Grace is pregnant. She won't believe that David is the father. She'll think I'm trying to stitch him up; make her hate him. "I should also tell you that . . . you look beautiful, despite all this mess."

Julia frowns. "No, Murray. I know you better than that." Her brow folds together suspiciously. "What were you really going to say?"

I've blown it. She won't let up until she knows. I shock her with something else entirely. "Will you have dinner with me?"

She shies her head, trying not to smile, even through all this. She's fighting it as if someone's pulling up a string attached to the corner of her mouth. It makes me do the same. "Bloody hell, Murray." She sounds like we did as kids. Incredulous but pleased when I did something that both thrilled and repulsed her. "What a stupid question. No. Of course not. We're about to get divorced."

"Please?"

"Maybe. With the kids. All of us. On Alex's birthday."

A furnace inside me ignites. Blood begins to flow.

"Can we go to that pizza place again, Dad?" Alex pipes up. He has clearly been listening to everything. I stand up and take a look at what Flora's been drawing. As soon as I am beside her, she whips the paper from my sight and shields it with her arms.

Can't I see your picture?

She shakes her head while her eyebrows tug together. It's a secret, she signs.

Oh, right. I understand. I won't look then.

"So." Julia presses on. "What were you going to tell me?"

"It was just the dinner. Really." I have to stick to my guns. She might even respect me for it. I knock back the rest of my tea. "Shall I make some more?" I hold out my empty cup.

"No, Murray. No more tea." She stands. "It's amazing, isn't it?"

"What is?"

"That everyone automatically thinks David is a sleaze, just because he was the victim of a schoolgirl crush."

"Julia . . ."

"Nah. Forget it, Murray. You're just the same as the rest of them." She signs to Flora that it's time to go. Our daughter isn't even looking; she's still drawing.

As I watch my beautiful Julia preparing to leave, in my head I tell her everything I know.

You see, my love, David and Grace had been meeting secretly, clandestine liaisons; the lust of a willing young girl easily soaked up by an older man. Grace went to see David to tell him she was pregnant. Witnesses saw them fight, have a disagreement. David knew his career would be over if it got out that he'd been sleeping with a schoolgirl, a teenage patient. Listen to me, Julia. The police have a victim, there is evidence, and above all there is a motive. For you, I will defend him, but I believe there is no doubt that David attacked Grace

Covatta with the intention to kill her or at least scare her off talking about the baby.

In my mind, I hug her close; hold her tight until it doesn't hurt so much. It's now that I should tell her about the bail. I don't.

"We're sinking," I tell her instead.

"But," she says — and her smile is our life raft — "I've got you to save me."

MARY

If I replay the words, relive that night, listen to the whispers inside my head, I can see that it was David's idea. I'll never stop wondering: had he planned it all along?

It was a tempting diversion at the time, I admit, and Jonathon didn't protest. We were all drunk; all looking for escape. We gathered up the champagne and glasses, clinking in our shaking hands, and Jonathon held the rowing boat steady as I climbed into its barrel-like hull. There were two bench seats and a pair of oars sitting in a puddle of water running along the boat's spine. I took the forward seat so I didn't have to row.

"Ahoy there," Jonathon roared as he leapt from the small jetty into the hull. The boat rocked precariously. He tossed the length of rope into the bows and lifted the oars into place. "I'll row," he insisted, and David didn't seem to mind. He sat next to me, staring with eyes hot enough to set me alight.

"Are you warm enough?" he asked.

"Yes, of course." I was certain I was melting. My skin was tacky. It was a humid night; the air expectant and heavy with moisture. "But I wish the rain would come."

I shifted the flimsy material of my dress a little higher up my calves so it wouldn't drag in the water swilling in the bottom of the boat.

We were all thinking it. The rain, getting soaked, shirts sticking, dress peeling, flashes of teeth and shattered laughter. It was the storm building, I swear, that lit the touch paper, started it all off. The electricity zipped over our skin.

Jonathon rowed hard and soon we were in the middle of the lake. Even though we were together, I felt alone — totally alone in the middle of the black water. Jonathon ceased pulling on the oars and we floated aimlessly, just the sound of water slapping the hull. The pulse of the storm hadn't quite reached us.

"I say we go over there, check out what's in that cabin. We can have another drink and watch the lightning." Jonathon's face glowed in the eerie light. I looked to where he was pointing and saw the outline of a small building. Suddenly, everything was daylight-clear as a strap of lightning split the dull sky.

I agreed. This was infinitely preferable to being mocked by a bunch of pompous students.

David also nodded his approval. He'd been quiet since we'd set out on the lake. I touched his hand to let him know I was there for him. However much his mother upset him, I was still his friend; his true, trusted friend. I squeezed his fingers, flashed a grin of excitement, briefly laid my head on his shoulder. I should have realised that by then, it wasn't my friendship he wanted.

"I'm worried about Mother," David said finally. "She'd drunk too much —"

"And you haven't?" I laughed. "Relax, David. Watching the storm will be fun." I pointed at the roll of thick green-grey cloud that grumbled across the sky. It felt as if the tip of my finger was connected directly to the heavens. A shard of electricity zigzagged between me and God. David finally admitted the sky was impressive.

Jonathon rowed on for all he was worth, puffing through each pull of the wooden oars across the still lake.

"Did you feel that?" A big plop of rain landed on my bare shoulder. I was gleeful. It was an adventure and all the attention was lavished solely on me. I was damn well going to enjoy myself. "It's raining."

"The only raindrop in the entire storm and it fell on you, Mary Marshall." David grinned. He always made me feel special, whether he was studying deadly pathogens or whispering poetry to me in the library. Just for that evening, I allowed myself to believe I was.

Within a couple of minutes the lake was peppered with mini explosions. The raindrops had turned to hailstones. "Oh, God," I laughed as my skin tingled. "Get us out of this, Jonathon!" The ice beads pelted my skin, the inside of the boat, our heads, our hearts. I helped pull faster on the oars. The sky had blackened so that it was hard to tell where lake ended and cloud began. We were in fits of laughter, and from the corner of my eye, I saw David drinking champagne from the bottle.

Finally we reached the opposite shore and spilled from the boat. We ran from the water and took shelter under some trees. By then the hail was mixed with rain and the first crack of thunder broke overhead. Our spines tingled together as the electricity fused our bones. It was the most thrilling feeling I'd ever had.

"Come on. Let's make a dash for the hut." I can't remember who said it. Just a voice threaded between the raindrops.

It wasn't much more than a gardener's shed. Jonathon rattled the padlocked door and pulled a face. "That's that then. Locked." We huddled under the shallow eaves to escape the downpour. Cold beads tracked down my skin, my neck, my arms.

"What a shame," I said, peering through the grimy window. "It looks so cosy in there." I squinted through the cobwebs and saw the outline of an old settee, a table, a rug. General clutter resolved through the murk.

"Boo!" Jonathon barked at me. I jumped.

"Oh God, don't," I squealed. "You scared the life out of me." I shook with fear and delight.

Then, silently, David withdrew a knife from his pocket. It was a fold-up knife with a bone handle, perhaps one that would be used for hunting — skinning a rabbit or stilling a writhing fish on a line. He picked and scratched uselessly at the padlock, then spotted the mallet leaning against the side of the hut. After a couple of blows, he had the metal strap hanging from shredded wood.

"Don't breathe too hard," he said. "The whole place is so rotten it could fall down any minute."

"Oh look," I said, breathless with excitement. I was the first to step inside. "Someone actually lives here." I felt like Goldilocks. We shuffled forward, gradually realising that it was indeed someone's home. "What if they come back?"

"If you ask me, it's the groundsman's place," David said. "He'll only use it when he's working this side of the estate, and on a day like today, what with the wedding and the bad weather, I doubt he'll disturb us."

"You're right," I said, relieved. I didn't want to go back yet. I fell on to the ancient sofa. I fanned my hand as a cloud of dust ballooned around me. "Come on then, crack open the bottles."

None of my behaviour that day was typical. Maybe the storm had opened a crevice in my brain and good sense had fallen out; maybe it was the idea of being holed up with David and his intriguing friend — they were so similar yet excitingly different — that thrilled me. I was out of my usual domain; I felt as if anything could happen.

With hindsight, maybe it *was* my fault. However attracted I was to David, I understood full well that as the older woman, I had a duty to behave. I'd made a pledge to myself and intended to keep it. There was fun to be had but nothing else. For me, that made it all the more exciting.

We drank more champagne. The glasses had miraculously stayed intact on our turbulent journey. "Anyone fancy something a little stronger?" The rain beat on the tin roof, and until I realised what David meant, I just listened to its rhythm. The pair of them —

two intelligent, handsome young men with opportunity spilling from them — made me giddy.

"Drugs?" I asked wide-eyed. My heart raced as if I'd already taken them. In the seconds that followed, I thought about the consequences as best I could in my dizzy head. Everyone at university did drugs, didn't they? For David and Jonathon, taking something to help them relax was probably as common as a cup of tea. Besides, it would only be this once, and David was virtually a doctor anyway.

"You're a medical student. I trust you," I said. I'd never taken anything before and wouldn't have even contemplated it if I'd not been so drunk.

I stood at the open door of the hut. I felt sick. I sipped my drink, proud of myself for finally living on the edge. Mary the farm girl had been left behind. I was in a different world with different people and I wanted to get a glimpse of who I really was; who I might have become had I been given the chance. I danced out into the storm and skipped away from the shelter of the surrounding trees. I sucked in the moist night air as the rain fell on my shoulders. I wanted to get thoroughly soaked.

"You'll catch a chill." I knew straight away that it was David behind me. His voice, his touch, his words, his scent blended together and affected me way more than any drug ever could. We stood and stared out over the lake. I was convinced I could walk across it. He snaked his arms around me from behind. I breathed in sharply but his clutch wouldn't allow it. "You're wet through already."

I laughed, gazing up into his young face. He was so beautiful; trying so hard to be everything he knew I wanted. And he was exactly that. A perfect score on my chart, but I couldn't have him. If I was to hold on to a shred of self-respect, then slipping any deeper into David's life, his psyche, his bed would only highlight the unbearable magnitude of what I could never be.

"I don't care. You're going to be a doctor. You can make me better if I catch a chill." A battle raged inside my mind and body. The overhead thunder and lightning drove our shoulders to our ears. We screamed out with laughter and fear. David bent his face down and kissed me.

My lips curled but then opened like blossom just as he retracted.

"Never again," he said when it was over. I mistakenly took this to be an apology, even though I didn't believe him. "I won't do that ever again." We both knew he would.

It was the most beautiful kiss I had ever had.

"No, you won't," I echoed. My voice faltered at such tragedy while my body prickled with desire. He pulled me on to his lips again, this time driving deeper. I mouthed my protest from beneath his passion. It had to stop.

When we separated, we were at arm's length. Lifetimes apart. "I've taken one already," David said quietly, holding out an envelope. "Have one. It'll help you relax."

David shook the envelope so that all the little pills inside it danced. "What are they?" I asked, not that it really mattered. I wasn't about to swallow one because of what it would do to me. No, I wanted to take one to be more like David; to make up for rejecting him, for never being able to have him.

"Ludes, sweetie. To make you feel even sweeter." David laughed.

I peeked inside the envelope. "Eeny, meeny, miny mo . . ." It was exciting. The champagne made me not care. Everyone took drugs, didn't they? Just because I'd missed the education train didn't mean I had to be a social dropout. "This one looks nice." I grinned and plucked out a pill. I held it up as if it was medicine to make the rest of my life better. Carefully, I placed it on the tip of my tongue, and before I could change my mind, I washed it down with the remainder of my champagne. "Ludes," I said, mulling the name. "It sounds like a game."

"Oh, it is," David confirmed with a twinkle in his eye. "Methaqualone. One of the best drugs out there."

For what seemed like lifetimes strung together, we stared at each other. I felt the pill dissolving in my stomach and then a crazy mix of champagne and drugs bleeding through my veins. Gradually, before my eyes, David turned into someone I didn't recognise. As for how I felt about myself, I was already transforming into the stranger that I would become for the rest of my life.

"Come on." David suddenly broke the silence, realising just how wet we were getting. "Jonathon will wonder what's happened to us, and we'll catch our death."

"I think I already have," I said in a voice that clearly wasn't mine.

Back inside the hut, David lay down on the floor, grinning, his heavy brows sinking over his eyes, his head crushing his shoulders at the open neck of his shirt. I don't think I'd ever seen him look so alluring. He fished a silver hip flask from his jacket pocket.

"Is that a good idea?" Jonathon asked. I hadn't seen him take a lude.

"Effects of this sedative drug include euphoria, reduced heart rate, slurred speech, amnesia, impaired perception and confusion. Prepare for a crazy time." David ignored Jonathon, sounding as if he were reciting from a medical textbook. He tipped the flask to his mouth and then passed it to me. It was heavy. It was full. I took my share and then some more.

Later, when the rain still drummed on the roof and the rotten wood of the hut vibrated from the thunder, we sang. David and I took turns to belt out every anthem we could remember, only with hindsight, we were barely opening our mouths or making a noise. Jonathon was cautious and sat next to me on the dusty sofa, keeping watch while we continued with our nonsense words and a made-up key. The storm kept time to our music while Jonathon grew bored.

I was grinning — the stretch of my mouth almost hurting my face — as I used all my strength to stare between the two men. All was good. The world was good, and being in the hut in the rain with the two most intriguing characters in the world held me as tightly together as any degree course at Cambridge could have done.

I locked eyes with David in a passionate stare. Both our mouths were still burning from the kiss. Jonathon didn't know what was going on. The thoughts that zapped between us were private and incomprehensible to an outsider. There was an unspoken pact between us; such a delightful agreement that we could hardly stand it in our euphoric state.

David had been right. I felt sweet. The pill had made me feel so sweet that I slipped off my shoes and stood up. "Who will dance with me?" I closed my eyes, wondering if David would take the bait. I waited for an age, and it wasn't until later, when I opened my eyes again, that I realised Jonathon had left.

JULIA

It's morning break time, and instead of marking homework, I'm making lists. The first list is of all the good things I'm sure of about David. I stop and smile. I half expect the list to go on for ever. Firstly, he likes me, *really* likes me, and perhaps one day soon he will love me. I could love him. I stop and chew the end of my pencil. I *do* love him, I confess.

He seems to adore the kids, especially Flora, and he genuinely cares for Mum. Only a man truly committed to me and my family would arrange private medical care for a sick relative. Next, he is a doctor. That's a good solid profession, and at his age he's proved his commitment to his career, unlike . . . My thoughts trail off. Comparisons still hurt.

"I like the way he looks," I say to break my last thought. I find him incredibly attractive, I admit. "And he takes good care of himself. We have great conversations. He irons out my insecurities. He is confident . . . interested in me as a woman . . . he can cook. Good sense of humour . . ." I'm scribbling notes fast. Finally I put a row of dots at the end and scribble "et al.".

282

Then, taking a deep breath, I tear off a separate piece of paper. I am going to make a list of all the things that are not so easy to understand about David. I can't use the word bad or negative. These are mostly things that I have learnt from Murray, so how much weight I place on them hangs largely on my judgement of Murray's motives. I must remember that to him, David is the enemy.

Number one, David is being held in custody. Secondly, he has been charged with a serious assault. I swallow. This isn't easy. Poor David has been the victim of unwelcome attention from misguided schoolgirls, including Grace. There appears to be a mix-up on my mother's medical file, but that's nothing to do with David. There is also uncertainty about who is actually paying Mum's medical bill, but I believe it's David. That's what he told me and I have no reason to think otherwise. I consider putting this on the positive list but decide against it. I don't want to be accused of weighting the argument.

I put down my pencil and hold the negatives in my left hand and the positives in my right. "Oh, David." I sigh. He seems a million miles away, stuck in prison. I read through both lists again. The one in my left hand weighs heavy on my heart and drags down my fingers.

As I read through the other, my spirit lightens and a smile creeps across my lips. "Of course," I say, feeling a thousand times better. "I forgot to write down the most important thing." I chew the pencil again. Putting this into words will be hard. Then, as I hear the first

283

trill of my mobile phone in my bag, I jot down on the positive list: *Feels like I've known him for ever.*

"Hello?" I scrabble my phone from my bag just as the bell for lessons sounds. "I can't hear you. You'll have to speak up." It's Murray, but reception is poor. I dash to the window for a better signal. Once, I used to covet his calls because we loved each other. "Can you hear me?" Murray sounds like twanging piano wire and so I dash out through the staff-room door and stalk the playground until his voice rings true in my ear. "Thank God," I say. "Thank God."

A minute later, I'm in the staff room packing up all the files I'm supposed to be marking. On the table, I see my two lists. I scrunch up the negative one and toss it into the bin. Along with all my doubts.

"Murray," I squeal. I want to hug him, leap in the air, muss his hair like I might do to Alex, kiss him, dance. For now, I simply manage a very sincere "Thank you."

"Really, Julia, I didn't do very much."

I remember Murray as he once was — in control, assured, motivated — and at a push, I could even believe he is that exact same person now, sitting behind his office desk in his suit. "I don't care a jot how it happened. I'm still going to believe it was all down to you. I need to thank *someone*." I'm so happy.

Murray watches the inane grin that overcomes me, transcending all the trouble between us. "When can we expect him out?" The words flutter around like party streamers decorating his dull office. "You should get Alex and Flora to do some paintings for the walls in here. How's it all going with you, anyway? And work? Any more juicy cases? Is Sheila still badgering you? How's your girlfriend?" I know I'm babbling but I can't help myself.

Murray raises his hands. "Slow it down, girl. There's a long way to go before David can sleep soundly." The way he dips his eyes, I know he's thinking of David and me slotted alongside each other in bed. "I need to know the conditions of bail and if all the charges are being dropped. I have a meeting tomorrow, so let's get that out of the way before you get too excited. You can't rush these things." Murray sounds vague, as if he's not telling me everything. He leans forward, and if I hadn't pulled my hands off the desk, I reckon he'd have taken hold of them. He clears his throat. "And Rose is fine, thank you. I will introduce her to the kids soon."

Again, he doesn't sound genuine; as if Rose — I'm assuming she's the girl I saw on the boat — is make-believe.

"As long as it's serious, you know, between you and . . . Rose." I say her name with bitterness although I still can't help thinking of pink petals. "I don't want the kids getting fond of someone only for you to dump her a minute later."

"Oh, that's great coming from you!" I duck as he slings harsh words. "You've mentally married Carlyle, virtually committed to him for life, and then he goes and ends up in prison — perhaps for the rest of *his* life. What has *your* haphazard devotion done to Alex and Flora?"

285

"They're fine about it," I say calmly. "They really like David." He's there for them, sober, I want to say but don't. "As for the arrest, I've already explained to them that the police probably made a mistake. Now, when I tell them he's being let off, they'll see I was right. It's all about trust, Murray." This is where we have always differed. I see reality. He believes in fairies.

"*Probably*, you see, Julia. What if probably comes true? What, indeed, if the police *have* made a mistake . . . *are* making a mistake? What if they are releasing a violent criminal?"

As well as seeing the shudder in Murray's shoulders, I feel it through the air. He's always been dramatic. "David said to have faith in the legal system. And look, he was right." I won't allow Murray this last-ditch attempt at slating David. Or is it a valiant attempt at saving us?

"Think about what we truly know about him, Julia. The facts. Just consider them."

"I would if I had hard evidence, but all I have is second-hand gossip." I stand up. I've had enough of this. "*Chrissie* said, *Nadine* said, *you* said, psychiatric hospital this, missing files that. Why you think David is linked in some sinister way to my mother is beyond me. He's trying to help her, can't you see? You're living in a kids' adventure book, Murray."

After a long pause, as if he's really considering something, mentally weighing up whether he should tell me or not, Murray finally hits me as hard as he can. He speaks slowly, calmly, which in itself frightens me. "Julia, now David is being released, however temporary that may or may not be, there's something else I want you to know." I shift from one foot to the other. I'll be late fetching the kids if he doesn't hurry up. He continues. "If this goes to court, it'll come out anyway."

I take hold of the chair. I feel dizzy.

"Grace Covatta was pregnant. Perhaps still is pregnant," he adds.

It only takes a second for me to realise he's lying. "Oh. Right. And who said that? Santa Claus?" I'm not listening to any of this rubbish.

"No, Julia," he says softly. "David said."

MURRAY

It was juvenile, I know, allowing Julia to believe that I am romantically involved with Rose. It was all Nadine's work, setting me up on a blind date in a rash attempt to get my life back on track. It didn't work. A part of me panicked when Julia found us together and I couldn't resist throwing in the bait to see if she bit. She didn't. It hurts that she doesn't care.

"God damn, Nadine, this is all so wrong. Can you name one part of my life that's right?" She looks confused, exhausted. A long shift at work has extracted the life from her. I stopped off at the hospital for a bit of sisterly comfort.

"Your beautiful children?" Of course she was going to say that. I feel a clench of guilt.

"That's why I can't bear the thought of Carlyle anywhere near them. Julia has to promise me that she won't see him when the kids are present." I doubt she will ever agree to that. "I'll do whatever it takes."

"Then do it," Nadine says as if it's easy. "As far as I can see, you have a limited number of options, Murray. First, you can win Julia back somehow and skip off into the sunset with your family. Secondly, you can dig the dirt on the doctor — if there is any — expose him, and hope that Julia sees sense. Or thirdly, you can close your briefcase, get on with your life, see your kids every Sunday and forget all about Julia Marshall once and for all." Nadine's voice gets progressively snappier so that when she mentions Julia's name, she's spitting her words on to the floor.

"An exit into happy-ever-after land with my family is very hard to imagine. Forgetting that Julia exists is . . ." I think, glancing at the ceiling, ". . . impossible."

"Then that just leaves option two. Expose the creep for what he clearly is." Nadine peels back the wrapper on a bar of chocolate that she has just bought from a machine. "Lunch," she confesses. "Or maybe it's breakfast."

We walk along the corridors of the hospital. Nadine blends into the walls, the very fabric of the building, with her white tunic, white trousers and soft-soled shoes. She belongs here. "Want some?" she asks. I take a square of chocolate.

"And how's Julia going to react to that? If what I suspect about Carlyle is true, even in the vaguest sense, Julia's never going to buy it. Not from me. She'll accuse me of ruining her happiness. And if it's not true, if he's clean, then how can I sit back and watch their happy ending?"

Nadine stops, turns and faces me squarely. "You don't. You hide your eyes. But for now, Murray, you need them wide open." It's what our mother used to say to us when we were kids.

289

"So I quit being his solicitor and become a detective. Is that what you're saying?" We're standing near the main entrance where all corridors converge.

"I didn't say that, did I, bro?" Nadine gives me one of her false innocent looks. "Just don't forget who I'm married to."

Nadine stands at the hospital entrance, teased by the daylight outside. The sky is blue, the frost shimmering across the tarmac. "Chrissie's findings were worrying, Murray, but perhaps only in the light of Carlyle's arrest."

I take over her thread. "But considering that he's been charged with assault, any slips he makes are magnified with suspicion. He couldn't sneeze without me thinking he had the plague."

"Exactly. I'm not siding with him, but you need to study the facts clearly. I'm sure there are times when you've done things so out of character that if a stranger saw, they'd get the wrong impression of you entirely. Perhaps even label you a criminal." There's a pause as we share a moment's recollection — the *same* recollection — that seems to take us a decade to wade through.

Julia didn't know who else to call. Nadine had to leave her work. The kids were tucked up in bed at our house and Flora was still so little, she couldn't possibly be left even for a moment. My memories of that night are largely patchworked together from Julia's outpourings, Nadine's calm telling of the tale, and a doctor's follow-up consultation to convince him I hadn't lost hold of my senses.

290

"Really, it was a one-off binge. Stress at work. That kind of thing."

"But you threw a chair at your wife."

"No," I say, laughing, trying to blow the whole mess back into insignificance where it belonged. Sadly, no one else saw it like that, least of all my wife. "The chair wasn't meant to go anywhere near Julia."

"But you threw a chair."

"I was drunk."

"Then you hurt yourself and knocked over two nurses."

"Not on purpose. I didn't mean to break the bottle."

"But you ended up in hospital having your arm stitched up."

"Yes, you already know that." Covering old ground seems pointless, except to me it isn't old ground. I couldn't remember a damn thing about my psycho-binge. I was desperate to know if I'd hurt Julia but she refused to answer my calls and barricaded the front door. She told Nadine she never wanted to see me again. If I'm honest, it was the beginning of the bad times. Before that, we'd never given much thought to my drinking. It was as integral to our lives as changing Flora's nappy or walking Alex to school.

They gave me antidepressants for a while; marked up my file so no doctor would ever treat me as a normal person again.

"I'm not the one in custody," I say before Nadine can chip me with her thoughts. The clatter of the hospital brings me back to the present.

"Assaulting NHS staff is taken extremely seriously. Essentially, your medical file may not look that different to Carlyle's police file." Nadine has her work voice on. Soothing yet firm, tolerant yet persuading.

"Thanks," I mutter, shocked she's comparing me to a suspected criminal. "It was all an accident. All because of the drink."

"Perhaps Carlyle has a similar excuse."

"Unlikely," I say. "He just says he didn't do it. Calmly and consistently. Anyway, I don't know why you're siding with him. Surely you want him locked up as much as I do."

"Of course. I'm playing devil's advocate, Murray. Besides, I don't think anyone wants him put away more than you because no one wants their family back more than you do." She stuffs the foil wrapper into her pocket and glances at her upside-down watch. "Look, all I'm saying is be careful. You're treading a thin line between being a lawyer and a vigilante. Don't confuse the two. And whatever you do, don't act desperate with Julia."

I agree, nodding, pausing as we wind things up.

"Julia has a theory," I say before we part. "That I suspect David is somehow connected to Mary in a bad way. *Sinister* is the word she used to describe it." I wait to see if Nadine agrees, if she thinks the same. It's just a hunch, after all, but she says nothing. "If I'm honest, Nadine, Julia's right. I do think that." When she stares at me blankly, her eyes dissolving from tiredness, I say, "Go home, sis." I give her a kiss on the cheek. She's done enough for me.

Nadine reanimates and fishes a pen from her pocket. She jots a number on my hand. "Chrissie Weaver," she says. "And remember, eyes open." Then she turns and walks off to her car.

Chrissie Weaver is younger than I expected, but as she rattles through her qualifications, along with all the prestigious places where she's worked, I become seriously impressed. I'm buying her lunch. An expensive lunch. It's her day off and it's the least I can do seeing as she has given half of it up for me.

"I shouldn't have this," she says, tapping the file. "Least of all be showing it to a stranger. But," she sighs, "Nadine's been a friend for ever, and when she told me her brother needed a favour, well, I couldn't resist." She shrugs her shoulders and her eyes sparkle. This is obviously exciting for her. I wonder just how much Nadine has revealed.

Chrissie is attractive and no doubt incredibly smart because she then tells me about a list of awards she's won for her psychiatric research work. "I just adore it," she says as if she's talking about a boyfriend. "When I get home at night I just want to be back at work. I take my laptop to bed with me. Most girls would be shopping on their day off. Me, I'm working on a research paper this afternoon." No wonder she refused the wine I ordered. In solidarity, I only pour myself a small measure.

Over the next half-hour, I hear all about her dedicated lifestyle and commendable work ethic and how another promotion is just around the corner, all the while pretending to appear interested when what I really want is to get my hands on the file marked *Mary Marshall*. It's tucked neatly inside a stripy canvas bag that rests beside Chrissie's feet. I salivate, and it's not because of the forty quid's worth of food that's just been placed between us. "What are you researching?"

She smiles, helping herself to a langoustine. She cracks its back. "Communication in dementia patients. Everything from Alzheimer's and Parkinson's to CJD."

"Fascinating," I reply with a good dose of pretend enthusiasm. It doesn't occur to me immediately. The wine is good and I study her over the rim of my glass. I don't like doing this, I really don't, but I have to. Flirting doesn't come naturally, not unless it's with Julia. "Such a serious subject for a beautiful young woman."

"Not that young." She laughs, and pops the pink flesh between her teeth. "I just look after myself." She's enjoying herself and that's exactly what I want.

"But still too young for an old bloke like me." Thank God I found this shirt; the one that vaguely suggests I have a sense of taste. "Just kidding," I add so she doesn't think I'm a total creep.

"Nonsense." Her pupils flicker large, then small, sizing me up, and for a moment I think she means it. Briefly I feel like Carlyle. Powerful, respected, dominant, and it gives me a bit of a rush. Then it strikes me. "Does your research work include . . ." What was it? I think. What did David call it when he brought Julia and Mary back to Northmire? ". . . whatever illness Mary Marshall has?"

Chrissie steals another langoustine. "These are totally delicious. I'm going to reek of garlic."

"We'll reek together," I say and really wish I hadn't. "So does Mary have the kind of illness that you're studying?"

Chrissie lays down the langoustine husk and sucks her fingers. "Sorry," she grins and peers at me over chunky-framed glasses that are way too big for her face. "When I looked through Mary's file, there was nothing to suggest that she had any actual pathological disease at all."

"Vaso something. Some kind of dementia that showed up on her MRI scan results." And we both chant it together: *But there weren't any MRI scan results*.

"You don't mean vascular dementia, do you?" Chrissie's tucking into the bands of squid heaped under a drizzle of scarlet sauce that nearly explodes my mouth. "I love Thai food, don't you?"

"Oh yes!" And if my lips weren't still tingling, I would lean across the table and kiss her right on the mouth. "Oh yes to both of those, I mean. Wonderful food and vascular dementia. That was it. That was Carlyle's reason for having Mary hospitalised."

Chrissie shrugs, more interested in the free lunch than solving my mystery. "It's very odd, don't you think, that he offered to pay for Mary's private treatment. The Lawns is incredibly expensive."

I pull a face. In every way, she's right. But she doesn't know the relationship between Julia and David.

It's odd on every count. "Strange indeed, although that's what's happened."

"But David Carlyle doesn't seem to be paying the bill, does he? His name's not on the account." This I already know. "And neither does there seem to be a need for treatment for vascular dementia. Not if Mary Marshall doesn't have it, and especially not at The Lawns, which, as we all know, deals purely with psychiatric patients." Another mouthful stifles her next suggestion. "What about getting Mrs Marshall another MRI scan? A second opinion?"

Hands up, I know she's right. I stuff my fingers into the napkin, wiping off sauce and garlic. "And round and round we go."

"Suck them," Chrissie says, winking behind the thick lenses of her spectacles so that her eyes look like giant clams. It's then that I know she'll do anything I want.

The boat stinks. Diesel, river sludge and stale spaghetti bolognese from last night's micro-meal blend together to make a perfect scent for my mood. An expensive lunch and Chrissie still hasn't given up the file.

"It's not much," I tell her. Excuses would be futile. I'm a man living alone. There is a certain expectation of slobbishness. "But it's home."

"It's amazing," she says. "You should see my flat. Four straight walls within four straight walls within four . . . You get the picture. This is so . . ."

"Grotty?"

"Romantic."

I must be careful. Remember Nadine's words. Eyes open. "Tea?" Julia would want tea now.

"Sure, but I can't stay long. You can take a look at the file while I drink tea but then I have to go." She says it as if I'm a naughty schoolboy allowed to have a couple of sweets. Only a couple, mind.

I jiggle the kettle. Just enough water. I try to light the stove. "Sorry. Out of gas. Juice?" My plan to buy time is not going well.

"Really, I'm fine. Take a quick look at the file and then I'll be off." She's nervous about handing it over, I can tell.

"Why not leave it with me? It's no trouble to drop it back at the hospital in the morning. You can trust me, you know, I'm a lawyer." I grin and hope that Chrissie sees the joke. She just stands still, looking worried.

"I'll wait." She settles down on the single chair by the fold-down table and taps away at her mobile phone. I end up dropping on to the beanbag with Mary Marshall's file resting on my legs, wondering how I'll ever make sense of all the medical jargon. A bottle of wine at lunchtime, even to an experienced connoisseur like me, tests my alertness score. But not so much that I can't whip up a plan to harvest the file for my own private use. A manila file is a manila file. My boat is littered with them from the office. Clients work their way into my private life any way they can.

"Nature calls," I say. Chrissie doesn't look up from her phone or notice that I take Mary's notes into the tiny washroom along with Mr A. Barrett's file on a case he's sure to lose, whatever I do. I swap the contents around and tuck Mary's papers behind the shower curtain before returning to the cabin.

"You know, I fancy some fresh air. Do you want to sit out on the deck with me while I read through this?" I wave Barrett's file in the air. Chrissie thinks it's Mary's. This is going to take some doing, but I'm up for it.

"Oh that would be nice. I can watch the moorhens." Chrissie wraps her scarf around her neck.

Perfect, I think, leading the way. As we mount the slippery deck, I hold my breath and waste no time in falling overboard with the file clutched to my chest. The last thing I see as I go under is Chrissie's mouth open, screaming, as she lunges for the precious file. Then I screw up my eyes in the murky water, doing exactly the opposite to what Nadine told me.

MARY

When I opened my eyes, David was standing in front of me, accepting my offer to dance. Pure pleasure. Pure excitement. He was forbidden fruit and this was the next best thing.

"Where's Jonathon?" I asked, glancing around the hut. In the seconds that I had closed my eyes, it was as if my entire life had changed. I laughed provocatively, nervously. I was alone with David. His body appeared twisted and enlarged in strange places, as if I was looking at him in one of those fairground mirrors. Sense didn't tell me it was the lude. Sense had long gone.

"He walked back to the party," he said. I think that's what he said. Didn't he want to play any more? I asked, but nothing came out.

"Can you dance the quickstep, then?" Some things are clear. Others are as if they have been dipped in melted toffee. I felt as if I had lost my bones. "Have you got them?"

David frowned. "Got what?"

"My bones." And then I heard my silly words echo down a long corridor that spanned the entire stretch of my life. David took hold of me and we danced. There was no music. "I feel sick," I confessed.

"That'll be all the booze you've had," David whispered, but then handed over his hip flask. I wanted to tell him he was bad; that he should be looking after me, but when I opened my mouth to protest, nothing came out. I was on the inside of a merry-go-round, watching out-of-control horses gallop past. David and I were suddenly riding the horses, the pair of us speeding up, everything spinning faster and faster. I wanted to tell him that I loved him.

"What you need to do," David suggested with heavy eyes, "is take another lude. It will cancel out the alcohol, for sure." He plucked another pill from the envelope and popped it between my lips. "Steady, baby," he crooned. "Down it goes." I relaxed and dropped on to the sofa. He would look after me. He was going to be a doctor.

Minutes became hours, or the other way round. The rain beat on the tin roof of the hut. I remember because it sounded the same as the beating inside my head. Nothing was real, yet everything was so vibrant, I could hardly bear it. Even my clothes became too much of an irritant to my sensitive skin.

"Undress me," I said, slurring. David looked at me as if I was speaking a foreign language. *Undress me*, I screamed, pulling at my clothes. *It hurts*. But it wasn't a scream at all. It was a useless cry in my head that no one heard. I rubbed at the layers of my new dress and pulled at the shoulder straps. Then I started laughing. I wasn't wearing any clothes. I was already completely naked. Wasn't I?

Mary, are you OK? Someone was talking to me. Was it my mother bending over me, stroking my brow? How would she know where I was? *I'm fine,* I replied, wondering if she could hear me. *I'm just taking this sweet, sweet trip on ludes.*

David was right. It felt good. Better than good. Nothing bothered me while everything ripped me apart. I knew I could fly. I wasn't Mary Marshall any more, and that, for the first time in my life, made me feel special.

Mary, are you sure you're all right? Perhaps it was my father, pleased as punch to see his daughter in such esteemed company. *A doctor, Mary. My, you are doing well for yourself.* But it wasn't my father. *Dad?* I asked into the void, helpless as a baby. Then everyone I'd ever known zoomed around me like colours on a spinning top. My eyes stretched wide as an album of my life flashed through the rickety shed. They all left their message of sympathy; all joined in the dance beat out by the rain; all screwed up their faces in shock. *Have we been washed away?* I heard myself ask, but no one replied.

Then I was struck by pain.

It took a hold of my heart and my mind and my body in equal measure and darkness pushed over my face. The first sting fell on my cheek. It came and went so quickly, it was only when the next one arrived that I remembered the first. I touched my face, smarting from the slap.

"David?" I asked. The fear was too slow coming. I simply didn't believe it.

Suddenly my neck was cracked back against the dirty sofa and I had to open my mouth wide so the skin on my throat wouldn't split. I screamed but nothing came out.

"Da . . . vid . . . no . . ." Fresh air whipped against my stomach as David's clever doctor hands ripped chiffon and lace from me that I already thought had been removed. I was confused. Time and reality skidded around me. I sent my arms to fight him off but they lay lifeless on the floor. I laughed. *I can't feel my arms*. All I could see was the cobwebbed wood of the hut's ceiling. A single bulb hung darkly from a central beam. The only light in my world was from the brightness of David's pills.

"Jonathon, Jonathon." I called out for help. I tried to lift my head, but the weight of it was too great. "Help me, Jonathon." No one, yet everyone, replied. Even the confusion was confusing.

Jonathon's gone . . .

I vomited and coughed, choking for my life. Suddenly I was on my front, face pressed to the musty boards in the stain of my own sick. David was thumping my back. He was trying to help me. He'd seen me choking and was trying to help me. A moment's lucidity. Maybe he wasn't going to hurt me at all.

"Please stop," I begged, but the taste of dust and grit choked me again. Then there was a great weight on my back and a pressure on my head so that my cheek was scuffed into the dirty floor.

Someone, help me . . .

Then my life split in two. My body was torn apart, every neatly stitched seam of my soul slashed to tatty threads. The size of him, the heat of him, the smell of him as he forced himself inside my body time and time again, the very core of him jetting into the very centre of me as I fell in and out of consciousness. I screamed for breath; screamed for help, but nobody heard. My nails scratched at splinters in the floor as David stole the life from me — each thrust a year eroded.

David. My doctor. My friend. I thought he loved me.

Then silence, the relief as he rolled off my body. I heard distant thunder, vibrating through the wood of the hut and into my bones. It was over. It seemed to have taken just seconds yet stretched from the beginning of time.

Surely it was all a mistake?

I vomited again, the vile taste a welcome wash to the sawdust in my mouth.

But fear was waiting for me, whipping me senseless again as I saw David's knife lying on the floor across the room — a discarded weapon, glinting, calling to him. Discarded but not forgotten. I shook with fear. I tried to speak but nothing came out.

"Shh," David whispered, leaning over me, watching me die, if not in body then in spirit. "Don't talk. Just don't speak. Shh. Keep quiet, Mary . . ."

It was the last thing I heard before I passed out.

JULIA

"My father called?" I laugh to cover a line of indelible sadness; a lifetime of making excuses to my friends at school, playing make-believe with myself that I had a dad. Truth is, I'm fine about it now. What you never had, you don't miss, right? "I don't think it would have been. Could have been," I add, baffled, excited, frightened. What if it *was*?

I let out another nervous laugh but only because of what she must be thinking. Did he walk out because of you? As a kid, dazzled by my mother's silence on the matter, that's what I always assumed. My father hated me and walked out on us. Mum couldn't bring herself to discuss it.

"Well maybe not your father then, but some older guy left an urgent message for you to call. It wasn't Murray." Ali crunched into an apple, oblivious to the spark of pain she had caused. She handed me a slip of paper. "And it certainly wasn't Alex's little voice." She winked. "OK. I'd better get on. Fancy a drink this Friday?" Ali headed up the school's admin team. We'd all be sunk without her.

304

"Why not," I say. "I deserve a bit of fun. Perhaps Murray can have the kids overnight and we can, you know, paint the town red." I felt silly saying it.

"You look like you need it. We'll eat first and then . . ."

But I don't wait to hear what Friday night could hold. When I see David's number jotted on the message pad, I gather my bag and scuttle from Ali's office like it's on fire.

In a quiet corner of the playground, my coat hunched around my neck, five rings seem like five hundred. "David?" I'm standing still but breathless, trying not to shiver but failing. "What's . . . what's going on?" I hardly dare ask if he's out.

"Julia," he says, and his voice is swift and smooth, like a bird. I glance up at the sky.

"Are you . . . are you really . . ." I can't say it. For these few seconds, there is hope. More hope than I've had for weeks, and if I'm right, then there's a chance my life will be allowed to heal. There will be hope for Mum again, hope for Alex and Flora to have some steadiness in their lives, and hope for me to rebuild mine. I blurt it out. "David, where are you? Are you free?" Stuffed inside my gloves, my fingers automatically cross and I screw up my eyes as if I can't stand to see his reply.

"I'm at home." And because of the poor reception, his words echo a thousand times down the line.

Screaming at Murray will not change things but I do it anyway. "You're bloody useless. Why didn't you tell me

305

he was being released today? I'd have been there. I thought you said it would be a while, that there were things to take care of. What happened about the bail conditions?" I'm on my way to get the kids; on the way to David's.

I step on to the deck of the hulk Murray calls home. "When are you going to grow up, Murray?" Then I fling myself at him and find my face pressed into the soft skin below his ear. It smells so familiar I have to pull back, frightened and ashamed. "Sorry," I whisper. The shouting's over. Just that little bit makes things all right for the moment.

"We were lucky," he tells me professionally, which is so unlike Murray it makes me think there's a problem. Knowing Murray as I do, I can tell he's holding something back. He sighs. "As you know, the evidence wasn't enough for the CPS to guarantee a conviction. Simple as that."

But it's not simple. Not to me. "That's a good thing then, isn't it?"

"For now," Murray says. "But as a condition of his release, David's not to leave the area and he has to report to the police station every three days. He won't be allowed his passport either. One tiny bit of evidence against him could reinstate the charges. The police won't rest until they get him back inside, Julia."

"God," I say, mulling all this over. "It's that unstable?"

He nods, swallowing. "There was one other condition of bail."

306

I'm waiting, freezing, thinking that nothing could dampen the joy of having David back. "Which is?"

"That he doesn't go anywhere near you or the kids."

For a moment, I think he means it. For a split second, I've dropped through the bottom of the boat and I'm standing chin deep in sludge, struggling to breathe. I splutter through my reply. "You're not serious, right?" Murray nods, as solemn as I've ever seen him. "And the court said that, did they? The police or the CPS or whoever else has a darned say over an innocent man's life?" I'm shouting again; a gradual crescendo.

"No, Julia. *I* said it."

The kids are excited to get out of school early. Patricia, my head teacher, was less than enthusiastic about my early departure so soon after my return to work, but I didn't wait around to hear much more than a shocked "Oh?"

"Did they catch the killer, Mum?" Alex, despite his seatbelt, is on the edge of his seat. "Will David be able to tell me stories of real-life baddies from when he was in prison?"

I smile and glance at the kids in the rearview mirror. They are my entire life, strapped up and safe. One of them a cop in the making, the other obsessed with dolls and her pictures. I love them dearly. "David's going to be tired and perhaps a little on edge, honey, so don't go giving him the third degree."

"What does that mean?" Alex is annoyed that I am halting his line of investigation.

"It means let him relax and don't question him." I brake for a dozy pheasant strutting across the road. We are nearing David's remote house. Strangely, the desolation makes me feel safe. "Right, here we are. Remember, lay off the questions and don't make too much noise." I sign this for Flora and help her out of the car. She collects an assortment of crayons and dolls from the back seat.

"Is this nowhere?" Alex asks, gaping around at the darkening landscape. Dusk still falls so early. We are not far from where I found Grace. I shudder. I can't afford to think of that now.

"Pretty much." Flora grips my hand.

The house lights glimmer squares of orange within the stone wall. It feels as if we've come home. The door opens the second I lift the iron knocker. David stands there, calm and reassuring, while a spillage of heat and the scent of good food draws us inside.

I fall into his arms when he holds them open. He feels a little thinner, a little warier. Finally he pushes me away and holds me at a distance. "Shut the door, Alex." He is engrossed in me.

"Oh David," I let out a part sigh, part cry. "This has just been the worst time. When we last stood here, the police —"

"Sshh. That's all over. Now I'm home, it feels as if I've never been away. I'm fine. I've suffered worse."

He is amazing and resilient; filled with determination more than I can imagine, and that's why I adore him. Briefly, I wonder what he means by *I've suffered worse*, but being a doctor, I expect he just means that he's seen worse in his job.

The kitchen is sparkling, not a remnant left to remind us of our last supper. In fact, something is cooking in the oven and I get a whiff of garlic and onions as the whoosh of the fan sends out comforting smells.

"Looking good," he says brightly, closing the oven. I stand gawping at his normality. He has just been released from prison yet is acting as if nothing has happened.

Soon we are eating, clattering knives and forks, conversation jostling for attention. Afterwards we settle in the living room. Alex and Flora are already sprawled on the floor, playing snap with the deck of cards Alex always carries. "Picking up where we left off, eh?" I nestle under David's arm, a little self-conscious in case the kids turn round and see us, but it has to happen sometime. They may as well get used to us being close. "I always knew you were innocent," I whisper into his ear. "The whole thing was preposterous, and how Ed could have —"

There is a finger over my mouth and a pair of dark eyes glinting at me, imploring me to not dwell on things. "Do you know what bothered me most about being in prison?" he asks.

I shake my head. There must be a thousand things: fear of never seeing the outside world again, violent inmates, terrible food, poor treatment . . . "I don't honestly know, David." And that's the truth. "I can't begin to comprehend what you've been through."

"What bothered me most about being locked up was not being able to see you."

David is suddenly on his feet, striding over to Alex. "No, no, no," he says. "Not like that." Alex thinks he's going to be told off and semi cowers as David looms above him. "Look, if you want to win, then you must sit like this." David lowers himself on to the floor and crouches so that his hands are positioned over the deck of cards. "Then you're ready to slam your hand down the second it's snap." David's face is inches away from Alex's. "OK?"

Alex slowly nods and a smile follows. "OK."

I sigh heavily, not realising I'd been holding my breath all this time. Flora's hands wiggle frantically at me. That's not fair. Will you be on my side, Mummy?

Of course, I sign back. I lower myself on to the carpet and gaze in wonder at the four of us. We are playing snap. Alex and David roar with laughter as Flora and I completely miss a turn. Flora sees the joke and scuffs the cards with her foot. Alex is about to fly at his sister but David grabs him and tickles him and for the briefest flash of time I see Murray playing with his son. I see us as we should have been; as we will never be.

"Did you hear something?" David suddenly freezes, holding his hand up to silence us. "I swear I heard something outside." He is on edge. It is understandable. "A crash or thump. It was loud." He is on his feet and flicks off the wall lights. He peers out of the window. "Jesus *Christ*," he says and snaps the curtains closed. When he turns, his face is ashen.

"What? What is it?" My heart skips as I stand up and rush to the window.

"Two vans. A bunch of people with banners. They're outside the house, shouting." David's voice shakes. The last time I saw him this scared was when Ed took him away.

I peel back the curtain. A dozen protesters line the front wall of David's property. "Oh dear God."

"Come away. Let me think." I can smell the adrenalin on his breath; hear his heart thump beneath his shirt.

"We must call the police," I say. "I'll phone Ed." But we're both thinking it. Last time he was here, David was carted off in a police car. "They're on your side now. The charges have been dropped." My hand on his arm does nothing to help. "In fact, they should have anticipated this happening and offered protection for you."

David paces the room, thinking. He's not really listening to me. He strides around the house locking the back door, the French door, pulling curtains closed and checking the catches of the old windows. "You need to get me out of here." His face is pale and his words equally washed out.

He means us, too, I tell myself. "But it's your home. You can't let a bunch of strangers drive you out within hours of being released." I lay my hands on his shoulders.

"What is it, Mum? Can't we play snap any more?" Alex asks.

"Not now," David says with the patience of a father. "Let me sort out this mess and then we'll have fun again." Alex seems satisfied. In the silence that follows, we are left with the angry shouts echoing through the walls.

Justice for Grace . . . Mur-der-er . . . Justice for all . . .

The sound of breaking glass makes my skin prickle. "Murderer?" I whisper, but David dashes from the room. I run after him to the kitchen and skid to a halt in the mess. Several of the small window panes are smashed and the thin wooden bars splintered.

Lying on the worktop is a brick with paper wrapped around it. David doesn't make a move so I pick it up. My hands shake with the weight as I pull off the paper. I read the words silently.

"Kids, get your coats on," I say, trying not to panic. I have to get them out of here. I pass the paper to David.

"Oh Christ," he says after a quick glance. On one half of the paper is a photocopied picture of Grace Covatta — her face made-up and grinning — and pasted beside it is a photograph of David, snapped as he was leaving prison. Across his harrowed face is a large black X drawn in marker pen with *Dr Death* scrawled underneath. "Why are they calling me a murderer?" he asks in a voice warped by fear. Then, "Let's go. We have to get out of here."

Back in the hallway he stops. "Look. It's me they're after, not you and the kids. If you leave by the front door, that will provide cover and I can slip out the back. I'll make a dash across the fields and in ten minutes I'll be at Hogan's Lane, where the road bridges over the river. Will you pick me up there?"

"Of course." I don't even need to think about this. My hands tremble. "You must take a torch and boots and a coat. Hurry. Get everything together." I'm urgent and panicking, yet totally in control. We will get through this. "But I wish you'd let me call Ed," I say. David shakes his head firmly.

In another moment, we say a second frantic goodbye.

"Remember, don't stop until you get to Hogan's Lane. I'll flash the torch three times as I get near the junction."

Then, rendering me speechless, David opens up a cupboard beneath the crooked stairs and fumbles around in the darkness. He takes out a small wooden box, opens it and pulls out a bone-handled knife — used for hunting or fishing, I tell myself. He flicks it open and closed so that the blade is just a silver flash. "Protection," he explains, pocketing it. He leaves by the back door.

Drawing a breath as if we are about to swim a mile underwater, I huddle Alex and Flora at my side and open the front door. They falter when they see it's a woman with kids. The cruel verses of their vitriolic chant fade and turn to random cries and jeers that come straight from the heart.

"Where is he?" a woman yells. I don't look. I wing my arms around the children as we scuttle down the front path with our hoods up and faces bent to the ground.

"I'm scared, Mum." Alex's voice is suddenly that of a much younger boy.

"It's OK, love. Just stay with me." I have the car keys aimed at the protesters as if I'm armed with a stun gun. I grapple with the front gate. We have to push through the gathering. "Look, please, just let us through." Flora is huddled inside my coat.

"Is he in there? Is he still in the house?" The woman's sobs stop me dead. I look up and my hood slips off my head. I stare into her vacant eyes.

"Yes," I lie. Then, "I'm sorry," although I'm not sure what for. The flash of recognition — perhaps from a parents' evening, perhaps when Grace was in *Romeo and Juliet* — quickly ends when the jeering begins again. I want to reach out to her, to talk to her, explain that things aren't as they seem. I want to tell her everything I know about David so that she understands he didn't hurt her daughter.

Alex pulls at my sleeve. "Mum, come on."

"I'm so sorry," I say softly. I look at the woman's fidgeting hands. Between her fingers she holds a tiny brown bear; a mascot, perhaps belonging to Grace. It takes all my effort but I turn away from her and hurry to the car. I hold Alex and Flora tightly by the hands.

As I fumble with the keys, there is more shouting — a muddle of anger and bitter threats of revenge. I hear Grace's mother sobbing. "Justice will be done," she wails and I block it from my mind until we are safely locked inside the car. The engine starts on the third attempt and several stones clatter off the roof as we drive off down the darkening lane to find David.

★ ★ ★

The telephone wakes me. For a moment, I forget where I am, but once I've located the clunky plastic receiver in Mum's spare room, I remember the day before with sickening clarity. David forced from his own home.

"Murray," I say, wondering if I'm still dreaming. "Why are you calling so early?" I am lying on my side, facing the wall. I hardly dare turn over to inspect the remainder of the bed. My eyes are wide and my cheeks flush with expectation. I am waiting for the warm hand to settle on my bare shoulder. I pray that nothing in my voice gives away what might have happened between David and me. As Murray tells me why he is calling, I frantically think back to the night that followed our arrival home.

It was late by the time we'd grabbed some food at a tiny anonymous restaurant. David was chilled from his dash across the fields. We returned to Northmire, exhausted, scared, determined, and once the kids were tucked into bed we sat and talked. David had bought some brandy and set the bottle on the table beside the fire. Having him at Northmire seemed somehow . . . right.

Oddly, he didn't want to go over the day's events or figure out how he could be protected from harassment in the future. I insisted we call the police for advice but he wouldn't hear of it. No, he was more concerned with talking about me. He asked crazy, irrelevant things about my childhood; he spoke of what he was doing in the world as I was growing up — only serving to highlight the age difference between us. For instance, when I was born, David was a second-year medical student at Cambridge University. Perhaps it was his subtle way of telling me there was no future for us together, that we were simply worlds apart.

"And your school years?" he asked. "Were you a good student?"

"Average," I replied, yet before I could expand, he had asked three more questions about my school days. Was I happy? Who were my friends? What made me want to be a teacher?

Then, "What about your mother, Julia? How did you get on with Mary as you were growing up? Did you fight? Were you close? Did you spend time together?" I never had the chance to answer. David poured more brandy, his eyes slurred with curiosity. And then he hit me. "What was it like growing up without a father?"

"Look, I'm tired. It's been a crazy day." My eyes vindicated my excuse. If my mother wouldn't let me discuss the subject, then there was no way I could talk about it with David. Not yet, anyway. "I'm going up." I left the room with my head bowed; a child sent to bed. I went to shower . . . promising to make up the spare bed for David . . . promising to see him in the morning . . . Perhaps a warm hand falls around my waist, igniting my heart . . . A soft breath on my neck, with the promise of breakfast. I wait for the memory of him on top of me, beneath me, inside me, to fill my mind. It doesn't come. I look round. The bed beside me is empty.

"Julia?" Murray says.

"Sorry," I say. "I'm tired. I had a late night." In my dream, David fondly strokes my hair. I can smell him, feel the soft brush of his skin against mine. "What do you want?"

Quite calmly, but in a way that makes me realise he's deadly serious, Murray says, "The children."

The toast burns and of course I blame Murray. It's better than screaming at him about this crazy idea he's woken up with. The kids look at me as if I have two heads and David refuses to leave the room in case I need support.

"Is now the best time to be discussing this?" I scrape the toast and a shower of black rains on the floor. "In front of them?" I add. Murray is infuriatingly calm.

"I just want you to know that I'm going to be filing for sole residency with limited contact. As far as I'm concerned, any agreement we already had about Alex and Flora in our statement of arrangement — sorry, *your* statement of arrangement — is now unacceptable. None if it was based on you shacking up with . . ." Murray knows when to stop. "Look, their lives are inside out at the moment, and until you sort out yours, they have no chance of stability. That's all I'm saying."

"Ha!" It's a half-sing, a half-scream. This is not Murray talking. "And you're in a position to provide a little steadiness, are you? On a sinking, rat-infested narrow boat?" I shake my head. "Why are you wasting your time, Murray? Just accept the way things are now. We are nearly divorced, the kids live with me, I'll never stop you seeing them and —"

"Then let me have them today."

"What?"

"Hand the kids over now and show me you mean what you say."

"Murray, you're being unreasonable." David is suddenly behind me, just where I need him. His fingers thread through mine.

"Julia, it's Saturday. The kids always come to me on Saturday." Murray shrugs and sighs.

I sigh too, shaking my head in despair. "It's just the way you said it, Murray. You're scaring me. Demanding them as if they are a couple of toys to hand over." I'm relieved as Murray weakens. "They are our *children*."

"Look, I just want to see them, OK? I miss them. I have a surprise planned and, well," he glances at David, "I didn't know what kind of weekend you two would be having, so . . ." He's said enough and bows his head. I'm squinting at him, squeezing David's fingers, trying to get a message to him to ask what he thinks. *This is the man I loved.* So why do I feel so scared about letting my kids go with him? It's the glaze of tears on Murray's eyes that does it. I always was a sucker for that.

"I'm sorry, Murray. I'm being stupid. Of course the kids can go with you today. Just don't talk of residency orders and courts and taking them away from me."

"Yay! A surprise," and Alex signs at Flora to tell her about the treat.

What surprise? she signs back.

Well, it wouldn't be a surprise then, would it? Murray signs.

"Can you bring them home by six?"

"It will be eight o'clock."

"Seven, then."

"No, eight," he says firmly, and I thank my lucky stars he's even agreeing to bring them back at all.

Alex clatters their breakfast bowls into the sink and grabs his coat. He skids to a stop at Murray's side while Flora gathers up her little bag of crayons and folded sheets of paper. She is harbouring quite a collection of pictures. She also packs up a couple of dolls and half a packet of chewy sweets. She's all set and excited by the promised surprise.

"Have fun then," I say wistfully, although quite pleased to have time alone with David.

The kids' excitement is such that when Murray bundles them out of the door, neither of them remember to give me a kiss goodbye and Flora forgets to take her coat. I run down the drive waving it about, the sleeves flapping a silent message, but either Murray doesn't see or he doesn't want to risk me changing my mind. I stop running and stand panting, watching them drive off, my lips aching from not having kissed my children goodbye.

MURRAY

I didn't float but the papers did. All those white squares rippling in my wake. It was a crazy plan in hindsight. And the stupid thing was, I thought she was holding out the pole to save me. But no, Chrissie was frantically trying to rescue each and every one of Mary's medical notes, fishing them on to the deck with the long boathook I keep on the roof. But her panic was understandable — she was the one who had signed out the file from hospital records.

"You've brought new meaning to the expression," I say. I'm huddled under my duvet with a shot of whisky. Chrissie eyes me warily through her glasses. Her eyebrows peek above the frames. She doesn't have a clue what I'm talking about. "I wouldn't touch him with a bargepole," I explain. "Meaning I'm —"

"Low-down dirty scum?" she suggests. I'm shivering from my heart out. She's not. She's sitting there wondering how someone could stoop so low. After she'd pulled the first couple of pages from the water, Chrissie quickly saw that they weren't from the Marshall file at all but rather to do with a petty fraud incident in Kent concerning a Mr Barrett. It only took her a second to figure it out, and while I was dragging my body from the freezing, weed-choked water, she was ransacking *Alcatraz* looking for the swapped papers. And she found them too, even before I got back inside the cabin.

"You don't understand." I was dripping everywhere, too cold to even know I was cold.

"Damn right I don't. Nadine said you were a decent sort."

"Decent sort of what, though? Did she ever tell you that?" I'm trying not to smile. Chrissie bows her head away, trying not to smile too. "This case is really important to me." I'm serious now. I can't help it. I take a step towards her but she backs away. I stink. "My wife — rather my nearly ex-wife — is . . . has fallen in love with a man who's . . ." She'll think I'm crazy for sure now. "Look, I'm just trying to save my kids from having a violent criminal for a stepfather. All right? Does that sound so mad to you?" I knock back the whisky.

"Completely," she says solemnly. "You are mad and what you are saying is mad. Everything about you is mad. Your entire life is mad. How long have you known your wife?"

"For ever. Since she was born."

"Have you always been this crazy?"

She makes me think. "Always. Completely," I answer honestly.

"Poor wife."

321

"Life isn't about charts and statistics and research and graphs and computers spewing out loads of useless information that —"

"If you'd shut up for a second, I was going to say that I like mad people. They remind me that I'm sane. That must be why I'm friends with Nadine." And, to my shock and surprise — causing me to pour another measure of whisky — Chrissie hands me the papers from Mary's medical file. "You have my number," she says, standing up to leave. "I can see this means a lot to you. Call me when you're done. But make it quick."

I'm speechless. Chrissie disappears through the hatch and *Alcatraz* wobbles a little as she steps on to the towpath. "Thanks," I say to her legs as she strides past the cabin window. "Thanks very much."

I swear Mary Marshall's pupils dilate when she sees me approach. Of course, it could be the sun glittering on the lake giving a false effect. Either way, she doesn't move. She is frozen solid.

"Mary, you have a visitor," the nurse says. The uniformed young woman paces about, stamping her feet and clapping her hands together at the shore. Her nose is red and shiny. The water's not frozen, but fingers of icy grass reach right down to the tiny waves that splash on to the bank. There is a single bench and Mary sits on it, staring out across the expanse of water.

"Hello, Mary. It's Murray. I've come to see how you are." I don't sit down. Instead, I squat in front of her so that she has no choice but to look at me. "How are you

322

feeling?" Just in case, I sign the words. Still there is no response. "Mary, I've been looking into your case and . . ." This is no good. I stand up and speak to the nurse, guiding her a few steps away. "Could I have some privacy with my mother-in-law? Would you mind giving us a few minutes alone?"

"I'm sorry, sir, I can't. Mrs Marshall is on twenty-four-hour observations. She's not allowed to be alone even for a second."

"How come?" Julia never mentioned this.

The nurse glances back to Mary. "It was since she tried to set her room on fire. Sister thinks she might try something similar again."

Sighing, I get my wallet out. "OK, how much?"

"I don't think —"

"How *much*?" Everyone can be bought, especially poorly paid nurses. I pass a twenty-pound note to her. She holds out her hand but raises her eyebrows. I pull out another twenty and there's only a moment's hesitation, probably for the benefit of her conscience, before she takes the money.

"A couple of minutes only," she says while glancing around. The hospital looms behind us; dozens of lit-up windows in the blank white façade. "I'll lose my job if I get caught."

"You won't get caught," I assure her and sink down beside Mary again as the nurse walks off around the lake. "We don't have long," I begin. "I know you can hear me and I know you understand. What I don't know is why you won't speak. The doctors and nurses, Julia, everyone who's seen you like this, they all seem to accept that you have some brain disease causing your silence. Mary, *I* can't." I push myself directly into her line of sight although she doesn't focus on me. "I want you to know, Mary, that you're not ill. There is absolutely nothing wrong with you."

I'm sticking my neck out, I know, building her up when I may, at a push, be wrong. Someone could have made a mistake. There's a chance that papers could be missing from the file; doctors' reports lying on a desk somewhere; a conclusive diagnosis yet to be reached. But I need her to have hope. I need her to speak. I need to know the truth.

"Mary," I continue, "someone I trust has done a bit of investigating. There are no records of any MRI test results on your file here at The Lawns. Those results were the reason you were admitted here." I recall Chrissie's words. I believe her. "After that, I had your NHS notes tracked down and, more specifically, we found the actual report on your scan." I take a deep breath, give her time to assimilate all this. "Your consultant, Mr Radcliffe, concluded in his report that there is absolutely nothing wrong with your brain. There is no clinical proof of you having dementia — vascular or otherwise."

I stand up to ease the cramp in my legs. The nurse is on her way back to our end of the lake. I squat down again. "Do you understand, Mary? Give me a sign if you can. Lift your hand, smile, nod, blink . . . anything." I wait as she absorbs this news with one eye on the white uniform tracking back to us. My words battle between Mary's ears, funnelling down into her brain, her mind, her understanding. There's more to Mary's mutism than mere cerebral bleeding.

Having left *Alcatraz*, Chrissie had done some more digging at my request. Thinking perhaps that the vital NHS hospital scan result was still somewhere in their system — at the very least they would have a copy — she set to work finding out. She called up an old boyfriend, a senior house officer working in accident and emergency. He would have access, she said, to all computer records within the hospital trust. Chrissie was prompt calling me back with his discovery.

"Marcus had no problem in tracking down what you wanted," she said with a slow twist to her words. She was creating suspense, presumably as punishment for my stunt with the file. "How are you, by the way? Did you catch a terrible chill?" Then laughter; an appealing giggle. "Have you dried out yet?"

"Chrissie," I said finally. "The report?"

"Marcus said that Mr Radcliffe's report on Mary Marshall showed absolutely nothing unusual. The consultant concluded that no further action was required. A letter was sent to her GP confirming all this." A pause, but I didn't say a word. I couldn't. "Marcus even studied the stored images that accompanied the report. Nothing. Zilch. As clear as a bell. And he would know." Chrissie paused dramatically, then said, "If she's got vascular dementia — or anything else for that matter — then I've got lung cancer and a missing leg."

"Chrissie, you're a star. An absolute shining star in heaven." I chewed my pencil. "And please, don't have lung cancer."

"There's more," she said expectantly, proudly. "Although it may be nothing. Marcus went one step further and called up the GP's surgery where Mary was a patient. Being a doctor, he won the receptionist's trust and made up some story about Mary being in his care. The receptionist told him that Mary had visited the GP recently. Marcus is completely mad too, by the way," she added as if that justified the extra digging, "and also desperate to date me again. Anyway, it turns out that Mary saw a Dr David Carlyle on the twenty-second of December for a routine appointment. Apparently she had an infected finger."

"Yes, yes, I knew about the infected finger," I said slowly, pondering. "But I didn't know exactly when it was that she'd seen Carlyle. Thanks, Chrissie." And our phone call ended after more well-deserved praise.

"A sign, Mary. I need to know you understand what I'm telling you." I clasp her hands and watch her eyes flick out across the water as if she is out there, cutting through the glassy surface. But she doesn't give me a sign.

Before the nurse returns, I think about the sequence of events. Julia discovered her mother mute on Christmas Day. During the time since Mary's visit to Carlyle on the twenty-second — that three-day period — something stopped her speaking. I transfer my grip to her brittle shoulders. "Mary, what *was* it that scared you into silence?"

326

And just when the tiny tremor on her jaw begins to pull at the muscles of her mouth, just when her blinking directs her stare from the water to my face, the nurse returns and insists that Mary has to go back on to the ward.

I turn and gaze out over the lake myself, in case Mary left any clues in the water.

If she hadn't called me ridiculous, if she hadn't mocked me, then I might actually have considered changing my hot-headed plans. But in my work, I see so many cases of clearing up the mess when it's too late, far too many instances of the children being left to suffer with inappropriate step-parents unnecessarily, that I simply can't help myself. I'm not losing my kids. When we leave Northmire, I take them straight to *Alcatraz*. And they won't be going back this evening as I promised Julia.

"What's the big surprise then?" Alex is disappointed, I can tell. "You promised there was a surprise and it's just the stupid boat."

"Ah, that's where you're wrong." We walk down the towpath. "We're going on a holiday." Alex hesitates, pulls a vaguely hopeful face, then signs what I've said to Flora. She gives a delighted squeak.

"Where to?"

This is as far as my spur-of-the-moment holiday plans have got. "To an amazing place," I say in a voice that implies a jungle trek, a desert island, a Disney resort.

"Do we get to go on an aeroplane?" Alex is still dubious but evidently willing to be tempted.

"Not exactly. Think of it more as a cruise."

"On the sea?"

I reckon he'd go for that — a glitzy jaunt round the Mediterranean or an icy fjord adventure. I stop walking and go wide-eyed and serious, staring intently at each of my children. "We're going on a cruise so dangerous, so intrepid that no explorer brave enough to attempt the journey has ever returned alive." I pause dramatically. I can almost hear Alex's heart beating. "The very mention of the River Cam sends chills of fear down valiant men's spines. Our mission . . . to make it to Pope's Corner and maybe even beyond by tomorrow night. We will be heroes and the world will be ours for the taking." I punch the air and cheer, conjuring an image of our homecoming for my son. I wait for his reaction and Flora just gawps at me, totally unaware of what's going on.

"Dad, I'm eleven, not three. And the holiday sucks. Does Mum know you're taking us on the stupid boat?"

He's clearly not impressed. "Of course." But I can see he doesn't believe me. "Look, let's just get aboard and plan our adventure. It'll be great." I'm desperate now. "We can even make a campfire tonight, if you like. We can cook sausages on it." For now, the Boy Scout cooking seals it and Alex grudgingly accompanies me on to *Alcatraz*, disappointed that his promised surprise is no more than a chug up the river. Before we board, I squint at the hull. She's drawing another inch, perhaps two. I pray we're not sinking.

328

★ ★ ★

None of it's planned properly, of course, but then in my experience it's best not to map out a course you can't follow. That's why a life on the water is so simple. There aren't many ways to go, and a three-sixty about-turn is fairly impossible in a thirty-two-foot boat on a narrow river. So what could possibly go wrong with this holiday?

"Can I steer?" Alex is shivering and wearing his coat with my waterproof jacket over the top. He looks like a semi-erected tent.

"Sure. Remember, left is right and right is left." That about sums it all up, I think, squinting through the drizzle.

Our view of the countryside is occluded by the low-hanging clouds and rain. Flora is sensibly tucked up inside the cabin, keeping warm under a blanket. She doesn't appear to have brought a coat. As soon as Alex told her of my appalling plan for a holiday, she took to sulking and working on her secret drawings. I make a mental note to ask her again about her brief moment of contact with her grandmother. I need all the clues I can get.

Hours later, just as the vague afternoon light gives way to a lilac dusk, perhaps promising overnight snow, I decide it's time to set up camp for the night. "Drop anchor, skipper," I call out to Alex. He is standing on the forward deck, being the figurehead of our journey, having made the death-defying walk down the narrow ledge along the side of the boat. His mother would faint at the sight. He turns and gives me a sullen stare.

"Don't be stupid, Dad," he calls back angrily, but when he sees my expression dissolve into hurt, he bows his head and makes his way carefully back along the narrow ledge, gripping on to the roof for all he's worth. With every step he takes, I imagine him transforming from boy to young man. I close my eyes for a beat and realise that I don't have to lose him, not if I tread carefully too.

"Want to take the tiller while I pull her in?"

"Sure," he says, grinning at the responsibility.

I peek down the hatch before I leap the few feet to the bank, making sure Flora is safe. She's absorbed in her work and frowns as she sees me spying. She cradles her picture with her arms.

"Slack off on the throttle, buddy," I call out over the engine noise, and Alex does as he is told, sliding *Alcatraz* to an easy stop at the bank. Between us, we secure the stern and bow to a couple of nearby trees. "It'll hold as long as we don't have heavy winds overnight. Who knows where we'll end up then? Down in the Amazonian rainfor —"

"Da-ad, I'm not a kid. You don't need to talk to me like I am. The boat's secure, OK? Nothing's going to happen. Nothing out of a storybook, anyway."

"Sorry," I mutter, and nod in agreement. Alex's face slumps when he discovers that, after pulling a shower of coloured wrapping from his pocket, he's eaten his last Fruit Pastille. There's no food aboard either, so unless they fancy eating tinned mackerel marinated in Jack Daniel's, it's going to mean a trip to a shop or a meal at a pub.

"But you said we could cook sausages on a fire." Alex is horrified when I suggest the pub meal. I'm already salivating at the thought of a pint, but in the interests of father-son relations, I must keep my promise. Alex will cook sausages on a campfire on the riverbank if I have to hunt all night for food and dry wood. I stare at the British Waterways map.

"According to this, we should be near Little Stretford. There's a track right here that goes directly into the village."

"It'll take ages to walk there and I'm starving. You said we could cook campfire food." Alex cradles his chin in his hands, leaning on the tiller.

"Buddy, I'm working on it, OK?" I reach into the cabin and pull my hat and gloves from a hook. The temperature's falling and it won't be long before a frost works over the land. "Are you sure you're not up for pie and chips in the local?" I can even smell the pint as the barmaid pulls it. "You sure you won't be too cold cooking outside? It might start raining again."

"We'll have the fire to keep us warm. It'll be an adventure. A proper surprise like you said." Alex opens the guilt tap full force.

I sigh, resigned. "Bangers and toasted marshmallows it is, then." I zip up my jacket. I can make this quick. "Look, can you show me how really responsible you are and look after your sister for twenty minutes?" Judging by the map, it shouldn't take any longer than that. I pray there's a village shop still open.

"Do I get paid? Baby-sitters cost money, you know."

"Will a pound do?"

"Five."

"Five? Two. Last offer."

"Three, and that's *my* last offer or you'll have to put up with Flora whining across the fields with you. And she doesn't have a coat and Mum'll go spare when I tell her."

He's right. "OK. Three it is, then. Get down inside the cabin. Sit with your sister. Don't fight and don't, whatever you do, leave the boat. Got it?"

"Got it," he says, saluting as new skipper. "And don't forget to buy ketchup."

Alex grins and disappears inside the cabin. I hear him slide the bolt on the door. I have a torch, a map, some money and an urgent need to get in my son's good books. With that in mind, I set off on the track that leads to the village, not thinking about a pint in the pub at all.

JULIA

My mobile phone vibrates in my pocket. I'm alone. David left a few hours ago. He was distant and troubled; no doubt deeply worried about the disturbance outside his house. I suggested he leave it another day, but he's gone home to check there wasn't any further damage. I made him promise that he would call the police if there'd been any trouble. I'm not sure when he's coming back.

I glance at my watch and pull my phone from my pocket. Thankfully Murray will be bringing the children home soon. I contemplate asking him in for a cup of tea. I need the company. As I answer the phone, I see that I have eight unanswered calls.

"Hello."

"Oh God, Julia. Julia. Oh my God. It's Flora. She's gone missing. Shit. I don't know what to do, Julia." Murray is shouting, hysterical, and his voice distorts and shatters my head into a million pieces.

I scream. "What do you mean, Flora's missing? Murray!" A wail comes from a place so deep inside me, it hurts. "But Flora is with you. She's safe with you, right?"

"No. Julia. Flora's gone. She's gone from the boat. Just gone. Nowhere. Flora is nowhere."

"Murray, shut up. What do you mean, gone? Where are you?" Of course, there's been a mistake. My hands shake so much that I can hardly hold the phone to my ear.

"We're on the boat. We were on the boat. We went on a trip today. I was getting food and when I came back she was gone." There's panting or wind or something rushing down the phone. Fear.

"Call the police. I'm coming to you. Where are you? Where's Alex? Is Alex safe?"

"I've called the police," he tells me as if it's all under control. "Alex is fine. He's beside me. Do you want to talk?"

"Yes!" Put him on."

Alex is crying, I can tell. Little sobs half hidden beneath bravery. "We were on the boat and going to have a fire and then Flora was gone."

"Christ. Did she fall in the water?" I snatch the keys from the table and head out of the door while still talking. "Where are you, Alex? Where is the boat? Did you go very far?"

"I don't know. It's all my fault. I want Flora." And then my son falls apart and Murray comes back on the line. I am hammering my car down the lane, driving in second gear because I daren't let go of the phone to change up.

"Julia, go to Little Stretford. Come along Main Street as far as you can go. Keep going down the fen

334

road. Keep going until you reach the river. Go over the railway. Keep going to the river. Hurry, Julia, hurry."

"Why . . . what . . .?" I can't speak. "What are you doing all the way up there, Murray? Where's Flora? Get her now. I'm coming to take the kids back. You can't have them." My voice tempers slightly and switches to automatic as I tear along the dark lanes. I continue talking long after the line has gone dead. "Tell Flora to pack up her stuff and get ready to come home. Tell Alex not to cry. Get Flora ready for me . . . I want my children back, Murray."

In ten minutes, I am breaking the speed limit through Little Stretford. Thankfully the speed of a car outruns a whole day's chug of a narrowboat.

"Dear God, let her be OK." Cottages and the village pub flash by as I follow Murray's directions. "Over the railway line," I say out loud. Then, "Surely there's been a mistake. Tell me this isn't happening." Stifled sobs spill out with my staccato breaths. "Please someone tell me this is a joke or Murray has gone mad. Maybe he's drunk." A slight relaxing in my chest. "Yes, maybe he's so drunk he didn't even notice Flora tucked up in her bunk." I bang the steering wheel and rock back and forth as if it will make the car go faster. I bump down the lane as it narrows, approaching the river. I pass over a railway crossing just like Murray said.

The lane funnels to a small gateway and I realise I'm going to have to abandon the car and run the last bit. I leave the headlights on to illuminate my passage to the river.

"Murray!" I call out when I think I'm close. "Murray, where are you?" I scream his name over and over until my throat burns.

"Here. Over here." Finally I hear him and see the flash of a torch beam sweep through the night. I push through long wet grass and finally on to the bank of the river. Murray's boat delivers beacons of light, vaguely warming, somehow promising that Flora couldn't possibly be far away. I see that the grass is flattened on the bank — a million panicked footprints.

"Did you find her? Is she OK?" My mouth is so dry I can hardly talk. I'm panting.

"No. She's still gone." Murray sprays torchlight into the night, across the river.

"*Murray, Murray!*" I scream. I lunge at him. Half because of hatred and half because he's the one I've always turned to when things are bad. He catches me as I slide down his body. "Oh, shit, shit. Did you run up and down the bank? Did you look in the water?" I point either way up and down the wretched river. "I told you not to take the kids on the boat. She could drown. What time did she go?"

My chest heaves up and down. The breath in me is enormous. I'm ready for anything. Ready to run for miles to find Flora. Any minute now, she's going to come striding back to the boat, angry with her daddy for letting her get lost. I tell myself this over and over.

"Between six and eight. Maybe half an hour either side." Murray's face is crinkled with worry; his cheeks burning red with panic.

336

My watch says eight forty-five. "Where are the police? Did you call them?" Then it strikes me. "Why don't you know exactly when she went? Where the hell were you, Murray?" No doubt he had fallen asleep after drinking too much. I try to catch the smell of his breath on the wind. "You said you were getting food? Where was Flora when you were cooking it?"

"We hadn't started cooking, Mum." Alex grips my arm as if he's caught in a gale. "We were going to have a campfire and cook sausages."

"What on earth were you doing, then?" I scream at Murray. I run to the boat and peer through each small window in turn. I dash back to Murray. "What were you doing?" I yell up close into his face. I smell beer.

"I was getting food. From the village." Murray bows his head. "It's no good standing around talking. I'll keep searching until the police arrive. You stay with Alex on the boat in case she comes back. Keep calling her name. Yell as loud as you can. She can't be far away. She's probably hiding, frightened she'll get told off."

I stare at him in disgust. "Our daughter is *deaf*, Murray, in case you'd forgotten." I turn away, unable to look at him.

Without another word, knowing there's no way back from this, Murray strides off up the river, leaving me in a silent stupor.

Flora had two hearing aids fitted when she was fifteen months old. They were so tiny I couldn't understand how they would help her hear such a big, noisy world.

And Flora was so tiny that I wasn't sure I wanted her to hear it anyway.

The first pair, she ripped out and threw into a puddle. We were out walking after a thunderstorm — Flora in her pushchair, Alex trotting alongside. She'd been tetchy all day; grizzling and moaning as if she was coming down with a virus. She batted at her head, rolling it from side to side on a pillow just like when she cut a tooth. In the end, I put it down to that — she was teething.

Flora's aids had been fitted the day before and it hadn't occurred to me that being bombarded with something so invasive, so unknown, was the cause of her misery. She heard the crackle of the thunderstorm long before we did. Every car that passed by was an earthquake. Birds squealed in the trees, the breeze howled through her head, and other children made a deafening din. At home, it wasn't words and happy sounds that she picked up. No, all Flora heard was a jumbled cacophony of pain, bangs and meaningless noises. She'd been thrown into a hearing world from her perfect silent one. To her, it was like being dumped on another planet.

She destroyed three further sets of hearing aids over the next two years. It was then I told the doctors she wouldn't be wearing them ever again.

"Ju?" Murray and I hadn't discussed it. After yet another hospital appointment, I told him of my decision.

"How would you like to suddenly be made deaf?" I asked.

"Well, I wouldn't, but —"

"So why should Flora suddenly be made to hear?" Flora knew some basic signs already. I'd been on a course. Alex was amazing with her, knowing exactly what his sister was saying even without their hands talking. "She is how she is, Murray. She hates wearing the aids. I think she . . ." It was difficult to explain. "I think she hears too much with them in. I think it's just too painful for her to hear the real world."

Murray thought about what I'd said. That evening he watched our daughter intently — playing, leaving a trail of toys around the house, interacting with Alex, beaming with happiness when a neighbour and her child called by. Flora splashed in the bath and she refused to go to bed without looking through a picture book. She hugged us both, pretended to go to sleep, and was downstairs begging for milk ten minutes later. She was just like any normal three-year-old.

"You're right, of course," Murray said, pulling me close. We'd just flicked off the light in Flora's room. Even through the half-darkness, we heard her loud and clear when she signed that she loved us. "No hearing aids."

That was how we learned the difference between language and speech. That what you're trying to say, that what is so important it must be heard, doesn't have to be spoken. Flora showed us that actions speak way louder than words.

By the time the police arrive, I can't stop shaking. It's a combination of fear and the freezing night that takes hold of every cell in my body.

"Tell us what happened, Mr French. As quickly as you can," the constable says. Murray came running back to the boat when he saw the flashing lights of the police cars.

"Where's Ed? Where's DI Hallet?" I ask him. He's too young to be dealing with this. "I want Ed here searching for Flora. He's my brother-in-law." PC Clough ignores me.

"Speed is of the essence, Mr French." Murray can barely speak.

"I . . . I went to the village. Just to get some sausages for Alex to cook on a campfire. The kids were in the boat. They knew not to leave. Alex was baby-sitting." Murray falters and glances at me. "He was happy to look after his sister. When I came back to the boat, Alex was on the bank collecting firewood. I'd told him to stay inside the boat but he couldn't wait to prepare the fire. When we went back inside the boat together, Flora was gone."

"Oh Murray, you stupid —"

The constable holds up a hand to silence me. "What times were you away from the boat and how far away from the boat was Alex when he was collecting wood?"

Murray thinks. Shame settles over him. "I was gone for a couple of hours, between six and eight, and Alex was maybe fifty feet away. That way." Murray points in a northerly direction. "Shouldn't you be out there searching? Have you got sniffer dogs coming?" he asks, deflecting the blame. "Have you got helicopters and searchlights? Please . . . do something." He isn't quite yelling, not quite crying. "Alex, why didn't you stay inside the boat with your sister?"

"Murray, stop it," I tell him. He can't blame our son.

"Dad, you were gone ages. I was bored and Flora was doing her colouring. I thought I'd surprise you and get the fire built for our cooking."

"Oh, Murray . . ." I bury my face in my hands.

"The village isn't a particularly long walk from here, yet you said that Flora could have gone missing between the hours of six and eight. Two hours to buy sausages?" PC Clough waits for a reply.

He's right. "Hell, Murray, why were you gone so long? Where were you that took two hours?" I push past the constable and grab my husband's shoulders. I inhale deeply at his mouth. I am sickened. "You were in the pub, weren't you?" My voice quakes, on the edge of erupting. "You left our children alone at night on a boat and went to the pub." I push myself away from him, disgusted by his behaviour. "Get out there and find Flora." I'm crying again. Tears that won't help find her.

"Mrs French, we have a number of officers doing just that. But we need to get the facts straight here."

"It's Mrs *Marshall*," I say, appalled at the thought of being Mrs French right now. "Facts? My daughter's missing and you're sitting here chatting. Please, go out and find her!"

The PC turns away from me. "Can you give us a detailed description of the child, Mr French? Anything that will help our officers. And we may need an item of clothing or something personal of hers for a scent."

"Yes, yes, of course," he replies slowly. None of this is real. He's sitting there saying these things but the words aren't real. "She's got blond hair that's slightly auburn in certain lights. It's quite curly and shoulder length. Her eyes are blue —"

"Greeny blue," I add. Can't he even remember what she looks like?

"And her skin is pale. She has a birthmark at the nape of her neck. She's about up to here on me." Murray stands and places his hand beneath his ribs, as if he's patting the top of Flora's invisible head. "So about four feet tall, I don't know. Maybe an inch or two more. Maybe less."

"And she's deaf. Profoundly deaf," I say. The constable gives me a worried look. "You will find her, won't you?" I grab the torch off Murray and tell Alex to stay with the boat. "She can't be far away. She probably wandered off looking for you, Murray. I'm going to head for the village."

"Until she's found, I assume abduction can't be ruled out?" Murray's comment freezes me. He sounds like a solicitor. For a second, all I hear is the water slapping against the side of the hateful boat.

"Indeed," the constable says. "We have to consider all possibilities. Is your daughter able to swim?"

"Yes, yes," I say, inspiring hope in all of us. "She's a good swimmer." Just how good a swimmer she is in the dark, in freezing temperatures, fully dressed, perhaps with a bump to her head, I wouldn't like to guess. I leave the boat and step out into the darkness to search for my daughter.

* ★ ★

Several couples are leaving the pub in the village. I run up to them like a madwoman, breathless and sweating even in the cold night.

"Please . . . help me. Have you seen a little girl of eight with blond hair? She's lost. Did she come into the pub?" Perhaps Flora knows her daddy too well and guessed that's where he'd be. A few more drinkers are leaving the building. I try them instead. "Did you see a girl tonight? Blond hair, pretty?"

"I wish," jokes one of the men, raising a laugh from his fellows. The sick feeling in my stomach erupts, forcing me to bend into the gutter while I retch up my dinner. "Go home, lady. Sleep it off."

I rush inside the pub. Everyone turns and stares at me. "Has anyone seen a little blonde girl tonight? I've lost my daughter. Please help. Please think."

"No, sorry," one woman says, followed by a few more headshakes and shrugs. They just want to get on with their drinking in peace. I see the blue staccato of a police car light in the street. I run outside again and flag down the officers.

"Any luck?" Of course they've had luck, I think, peering through the back window, praying I'll see Flora sitting there.

"Sorry. No news yet. The dogs have arrived and are going to search down at the river." And they drive off.

"Excuse me, have you seen a little girl? She's eight years old with blond hair?" A man is walking his dog.

"No, but I can help you look. Where did you last see her?"

In my mother's house this morning, I want to tell him. She left with her father and didn't remember to take her coat. I didn't even get to give her a kiss goodbye.

"She was on a boat on the river with my husband. He walked up to the village, and when he got back she was gone. I thought she may have come looking for him."

"An eight-year-old left alone? Oh dear," he says. "I'll keep a lookout. I'll walk all around the village again. He hasn't done his business yet." He points to the old Labrador and shrugs.

"She's called Flora," I tell him. "And she's deaf." I start running one way, then another. I've lost my bearings, and when I see another police car, I charge after it back to the boat.

The riverbank is swarming with uniforms. Two dogs sniff at the night air. Their tails are high and they strain at their leads, excited by the prospect of a search. Floodlights illuminate the area as if it's daytime, and radios crackle inaudible messages into the sky. I wonder, amidst this riverbank mess, if anyone is actually searching for Flora.

"Murray . . . what are you still . . . doing here? Why aren't you out looking?" I nearly fall as I go down into the boat's cabin. I can hardly speak I am so out of breath. One officer, a higher rank judging by the plain clothes, stands beside my husband in the cabin. He turns to face me.

"Oh, *Ed*," I wail and fall into his arms. "Thank God you're here. Now we can find Flora."

344

"I've been looking for her," Murray snaps back before Ed can speak. "The sniffer dogs have just arrived. I've been looking for some clothing, her bag, anything of hers to give the dog handler, but there's nothing here."

"Well, she didn't have a coat with her, Murray. You drove off from Northmire without it. She just took her bag of crayons and paper and goodness knows what else. There must be something of hers around here." I glance about but see little evidence of my daughter. The fold-down table has lines of crayon smudged on its cracked varnish, and there is a half-finished cup of orange squash sitting beside some sweet-wrappers. I imagine my daughter, absorbed, head bent over her work, sucking on a sweet, her little eyelids batting in concentration.

"Oh Flora," I say pitifully, and then, under the table, I see something that makes my heart skip. Her little rabbit. Her dirty, torn, faded and battered pale pink rabbit. "Look, what about this?" I bend down.

"Don't touch it." Ed scares the life out of me. "I'm about to seal off the area. If nothing transpires soon," he adds, for a quick shot of hope. "Leave everything exactly where it is." He speaks into his radio and I realise he is going to make *Alcatraz* into a crime scene. The chances that Flora has simply wandered off are growing slimmer by the minute. He is considering the worst outcome.

"Be careful with it then," I say. "She loves it. She can't sleep without it." Then I wonder how Flora will sleep tonight. "Oh God, Murray. What if someone's taken her? Or what if she's curled up in a hedge and lost and freezing half to death?"

"What if," Ed snatches the speculation from me, "you take care of your wife, Murray, and leave the worrying to us?" He tries to sound sympathetic but this is the second time I've seen him at work recently and there's none of the real Ed in him at all.

I don't bother correcting him about "wife". It somehow offers a little comfort. "I have my most capable men on the job," Ed says. A vein pulses on his neck. "We've started work on this quickly. The first couple of hours are the most important."

"But she could have gone missing as soon as Murray went to the village." I look at my watch. "That's up to five hours ago now. So much can happen to a child in five hours." Then my mind tries to destroy me with images of everything that could have happened to her. "Oh, Ed. *Please* get her back." The tears crash down my face. "Tell me she's just wandered off and is in the next field. She won't be able to hear us calling her. She'll think we're not searching for her."

"That's a highly likely scenario, Julia, and her deafness doesn't help the search, I admit. Our dogs will soon pick up a trail." Ed reaches out and gives me a brief hug. "Mike, is your team ready?" A man and a dog have come aboard.

The dog's nose calmly scans the air before she bows her snout and leads her owner off the front of the boat.

"That's odd," Murray comments. "Flora would never leave the boat at the bow. The climb over the side is too high for her."

"Does that mean that someone took her off?" I rush to the forward deck to see where the dog is leading her owner. I see the zig-zag beacon of the officer's flashlight and hear the other dog bark in anticipation on the bank. It is quickly silenced.

"Why didn't they use Flora's rabbit for a scent?" The forgotten toy still lies on the floor inside.

"Flora's trail will still be fresh for the dogs," Ed explains. "We have a dog that's trained for water search. If necessary." He adds the last bit for my benefit, I know. I push the image of Flora in the water from my mind. She needs me to be strong. "I'm going to brief my men with an update on the search plan and put a police diver on standby. Sit tight." Ed gives me a wisp of a smile before leaving me alone. Beside me, a thousand miles away, Murray is buried in his own misery, drowning in guilt.

"Come on," I say to him. We have to stay positive. "Let's search a wider area. Where would a little girl want to go on a freezing cold night?"

Murray opens his mouth, but before he can answer, I stare out into the night, wide-eyed, and whisper to him, "*Home.*"

MURRAY

I hold my breath and stick my face out of the window, squinting because the freezing air stings my eyes. I scrutinise every inch of the verge and hedgerows as Julia cruises slowly along the country lanes. Alex has been instructed to look anywhere and everywhere as we drive home with the headlights flashing beacons in the night.

"What if she walked across the fields?" Alex asks. "She'll get lost. She might get killed by the man that hurt that girl." We'd all been thinking about Grace Covatta, but no one had dared mention her name. Not in the same breath as Flora's.

"That won't happen," I reassure my son. "Not to Flora." And after Julia gives me a sharp look, I turn back to scan the dark lanes. When all I can see is my own gloomy reflection in the glass, I can't help wondering if Alex might be right.

Alex is a good boy. He's mature for his age, smart at school, and only occasionally pulls stunts that remind me he's an eleven-year-old boy. I really trusted him to look after his sister. And I wanted him to know that I trusted him. The thought of dragging Flora across the fields in the dark was less appealing than leaving her cosy and content with her brother inside *Alcatraz*. She would have towed along behind me, moaning, and ended up on my back, shivering in the frost. Besides, I'd promised to be quick.

The walk to the village didn't take as long as I'd expected. I marched around a couple of unfamiliar lanes and was about to ask someone if there was a shop in the village when I spotted the pub. It was warm, inviting and promised a moment's salvation. I would drink quickly.

"A pint of that, please." I gestured to a local ale. Nothing about what I was doing felt easy. Leaving Alex in charge was like going out without shoes on. It wasn't something I'd normally do, but I'd resolved to make him feel grown-up; just give him the first sniff of responsibility. And what could possibly happen? I'd thought as I walked away from the boat. The benefits of keeping the kids warm and comfortable inside *Alcatraz* outweighed any risks. I knew my kids. They wouldn't leave the boat unless there was a real emergency.

"Two eighty-five, please, mate."

I handed over a twenty-pound note. "Is there a shop around here? I'm after some sausages. Perhaps a tin of beans and some bread." I sipped my pint. It was good.

The bartender glanced at the clock. "You'll be lucky to find it open now. If that's all you're after, I reckon my Margaret will have something in the kitchen for you."

"That would save me much flack from my son." I grinned and drew a large mouthful of the beer. It dropped right down inside me as if it belonged there.

"Off the boats, are you?"

I nodded. "Yes. My son wanted to try a spot of outdoor cooking tonight. It's a boy thing." I rolled my eyes and dipped down to the halfway mark on my pint while the man called for his wife. He instructed the middle-aged woman to search the kitchen for what I wanted, and as if by magic, she quickly reappeared with everything Alex could want for a campfire supper.

"That's great. How much do I owe you?"

"Don't mind the money. Just try a couple more of my ales and we'll call it quits, eh?" The barman was already pulling back on the polished pewter arm of a beer I'd never even heard of. "Drink up," he said. "And tell me what you think of this."

And so I did. At least four more times over the next hour, and with each pint consumed, the urgency to get back to the boat waned by an exponential amount. The kids would be fine. Alex would come looking for me if there was a problem. It was only when Margaret emerged from the kitchen again at least two hours after I first sat down at the curved bar that I decided I should be on my way. The beer had loosened my world.

"Good to see you then, Dan."

"Don," the barman corrected.

"And thanks for the sausages." I slowly turned around looking for them, and eventually found the wrapped packet under my stool. I felt dizzy and sick. The beer was stronger than I was used to. "See you again maybe. And thanks for all this." I held up my loot and set off for the river. Ten minutes later I dashed back into the pub for my jacket.

I finally found *Alcatraz* through all the fields, but only because of the whistling. "Alex?" I called out. "Is that you? Where are you?" I saw the line of my boat's windows through the hedge and I soon emerged on to the bank. "Alex," I called out again. I was annoyed that he'd got off the boat.

"Over here, Dad." He was a little way up the river. I heard him panting and the thud of his quick footsteps pounding the bank as he ran back to me. "I was just getting the firewood ready. You were gone *ages*. Did you get the sausages? We're starving."

"I sure did," I said proudly, and held up the paper packet that Margaret had kindly given me. "And I made some new friends." The beer filled my belly and my brain banged against my skull. By choice, I usually drank whisky. "You should be inside keeping warm. Let's go and get Flora and she can help light the fire." We stepped aboard. "You shouldn't have come out," I muttered. "I told you to stay in the cabin with your sister."

None of it mattered now. I was back. With sausages. We were going to have a fun evening. No more ticking-off.

"She's probably asleep by now. She was bored," Alex said.

I went into the cabin, and because of the alcohol, I didn't feel that first stab of fear that every parent suffers when they can't instantly locate their child. Last time

I'd seen Flora, she was sitting at the table colouring. "Where is she, mate?" I went to the tiny bathroom and pushed against the door. It swung into the cubicle, proving it empty. "Shit," I remember saying, although I still trusted that she was on board. "Were you playing hide and seek?"

"No." Alex reddened. He knew what was coming.

"She must be in here somewhere." I went to the front of *Alcatraz* and flung open a couple of storage lockers big enough for a child to hide in. Nothing except the stale whiff of damp tarpaulins and ancient rope. I opened the semi-glazed door to the forward deck and checked right up into the point of the bows. Nothing. I must have missed her in the kitchen. The ale did its best to dampen my instincts, but my heart still raced against the sluggish effects.

"Flora, where have you gone?" It was a cross between fear, worry, frustration and a belief that my darling little girl was having a game with me. It wouldn't have been the first time I'd spent ten minutes hunting for her.

"She was here, Dad, honestly. She was just colouring and then she played with her dolls."

"Flora!" I yelled, even though I knew it was futile. Perhaps the vibrations of her name would send her scurrying from her hiding place. My search gathered momentum, and soon every single stowage space had been ransacked. I even shone the torch down into the engine compartment. I made a mental note to run the bilge pump when Flora turned up. There was more water in the hull than ever.

"OK, buddy. We'd better go and look on the bank. She must have followed you outside."

"Probably," Alex admitted. "Although I told her to stay in here." He touched my arm ever so lightly, and for a second I thought that it was Flora creeping up from behind. "She'll be all right, won't she, Dad?"

"Of course," I said. My mouth was so dry that the words came out flat.

MARY

The groundsman found me in his hut. I was lying in a cone of sunshine, vomit and blood. The difference between consciousness and what lay beyond was unfathomable, although I had been passing between both for hours.

"Sweet Mother of God." He loomed over me, making me stiffen with fear. "What happened here? What happened to you, lass?" A rough hand touched my cheek with the lightness of a leaf.

I flinched and stared up at him. The tongue in my mouth was a swollen cut of meat. It pressed painfully on my teeth, allowing only the tiniest space for air to pass through the back of my throat. Swallowing was impossible. And the soles of my feet, paddling in pools of blood, burned with the grooves that I knew had been carved into them. I couldn't speak or flee. I was an animal in shock, waiting for this man to assault me or save me. I didn't care which, as long as the pain could end.

When they arrived, the police were puzzled. They stared down at me, asking me questions I couldn't answer. An ambulance crew was summoned, and after a great deal of gawping and pondering, chatting with the groundsman and Mr Boseley-Greene about how such a terrible thing could have happened at his daughter's wedding, they finally carted me off to hospital.

I was an inconvenience, an embarrassing remnant of an otherwise perfect day, and until I was in the ambulance and wrapped in a rough wool blanket, I had remained naked and bloody. The suffering went on as if David had carefully orchestrated all this misery; all my life of misery.

In hospital, answering the detective's questions was impossible. I couldn't speak. Memories were a road accident in my mind; an evening exploded into incomprehensible fragments of delight, pain and terror. And because of the drugs, I was still peering through fogged glass. Nothing was visible; nothing was real.

I told the police what had happened by jotting down broken sentences, barely legible scrawl, on to a small notepad. If I filled every page, there wouldn't be enough space to tell them the truth.

"Rape, Miss Marshall, is a very serious allegation. And at a wedding? The young man you are accusing is particularly upset by what happened to you. He went to the police station voluntarily when he was informed what had happened. Are you *sure* you have got your facts right?" The worn-out detective watched a pretty nurse walk down the ward, more interested in her starched white uniform and neat, long-legged steps than he was in taking a statement from me.

I stared at him from my hospital bed. He had no idea how I was feeling. I wanted to tear myself inside out, set fire to my remains. I hated myself. I hated what David had done to me. The concept of trust, of friendship — *of a future* — had been destroyed.

I picked up the pencil and wrote again. No one had asked about my injuries. I screwed up my eyes as I handed the page to the detective. I could still feel David's knife cold against my skin.

"He attacked you with a knife?"

At last, a glimmer of interest. I'd been in hospital three hours and no one had asked where my wounds had come from.

My legs were suddenly exposed as the detective stood and whipped back the sheet. "The doctor mentioned lacerations to the lower limbs. Nasty." Then he peeled apart my lips and gawped into my mouth before shying away.

He did this to me, I scribbled, underlining "he", and handed the paper over.

"Assault is an entirely different matter, miss. Will you please confirm that you are claiming that Mr David Carlyle assaulted you with a knife?"

Yes. Yes. And I underlined it again. Wasn't the rape enough? I wanted to add, but the detective pocketed the paper. He sighed, weary, and started to leave.

"Did you have too much to drink, Miss Marshall? Were you leading the young gentleman on? Free love and all that. Young people of today, it's a tragedy."

Wait, I scribbled on a fresh sheet. It's the truth. Believe me. My hand shook as I wrote. I held up the pad. He didn't look.

"The nurses will take it from here, Miss Marshall."
He smoothed out his uniform. "A word of advice.
Perhaps stick to Coca-Cola next time." The wink, the
fat lips squashing into a doubtful, semi-formed leer
stayed with me for ever.

Murray tells me I am not ill. He watches me as I stare
out over the lake, my eyes settling on the surface of the
green water as if there are secrets submerged that only
I know. He's right, of course.

"Mary, what *was* it that scared you into silence?" He
takes hold of my hands. The first warmth I've felt in
ages. I want to tell him everything — what David did to
me — so he can rescue his wife and children. But for
Julia to know the truth would cause irreparable
damage. It should have been said decades ago; I should
never have kept quiet. It's too late now.

A heavy blink takes the place of any useful reply. As
much as I need to speak, I can't. My entire life is
jammed in my throat.

Help me, Murray, I scream in my head. Save your
family from this man, from the truth. I can't stand it
that David has walked free a second time.

I turn back to the lake and see the nurse returning.
Panic fills me. I try so hard to open my mouth, to
muster some words, a noise, anything. But I am only
capable of deafening silence.

Someone has to stop him, Murray. I beg my
son-in-law to hear me. *Because this time, he's come
back for Julia.*

357

★ ★ ★

The trial was a mix of journalists, nausea and confusion. My parents took the same place in the public gallery every day and watched stoically as my life was dissected like a cadaver in front of a judge and jury. I couldn't bring myself to look at David as he sat rigid in the dock with an officer attached to his side, but I knew he was there, occasionally flicking his eyes to me. The air was filled with his intelligence, his charisma, the scent of his body, and now the stench of his fear. David didn't want to go to prison. I was already there.

"Court rise," the usher instructed, and as I stood, I felt dizzy and sick. Although I wasn't showing yet, I was four months pregnant and the nausea was giving no sign of letting up.

"Ladies and gentlemen of the jury," the prosecution lawyer began. "Over the coming days, you will be shown comprehensive evidence why this young man, David Carlyle, saw fit to rape the woman he claimed to love."

There was a theatrical gesture to the dock, and I bowed my head. It had been a wedding. We'd been fooling around, playing games, and it should have been fun, silly, happy. It was meant to be an escape from the life I had into the one I so desperately wanted. Instead, I'd been delivered a future so far removed from anything I'd ever planned, I didn't feel vaguely like me. I was going to be a mother.

Gerald Kirschner, my barrister — a man as wide as he was tall, with greasy strings of hair criss-crossing his scalp — strode the floor in a pale suit and recounted my sorry tale. He gestured regularly to where I was sitting as he gave the jury their first glimpse of that terrible night. My parents had sold off most of Northmire's land to pay his fees.

"On the twenty-fourth of June, the life of this young woman changed for ever. Mary Marshall, an intelligent woman with her whole future ahead, was brutally raped and attacked." Kirschner paused, hoping for a couple of gasps or raised eyebrows. He didn't get any. He wasn't very good and the jury already looked bored. "The man accused of this despicable act is in the courtroom today, and it is my job to prove to you beyond all reasonable doubt that David Carlyle, supposed friend of the victim, is guilty of this heinous crime."

He went on, detailing the events of that night in such a monotonous way that even I fancied it as a made-up tale. I spread my hands on my slightly swollen belly just to prove to myself that it was all real, that I hadn't fabricated the story to get attention. The baby inside me was a product of hate. How would I ever love it?

Shortly after the opening statements, Jonathon was called to the witness box. I felt a pang of regret muddled up with fear as he settled into the small wooden cubicle. What if that first policeman back at the hospital had been right? What if, in my drugged state, I'd offered up my body as fair game? Jonathon would confirm this — my flirting, my clear attraction to both of them as we rowed across the lake, messing about in the hut, the drugs, my nakedness, the dancing.

I was conning myself. David had wanted me for many weeks, and while I'd been there for him as a friend, I'd never been available in any other way. We had been playing mind games, which perhaps I had enjoyed more than him. After all, a starving person is bound to scoff a meal. When it came down to it, perhaps what had happened to me wasn't rape, rather just plain old sex.

"Mr Felosie," Mr Kirschner addressed Jonathon, "can you tell me when you first met Mary Marshall?" He cleared his throat and withdrew a yellowed cotton handkerchief from his jacket pocket.

"At the wedding." Jonathon replied nervously. He was a far cry from the confident young man I'd met in the summer.

"You're going to have to speak up, Mr Felosie, so that the jury can hear you. And please use full names to avoid confusion." The judge sounded weary.

"I first met Mary Marshall at Amelia Boseley-Greene's wedding."

"And who was Miss Marshall with that day?" Kirschner stood squarely before the witness.

"She was David Carlyle's guest." His voice settled into an audible volume. So far he sounded believable. So far, everything he had said was correct. Why then was I holding my breath?

"Can you recall Miss Marshall's mood at the wedding, Mr Felosie? Was she happy, sad, outgoing —?"

"Objection," David's lawyer called out. "Leading the witness."

"Sustained. Be careful, Mr Kirschner. It's early days and you should know better."

Gerald Kirschner nodded and dabbed at the sweat on his top lip. "Just describe Mary's mood, please."

"She was very shy and introverted when I met her. It was like she didn't really want to be there. She didn't know anyone. She seemed overwhelmed and in awe of David and his rowdy friends."

"Can you remember who Miss Marshall spent most of her evening with while at the wedding reception?"

Jonathon took his time. He stared at me across the courtroom, recalling that night and how I had clung to David's side, how I had met his friends for the first time, how I had met him. We made a neat trio — David, Jonathon and me.

"She spent her time mostly with David Carlyle." He swallowed, daring himself a look at David. "Mary Marshall stuck to him like glue."

"Can you tell me about their previous relationship?" Kirschner was breathing heavily, as if even the act of standing up while speaking was too much for his body to manage.

"It had been ages since I'd seen David." Jonathon hesitated. "But . . ." Another pause, as if he was unsure ". . . but as I left the hut to go back to the party, I saw them kissing by the lake. I assumed they were very close." He cleared his throat. "And earlier, David confessed to me that he loved her."

My lungs inflated suddenly and I turned to David. But blank face, square shoulders, he stared straight ahead as if the thought had never occurred to him.

"Didn't you find it odd that David had brought Mary to the wedding? It was a society event after all, and Mary was just a café waitress."

I squirmed and lowered my eyes from the courtroom. Everything I had ever wanted was crushed in an instant. So there had been sex, I told myself. Big deal. It was rough sex, unwanted sex; sex where no meant yes, and yes meant I was a slut. The feeling of self-loathing, the same feeling that had consumed me the moment David pulled from my body, rushed through me again. I'd learned to suppress it, numb myself, although that meant being numb to everything else too. The baby growing inside me was the only reminder. Until now.

"I suppose it was a bit unusual," Jonathon said. "David usually socialised with women of a higher . . ." He glanced at me uncomfortably. "Of a different class."

By then, I didn't care that Kirschner was blowing apart my case. We'd only met that morning for a brief chat in his private chambers while he sweated his way through several handkerchiefs. "So would it be fair to say that David had brought Mary Marshall to the wedding as a . . . novelty?"

"Objection. Leading again."

"Sustained," the judge ruled.

"Let me put it this way then, Mr Felosie," Kirschner continued. "Is it true that David Carlyle's friends mocked Miss Marshall because she worked as a waitress? That they took delight in belittling her, as if David Carlyle *had* brought her along as a joke, a plaything, a toy?"

"Ob-*jection*!" The defence lawyer leapt to his feet, but by then, Jonathon had already said a firm *Yes*, the single syllable echoing throughout the court.

"No further questions." Gerald Kirschner retreated. My stomach curdled. David's lawyer was going to crucify me.

Leaving The Lawns is as easy as melting into the walls. My constant observations were reduced to hourly checks when they realised I wasn't a threat any more, allowing ample opportunity to prise myself from my chair and walk right out of the hospital. I didn't care much for the food anyway.

The long trek home wears out my soft slippers. I get on with it, briskly, just as I have got on with everything else in life. When I reach the main road, I follow the track beside it to guide me home. It's surprising, really, who doesn't notice an old woman wearing a dressing gown and a face of grim determination striding through the night. What choice do I have this time but to put things right myself?

Still speechless, with my voice a million breaths away, I walk into my kitchen. It doesn't feel like home any more. Strangely, the back door is wide open and there is no sign of Julia, the children or Murray.

I stalk through the cold, dark rooms searching for a familiar face. I am startled by something — a noise, a swish of air through the blackness. Someone moving, someone there. I turn, frozen from fear by the brush of cloth across my cheek. Knowing exactly where it is, I reach for the light switch and illuminate Gradin. He is motionless, like a character from a cartoon strip. We stare at each other, and in a second, I see that his hands are covered in blood.

JULIA

"Mum," I scream with surprise and relief at seeing her. "What are you doing at home? Did Flora come here? Have you seen her anywhere?" The barrage of questions is hedged by hope. I drop to my knees in front of her, praying for her to speak. "Just tell me, Mum, have you seen her? She's gone missing."

Then the tears come again and my head is level with my mother's muddy feet. I drop into a puddle of despair. She doesn't reply, but gets up and wheezes her way around the kitchen as if she's never seen it before.

"Mary, stop. Please answer Julia." Murray folds my mother into the fireside chair and covers her with a blanket. "I don't know what you're doing out of hospital, Mary, but Flora has gone missing. She was on my boat and then she was gone. We thought she may have come back here —"

"Oh Murray, listen to us. There's no way she'd even walk ten paces in the dark by herself, let alone set off through the countryside at night." I'm striding about the room, not knowing what to do with myself. I claw my fingers down the wall. Old plaster and paint splinter under my nails. "No, she's either been taken or

drowned. Either way, Murray, our little girl's gone."
And finally my pinballing comes to a stop when Murray
catches me in his arms.

Ed arrives at Northmire with an update. Police
headlights arc across the courtyard. I'm perched on the
chair beside my mother, shaking, staring at her
blankness, wondering if *I* will ever speak again either.
It's a good way to block out all the pain. Murray called
The Lawns to inform them that Mum was safe at
home.

"The dogs haven't picked up a strong enough trail
yet. The handlers thought they were on to something a
couple of times, but both petered out in the village. If it
is Flora's trail, then she certainly headed for the
village." Ed fills us in with the latest.

"She was looking for you," I whisper. With one more
ounce of guilt, Murray will collapse.

"It could be the wrong trail, or it could be that she
got into a car. So many people have crossed the path
now that anything fresh is long gone." Ed is showing
the strain. It's his niece that's missing.

"Ed, what are the chances? Be honest with me. She's
your family too."

He replies without hesitation. "Every minute counts.
But it's still early days."

I sit up, incredulous. "I thought search dogs worked
miracles. I thought if you gave them a scent, however
vague, they'd find someone hundreds of miles away.
Why can't they find Flora?"

"These dogs are general-purpose dogs. I've ordered two specialist dogs for first light, Julia." He sighs and just gets on with telling me. "One of them is a cadaver dog and an expert at water search. The divers are on their way too. It's time to scour the river." He says this with a note of apology, as if it's his fault, as if he's already breaking bad news. As if he's found a body.

"How can they search in the water?" Murray asks. I didn't realise it, but he's been holding my hand.

Ed closes his eyes and I know he doesn't want to answer. "The dog will be taken on a boat and will indicate scent on the air to its handler if it picks anything up below the surface of the water." He speaks quickly.

"Yes, but *how*?" Murray asks.

Another pause. He's thinking of a way to say this. "Decomposition. The scent percolates up. The dog will catch this and the exact location will be marked until divers can investigate."

"She's not dead," I whisper. I stare straight ahead at Mum. My mind runs through a film reel, spinning in fast-forward from Christmas Day to the current nightmare. My mother has always known what to do, has always been the mender of troubles, the fixer of crises, the healer of wounds. Now she is inert, a hindrance.

For the first time in my life, I hate her. Behind those lips are a thousand words just aching to be told, and perhaps just one of them might help find Flora.

Alex crawls between his dad and me, exhausted, pale and yawning. I kiss his head, already missing the second one I would stamp on his sister. Ed's telephone rings. Someone saw a little girl.

MARY

Perhaps I should just go back to hospital and allow the good doctor to plan my treatment. After all, he did this to me. He took apart my young life, unravelling each stitch of time that I'd spent twenty-seven years knitting together. It would seem fitting for him to clear up.

In the day room at the hospital, amongst the jigsaws and empty coffee cups, an inch of newsprint told me that the case against David had been dropped. He has walked free once again. Therefore, so did I. Straight out of hospital. Two pages earlier, the newspaper also reported Grace Covatta's death. There was a small picture of her, smiling, living her normal life. She looked a bit like I once did — happy, hopeful, in love with David. *Battered Teen Loses Coma Battle*, it read. The doctors had shut down her system. Nothing will wake her now; not even a kiss from David.

I think about myself. Similar to Grace, I have shut down my mind, my voice, my soul, in order to heal. I doubt that a handsome prince will come knocking on my door. The final sentence of the newspaper report revealed that the police aren't hunting for Grace's attacker any more. They are searching for her murderer.

★ ★ ★

Day two of the trial saw a selection of witnesses called from the wedding party. Most of them told a bland tale. Most of it was correct. Most of it made me sound like a girl without hope, without a future, intent on hanging around with a younger, hipper crowd; putting herself about, behaving like a floozy. After a while, I started to believe it myself.

"All rise." The court shuffled to a stand as the judge entered after lunch recess. It was my turn to take the stand. As I approached the witness box, I threw up all over the floor. Sixteen weeks of pregnancy added to a deep fear facing the court delivered nothing more than watery bile. I hadn't eaten properly for days.

"Silence in court!" The crowded gallery broke into a flurry of noise and commotion. I remember hearing the snap of the gavel on the judge's bench and the insistent call of the usher attempting to quieten the onlookers. "Silence in this court!" And there I stood in the box, a bunch of tissues crumpled at my mouth, a bucket in case it happened again, and two barristers ready to pull me in opposite directions. However much I tried, I couldn't utter a single word.

The house is quiet. First light, and Murray and Julia have resumed their search for Flora alongside the police. They will watch from the bank, maybe hand in hand, as the rubber-suited bodies of divers sink beneath the river's murk; holding their breath as if they too are underwater. They can only pray that the divers resurface empty-handed. I pray too.

Through my bedroom window, I watch as the night lifts and refreshes the fields with a weak frost and a skim of hope. The bright sun makes everything look better. Two tears roll down my cheeks. One for Flora and one for me — each of us encased in our own silent worlds; each of us lost.

There is a noise, someone on the landing. "You tell her then, stupid," Brenna says angrily. It seems like a million lifetimes ago since I first took them in. Even with the door closed, I can see Brenna shoving her brother towards my bedroom.

"No, Baby, you do it. She'll be cross." Gradin's words are slow and stretched, as if he's talking with a gobstopper in his mouth. Then there's a tunnel of whispering.

"You stupid boy. We'll both go to prison now." There's crying, and when I open the door, the teenagers jump like baby deer. "Mary," Brenna says almost flawlessly. Her eyes dart from me, into my room and back to me again. She looks well under the circumstances. In all of this, Julia has done a good job of looking after them. "Are you better? Are you home from hospital? We miss you." She's covering something up, that's for sure.

I glance at Gradin. His nails are still encrusted with a bronze paste of congealed blood. I take him by the arm and lead the boy to the bathroom.

"What are you doing to me, Mrs Marshall? I don't want to go to the toilet."

"Oh shut up, Gradin, and do as you're told." Brenna leans in the doorway, chewing gum, liking the fuss. She

370

watches as I roll up her brother's sleeves and plunge his arms into a basin of scalding water. I scrub his hands, his nails, from fingertips to elbows, with coal-tar soap. He doesn't protest, just watches as the water turns rust-coloured. I pull the plug, swill out the basin and remove his sweater. Whatever he's done, I don't want any trace of it in my house.

"Miss Marshall, I do hope you are feeling better now." David's barrister was slick in his grey suit with lapels that stretched to his shoulders. He wore green-brown shoes and I remember thinking that they were the same colour as my vomit. His moustache annoyed me. It looked false. "Perhaps we can start with you telling the court a little about yourself. I'd like to know your background, your friends, your ambitions."

Gerald Kirschner struggled to his feet from behind the table. He muttered some legal stuff that honestly I didn't understand. He was trying to object about something but all I could hear was the pounding of my own heart and the defence's cross-examination.

"When you're ready, Miss Marshall," the judge said. He was a patient man, I could tell that much, but surely not endowed with enough patience to endure my sorry tale. "I'd like to hear this. You must answer the question."

I stared at those sickly shoes. Then at the dark patch on the wood where the court janitor had magically appeared with mop and bucket. I swallowed. My lips buzzed and the place where the words usually were, the holding bay before speech, was totally empty of anything to say. It was as if my entire vocabulary had been erased. Simply, I was lost for words.

"It's important you answer, Miss Marshall, for your own defence." The barrister was cruising. "How much alcohol did you have to drink on the night of the wedding, Miss Marshall? Did you take any drugs that may have reduced your inhibitions? Were you dressed provocatively that evening? Is it true that you always denied Mr Carlyle sex, even though you outwardly flirted with him? Can you describe your relationship with the accused? How long have you known him? Did you pursue him if he avoided you? Were you hoping to have sexual intercourse with David Carlyle that night? Had you intended on charging for your services?"

The barrage went on, peppered only by the futile protests of my barrister, who had virtually given up on me and plainly wanted to go home. And that was exactly what I wanted as well. To go home. Back to Northmire, to erase and forget. I didn't care that David had raped me. I didn't care that no one believed me. I didn't care that I had a baby growing inside me. I didn't care that it was going to be Julia.

"One last question, Miss Marshall. Can you tell the court what happened after the rape?"

I took a deep breath and peeled my dry lips apart. I turned to face David and a few words finally came out. They were glue in my throat. "He attacked me."

MURRAY

Perhaps if I find our daughter safe and well — immersed in some massive game of hide and seek — Julia will forgive me and love me and take me back and, oh, in the craziest of dreams, we could be a family again.

"Ju, we mustn't give up. Flora is out there waiting for us to find her. I don't believe she fell into the river. She can swim." I twist my fingers into the cold knot of Julia's fist and make her hold my hand. Reluctantly, she lets me in. "Ed's team are still investigating the sighting." We stand on the ragged bank of the river. Light spreads across the countryside, giving me hope in my heart.

"Wouldn't it be easier if they just find a body?" Julia's voice is colder than the dawn. It has been the worst night of our lives. She snaps her head at me briefly before looking back to the river — a way of settling the blame without actually saying it. She stares straight ahead, trying not to cry and trying not to watch as the dog on the police boat sends his handler into a spin.

Ed strides along the bank and stops beside us. "The diver is going in."

"Does this mean the dog's found something?" I don't want to know and I don't want to hear. This is the point at which our lives could change for ever. Our daughter's waterlogged body could be dragged to the surface; her blue limbs and sagging clothes hanging beneath her.

I turn and stare at the countryside around us. Police crime scene tape decorates the trees and hedges, cordoning off a wide area around *Alcatraz*. Several officers stand sentry to ward off the gathering press, and a space-suited forensics team picks through the undergrowth. My boat sits semi-submerged in the water.

There is a shout. The search dog barks and its tail wags feverishly. I can't watch. I walk off a few yards. I drop down on to the frosted, trampled riverbank — not caring that the freeze soaks instantly through my clothes, or that the officer nearby sees the hot tears cut down my cheeks; not noticing, at first, that my hand has struck something hard, something cold and something plastic in the long grass. It takes me a moment, but when I realise that it is man-made, that it isn't a rock or a twig or even a piece of dropped litter, my mouth opens long before I am calling out for help.

"It's Flora's doll," Julia squeals. "Give it to me." Her face crumples into a frown as she stares at it.

"Alex said she'd been playing with her dolls." I scan the riverbank for my son. "Alex, come here." He is studying the policemen at close range, but comes to me immediately. "What game was Flora playing with her dolls last night?"

"I dunno," he says, and shrugs. "Something stupid like mummies and daddies, except Ken was the grandad. I told her he was too young to be a grandad." He eyes the doll sadly.

Suddenly there is another shout and some splashing in the river. I see a diver bubble to the surface shaking his head with his thumb pointing downwards in signal. As the father of a deaf girl, I am not sure if that means it's good news or bad.

It was a split dustbin sack of decomposing fly-tipped rubbish, destined to get caught around the propeller of a passing boat.

The police helicopter spends three hours scouring the countryside. Fuelled by finding Flora's doll, Julia, Alex and I beat down every inch of every field around *Alcatraz*. As of eighteen minutes past eleven, the police haven't found anything else suspicious in the water.

"Oh Murray," Julia says, stretching her back before dissolving into my arms. "What are we going to do?"

The sickest of feelings crashes through me. It comes in waves from the tiniest little breakers to all-engulfing tidal waves of despair. Julia looks up at me and Alex stands by my side. What have I done to my family?

Much of it was medical jargon that I didn't understand, but I read it carefully anyway. I'd recovered from my dip in the river and, piecing the whole file together — even allowing for the unfamiliar language — it didn't take a doctor to realise that Mary had been given a psychiatric treatment plan at The Lawns. I couldn't comment on the medication prescribed, but the assessments and therapies recommended seemed more suitable for someone with depression than a woman with vascular dementia. It had all been overseen by Dr David Carlyle, even though he didn't hold a position at The Lawns.

"Chrissie," I said when she answered. It was my smooth voice, the one I usually reserved for Julia when we had an evening alone. It felt treacherous using it on anyone else. "How are you fixed for later?"

"But I've only just seen you."

"I know. I can't keep away . . ."

"You want me to explain Mary Marshall's notes to you."

"Bingo."

"Eight o'clock. The Bull's Head at the end of the road where you're parked."

"Moored," I told her.

"What?"

"You park a car and moor a narrowboat."

"See you later." And she did, informing me quite clearly of what I suspected as she sipped on a pint of Guinness. She eyed me over the rim, enjoying my surprise at her choice of drink as I settled next to her with Mary's file and a double Scotch. I spread the papers out between us.

"An awful lot of thought has gone into this treatment plan. There's six months of intensive therapy booked, as well as a cocktail of prescribed drugs. Professor Joseph has been assigned for the therapy sessions. He's highly respected in his field, very sought after, and also very expensive."

I shrugged. "What *is* his field exactly?"

Chrissie sipped on her drink before answering. "Dr Joseph offers counselling and therapy for victims suffering post-traumatic stress disorder." Another draw of the pint. "All his patients are rape victims, Murray," she said matter-of-factly, wiping her lips, and watching as my eyes narrowed in confusion.

"Rape victims?" I said, trying to figure out what that had to do with Mary Marshall; trying to work out how such a terrible thing could fit into the life of a woman I thought I knew.

JULIA

"Alex, get down on your hands and knees and search for any tiny little thing," Murray says. Ed takes Flora's doll and seals it inside a plastic bag.

"If Flora's been taken by the bad man, there could be fingerprints on that doll." Alex is worried about his sister. He is pale and has lines on his face that shouldn't be there on an eleven-year-old boy.

"You're right," I say, "and we're going to find her."

Murray and I crawl along the wet bank, peeling apart clumps of twitch grass and nettles, not caring that our hands mottle with white weals. Ed radios for the forensics team to come over immediately, and in the same breath orders us away from the river. "This is a crime scene, Julia. You have to leave."

I give him a look which tells him he'll have to drag me away if he wants me gone. We have searched maybe twenty feet further on from where the doll was found when Murray calls out. He holds up a tiny orange square of waxy paper.

"Flora," I whisper, carefully crawling back to Murray along the track I have made and already searched. I'd bought the kids a packet of sweets each and Flora

378

chose those chewy ones. "But Flora would never drop litter."

"She would if she was making a trail," Alex chipped in expectantly. "Like when we play imaginary games."

Flora is a survivor and would never set forth on an adventure without leaving a trail to find her way home.

"She's leaving us clues," I cry.

"What else do you know, Alex? Where did you go in your imaginary games?" Murray takes Alex by the shoulders. "And what has Flora been drawing so secretively recently?"

Alex shrugs. "I dunno. She just kept drawing pictures of a man. She wouldn't let anyone see, but I sneaked a look."

Murray frowns, glances at me. "She was being very secretive about her pictures. It may be nothing, though."

I nod, not knowing what to think. "We must keep searching the bank." It's then that I feel a hand grip my arm.

"Come on, Julia." Ed is giving me no choice. He leads me back to the path, away from the river. "Any news and I'll call you immediately."

As we stand alone, just the three of us, Murray's hand slips easily into mine. Before I know it, his fingers are pressed to my lips. I am shaking. "The doll and the sweet-wrapper mean she left by herself; that she wasn't taken. Someone has to find her soon."

"Julia . . ." He swaps my lips for his on the tangle of our fingers. "We will find our daughter," he says, but I swear it comes out as *I love you.*

★ ★ ★

379

Nadine takes care of Alex while we are at the police station. However many blankets and cups of sweet tea they give me, I still shiver. Murray is beside me, doing all the talking, being strong for us both as the afternoon light wanes into dusk. Nearly a second night without Flora.

"I've released a statement to the journalists. They're on fire around here as it is, since Grace died and Carlyle walked." Ed bows his head when he realises I didn't know. "Hell, I'm sorry, Julia."

"Grace . . . is *dead*?" I think of the crowd outside David's house; Grace's mother, their chant of revenge.

Murray holds me. No one says anything for a moment, which is confirmation enough. Grace is dead. She was murdered.

"The press may be of some help," Ed continues as gently as he can. "We've set up roadblocks and are interviewing motorists. I have a team going door to door in the village speaking to the locals, and you'll be relieved to hear that the river around the boat has been thoroughly searched and is clear."

"Just around the boat?" I ask, wondering how to layer Grace's death on top of everything else.

"We can't search the whole river, Julia. Not yet." Ed paces back and forth. "Read over your statements, please. Make sure everything is accurate. Especially you, Murray. You were the last one to see her."

"Not really," I correct. "Alex was with her last. When we found the doll and the sweet-paper on the bank, Alex said he thought Flora was leaving a trail like they do in their games. She set off with the intent of going somewhere, Ed." My voice falters. "We have to think like a child."

"Then get Alex in here immediately," Ed demands, and instantly Murray is telephoning his sister.

Alex has mushroom-coloured rings beneath his usually sparkling eyes. This is way more than make-believe games and he knows it.

"Mum?" he says nervously.

I cradle him on my knee as if he is five years old again. He doesn't struggle or pull away like he would normally if I showed too much affection in front of other people.

"Uncle Ed just wants to talk to you about the time when you were alone on the boat with Flora."

Alex nods. "OK."

"Alex, you told your mum and dad that Flora was leaving a trail. In your games, where did you and Flora pretend to go?" Ed is standing somewhere between detective and uncle.

"Anywhere. Sometimes it was the seaside. Sometimes the moon." He reddens. "I only played those babyish games because Flora made me." He shifts uncomfortably on my knee. "She wanted to play a different game on the boat, though. But it was boring and so that's why I went out to get wood for the fire."

"That's good, Alex." Ed crouches in front of us. He's pure uncle now, his eyes probing his nephew. "And what *was* the game that Flora wanted to play on the boat with you?"

Alex sighs, as if we should all know. "It's because of those silly pictures she was drawing. Grandma told her to do them."

"Mum told her? But you know Grandma's not speaking, Alex. How could she tell Flora?" I glance at Murray, then Ed, hoping my questions will tease out the reply.

"That's not a game, though, drawing, is it?" Ed remains patient. "Where did Flora go in the game she wanted to play on the boat?"

"Oh, that's easy," Alex says. "She was off to find her grandad."

"Grandad?" Murray says. The kids' only grandfather died before Flora was born.

"No-oo," Alex says as if we are all stupid. "Her *new* grandad. The one Grandma told her to draw. She didn't talk, of course," Alex continues, anticipating the next question. "They were signing together. In the hospital when you were busy with the nurses. She said that Grandma told her a secret."

"She did?" I edge forward on my seat with the weight of my son bearing down on my legs. "Alex, it's so important that you tell us exactly what those secrets are. They might help us find Flora."

There is a pause, and it feels almost as long as the time Flora has been missing all over again. Finally, looking worried and pained as if it's all his fault, Alex speaks. "I don't know. Flora wouldn't tell me because I wouldn't play her silly game."

The breath I've been holding escapes and my shoulders flatten. The three of us converge our thoughts and Ed drives us in a police car back to Northmire. My mother, the woman who has not uttered a word for weeks, is the only one who can help us. Whatever it takes, she is going to have to speak.

MARY

The week after it happened, a few papers and a couple of society magazines ran the story. A socialite wedding with rape and assault thrown in for good measure filled a couple of columns — and, given the recent anonymity laws for complainants of sexual offences, I was protected from being named in their sensationalist articles. No one would ever know who David Carlyle had allegedly raped.

Months later, when the case came to court and a verdict was reached, my story hit the papers again. David's photograph — his face surprised, slashed by relief, creased with unbelievable luck, good fortune, perhaps even remorse — made it into every newspaper in the country. That was the day on which he was acquitted.

"How do you feel about the jury's decision, Mr Carlyle?" The reporter pushed a microphone at David's mouth. I sat alone at Northmire watching the morning's events on the evening news.

"Relieved," David replied solemnly. "Thankful it's all over and I can get on with my life." His voice sent shivers through me — the same shivers of anticipation that I used to get when he strode into the café, or when he grabbed my wrist and pulled me close. The passion, the intensity, it was all still there. All still David.

"Did you expect a not guilty verdict on all the charges?" The microphone was under David's nose again. While all this was going on, I had been escaping from the back door of the courthouse. A police officer draped a blanket over my head and I was driven back home by my parents. Blanket or not, I was guaranteed a lifetime of anonymity. No one would ever be able to find out the name of the woman who had cried rape; cried wolf. I was destined to a lifetime of silence.

"Yes," David said easily. "I trusted the jury to find me not guilty." Every nervous, overstated blink he made represented a minute of the torture I had been through. How could they have let him off? Why was I still the victim, the nuisance, the silly girl who had caused all this trouble? He raped me, and afterwards he attacked me with his knife.

In court, the rape charge had been dismissed. The defence barrister convinced the jury that I had been on the lookout for sex; a predator. I was flaunting my body and willingly indulging in mind-altering substances. In short, they believed that I had asked for it.

As for the slashes to my tongue and feet, the jury ruled that there was no evidence to uphold this charge either, especially in the light of my unreliable claim of rape. "It's equally as likely that Mr Felosie or the groundsman or anyone else at the wedding party harmed Miss Marshall," the defence stated in the closing argument. "That's not to say the attack wasn't

385

brutal and the perpetrator shouldn't be brought to justice. But fingerprints on a hunting knife owned by my client are hardly grounds for conviction."

"What about the drugs, Mr Carlyle? As a trainee medical student, what are your views on the use of the sedative methaqualone for recreational purposes?" A microphone was pushed at David's mouth.

"No comment."

"The jury found you had consensual sex. Is it true that the woman concerned is now pregnant? Will you be supporting mother and baby?"

As I watched the news that evening — the way David's expression changed, stopping his life for just long enough to realise the implications of this revelation — I could tell that he didn't know, or perhaps hadn't even considered that I was pregnant. Indeed, I had told only a few people about the baby and I was too ashamed to confide in my barrister, even if it would have helped my case. I had no idea how the journalist found out.

"No . . . no comment," he said and walked off into the crowd.

I flicked the television off, wiping David Carlyle from my life. For thirty years, I lived without him.

I didn't take the bus immediately. I stood at the stop — as still and cold as the metal post itself — and stared blankly at the road while the different-coloured cars blurred through my field of vision. When the bus arrived, I let it pass. Other passengers filed past me and I watched the number fifty-eight disappear down the road. My infected finger throbbed. I squeezed the tip of it as hard as I could stand. A yellow globe of pus burst from the side of my nail.

Without another thought, I walked back to the surgery and waited in the car park behind a thicket of bushes.

I was infected, certainly, but the pus wasn't limited to my finger. I knew I had to see David again. I wanted information. I wanted to know that he'd had a miserable life; that he'd suffered for what he had done to me. I didn't think I could live if I knew he would be going home to a happy house, a wife and two kids after work. Despite my tough exterior, the years of bringing up Julia, the foster kids, the farm, and finally, my grandchildren — despite all this, I had never recovered from what happened. Perhaps harder to understand was that he'd got away with it. David had walked free while I was imprisoned for ever.

Two and a half hours later, David Carlyle emerged from the medical practice wearing a green waxed jacket over his suit. His mobile phone was pressed to his ear. My heart stuttered with fear and intrigue. He gestured as he spoke, and even from a distance I saw that he looked angry . . . then appeased . . . then perplexed — a rainbow of emotions on a face that I remembered thirty years younger.

After ending the call, David unlocked his car, placed his doctor's bag in the boot, and locked the car again. He walked off down the road towards the centre of town. In a snap decision, I followed him, holding back just enough so that he couldn't hear the beat of my footsteps, but close enough to catch his scent on the breeze. My heart was pumping revenge.

David went into a café, a little place with gingham curtains and the smell of scones baked into the bricks. I waited outside in the cold. Several times I walked past the window and caught a glimpse of him sitting alone, sipping tea, glancing at his watch, sliding out of his jacket. And suddenly I was back there, at Café Delicio, so firmly planted in the past that it took all my strength not to go inside and take his order.

I would have watched him, hunched over his books, demanding eggs and coffee, while he told me jokes, held my wrist as I wiped his table, breathed warm words into my ear as I delivered his food.

"Mary," he would say, "I'm learning about lovesickness. Can you recommend a cure?"

I would stare fondly, using the tea towel as a buffer between us, wiping my hands over and over while he tormented me with his eyes and a grin that showed a trace of his crooked tooth, before flicking him on the shoulder and walking away, my own smile widening once my back was turned.

I bumped into a young girl, a pretty teenager obviously in a hurry.

"Sorry," I said, spinning a half-circle from the collision, but she didn't reply. Her hair spread as she tossed it back, just like mine would have done. She stepped inside the café, breathless, beautiful, hopeful. I watched through the window as she wove a seductive dance through the tables. She arrived at David's side, her face lighting up as she sat beside him. She left a kiss on his unanimated lips. David stared blankly ahead in just the same way he would often ignore me, hoping I would tease out the reason for his bad mood.

That was the first time I saw them together. I wondered if the girl might be his daughter, but the passion stitched into her expression showed me she was run aground with love for him — a love that no girl should have for her father. David continued to be cautious, nervous, as if someone was watching him. Perhaps, deep down, he knew.

My mother was content. Finally there was going to be a baby in the house. I'd strayed so far from my parents' plan of marrying a local boy, becoming a farmer's wife, rearing dozens of happy children alongside a prize-winning herd of dairy cows or acres of wheat, that being raped and getting pregnant, shaming the family and bringing the child up alone, was by then a perfectly acceptable alternative.

"No matter." Mother said this about pretty much everything, from a broken cup to my shattered life. "You can live here with us."

And so that's what I did. My life in Cambridge, my foray into the world of academia, my attempt at snatching a slice of it for myself, became a rancid memory consigned to the back of my mind. No one ever spoke of it, and my plight was protected from discovery by the anonymity law. My name hadn't been in a single newspaper. Plus, my mother made it her life's work to shield the world from my disgrace. She became adept at fabricating stories about my condition.

Each time someone asked, she told a different version so that no one ever really knew the truth.

"Mary's poor husband was the victim of a hit-and-run accident." This usually shocked those interested into silence.

"The baby's father was killed in action." No one ever asked where, for fear of not knowing about a far-off war.

"Mary's an agoraphobic, don't you know?" Most people didn't.

"He left her for another woman. And with a baby, too." Instantly, my absent husband was dirty scum.

"She has to cope with a new baby *and* a terminally ill husband in a hospice." This was reserved for the local shopkeeper and spread, in various forms, within hours of its release.

But with the help of the vicar and the circle of women that my mother set up around me as a steely barrier of maternal strength, a more realistic back-story was used to explain my sorry situation. "Mary fell in love with a man who betrayed her." It kept their questions at bay; it matched and explained my demeanour; it allowed me to grieve while taking the support of other women — in particular the mother of a pair of children named Murray and Nadine. Without her help, I don't think I'd have got through my pregnancy.

"Breathe like we practised," Shauna said through the cotton of her mask. Her eyes were wide above it. She had rushed to Northmire when my mother called to tell her the time had come.

Shauna pulled the mask off her face and showed me how to breathe, patiently timing each inhalation to coincide with a contraction. I followed her instructions as best I could. For hours and hours she bathed my face with rosewater. She allowed me to squeeze her hand until it nearly burst and took nothing personal from the insults and screams of hate and pain I threw her way.

"It's a baby girl," Shauna exhaled as the final contraction spewed out my daughter into the midwife's hands a full day and a half after I had gone into labour. The baby was placed on my deflating belly but I couldn't stand to look at her. As a reminder of that dreadful night, as a permanent receipt of my relationship with David, how would I ever be able to hold or love or care for my baby?

But, I later thought, being a girl, being so innocent, perhaps she wouldn't look too much like her father. If I'd delivered a son, I doubt I could have taken him as my own. As the minutes rolled into hours and the pain of childbirth, indeed the pain of the last nine months, diminished with every wail of my poor neglected baby, I mustered the courage to sit up and peek into the crib. The midwife pottered around, unwilling to leave until I showed some maternal instinct.

"Go on. She's beautiful," Shauna said, encouraging me to take a look. She'd cleaned me up, made a tray of tea, washed and dressed the baby while telling me about every tiny feature, every finger and toe, every hair on her head and lick of the air as her perfect mouth searched for my milk. I lay there with my eyes closed until finally intrigue and instinct won over anger and bitterness.

"She *is* beautiful," I whispered. My daughter had the palest skin gilded on to a squirming body. Her tiny fingers haphazardly scrutinised the soft blanket wrapped around her, while her feet, balled up in wool, kicked against cloth instead of my womb. "Truly the most beautiful baby alive."

At the sound of my voice, her huge eyes lolled up at me. For the briefest moment, we fell into each other's minds. Mother and daughter locked up for ever, just like that. "I will call her Julia," I said, and reached into the cot. I gently picked up my baby. "Shhh, be quiet, hush now," I whispered in her ear, and later, when we were quite alone, I told her who her father was, and promised I would never let him hurt her.

Julia and Murray and Alex blow into the kitchen like litter on a squall. They are exhausted, bereft, frustrated and angry. Flora is still missing. I am desperate with worry yet unable to help. What must Julia think of me, sitting here doing nothing?

"Mum, are you OK?" Julia says in a breathy way that tells me she has forgotten all about me. My heart aches for her. A moment later and Ed lets himself into the kitchen, and by now we are quite a crowd because Brenna and Gradin have come to see who's here. "Ed wants to talk to you, Mum. I do as well. We all do."

Julia's words are brittle. Her eyelids fold down over her pupils and I imagine for a moment what it would have been like to lose her when she was a child. They don't notice, but the skin on my arms dapples with goose bumps. Losing my daughter would have been a waste of all my pain. What I went through is only justified by her existence.

"Mrs Marshall, I need to take a statement from you regarding your granddaughter. I know you're not well, but we would greatly appreciate your help." Ed has always been formal with me when we've met at family gatherings. Once, maybe twice a year at most — Easter or a birthday. He pulls up a chair. "As you know, Flora is still missing —"

And it's just then, just at that point where everyone is holding their breath, waiting for me to provide all the answers, that Gradin rips the kitchen apart.

"*Nooo-ooo!*" he yells over and over, tearing down the generations of family life that make up the room. The patchwork of memories is snatched from the walls or smashed on the floor or toppled from a height. Gradin whips round the kitchen like a tornado without a weather warning, kicking and ripping and breaking up everything in his path. In a moment his hands and face are bleeding, but this doesn't stop him hurling a wooden chair through the old paned window above the sink. Everything he can lay his hands on gets thrown into the courtyard, and it takes Murray and Ed several minutes to catch, restrain and calm the boy. Alex huddles terrified beside me.

"Oh my God, oh my God, oh my God . . ." Julia wails as she crunches through the wreckage. Gradin has pulled down the dresser and with it at least twenty place settings of crockery. "I can't stand any more of this, no, no, no . . ." And my daughter is on the floor, crying with the same needy emotion as when she slithered from my womb.

As Ed and Murray deal with the boy, I recall the day when Brenna and her brother first came to stay at Northmire. I accused them of stealing thirty pounds. If tipping up the table was his reaction to a false accusation before, then I wonder what he has done to warrant this extreme explosion.

"That's it, young man. You're under arrest." Ed straightens from the kick he received in the leg, and he doesn't know it but there is a cut beneath his left eye. "I am arresting you for criminal damage and assaulting a police officer. You do not have to say anything, but it may harm your defence if you fail to mention when questioned something which you later rely on in court. Anything you do say will be given in evidence."

"Baby?" Gradin is shivering, quiet now, and his doleful eyes — as calm as they have ever been — hang heavy in his face. "Help me, Baby. Don't let them put me in prison." His words are laboured and without any trace of comprehension. Ed snaps handcuffs closed behind Gradin's back.

"You done it now, you stupid idiot. What you go and do that for?" Brenna leans on the door frame and gestures at the mess. She's trying to detach herself from her brother, his actions, their lives, herself. Brenna doesn't know how to help him, but like me, she knows this is bad. She knows that Gradin is disturbed by a secret he's struggling to keep to himself. It was the guilt, not Gradin, that did this to my kitchen.

Ed uprights a kitchen chair and bends the teen on to it. "Stay there and don't move." Gradin is so scared he can't even breathe, let alone run for it. Murray stands guard, but I can see he really needs to help Julia, who is still on the floor. Ed crouches at my side and takes a deep breath. "Mary . . . Mary," he pleads.

In my head, I sing: *Quite contrary . . .*

MURRAY

I pick up her shoe. I pick up her bracelet, likewise her cardigan, her hairband and the pile of snotty tissues that lie strewn around her. Then, piece by devastated piece, I pick up Julia.

"Mummy, are you OK?" Alex always calls her "Mum". He strokes her limp wrist. Julia flinches briefly.

"Mummy's upset about Flora," I tell him, and swallow the knot of fear that's worked its way up my gullet since Ed left Northmire with Gradin. "And all this mess doesn't help either."

"I can clean it up," Alex offers, and briefly I smile.

Instructing Alex to take charge — because I believe in second chances — I shrug into my coat. "Look after your mother, son. Keep her and your grandma warm and make them a drink. If you can find a cup. Don't answer the door unless it's me or Uncle Ed, and stay near the telephone. I'm going to find your sister." I pat his shoulder, then opt for a kiss on the head.

"Go, Dad!" Alex cheers as I leave the house. A second later I return for the car keys. I wink at Alex and blow a silent kiss at Julia. It gives me the shock of my life, but she blows one right back.

★ ★ ★

Ed is in his office, alone, smoking, bent over his computer as it rattles through a search. He looks up when I walk straight in. "Is the desk sergeant asleep again?"

"It's all right. He did his job." I sit down opposite, entering Ed's frustrated cop zone of smoke and despair. "You look nearly as bad as me."

"I have an entire team out there searching for Flora. It's headed by one of the area's best detectives. I've requested special police abduction experts to join the case. They'll be here in the morning. And Murray, I'm ordering a wider search of the river for tomorrow afternoon." Ed hangs his head.

"She's not dead," I say.

"It will have been a couple of days by then, and if she did have an accident and fall into the water, then . . ." he looks away, "then decomposition will bring her to the surface. It's the earliest we could expect that to happen. I'm sorry, Murray."

No one should be sorry. Not yet. That word, that single word, brings me to my feet with my hands slammed firmly on Ed's desk. "She's alive," I say, my voice as tight as a noose. "Just find her." And as if by magic, Ed's computer ceases its rattling search and spews up a list of names. At the very top of it is Dr David Carlyle.

I pull the small metal flask from my jacket pocket but it's empty. I chuck it on the desk and it skids on to the floor. "There's some Scotch in the filing cabinet if you're in need." Ed looks like he could use one himself.

"No. Nothing. I don't need anything." My body is screaming for a drink. It will help me concentrate. It will help me piece all this together with Ed, who has agreed to let me stay on at the station. Any news about Flora and we'll be the first to know. "Tell me again what the computer searched for." A grizzled batch of eighty-four known criminals and suspects slides up and down Ed's monitor as he plays with the mouse, thinking, pondering.

"Local offenders, ex-cons, anyone released from custody living within a ten-mile radius of Northmire. Some of these names go way back."

"But not Carlyle's," I say. "He's new to the area."

"That's where you're wrong." Ed pours two Scotches anyway. "Technically I'm off duty so this doesn't count. And technically I shouldn't be talking about Carlyle."

I slide the tumbler of whisky away. "Not for me." I shift my chair to get a better view of the computer monitor. I will not drink. There is something bigger in my life now.

For a second, Ed is protective of the screen and he tries to tilt it away. The files are confidential. Maybe it's because he understands my pain as a father that he finally twists the monitor so I can see it and allows me to take control of the mouse.

"I shouldn't be telling you this either, but Carlyle was tried on suspicion of rape back in the seventies." A mug shot of him resolves on the screen. "I'm sorry I had to keep that from you and Julia." He shudders as the Scotch hits his throat. "Jesus, I shouldn't be telling you now, but under the circumstances . . ." Ed sinks his head into his palms.

I am stunned. I stare alternately at Carlyle's face and the tumbler of whisky. Neither is attractive. "He's got a violent history?" I stand up; sit down again. "Rape? Why didn't I know about this? I'm his damned lawyer." Not a very good one, it would seem.

"Nineteen seventy-six. He was acquitted on two charges. The complainant cried rape but Carlyle insisted it was consensual and the jury agreed. There was an assault charge as well but the records are patchy. I can't find any details of what kind of assault supposedly took place. Anyway, it appears there wasn't enough evidence to secure a conviction on that either." Ed knocks back the shot in one. "Don't feel bad, Murray. Why would Carlyle tell anyone about his previous charges if he didn't have to, even if he was acquitted?" He paces the room, leaving footprints of guilt because he hadn't spoken up, because he hadn't warned Julia. "And don't think we haven't paid him a visit since Flora went missing. He was top of my list." Ed answers my next question. "No sign of him."

Carlyle was with Julia the morning Flora went missing, I want to say. And I want to grab Ed by the collar and demand why he didn't warn us earlier about these charges. But all I can manage is, "Who was he supposed to have raped?" A sick feeling sweeps through me.

Ed's face snags with worry lines. "I don't know. Not without a judge's warrant, and that takes time. An anonymity law was passed in the seventies protecting the identity of women who claimed rape. It was meant to encourage more women to report the crime; meant to secure more convictions. Whoever it was, speaking up didn't do her any good. Anyway, this is hardly relevant to finding Flora."

"I suppose not," I say, mulling over this incredible news.

"Look, Murray, I arrested Carlyle because of pretty strong evidence in the Covatta case. The CPS chucked it out when the DNA evidence, my best shot at a trial, didn't stack up. The samples harvested were from a third party. Not Carlyle, in other words. And there was no way the Crown Prosecution was buying the previous allegations as current evidence. The man was *acquitted* back then. Believe me, I'll get justice for Grace and her family, but not before I've found my niece. If I'm honest, I don't think Carlyle's got anything to do with her. What would he want with an eight-year-old girl?"

"That's where you're wrong. There's a common denominator here, Ed, and we're overlooking it."

"We? When did law school start giving out police badges?"

I ignore him. "It's Julia. My wife, your sister-in-law. She's the one person that links all these incidents. Think about it."

"Murray, just so you know, before you go any further, I was running this computer search for another detective working on a different case. Carlyle heads the bill because he's the most recent arrest with certain other credentials in this locality. This wasn't for Flora's case."

400

"I said *think about it!*" I didn't mean to yell. "Grace Covatta is assaulted. Who finds her? Julia. Which school does the girl attend? The one Julia teaches at. Christ, Grace is even in her English class. With me so far?" I pause; fight away the urge as the Scotch catches my eye. I turn away. "Carlyle is arrested for assaulting Grace, and who is he dating? Julia. While all this is going on, Mary Marshall — *Julia's mother* — refuses to speak, and the last person she saw before she was struck dumb, apart from the foster kids in her care, was David Carlyle. A little girl goes missing, and who does she belong to? *Ju-li-a Mar-shall*." I couldn't say it any clearer.

Ed is silent. Calmly he sits beside me and stares at Carlyle's computer file. "Déjà vu?" I suggest. "Carlyle walking away, free as a bird yet again? I'm gasping for air — knowing I'm drowning, knowing how to swim, but my hands and feet are tied. Above me I see Flora's face, begging me to save her.

"I suggest you find a friendly judge to get you a warrant," I continue. "We need to know who it was Carlyle raped thirty years ago." A sick feeling spreads through my entire being as I remember what Chrissie said about the treatment plan set out for Mary.

But my thoughts are interrupted when Ed's phone rings. Connected or not to the disappearance of my daughter, I want Carlyle put away — away from my family for good.

Ed hangs up. "There's been a possible sighting of Flora near Hogan's Lane. A woman is being brought in to the station to make a statement."

"Hogan's Lane," I say, chewing over the name although not initially remembering why it should sound familiar. "Hogan's Lane . . . Get me a map."

In a second, a detailed map of the area is on Ed's screen. "Now tell me I'm crazy." I jab my finger at the monitor. "Hogan's Lane. Carlyle's house."

JULIA

How am I supposed to do anything? How am I supposed to do nothing?

"Alex, do you know anything at all that could help find Flora? Was she behaving strangely when Dad left you on the boat?" I've asked him a thousand times already. Alex is pale and shivering and his eyes have dark rings round them. He is sitting opposite Mum beside the kitchen fire, which went out hours ago. I am crunching through the wreckage of Gradin's outburst as if maintaining constant movement will help find Flora. But it just wears me out.

An entire day and night without Flora.

To stop myself thinking about where she is at this precise moment, I rummage through Mum's kitchen cupboards and find a bottle of cooking sherry.

"If it works for your father, then it'll work for me too." I glare at Alex when he stares at me, shocked. I don't even bother to use a glass — there aren't any — and neck straight from the bottle. I choke, but a couple of decent swigs later the alcohol loosens my thoughts enough to figure out a plan.

"I'm going to David's house," I say, wondering if I'm already over the limit. I crouch down next to Mum, deliberately pushing my face near hers. I swear she recoils from my breath. "Will you be OK while Alex and I are out?" I glare at the woman in whom I have placed my trust for the last thirty years. She is a stranger. I take her shoulders and shake her. "Mum, do you understand me? I need to be with David for a while. Can't you just say one word, for Christ's sake? You owe me that." Through her pupils, I see a thousand thoughts flashing in her mind. If only she would translate them into words. It makes me think I'm going mad, but as we leave, I swear I hear her say *Goodbye*.

The Land Rover is ancient and probably hasn't been started up in years. It's a long shot, I admit, but I'm desperate. It sits in the barn looking as if it was last used in the Second World War. Mum doesn't go out of the village very often, and then she usually takes the bus. "We'll damn well walk if we have to." Murray has taken my car because his is still being repaired.

The keys were always left in the ignition, and after all these years I half expect them to either be lost or rusted solid. Alex climbs in beside me. I remember as a kid it was a treat to ride in the Land Rover. Sometimes Murray and Nadine would come with us, their mother having packed a picnic. We'd bump along, singing, the canvas roof rolled up under our feet, our hair tangling, Mum smiling from within her headscarf.

Miraculously, oddly, the key turns, and after a couple of attempts the vehicle starts as if it's used every day. "Thank God," I say, and leap out again to fling open the huge wooden doors of the barn. The headlights form two cones in the dark winter afternoon; beacons for Flora as we trundle down the lane towards David's house.

A family constantly changes, I told myself. It was nothing to worry about. These things were sent to try us. Good times out of bad. I jollied myself along because essentially things were happy in our household.

Flora fitted right in at her new school. She was learning fast and had made new friends. Alex was picked for his school football team, I'd been promoted at work and taken on extra hours, while Murray was getting stuck into his new job. His boss was a powerful woman, clearly keen for him to do well.

On that wave of hope, the relief that my family was settled, content, doing what families do best — muddling through the days in a blur of homework, cooking, bills and washing — Murray went and kicked a hole in it all by drinking even more. Were we too settled for him? Was family life just too content, forcing him to smudge it out with Scotch every night, every day, every morning?

"You need help, Murray. More than I can give you." It splashed the tiles, my clothes, the floor, as I glugged two nearly full bottles down the sink. I'd found them amongst the kids' outdoor toys in the garden shed. "Get help or get out." That was the first time I threatened divorce. I would need to say it a thousand times more before he finally believed me.

405

Over the years, I tried everything to stop Murray drinking. We went to group meetings together but he refused to speak about his problem. I booked counselling but he didn't show up. I took the kids and went to stay at Northmire for a week, but when I came back, the house was full of empty bottles. I tried talking to him about it but we ended up fighting. I tried ignoring it, but he still drank and drank.

"You saved me from drowning, Murray. I want to do the same for you." If I didn't know the reason why he drank, I stood no chance of being able to fix things.

"It's simple," he once said, although back then I didn't understand. "I'm so frightened, so terrified that I'll wake up one morning and it'll all be gone. All this." He had tears in his eyes. We were in our kitchen. The kids were scoffing food. Murray spread his hands wide around the room, around all of us. Back then, I didn't know what he meant.

"He was right," I say over and over. "He was right, he was right, he was right." I'm crying, hardly able to see the road ahead as Alex and I speed to David's house, to sanctuary.

"Who was right?"

"Your dad. He was right about it being the most terrifying thing in the world. Enough to drive him to drink."

"Mum, what are you talking about?" Alex is concerned about me. I am crying, sobbing, driving, talking nonsense.

406

"I understand him now, really I do." I pull the Land Rover back on course as my blurred vision takes me on to the verge. "About how losing all this is so terrifying that you can't stand to think about it. That's why he had to take the edge off his life. It was simply too good."

"Losing what? What was too good?"

"All of this, all of us. Our family. Dad, Flora, you, me. Tell me we can't be the only ones left, Alex?"

MURRAY

The car sits slewed to a halt in the mud, blocking the top of Hogan's Lane. I leave the headlights on because down here it's pitch black.

"Flora!" I scream, praying that somehow the vibrations of my voice, my need, my fear will get through to her. I regret not waiting to hear the woman's statement at the police station. She would have given a more precise location. The lane is several miles long, and being so familiar with the waterways, I know the River Cam snakes very close to here.

I stop and stare out into the night. For all I know, the woman could have seen Flora yesterday. For all I know, it wasn't even Flora she saw.

When the light from the car peters out, I rely on my torch. I'm still on the lane, trudging down the wet verge, flashing the light in a wide arc, not missing any spot. Several times my heart skips at the shining discs of animal eyes; several times I lunge at the hedgerow in case my daughter is hiding there. If I have to, I'll search the entire world with a flashlight to find her.

I pick up speed, running down the lane, and ahead I see a bridge; a familiar bridge, one that I passed under on *Alcatraz* not so long ago. In my mind I form a mental map. I am near the river. If this is the bridge with the yellow graffiti on its side, then — I stop running in order to concentrate — then over there, right across those two or three fields is . . . My heart skids into overdrive.

"So over there," I whisper into the night, "is David Carlyle's house." In response, an owl flaps from a tree, scaring the life out of me.

I point the torch in the direction of his property. I can't see a thing. I continue down to the bridge, and before I can pick out the arched brickwork by torchlight, I spot the jagged shapes of the graffiti spray-paint on the bridge. In my mental map, I recall the head of the tiny lane where I left the car when I illicitly visited Carlyle's place. I leg it back up the road to fetch Julia's car.

Wherever I turn, Carlyle is always there.

Five minutes later, with the car left in the gateway the other side of the river, I'm striding down the remainder of the lane to David's house. There are two criss-crossed squares of light in the blackness.

In the front garden, I pick my way across frozen flower borders to get a glimpse through the small gap in the curtains. I press my face close to the cold glass.

It takes a few seconds for my eyes to adjust to the light. At first I don't believe what I see in the orange glow of a coal fire and the cosiness of someone else's private room. When I'm sure, when I know what I'm seeing is real and not a mirage of hope or paranoia, I pick up a garden rock and smash my way inside.

JULIA

The Land Rover carries us noisily along the lane, and at first I don't hear my phone ringing. It's Alex who alerts me to it. I pull over, fumbling to answer in time, but the phone slips from my hand into the footwell of the Land Rover. I miss the call but see it was Murray. My heart flips in my ribcage, making me feel sick. I kick aside the newspaper lying at my feet — a recent edition with a familiar headline scrunched and muddy.

I call him back. "Murray, what? It's me. What did you want?"

Breathlessly, beautifully, precisely, my husband tells me that he has found our daughter. Flora is alive.

David's house beckons to me across the countryside. From half a mile away, the flatness of the land shows that the property is flanked and lit up by at least half a dozen police cars. Redemption, at last. I sincerely hope that Ed is there to witness David's good deed.

"I'm coming, baby," I say with tears obscuring my view. Alex is asking a thousand questions that I can't answer.

410

"Who found Flora, Mum? Is she hurt? Did David get arrested again?" He peers ahead at the pulsing blue lights.

"No," I say. "*He found* Flora. That's why she's at his house, thank God. Won't this thing go any faster?" I have my foot digging down on the accelerator but still we chug along at thirty miles per hour. Eventually we push down the final narrow section of lane and I see my car parked haphazardly in a gateway, as if Murray dumped it in a hurry. Odd, I think, that he didn't drive right up to David's house.

I skid the Land Rover to a halt beside a police car and fling open the heavy door. "Hurry," I call to Alex as he unbuckles himself and runs up to my side. I grab his hand and suddenly we're inside, shoving between startled officers, tearing from room to room.

"Flora!" I cry out. "Murray, where are you?" I follow the sound of his voice and turn to the kitchen. Pushing past Ed, I skid to a stop just inside the room, and there, sitting on her daddy's knee at the kitchen table, is Flora. My angel.

Nothing exists around me. I fall to the floor at Murray's feet, pulling our daughter into my arms. I press as much of her body against me as I possibly can. Just to make sure she is real. Just to make sure this isn't a dream.

Her hair covers my face as I press her head to my lips. Her skin feels soft against me and her little arms wrap around my neck. I whisper in her ear that I will never let her go. She can't hear but I know she understands.

I've been on an adventure, she signs. My hands shake too much to sign a reply. I love you, Mummy, she says over and over with grubby fingers. I kiss each and every one of them — they taste so sweet — and I tell her that I love her too.

After a few more moments of greedily drinking in my daughter, I am able to communicate. We didn't know where you were, I tell her. We were so scared. But David found you and that's all that matters. I cast my eyes over her body, hardly daring to look for signs of harm.

"No, Julia —" Murray stands, but doesn't get a chance to speak in response to my signing.

"Thank God it turned out right for you." Ed butts in, awkwardly breaking into our reunion with an inappropriate voice.

"Julia, it wasn't David who found Flora." Murray joins his hands somewhere between our daughter and me. I hear him but I don't understand him.

"Well who did find her, then?" It doesn't sound like me talking. I try to convince myself that it doesn't matter who discovered her, just that she's OK. "I . . . I thought that David rescued her. That's why you're all here."

"No, Julia." He closes his eyes. "David *took* her." Murray reaches out for me as the blow hits the side of my head.

I can't have heard him correctly. But when I watch Flora's hands in front of my face, she signs, Mummy, don't be cross. David didn't hurt me. We went on a holiday. Alex couldn't come.

412

I feel like I'm going to faint.

"We're going to need to speak to Flora while everything is still fresh in her mind," Ed says solemnly.

This can't be true. I know the police have to get on with their business — Flora went missing after all — but that means acknowledging what they are saying; that David has done something . . . wrong.

"Julia, Flora must be checked out medically." Ed stops. He stares at me, willing me to understand what he means. As Flora's uncle, he can't bear to think of what might have happened to her.

Not *David*, I think, or perhaps I whisper it, because the words shatter around me. He adored the children. We were good together. I loved him. Suddenly the present tense slips into the past. "David took Flora?" Murray catches my brittle words as they leave my lips.

"It's going to be OK," he tells me. He pulls me close and it's then that I know we've never really been apart.

"We have to get to work on statements," Ed continues.

I sit on the floor with Flora nestled within each of my limbs. I can't hold myself up any more. Then it occurs to me. "What about . . . where is . . ." I just can't think of it. I can't allow the thought of what has happened — or indeed *why* it has happened — to have space in my head. "Where is David?" I finally get out. Ed glances out of the kitchen door, perhaps so he doesn't have to look me in the eye.

"He's being detained by my officers." He indicates beyond the hall, meaning David is still in the house.

Are you OK, Flora? Alex signs tentatively, as if she's come back someone else entirely. He kisses her on the head but she bats him away. What happened to you? Alex asks, unfazed by her rejection.

Nothing, Flora replies, shaking her head so that her curls flick my face.

Did you run away? Did the bad man get you? Alex asks.

Flora shakes her head and simply refuses to reply.

Ed announces he wants the house cleared for the forensic teams to start work. He is weary; he wants to get home to Nadine; he wants to be an uncle, not a detective.

I pick myself up off the floor. Both here and wherever David took Flora, they will be looking for tiny traces of my daughter mixed up with bigger pieces of David. Cell by cell, they will reconstruct the last twenty-four hours, whether Flora is prepared to tell us what happened or not. I heave her against my hip and walk outside to the waiting ambulance. The night is a dazzling cocktail of flashing lights, uniforms and authority. Murray and I stand with our children in the cold, somehow lost in the unfamiliar landscape of police business.

Then my world falls silent as David is escorted out through the house. I stare at him, our connecting eyes freezing in the frantic scene around us. He is handcuffed and winged by two detectives, who lead him right past us — just like before. I'm not sure if it's the bitter wind that ruffles my hair, or David's wake.

There are so many questions that I will never get to ask. He is ushered into the police car and driven away into the night, his eyes shining brilliant dots through the glass.

Flora straps her legs around my waist so tightly I can hardly breathe. Murray pulls Alex to his side, linking us all together. "Are you scared?" I whisper to my husband.

"Not any more," he replies as the police lights vanish completely.

"Me neither," I reply.

MARY

I couldn't sleep. That particular night, my dreams were filled with images of him and her together in the café. It was as if the last thirty years had never existed, as if Julia and Alex and Flora were fragile parts of a forgotten reality; as if the only person I'd ever known was David. Life was an illusion and it was up to me to decide which parts were real.

I'd tried to forget him; I'd packed him away in the depths of my mind, and for three decades I believed I'd succeeded in obliterating him from my life. I got on with being Julia's mother, running the farm, and later the fostering. I was busy, I was active, I was doing something good for society, and that, in turn, helped me forget.

But if I'm honest, David was always there — in my thoughts, on my skin, inside my house, in my dreams. After my parents died, I got rid of the old radio and television set at the farm. I would see him in every male actor; hear his voice in radio plays. He had wrapped his genes around my daughter and then my grandchildren. In truth, he was with me every minute of those thirty years.

416

I kicked the blankets off me. The house was freezing yet I stood at the open bedroom window without shivering, staring out across the flat land. An unrelenting wind dragged horizontal rain over the fields. I glanced at the clock. Four thirty a.m. The rain was turning to snow.

I stared over the barn roof in the direction of David's house. It was too far away to see, of course, but not so far away that I couldn't feel the warmth of his breath on my neck as he slept. I'd overheard him talking to Julia about his impressive country home, remote yet close to the surgery. The area was as familiar as the lines on my hand, so identifying David's house would be easy. It was the Grangers' old place a little way up the river — a derelict farmhouse that had fallen into disrepair before an opportunist renovated it and sold it on.

Julia had been excited about having dinner there from the minute she was invited. I didn't begrudge her that — it was what I'd been chasing, after all. Plus, she was keen to show the children David's spacious home — perhaps one day theirs to roam. Julia was intent on slotting into David's life where I had failed.

How could I stop her seeing her father, yet how could I tell her who he was? After all this time, she would hate me for not being honest with her. As a baby, she needed only me. There were no questions asked, no judgements made. The questions came when she started school. I'd already decided, virtually from the minute she was born, that Julia would never know about her father; she would never know what he had

417

done, where she had come from, the pain he had caused. How can a mother tell her daughter she was the product of rape?

I hated lying to her. I hated that if I was honest, I would have to tell her how David was found not guilty, how I was accused of flaunting myself, of getting what I deserved. With David innocent, it went without saying that I must have been lying. Appropriate, then, that I have lied to my own daughter all her life.

Of course, once David was back on the scene, there was always the risk that he would tell Julia the truth. It was a chance I had to take. Having found out about my pregnancy after the court case, he would have easily deduced that Julia was his daughter. Her age, her looks, and being an only child were as good as a birth certificate. He knew exactly who she was. So what did he want?

"I'm here for you, Mary," he'd said when he telephoned Northmire the same day I first saw him at the surgery. "And Julia." I hung up immediately. He stopped calling after a while, but not until Brenna promised to pass on a message that he wanted to help me. Too late for that, I replied silently.

The lie to my daughter had developed over thirty years; the clean-cut, hard-edged, no-nonsense con that prevented her from ever asking about her father held watertight. The more time that passed, the stronger the lie became. But with David in her life, it was just a matter of time before the dam burst. Me, I wasn't going to be a part of it. The thick silt stirred up from the bottom of my mind got stuck in my throat; prevented me from talking; a safety valve about to blow.

The snow spread a silent blanket across the fields. Impulsively, I pulled some old clothes from my cupboard — a sweater, some torn trousers, my work boots — and got dressed. I went downstairs as quietly as I could. I avoided every loose and creaking floorboard and only opened the doors as far as necessary before the ancient hinges had a chance to creak. I unhooked my overcoat from the peg and shrugged it on as I stepped out into the flurries of snow.

In the yard, a newspaper fell from my coat pocket. I remember wedging it in there on my last walk back from the village shop. After that, they collected at the gate until Julia fetched them in. It seemed an age ago. I didn't want to leave a trail, so I picked up the newspaper and took it with me. The cold air took my breath away.

Decades of a prison sentence I never deserved — the sentence *he* should have suffered — sent me out to the barn, marching across the courtyard as if I was setting forth into battle. I quietly opened the large double barn doors, remembering how Julia used to cling on and take a ride when she was a child. I sighed it all away.

The Land Rover only ever started fifty per cent of the time. "If it goes, then it's a good omen," I whispered, climbing in. It smelled of straw and dogs. I tossed the newspaper on to the floor. I turned the key, which had almost frozen into the lock, and after a second's sputtering it banged to life. I drove away from

Northmire, praying that the rattling diesel engine wouldn't wake anyone.

The house was smaller than I'd imagined. In fact, to me David still lived in his university room lined with books, smelling of cigarette smoke and Earl Grey tea. His property sat squarely behind a low fence at the end of a narrow lane to the east of the river. I let the engine die and rolled to a stop about a hundred yards away. I didn't want him to hear me coming. I didn't want him to plan excuses. I wanted it straight. I deserved that much. After all this time, I wanted to know *why*.

I got out of the Land Rover and walked through the bitter night. Something, perhaps a fox, scurried across the lane and disappeared into the hedge. I felt strangely calm as I approached David's house. All the curtains were closed.

He would be sleeping. I would knock. He would answer. I would ask him why he did it. Everything would be resolved.

Something halted me — I don't know what — but I stopped and stared across the fields. There was only the faintest hint of moonlight as the snow clouds broke apart. The blizzard was short-lived and had dusted the land. The subtle light picked out the edges of several trees, the white gable wall of David's house, and the memories that raced through my mind. They were all I had left.

Suddenly the front door of David's house opened and loud voices rang crisply through the night. I was close but not so close I couldn't abort my arrival without being spotted. Someone came running out of the house, slipping over on the snowy path. There was crying, shouting — a female voice — followed by lower male tones. I saw a struggle, more crying, swearing, and David's voice booming through the night.

"Take my coat at least," he called. "I can't let you back out into the night like this. It's freezing. Shall I call your parents?" His figure was silhouetted in the hall light as he reached inside and passed her a coat. He bent down and helped the girl to her feet. "Look, I think you should come back inside." He was almost begging — something David never did — and his voice carried cleanly through the freezing air, weaving through the hoar frost. I didn't understand what was going on, but even in the dark I could see that the young girl was the one from the café.

"You can't stop me leaving," she called out. "I'm going home." The girl glanced back over her shoulder, perhaps hoping for David to come after her as she teetered off wearing a silly short skirt and heels. She hadn't bothered to put on the coat but had it slung over her arm. David watched her walk as far as the end of the path, and then, shaking his head, he closed the front door.

The girl came down the lane, heading exactly where I was waiting. I froze in fear. In a moment, I would be spotted.

So then I did it. I spoke. I spoke to save the rest of my life; the rest of Julia's life. One word, and it fell out as if I had never said anything ever before. "Hello." I was pre-empting her thoughts with my stuck-together voice. I coughed, clogged and uncertain about the noise I had just made. If I hadn't done it, she would have seen me and become scared.

Twenty feet away, the girl stopped dead, not expecting to meet anyone at this time of night. Her neck stiffened and her shoulders hunched. One ankle twisted to the side because of her ridiculously high-heeled shoes. She looked like a hooker. She looked like me thirty years ago. I knew because of the pain weeping from her eyes.

"Who's there?" she asked, relieved to hear the figure blocking her way was female.

"I'm an old friend of Dr Carlyle." My voice crackled. The words rose from my chest like a slow-erupting volcano. I had to stay calm, in control. "Are you OK? Can I give you a lift?" I asked before she could question my presence at such an early hour. She clearly wanted to go home. I would take her and then come back to confront David.

"Yeah, yeah, actually, that would be great. My parents will kill me." She was still nervous, still incredulous, hesitant, but her need for assistance outweighed her fear of strangers. She relaxed a little.

"Why don't you call them?" All the while, my mind was spinning back and forth between now and then, him and her, David and Mary, rolling us together as if thirty years had never passed. What had he just done to her? She was dishevelled. Upset. I was watching it happen all over again.

"Out of battery." She held up a silver phone as she approached me. Her face was blotchy and streaked with make-up. She'd been crying. I remember crying; alone, violated, bereft, in pain, dirty, ashamed.

"Come on then. Climb in." I led her back to the Land Rover. I prayed that once again the engine noise wouldn't give away my presence. "What's your name?" I asked as I started the engine.

"Grace," she told me. "Do you have a phone I could borrow?" She took off her shoes and rubbed her bare feet. They were violet from the cold. She pulled the waxed jacket that David had given her around her shoulders; the only sensible thing she was wearing.

"Me? A mobile phone?" I laughed. "No. I don't have a phone." And after a three-point turn in the gateway, I drove off. In the rearview mirror, silhouetted against the house lights, I saw the outline of a broad male figure, watching us disappear down the lane.

"So, tell me." I still wasn't used to the sound of my voice. "What's a young girl like you doing roaming the countryside at night?" It was as if I was talking to myself all those years ago; as if I was looking into a mirror from nineteen seventy-six. There was so much I wanted to know. She would help me understand.

"It's a long story," she mumbled.

"I bet I've got a longer one," I replied. We bumped along.

"You have to turn right at this junction," she said. There was already a quake in her voice. Just a hint of fear. The moonlight made her nose seem bigger, her cheekbones prominent. I glanced at her lips. Lips where *he* had been. I wanted to scrub her clean.

"OK," I whispered, turning the opposite way. There was a pause; a moment for her to decide what to say.

"Are we going somewhere else first?" Her hand crept on to the door handle.

Truth was, I didn't know where we were going. Maybe I wanted to drive the rest of my life away with Grace — *me* — as my passenger. I would be safe then, perhaps prevent it from happening. I could ask her about David, find out if she'd met Jonathon, if she still worked at Café Delicio, if she was studying at university and finally going to make something of herself. I could tell her not to go to the wedding; I could tell her to turn the open sign to closed on the café door when David walked by. I could tell her the pain never goes, never lessens, never stops ruling every decision of your life. I could do all that.

The more I drove, the clearer it became — resolving like the dawn would do in just a few hours. Behind us, a car came down the lane from the direction of David's house. To begin with, the headlights were fireflies in the hedge but turned into bright moons as they neared. In my mind, I imagined it was David following us. In my mind, I imagined everything worked out fine.

MURRAY

Flora refuses to let go of her mother.

"You can come in with her if you like," the nurse says. She holds out her hand to our daughter. Flora pushes her face into Julia's shoulder.

"Is it really necessary?" I ask when we are inside the cubicle with the doctor.

"If there are signs of . . ." she mouths the word "abuse" above Flora's head, "then the police need to know. Action can be taken. Flora will need treating. Counselling." She speaks in a gossamer-thin voice. Mostly mouthing.

"She's deaf," I say. "She doesn't know what you're talking about."

The doctor closes her eyes for a moment. "I need to check for vaginal interference. Trauma. Bruising. We will need to take photographs. Swabs." Her words are suddenly loud, clipped. Determined.

"No way," Julia says. "There's no way David would have hurt Flora."

Did David hurt you, Flora? I sign. Flora is lying on a white couch and is wearing a hospital gown. She had to take her clothes off standing on a sterile plastic sheet to catch any forensic evidence that might fall from her. Her clothes were bagged and labelled. Even her doll was taken from her. Did he hurt you? I sign.

Flora shakes her head and signs, I didn't mean to leave the boat. It was boring. David found me on the lane.

"Did you see that?" Julia says. "David didn't kidnap her at all."

I slip my arm around Julia's waist. She hasn't said she wants me back. She hasn't said she doesn't. A part of her still believes that David is innocent.

Flora has tears in her eyes as she lies back on the couch. I just catch her hands quiver *sorry* as I leave the room. It is no place for me as the doctor begins her work.

Twenty minutes later, the paediatrician calls me into her office. Flora nestles on Julia's knee. She is licking a lollipop but her tired eyes keep drooping shut and her head falls forward.

"Good news, Mr and Mrs French." Julia doesn't correct the doctor about our names. A good sign. "Your little girl is fine. The only trauma she seems to have suffered is guilt at having wandered off. Other than that, she's perfect. I'm going to get a child psychologist to assess her. To be on the safe side."

Julia and I nod in unison. It's the first thing we have agreed upon for as long as I can remember.

Ed is waiting for us in the department reception. "Are you here as Uncle Ed or Detective Inspector?" There's the seed of something in my voice now that I know Flora is unharmed. It's hope; it's the first glimmer of good in months of mess. Already my eyes are stinging from the brightness of it all.

"I'm here as both," he says. "And with that, I advise you all to go home. Together." Ed's eyes sweep around my family. He has been looking after Alex while we attended to Flora.

"I got to ride in Ed's police car, Dad. And he let me talk on the radio." I ruffle my son's hair and he pulls away. "Not cool, Dad."

"Talking of cars," I say to Julia, sighing at the logistics, "your car and your mother's Land Rover are still at . . ." I don't know what to call it. I don't even want to say his name. "Need picking up from . . ."

"We'll fetch them tomorrow," Julia replies. She drapes her coat over Flora's arced back. She is clinging on round my neck, just about asleep now. "Let's get home," she says, and Ed offers to give us a lift, although I can't honestly say I know where home is any more.

The rock had landed on a polished side table, smashing a lamp and a vase. David swung round at the sound of breaking glass but Flora didn't stir. Her back was to the window and I was careful to avoid her, but I had to get in somehow. Carlyle was hardly going to open the door to me. Flora was looking at something — photographs — and it was only after I pushed in all the glass with my coat wrapped around my arm that she turned to face me. I leapt through the window, banging my head on the stone lintel.

Get back! I signed to her, but my coat got in the way of my hands and the urgent warning was lost. David stood, his mouth gaping, choked with excuses. He didn't attempt to defend himself. He just stared at me, almost as if he was pleased to see me.

"You bastard!" I yelled, and strode up to him, swinging a punch on each side of his face. Then I rammed him in the guts with my foot and fists and would have done more but Flora was close up, watching, stunned, crying. Her hands got tangled as she tried to sign. I pushed Carlyle down on to the sofa. He didn't fight back, not even when I dialled Ed's number. The police were on the way.

"What have you done?" I yelled at Carlyle, but he didn't reply. I towered above him, giving him no chance of escape. Strangely, calmly, he picked up the photograph album that Flora had been looking at and flipped quietly through the pages. When I saw the pictures, I felt sick. Each leaf was crammed haphazardly with photographs of Julia, Mary, the kids, even me in places. They were stuck in roughly with Blu Tack or tape, as if they had previously been displayed somewhere else.

It's OK, honey, I signed to Flora. Uncle Ed's coming to help us. The pain of not being able to hug my daughter properly until the police arrived was agony. My hands itched both to thump Carlyle again and cradle Flora.

Are you the bad man because you hit David? Flora's hands shook as she signed. She wouldn't look at me.

Will you go to prison now? she asked. I shook my head, watching as David turned the album pages.

No, but I should, I thought. Pictures of my wife and kids flashed before me. It was as if Carlyle was showing me what I had been missing all these years by having my nose shoved in a bottle. If I'm honest, Flora, I sign, I think I've just been released.

The house smells damp and it's freezing. I swear it's actually warmer outside in the orange glow of the streetlights than in here. I turn on the central heating and the boiler makes a grinding noise, but after fifteen minutes — the same length of time it takes to knit my family together with hugs, smiles, tea and blankets — we feel a layer of dry heat creeping through the small house.

"So," I say. Julia sits opposite me at the kitchen table. She wanted to go home to Ely. She wanted me with her. Ed stopped off with us at Northmire on the way home to check on Mary. She was sleeping, the breath falling from her chest steadily. Brenna and Gradin were settled in their room and complained bitterly when Julia insisted that they come with us back to Ely.

"We won't do anything wrong," Brenna said. She nudged her brother but he didn't speak, still suffering the trauma of a few hours down at the police station. Ed didn't press charges in the end, although he's convinced there's something troubling the boy; something he's bottling up.

But Julia insisted that the pair come home with us. "We can't possibly leave you." And she packed up a few belongings.

"Do you think she'll be OK?" Julia asks about Mary as we sit in the kitchen.

I nod, thinking how beautiful my wife looks, how unusual this is. Us, together, calm, at home.

Then she says, "Just one night. That's all I need. Just one night at home, normal, as it used to be. The four of us."

"Four plus two," I say, laughing. "They're all crashed out. All exhausted." And I know what she means about the one night at home. If it's all I get, I will stretch out the memory for ever.

She cradles her mug in her hands. "Oh, Murray," she says. Then she calls out my name, but not so loud that she will wake Flora. Beneath the table, her foot curls round my ankle.

Earlier, our daughter couldn't wait to climb between her own sheets. She surrounded herself with soft toys, and Julia and I kissed her simultaneously on each cheek, just like we used to. Then we looked in on Alex. He was reading, waved a hand at us without looking up. "Some things never change," I whispered to Julia as we went downstairs.

"And some things do," she replied.

Now, as we sit in the kitchen, Julia finishes her drink. "I'm so tired I could sleep for a thousand years."

"Then do," I reply. "I'll sit and wait for you."

JULIA

There's a stack of mail to sort through, but this particular letter arrives alone on our first morning home. I tear the seal and slide out the papers, skimming the formal letter before studying the official document. Everything is in order with the divorce. It's nearly final.

Murray left early and went back to Northmire to persuade Mum to go back to hospital. All the kids were still asleep so he'd insisted I stay here with them.

"Nadine's offered to ferry the cars back with me. She wants to help. I spoke to Ed first thing too." Murray had hesitated. "Kidnap charges have already been brought against . . . him."

I toss the divorce papers on the table. Flora stands in the doorway, sleepy, rubbing her eyes. She seems quite unaffected by what happened to her. Alex pushes past and makes for the food cupboard. I slide the papers back in their envelope, so he doesn't see.

Hey, darling, I sign to Flora. Did you sleep well? I know she did. I went into her room six times during the night.

For the briefest of moments, everything feels normal. We are in our kitchen, the breakfast scrabble about to begin. If Murray was here, he'd be hunting for a clean shirt. Alex would be catching up with missed homework, and Flora playing with dolls when she should be dressing. Me, well, I'd be the one ironing the shirt, conjugating French verbs on the fly, insisting Flora get ready for school. Somehow, I'd suddenly be dressed and ready myself, and with the chaotic disorder of the universe empowering us, we'd tumble into the car and be delivered at our destinations. The day would begin. The day would be normal.

I can't stand to think of things not ever being normal. Murray back at the boat, Mum alone at Northmire with no one around to hear if she speaks anyway, me and the kids alone again.

"Murray," I say, pretending he is here. He turns, hopeful, his face fresh and untouched by alcohol. "What about if . . ." I hesitate. "Maybe you could, or rather we could, give it another go." It doesn't come out right. "How about, for the kids' sake, we try . . ." I pause. He wouldn't like that. "Maybe we could see someone . . ." He definitely wouldn't like that. I grab him by the shoulders. "Murray French, I love you. I love you, I love you," I say, and this time he understands completely.

"Mum, who are you talking to?" Alex spoons cereal into his mouth, grinning.

"Your father," I say, not letting go of Murray's shoulders.

"But he can't hear you."

"Oh yes he can," I say, dropping a kiss on to his invisible mouth.

MURRAY

It's propped up on the kitchen table at Northmire, leaning against the pepper mill as if someone forgot to drop it in the postbox. A small white envelope with *Julia* written on the front makes me pause, frown, pick it up, turn it round and round, run my finger beneath the unsealed flap.

I stand it up against the pepper mill again, shrugging, but stop in the doorway. It's Mary's handwriting.

"Mary," I call out. Not because she will reply but so that she hears me coming and isn't surprised or half dressed. I suspect she will be in exactly the same position as we left her — asleep in bed. Today she will have to go back to hospital. Thank God that Julia had one night away from all the mess; one night with me. I stop halfway up the stairs and take a moment to relive our closeness.

Upstairs, I open Mary's bedroom door a few inches. I am right. She is sleeping. She looks childlike, as if her life has rewound to the beginning — her skin strangely smooth, bloodless.

"Mary," I say. "It's Murray." I pull back the curtains. Light floods in.

The sheets are bound around Mary's body, pulled tight across her chest. Her hands lie clasped over her waist. Her hair spreads on the pillow, more silver than ever before. The medication bottles sit empty on the bedside table.

"Oh God, Mary. Mary, no!"

I shake her. She is lifeless.

I don't touch anything. I can't, because my hands are shaking. I leave the room, already tainted with a faintly sweet smell. Gasping for air, I run downstairs. I stop in the kitchen, panting, thousands of memories spilling in my way, tripping me up, as if the house just doesn't have room for them any more.

The letter for Julia still sits pristine and white on the table. I think about the consequences if I open it; think about them if I don't. I sit down because my legs won't hold me. As I unfold the paper, Mary Marshall speaks loud and clear.

Dear Julia,

When you read this, I won't be here to explain. Read these words carefully and without prejudice, and whatever you do, don't believe for one minute that I wasn't totally in control of myself. Have you ever known me otherwise? Can't you tell already that it's me speaking, finally, clearly, effortlessly? My handwriting, although a little shaky. My words, perhaps a little pompous. My decision — a coward's way out.

But preferable to the lie that I have lived for thirty years. The truth, Julia, was harder to say than the deceit

434

I have spun around us. I couldn't have you find out from him; but then I didn't have the courage to tell you myself. You would have hated me. I have truly been bound up by my own guilt, my own shame . . .

When I'm finished, the letter flutters to the floor. Mary's words escape; butterflies set free.

The guard at Whitegate Prison remembers me. There are no planned appointments, no scheduled visits, no meeting cell booked. I've come straight from Northmire, leaving Mary in bed. No one except me knows that she took an overdose. I must be quick or Julia will come looking for me at the farm. I need to be the one to tell her.

"Back so soon?" he asks. "You'll have to wait, I'm afraid. I'll need to phone through for special clearance if you haven't got this booked in."

I think he takes pity on me. T-shirt, jeans, trainers. My zip-up coat is muddy from searching the fields. My face is layered with sadness. Sheila would scream at me to smarten up, to buck up. There's no point in telling her that he's not my client any more. No point in telling the guard, either. I'll never get through security then.

"OK, you're in. Let's get started," he says a few minutes later. The front desk guard begins the necessary paperwork. I place my hand on Mary's letter. It's folded into my coat pocket. In the end, Mary had her say.

★ ★ ★

He sits at a table set squarely in the middle of a small room. There are no windows and, as usual, the guard leaves us alone. "Thirty minutes," he says, and I want to tell him that Mary's story will take at least that number of years.

"Carlyle," I say. It's impossible to tell if he shows remorse. His plain prison clothes, his plain expression, his plain posture give nothing away. "I'm not your lawyer any more."

"Hardly worth a visit to tell me that, was it?" His voice is unemotional and he barely moves as he speaks.

"I know who you are," I state calmly. Inside me a storm rages. "I know you are Julia's father. What I want to know is *why*." My voice is barely above a whisper but deafening to Carlyle. He flinches. I lean over the table. I don't know if I'm asking why he kidnapped my daughter or why he raped my mother-in-law.

I never knew why he hurt me, Julia. I never understood why your father turned into someone else that night I've always blamed myself . . .

He sighs. "Flora?"

I nod. A good place to start.

"Because she is just like Julia. I missed her childhood and saw Flora as a second chance." He lays his hands flat on the table. His answer is slick and prepared. "And because she doesn't speak and I don't sign, we had a silent understanding. I never planned to take her. I certainly never meant to keep her longer than an hour or two, but how can you cram a missed childhood into

436

such a short time? She's my grandchild. It was wrong, I know —"

"Wrong?" I yell. "Wrong doesn't even come close to the agony you caused my family." I want to punch him, throw the table at him, beat him to a pulp. But it wouldn't help. Flora has already confessed to wandering off the boat.

I was bored, Daddy. I went all along the path and on to the road above the bridge to look for you. David was passing in his car and stopped to take care of me. Flora's hands were frantic as she signed and I had to make her slow down.

"And it's because I love her," Carlyle continues. Now I'm not sure if he's talking about Mary, Julia or Flora. Three generations of Marshall women. Does he love them all?

"Back then, I wanted her so much it hurt. But there was a gap between us — not just our ages, but a gap in time, a gap in the universe. She stood one side, I stood the other. Our destinies were lifetimes apart and I couldn't bear that. I never meant to hurt her."

I adored your father once and I know that, in his own way, he loved me. I want you to know that there are remnants of love in your blood, Julia. Leftovers from an affair that was never meant to be. It's the most tragic love story, isn't it?

"Mary," I say. He's talking about Mary. I picture them both — him the cocksure medical student, her struggling to make a living. Mary's letter mentioned her days in Cambridge, "I know what you did to her. It was brutal. And I know that Julia is the result."

Carlyle stiffens. His skin washes grey and yet somehow he still maintains that proud posture, the respected doctor. "You're right," he tells me. "Julia is my daughter." I expected regret, but his words are laced with pride.

"She was falling in love with you, you fool. Did you know that? Were you in love with her? Are you some kind of sick —"

"Stop!" His breathing quickens. The muscles banding around his jaw pull tight, making it difficult for him to speak. "I didn't know she was going to fall for me in that way. When she called me on Christmas Day, it was clear she needed more than a doctor for her mother. She needed someone strong. A father figure and . . ." He trails off, having the decency not to bring my relationship with Julia into this.

"It was my opportunity to get to know the daughter I'd been denied," he continues. "I confess that I moved back into this area to make contact with my . . . family. I hoped that after thirty years, Mary would allow me into their lives. I didn't expect her to come to my surgery that day. I'd planned to approach her at some point, but not like that. I didn't even know she was registered at the practice.

"Later that day, after her appointment, I called her but she refused to speak to me. Then, when Julia called me out in a panic on Christmas Day, I saw that something was very wrong with Mary, as if something had short-circuited. After all these years, she was still suffering. I was determined to help."

So your father put me in The Lawns to make amends for what he did. It was his misguided way of cleaning up the mess he'd made. Part of me liked being there, as if the rest of the world didn't exist. It was some sanctuary from the pain. But I was so desperately worried that he would tell you everything, I had to find a way to stop him destroying you. Destroying us. I admit, I wanted revenge.

I'm more certain than ever that Julia mustn't know any of this. I'll do whatever it takes to keep her out of the courtroom. "I know Mary wasn't ill — not in the physical sense. You'll be struck off the medical register now anyway, but it was a pretty low act concocting a nonexistent illness."

"I wanted to make sure she got the treatment she needed. It was my fault she'd ended up in that state. None of this was planned with malice or much forethought. I had to help Mary, to make amends. But I also knew that she would never agree to go to a psychiatric hospital. And to convince Julia as well, there had to be a serious medical implication for her mother," He sighs. "After all this time, it's as if another person did those . . . things. I'm a different man now."

"I suppose you've left the Marshall family with a hefty bill." It gets better. I see the remainder of Northmire's land carved up and sold off to pay the debt. I see a disturbed man.

"No," he says urgently. "The account is taken care of. There is a trust fund. My parents left me a large amount of money and I immediately invested it for Julia. That's what parents do for their children, isn't it?"

Part of me wants to ask how much; part of me doesn't even want Julia to have the money.

He second-guesses my thoughts. "She won't need to worry about her future. The trustees will be in touch."

That can't happen, I think in a panic. I was working this out, about Mary, about keeping Julia safe, about keeping quiet. How can I destroy my own wife? The death of her mother will be pain enough, let alone finding out about her father — the man she fell in love with. "If you want to do something for Julia, then you'll never tell her who you are. You'll never make contact with her again. You won't reply if she approaches you, and the money must go to a charity. One that Mary would approve of." I think quickly. "A charity for disadvantaged kids. Give the whole lot away."

He doesn't protest. My fingers slip round Mary's letter tucked in my pocket.

Nothing can compensate for what happened, Julia. All the money in the world couldn't heal me. And in turn, I have created a debt so huge to my own daughter, I am left with no option but to default.

"And what about those photographs you have of Julia and the kids? Are you some kind of stalker?" Anger rises in me again as Carlyle returns with a swift answer, as if he was already on trial.

440

"From time to time I watched Julia." He swallows and his jaw clenches. "I was working for a medical agency, and whenever I could, I travelled to Cambridgeshire. I wanted to know that she was OK. That she was happy."

"From time to time? By my calculations, you've been around every street corner, behind every lamppost, spying on my wife every month for the last three decades." I don't want him to see the veins on my neck stand out. I glance at my watch. If I'm too long, Julia will worry.

"Is it so wrong to want to see your daughter grow up?" He asks a question I can't refute. "The photographs were all I had. When Mary and I . . . when Mary got pregnant, it was not an act of hate on my part I just wanted her so much; so much that it hurt." He pauses, reliving it. "I was stunned that it went to court and even more stunned to learn that she was pregnant. She was pregnant with my child."

In my mind, the punch lands cleanly on the side of his face, toppling him back off his chair with a broken jaw. "You gave up your right to fatherhood when you raped Julia's mother."

"I was eighteen. I was stupid and irresponsible, and at the time I truly believed Mary wanted me to . . . to . . ." Carlyle actually has the guile to show remorse. His delusions don't wash with me. "We'd been drinking, taking drugs. She said no but . . . but she always said no. That was the thing with Mary. Sometimes no meant yes." His head sinks into his hands. "I don't know any more," he whispers.

Looking back, Julia, I blame myself for what happened that night. The jury said so, didn't they? Your father raped me, and the dirt, the shame, the guilt has stuck to me ever since. There's no washing it off. It was a game gone wrong. I was out of my league and made an incorrect move. I lost.

Suffering that blame has stopped me from healing. I've lived my life on a tightrope, just waiting for someone to trip me up. And I was balancing just fine until I saw your father again.

"Whatever Mary claimed about the ... the sex, I wasn't responsible for her wounds." Carlyle speaks freely, anticipating my questions. "After ... after we'd ... when it was over, I went back to the wedding party. It had stopped raining. I walked rather than take the boat across the lake as we'd done earlier. It was quicker. I assumed Mary would join me once she was dressed. Looking back, I shouldn't have left her alone at night. I was drunk and didn't realise how much she'd had. Combined with the drugs she'd taken ..." Carlyle wipes his hands down his face. "Mary's perception of what happened is so different from what I intended. But I did not cut her afterwards. I swear I did not do that to her."

It was a release, Julia. Can you understand that? An attempt to replace the wretched pain inside me with a greater one. I was trying to fool myself and of course, everyone else. It was the poison coming out and I wanted your father to take the blame. If I'm honest, there's only one way to escape now.

After it happened, I lay on the floor and cried. I was sick; I was alone; I was scared. I had been ripped in two and there was no one there. No one came looking for me; there was no one to care for me. David was back at the wedding party. No one even missed me.

Across the room, I saw David's knife still lying on the floor. He'd jimmied the lock with it earlier. My stomach cramped as I reached for it. Several hours passed. I turned the knife over and over in my hands. I licked it. I wiped it down my forearm. I hated myself I had allowed David to take me in a way no woman should. If I couldn't have my life any more, why should he have his? I was scared no one would believe me about the rape. I had to make sure he was put away for good.

Sitting cross-legged on the floor, I pushed the blade into the sole of my foot, Julia.

It felt good.

I did it again and again. The silver edge slipped in easily. The pain of my cuts overtook the pain of what your father had done to me. It focused my mind. I was anyone but David's victim.

The blood flowed.

I was numb, but already a plan had formed. I would tell the police that David attacked me. It cut both ways — a release for me and a prison sentence for him. It was his knife. He had already raped me. Then I would tell them he tried to silence me by cutting out my tongue. I stuck the knife in my mouth. It was agony, but then the pain eroded into a peace I never anticipated.

"Yes, I know you didn't hurt Mary with that knife," I say. I have Carlyle's full attention.

Slowly, slotting together the pieces, his eyes squinting, he shakes his head. "How did you know that Mary was hurt with a knife?"

"I know more than that. I know it was your knife." I dodge the question. "And it was Mary that used it. She did it to herself."

Shock seeps over Carlyle's face — every molecule soaking up the implications. His mouth forms an open bow; an expression of realisation, understanding even. I continue. "She hated herself after what you did to her. She felt dirty, wretched, as if her life had ended. Nothing surprising there. She'd been raped." If there was a window in this pit I would be at it, staring out, gripping the sill to stop me thumping him.

"I let her down," he says. "I can understand why she did it. At the trial, part of me believed I deserved to go to prison. Part of me even hoped I would."

"Oh you'll be going to prison all right." I circle the table, my fists itching to take a swing. "For the kidnap of my daughter at the very least. And DI Hallet still has your card marked for Grace's murder. Fine retribution, don't you think?"

"I did not kill Grace Covatta," he says. Back to the expressionless state. Carlyle banks his shoulders defiantly. "I was so sorry to learn of her death."

I check the guard is out of earshot. "I doubt if —"

"I saw Mary with Grace on the night she was attacked." He interrupts with flat, emotionless words. I let him speak. I need to know what he knows.

This time round, I needed justice, a resolution, Julia. Can you understand? I couldn't let David get away with it again. Not with this young girl; not with the black mascara tears on her cheeks, her freezing feet, her hopeless devotion for a man who should have known better. Grace Covatta got into the Land Rover of her own free will.

"Grace was a patient of mine. A problem patient. She had trouble with her parents; she'd got herself pregnant. I'd diagnosed depression, too. She came to see me about once a month to begin with. I would listen and advise. She trusted me. But then her visits became more often — once a week, sometimes three times a week. Then she started calling me at home, insisting we meet. I was worried that it wouldn't look good professionally. People at the practice were talking. I was stupid. I cared for the girl. I met with her a few times out of the surgery, and from that she assumed we had something going. In the end, it was her crush that killed her.

"On the day she was attacked, Grace called me a dozen times, making a terrible nuisance of herself." Carlyle shakes his head at the memory. "I suggested she change doctors but she got hysterical and told me she loved me. She threatened to tell her parents that the baby was mine if I didn't let her come to my house that night. I didn't know what to do."

"And was the baby yours?"

"Of course not," he replies indignantly. Against my better judgement, I believe him. "During that night,

445

there was a terrible noise at my door. It was Grace. She was in a state. When she threatened me again, I explained that a simple paternity test would prove I wasn't the father of her baby. I took her in for a short while but then offered to call her a taxi or phone her parents. She wanted none of it. She became hysterical again and took off into the night. She was wearing very little and the weather was atrocious. I was worried about her freezing to death and insisted she take my coat." Carlyle takes half a glassful of the water that's set between us. He is sweating as if the story is a cross-country run.

"But just as I was going back inside, I heard voices in the lane. I strained to see who was out there. Someone was with Grace. I walked to the end of the front path and listened. She was definitely talking to someone."

"Who was it?" I have to know if he knows.

I made up some stupid reason why I wasn't driving her home straight away. She was a little nervous but relieved to have a lift. It made me wonder what had happened inside David's house. Why was she so troubled? Memories that I thought I had locked away fell as fresh as the snow on the fields.

On a whim, I veered the Land Rover round and doubled back towards David's house. She asked where we were going but I couldn't reply. I didn't know. I turned down Lightning Lane, which I imagine is etched on to your mind like a tombstone now. It's where we used to walk the dogs; where all the village kids used to smoke, do you remember? I parked but left the engine running. I couldn't risk breaking down. I got out of the car and told Grace to do the same. By then, she looked puzzled, frightened, but clearly relieved to be out of David's house.

"I couldn't tell who was out there with Grace. It sounded like a woman's voice. Then a vehicle started up. A big, noisy thing. When the lights came on, I could just make out the rear numberplate. It was unusual and easy to remember — an old-style or private plate. I ran after them, hoping to identify the driver. But I was too late. They drove off." Carlyle stops as the guard suddenly knocks and opens the door. I nod at him and he leaves again.

I told her to walk with me. It was crazy. She put those silly heels back on and wore the borrowed coat from David slung around her shoulders. She told me her mum would go spare that she'd been out nearly all night. Her face was as alive as mine had once been — eager yet refusing to see the truth.

We walked on for a few minutes and she kept stumbling in her heels. I suggested she take them off. She tossed the shoes away with abandon. Her toes sank into the iced grass and she giggled and shivered at the same time.

"Don't get in the rowing boat," I remember saying to her, and she asked what I meant. By then a thousand other words were queuing up and I couldn't answer.

Speech was a novelty and didn't have to make sense or fit an order.

Grace said she wanted to go home; she looked scared — what with the moonlight reflecting from her cheeks and her skin mottled blue.

"I can make everything better, if you follow me," I told her. "I know what he did to you. I can heal you. He won't get away with it again."

She didn't understand me, I could tell, but despite her nervousness, she walked on. I think she'd been drinking. Her lips were frozen into a lopsided grin and I doubt that she knew what the next thirty years would hold if I didn't help her now.

"I know about you and David. I know what he just did to you."

"He didn't do anything," she replied instantly. She was so immature. So naive; that nervous laugh. She was trying to protect him.

"When Julia was showing me around Northmire Farm a few days later, I saw that same vehicle in the barn." Carlyle stands up and paces about. "I know it was Mary out there that night with Grace. It was her Land Rover I saw in the lane."

Eventually we approached a hedge and couldn't go any further without hurtling down the deep dip that the local kids believed was an old Roman amphitheatre. You know where I mean — that unusual hole in the fields. By then, Grace was several paces ahead of me. I picked up a heavy branch and swung it at her head. She fell to the ground instantly. Blood wept into the snow.

She remained on the ground as I worked. Another blow and she was unconscious. I dragged off the jacket and flung it into the darkness — then the rest of her clothes. I couldn't stop, all the while vowing vengeance. The branch battered her again. The knife — you know, the one I always keep in my walking coat pocket — made quick work of her feet, her tongue.

It was all done, just as before. A perfect replica.

I pulled the knife from Grace's mouth. I ran.

David would be punished for sure this time. His coat was a few yards away. His DNA was all over Grace. I didn't care about anything else. It was my chance.

I got into the Land Rover. I drove.

Home, behind the barn, I burnt Grace's clothes. I wrapped the knife in the newspaper and hid it in the back of the Land Rover. No one ever used that old vehicle.

I went inside and undressed, hiding my muddy clothes balled beneath the bed. I tried to sleep but couldn't. I stared at the ceiling. I waited for David's life and my misery to finally end.

I never meant for her to die, Julia, I swear. But when I saw David and Grace together, something twisted inside me. Something drove me to believe I could put things right. By hurting her in the same way I'd done to myself thirty years ago, I believed the connection would be made and your father would be put away once and for all. No one could get away with it twice.

I am so very, very sorry.

I take a breath and a second's thought. "Then why didn't you tell the police all this when you were arrested the first time?"

Carlyle shakes his head. "You really don't understand, do you?"

"Enlighten me."

"I still love Mary. I've always loved her. If it had been necessary, I would have gone to prison instead of her. There was no way I was pointing the police in her direction. She'd suffered enough."

"Loved," I say quietly, and at first he doesn't understand. "You *loved* Mary Marshall. She's dead, David. She took an overdose last night." I can't watch the landslide of pain on his face. I believe that somehow, in his sick and twisted way, he did love Mary; I believe that he is hurting as much as if I'd been told the same news about Julia.

"Mary . . . is *dead*?"

I nod. "And so are her secrets. She'll never tell now. And you will be going to prison for a few years on her behalf." It seems Mary got her revenge, even if it did cost a young girl's life.

Carlyle sits down heavily as if his bones have dissolved. He doesn't say another word, and that's how I know that Mary's secrets will be safe.

The fresh air outside the prison expands my lungs. I leave swiftly, stopping only once on the way back to Ely. Torn into a hundred pieces, I scatter Mary's letter into the river from the top of a bridge. Julia must never know.

"For heaven's sake, Murray," Mary says to me in her disapproving voice. "Did you have to make such a mess?" And she wags a finger at me, as if I'm still a kid.

"Just trying to clean the mess up, actually," I reply as the pieces spread and float away in the wake of a boat. I wait until the last one disappears from sight before going home.

Julia opens the door before I reach it. Her face is thin, her body bird-like. Somehow she is in my arms and we are standing alone, the kids oblivious to their mother's pain as I tell her about Mary. There's a little hiccup and she digs her fingers into my shoulders.

I kiss her head and she cries. Then there are the hours when she says absolutely nothing at all.

Little piece by little piece, day by day, Julia remembers her mother. She remembers the scolding she got when the rope swing broke and she fell into the mud. She remembers baking summers in the orchard, her mother halfway up a ladder collecting apples in a basket. She remembers winters at Northmire, huddling beside the range as her mother stirred a pot of stew as big as a cauldron. She remembers her mother at our wedding — stiffened in an outfit that she marched straight to a charity shop the next day — and she remembers her mother bent over the kitchen table at night, spied on through a crack in the door as she sobbed and sobbed.

To gradually ease the pain, Julia remembers her mother. Not once does she remember her father.

JULIA

"I thought I'd find you here." Flora's mittened hand is squashed inside mine. Alex thwacks a branch against the hedge. He didn't want to come down to the river ever again but I told him that would be silly. Murray stands, hands on hips, staring at the water. "How did that happen?" I ask, not at all surprised. I stifle a laugh.

"It's gone. Completely gone." He smacks his hands against his thighs; a windmill of despair.

"Not true," I tell him. "Look, you can still see the chimney." I'm right. The brass-ringed funnel top pokes through the surface of the water. "There's a bit of roof still showing, too. And see, there's one of your boots floating away." Then I laugh. The first time since Mum died. I can't help it. She would have laughed too.

"*Alcatraz* has *sunk*." Murray sounds incredulous. Almost relieved. "It was my home."

Did the bad man do that to Daddy's boat? Flora signs, worming her hand free from mine. By gripping her so tightly, I am stopping her communicating. But after losing her — so very nearly losing her — how will I ever let her out of my sight again?

No, sweetheart, I explain. The bad man has gone to prison. Daddy's boat sunk because it wanted him to come and live with us again.

Flora grins, apparently satisfied with my explanation. If only things were that simple. If only it had sunk months ago. "Well, it's not your home any more, is it?" I remind Murray. Now the funeral is behind us, we have moved into Northmire. The house in Ely will get sold. We will visit Mum's grave on her birthday, at Christmas, whenever we need her. We'll take flowers and the children will leave her homemade gifts.

I squeeze Flora's hand. The four of us walk away from the river and I'm the only one to give a quick glance back. Murray, Alex, Flora — they all dart ahead, dodging the puddles, racing to the bridge. One last look, just to make sure it's really gone; just to make sure he'll be coming home with us for good.

There was a candle, the table was set, and I'd cooked a meal. Our first time alone in ages; our first night at Northmire with just Mum's ghost for company. Nadine had offered to have the children. She said she needed all the practice she could get for when she and Ed adopt. The application is already in; the chance of a baby in their house is a breath away.

"It's a start," I said to Murray when he saw the table, thinking just how close to the end we'd come. I served the food. "Do you think Mum would approve?" I'd rearranged some furniture and Murray had plumbed in a dishwasher that morning. A radio stood amongst photographs propped on the dresser. We had plans.

"No," he said laughing. "She'd kick and scream." Suddenly, we both heard her barging around the house, cursing at the television in the bedroom, shaking her head at the music coming from Alex's room.

She'd notice the changes; she wouldn't approve. That was Mum. "She'd be happy for Brenna and Gradin, though," I added. "Although not so pleased about her chickens." Reluctantly, before the brother and sister were introduced to their new family, Gradin took me aside. Growing up about ten years in as many minutes, he confessed to culling a couple of Mum's birds. "I was angry," he said. "They pecked me and stopped me from sleeping." Brenna and Gradin are seeing their mum at weekends now, living with a new foster family, hoping to rebuild their lives.

"This is good," Murray said, and I didn't know if he was talking about the food or us. "Sheila called me from the office earlier," he continued. He took a sip of water and closed his eyes for a second. "With news."

Since Murray told Sheila that he didn't want the Carlyle case, he'd been waiting for the call to clear out his desk. But, probably using up her entire lifetime's supply of empathy, she'd allowed him several weeks' compassionate leave. I held my breath; fork halfway to my mouth.

"I've been offered a partnership."

"Wow," I said, trying not to sound too excited. "But?"

"No buts. Dick Porsche left. Gone with dream-girl to Sydney. As of Monday, I have an office with a view."

454

"Whatever reasons you gave to Sheila about dropping the case must have convinced her that you're good at your job."

Murray eyed me over the rim of his water glass. As he drank, I didn't have that feeling inside — the one that would prepare me for the drunken hours ahead, not knowing if he was going to be happy or morose; kick up an argument or sleep it off.

"Sheila . . . understood," he replied, and I didn't question what he meant.

The talk of solicitors reminded me of the envelope that had been in the pile of mail waiting for me at Ely. After we'd eaten, I fetched it from the kitchen. "This came." I withdrew the document and ran my finger over Murray's signature. It confirmed that he had received my divorce petition. It confirmed he agreed.

"It's what you wanted," he said, clearing the plates and running a bowl of water. "So I signed it."

"No. It wasn't what I wanted. It was what I had to do. For me. For the kids." I watched him and couldn't help the laugh. "Er . . . Murray." He turned around from the sink to see me pointing at the new dishwasher.

It took him a moment to realise. "Old habits, eh?"

"Exactly," I replied, and took the plates from him. My arms slid easily around his neck.

Later, when we came back to the dishes, I tore up the divorce papers and dropped them into the bin. Now all we have to do is pick up the pieces.

The first fingers of spring flourish into colour and hope; little stubs of daffodils have shot to brilliant swathes of yellow these last few weeks, while patches of folded green buds erupt on the trees. It's a nice day for a walk. The sky is clear.

"Watch this, Dad." Alex has made a dozen paper aeroplanes and is chucking them in all directions. We have been to visit Mum. The first time since the funeral.

The cemetery is half a mile outside Witherly. It was a pensive walk there for Murray and me; a chilly scamper for the children and Milo. As we approached the neat lawns and ordered rows of headstones, Milo slowed instinctively. He fell alongside me and allowed the lead to be hooked to his collar. We only stayed for a few minutes, long enough to replace the flowers; long enough for the children to leave a picture for their grandma.

"Give me a moment," I say to Murray, and he nods, watching me walk through the cemetery. Alone, I pay a visit to Grace. My brilliant pupil. I kneel down and tell her that her classmates planted a garden in her memory. "You won't be forgotten," I say, laying down some flowers. Then, shivering, I leave her to rest.

Murray pulls off his scarf and winds it round my neck. "You need to get away. Let's book somewhere for the Easter break."

"Let's," I reply, smiling up at him as we walk home. "Depending when . . . when the trial is." The word narrows my throat. Kidnapping charges were brought against David, and Ed is determined to nail him for Grace's murder. Murray says he won't be leaving prison for a long while.

456

"Look at Alex. Have you noticed how he's really grown up these last few weeks?" Murray asks, changing the subject. We watch as Alex smoothes out a paper plane that Milo caught in his mouth. "He's realising that things don't stay the same for ever."

"Yes, but it's hard when that thing is you," I say, laughing. Flora pulls off her mittens to talk, trotting in front of me.

Where's my grandad? she asks. Is he with Grandma? Her nimble fingers dig straight into my heart. She bounces around, pretending to be Tigger.

Perhaps, I sign slowly, wondering if the world is on a big, repeating loop. And there I am, whisked back in time twenty-five years to my first day at playgroup when I'd painted a picture of a father I didn't have. Murray falls out of step with me, chucking planes about with Alex.

"Oh Flora," I say, taking her by the shoulders. She catches the breath of her name on the wind and watches my lips as if she can read them. I tell her about the day my mother insisted I never mention him again; about how upset I was; about how I learned to live with the hole in my heart. I so desperately wanted a father.

So haven't I got a grandad then? Flora signs.

No, I reply. She is confused. I never knew my father, your grandad. And you already know that Grandpa French died a long time ago. I hug her close, wishing I could have had just one day with my father, to get a glimpse of the other half of me, to show him my children. He would have been proud. Now Mum is gone, that will never happen.

I'm going to do a picture of him for Grandma, Flora signs. So that she won't be lonely.

Come on then, let's go inside and you can get started. I refuse to let the tear in my eye drain on to my cheek.

The kitchen is warm. Boots are kicked off and coats dumped on chairs. The promise of cake and drinks follows, while Flora settles at the table, unfolding her bundle of pictures. She spreads them out for all to see and sets to work with her colours. I peer over her shoulder.

What are all these? I ask. There are at least a dozen drawings of different men, each one with a different look. I pick them up, amazed at the detail.

They're my grandads, she says proudly. They don't have to be a secret now Grandma's gone to heaven. She told me to draw them.

I frown, remembering the workings of a little girl's mind. It was so hard to understand why someone wasn't there — especially when you knew that he must have been once.

I sit down next to Flora and pick up a couple of crayons. She will get her grandad. What colour hair do you think he has? Brown, grey, bit of both?

Flora nods and begins to draw. Between us, we create the perfect father, the perfect grandparent; always there.

Look, Daddy, Flora signs. She holds up a picture of a man with one arm longer than the other. He's wearing a bright green cardigan and smoking a pipe. He has a little dog and is standing on a strip of blue grass.

458

Murray comes up behind me, slipping his arm around my shoulder. He's a fine-looking chap, he tells Flora. She grins. Alex comes to see what all the fuss is about.

"I want to draw too," he says, settling down next to his sister. Within a second, Murray has grabbed some crayons and there we are, the four of us, scribbling and colouring for all we are worth; chattering and squabbling over colours, comparing sketches and laughing at our mistakes.

Before long, we have a stack of papers, each with a father or a grandfather staring out of the page. Some stand tall with proud eyes and long noses, while some are hunched and old, bent over a walking stick. All of them ours. All of them make-believe. I spread them out on the table.

"Enough to last a lifetime," I say proudly. "Now no one in this family need be without a father again."

And Murray looks at me thoughtfully across the table, a crayon pressed against his lips, as if he's about to say something so life-changing, so huge, it got wedged in his mouth on the way out.

What? I ask, frowning and signing at the same time.

"Nothing," he replies too quickly. "Really, nothing."

Odd, then, that I understand his silence completely. Odd, then, that for the first time in ages, I feel the first glimmer of happiness.

Also available in ISIS Large Print:

Blood Ties

Sam Hayes

January 1992. A baby girl is left alone for a moment. Long enough for a mother to dash into a shop. Long enough for a child to be taken.

Thirteen years later, solicitor Robert Knight is delighted that his stepdaughter has won a place at a prestigious London school for the gifted. The only puzzle is his wife Erin's reaction. Why is she so reluctant to let Ruby go?

As Erin grows more evasive, Robert can't help but feel she has something to hide, and when he stumbles across some mysterious letters, he discovers she has been lying to him. Somewhere in his wife's past lies a shocking secret — one that threatens to destroy everything . . .

ISBN 978-0-7531-7932-1 (hb)
ISBN 978-0-7531-7933-8 (pb)

ISIS publish a wide range of books in large print, from fiction to biography. Any suggestions for books you would like to see in large print or audio are always welcome. Please send to the Editorial Department at:

ISIS Publishing Limited
7 Centremead
Osney Mead
Oxford OX2 0ES

A full list of titles is available free of charge from:

Ulverscroft Large Print Books Limited

(UK)
The Green
Bradgate Road, Anstey
Leicester LE7 7FU
Tel: (0116) 236 4325

(Australia)
P.O. Box 314
St Leonards
NSW 1590
Tel: (02) 9436 2622

(USA)
P.O. Box 1230
West Seneca
N.Y. 14224-1230
Tel: (716) 674 4270

(Canada)
P.O. Box 80038
Burlington
Ontario L7L 6B1
Tel: (905) 637 8734

(New Zealand)
P.O. Box 456
Feilding
Tel: (06) 323 6828

Details of **ISIS** complete and unabridged audio books are also available from these offices. Alternatively, contact your local library for details of their collection of **ISIS** large print and unabridged audio books.